The Witch's Arcana

THE WITCH'S ARCANA

S. L. VELA

This is a work of fiction. All of the characters, organizations, and events portrayed in this novel are either products of the author's imagination or are used fictitiously. Any resemblance to actual persons, living or dead, or actual events is purely coincidental.

THE WITCH'S ARCANA

Copyright © 2024 by Samantha L. Vela

All rights reserved.

No part of this publication may be reproduced, distributed, or transmitted in any form or by any means, including photocopying, recording, or other electronic or mechanical methods, without the prior written permission of the publisher, except as permitted by U.S. copyright law.

Published in the United States by Corvus Books
For permission requests, email connect@corvusbooks.com

ISBN 979-8-218-57250-1 (paperback) / 979-8-218-57251-8 (ebook)

First Edition: December 2024

Cover art by Samantha L. Vela

*This one is for my beloved students of
Lyndon B. Johnson High School.*

*Be fearless, be persistent, and persevere.
Take valuable chances in life.*

Here's to the Wolfpack!

CONTENT WARNING

This book includes horror elements and topics that may be sensitive to some readers, including death, self-harm, mental illness, witchcraft, and tarot. Reader discretion is advised.

PROLOGUE

Flashes of lightning across the dark sky cast serrated shadows through the stone walls of the Regnum Noctis Hotel. Amidst the bedlam which unfolded in the locale, the consistent growling thunder served as mere background noise. The night of All Hallows' descended, wrapping the kingdom in a shroud of unease.

Loud whispers from the housekeeping staff echoed through the hotel's corridors. In the grand lobby, the guests loitered with frantic purpose, unable to find peace. Their elaborate costumes and masks transformed them into a haunting display of spectral figures. The collection consisted of shapeshifters, mummified creatures, vampires, and the undead. In the lobby, the chandelier's flickering candles cast unsettling silhouettes on the walls, intensifying the growing tension as guests circulated one rumor after another about the recent incident. Their voices conveyed the cacophony of fear and speculation.

A circle formed as they gossiped about the current event—a man confined in the cold, damp holding cell on the lowest floor of Regnum Noctis. His fate lay in the hands of the kingdom's royal family, and the entire community held its breath as they waited for the verdict.

Rumors spread among the staff about the impending tragedy awaiting the unfortunate soul. They speculated his execution would take place that iniquitous evening—further contributing to the eerie atmosphere of All Hallows' Eve.

The captive man would be a new soul to join the ranks of the dead.

Citizens experienced dread for the man, and they felt intimidated by the law of the land, but their chaotic emotions also harbored excitement because they didn't sit in the offender's seat, awaiting the leader's judgment, which stemmed from pure greed, convenience, and corruption.

As a whole, the community believed in the laws of their realm and in their judge, who also held the title of the kingdom's crown prince. The gossip, along with the judge's handsome appearance, wisdom, and power, invited twisted entertainment. The judge's strict sense of justice and protection for the realm blinded them. If someone accused another of a capital crime in the Kingdom of Follyn, everyone would shun the accused.

Another shapeshifter opened the hotel lobby doors, letting in frost from outside. The guests recognized him as the location's manager. He held a large key ring, which contained many keys of different shapes, sizes, colors, and designs. The grave situation led the family to detain the man in the dungeons of the premises instead of moving him to the town's jailhouse. Given the seriousness of the jailed man's offense, the royal family conducted his trial the night of his arrest. He wouldn't have a hearing in the town's courthouse. The authorities arranged an immediate sentencing within the basements of the fortress-like hotel, in what the royal family called an emergency-sentencing-chamber.

The room above the chamber served as a witness room. Hotel guests became welcome spectators in the emergency executions taking place in the venue—on the condition that the establishment's manager opened the witness room for the event.

"What took you so long? Results are about to be revealed!" A bloodsucker directed his impatient words to the manager.

Two mummified guests ran down the stairs to the lobby. The one in charge instructed the other. "Make haste! We'll miss out, man!"

The anxious audience agitatedly asked the manager to hasten as they followed him toward the witness room. Stealthily, the observers entered a room with glass walls and floors, providing a view of the scene in the unsettling Follyn death chamber.

The chamber's glossy black tiles and marble walls gleamed with immaculate cleanliness. The deep black tiles absorbed all light, while the polished surfaces reflected everything like a mirror, capturing the faintest details of their surroundings. This created a disorienting effect. The stone walls, streaked with veins of white, radiated a dim glow, reflecting the light from the polished surfaces. As one moved through the space, the reflections shifted, creating new distortions and giving the impression that the chamber itself was alive, watching along with the spectators in the glass room above.

The crown prince sat in the judge's chair, as usual. Considering his training to take over for his father, the current king, the family agreed he fit best for sentencing severe cases. However, at the moment, the royal family erupted into discussion.

The judge's laid-back posture suggested nonchalance towards the event, yet the faintest ghost of a smile on one side of his face and the glint in his sapphire, reptilian-like, slit pupils betrayed his true feelings of entertainment. He was a master tactician, skillfully controlling his pawns and maneuvering his world like a grand chessboard. His wicked, intelligent mind and his indoctrinated faithful followers helped him keep the realm in line and maintain his prime position of authority. He did not tolerate the *evil* seeds who spread opposing opinions and questioned the laws of Follyn because he wanted to prevent such concepts from contaminating the "good" subjects. He kept this in check through noisy discussions in the courtrooms or the witness room where he placed his spies—starting with the hotel manager.

During those excited discussions filled with adrenaline, many individuals made promises to take certain actions against the kingdom's laws. Potential enemies came to light. Creatures spilled information which showed their loyalties. They engaged in heated arguments for or against the crown prince's ideas, and sometimes, they spoke of details of plots planned against him. In rare cases, such as the current one, even his fellow family members showed their loyalties and capabilities in the confines of angry discussions. All of this excited talk allowed the prince to gather information on his next potential victims. With fluency, he analyzed nonverbal cues and whispered comments. He paid a sharp attention to detail.

As such, the foolish imprisoned man, disguised as a shapeshifter, didn't consider the Crown's careful observation. The judge knew the accused wolf meant no harm. However, he possessed one of the most forbidden pieces of text, and the poor, innocent fool did not intend to turn it in to the royal family of the territory that captured him. Therefore, they justified carrying out his execution without delay. The monarchs aimed to demonstrate their authority, which became more crucial when handling matters on these enchanted objects. Any other person determined to awaken the contents of the text posed a severe threat to their power. In fact, the poor sucker who possessed the card might have escaped if he awakened the contents of the text with expert precision and fought with it. The Follyn royals planned to use the captive man as an example, making a resolute decision to apply the same punishment for all future offenders.

Once the crown prince settled the offender's sentence, he expected facing another conflict with his family. Each of them desired the power of this text, after all.

"Seems like there is an uproar inside as well," whispered a bloodsucker.

The witnesses fell silent, captivated by every word from the royals in the chamber.

During the royal family's debate, the bang of the gavel reverberated in the chamber three times in a row.

Did he have to strike the gavel multiple times?

No.

It always took a single *bang* to get everyone quiet in an anticipatory wait for the last words to be said by the judge.

The magistrate looked down at his victim. "We are all aware that capital crime comes with capital punishment."

The viewing audience couldn't contain their emotions and disrupted with shouts, gasps, and cries.

"Quiet!" exclaimed a bloodsucker, but he voiced it too late. The disturbance in the witness room drowned the judge's final words, and for the last time that night, he slammed his gavel into the podium.

No one needed to ask the verdict—everyone sensed the tense ambience, and while many approved, hotel guests from neighboring kingdoms and acquaintances of the accused man hid their silent wrath and distaste for Follynean practices—those of the crown prince in particular.

The judge of the realm, also being its future leading guardian and master of the realm, took the steps down from the dark room's podium and lifted his arm towards the chained shapeshifter. Two executioners held him in place—each of whom held one of the shapeshifter's arms out in order to expose his chest. Upon the wave of the crown prince's hand, the executioners dragged the criminal's body towards a beautiful porcelain tub in one corner of the chamber. Despite the offender's cries, the executioners chained his arms and legs to the edges of the decorative outline of the tub—the intersections of floral-patterned metallic swirls. Above him, towards the right of his body and a tad below eye level, rested a large, sharp blade. Operating in a manner reminiscent of Poe's pendulum, it only needed one swing from right to left to decapitate the criminal's head.

The executioners lowered the weapon until it aligned with his head.

A hint of a smile broke through the vicious crown prince's face while he viewed the villainous outlaw's defeated expression. He didn't cry, and he didn't yell for help as others did in his position. He recognized that any pleas for help would be in vain, or maybe his pride forced him to accept his deadly fate. A flash of regretful melancholy lingered in his eyes as he faced the onlookers above him with quiet resolve. The judge, possessed by the devil, enjoyed the prisoner's last moments of societal scorn. He took perverse pleasure in witnessing people lose their battles to Death right in front of him. The thrill of resisting the sight and scent of blood kept his emotions alive, a constant battle between desire and self-control. The mere sight ignited his urge to indulge, yet he fought to maintain his composure.

With a lift of his hand, the judge signaled the release of the blade. With a single motion, the large blade swung left, clicking into place.

Its mission ended in success.

Crimson liquid dripped from the sharp object.

The shiny white porcelain tub held a pool of the criminal's blood, and the eerie chamber became decorated with splatters of the runny ruby-like fluid.

The outlaw ceased to exist.

A shapeshifter's possession of a single card turned the beautiful, bewitching night into chaos.

I sprinted up the endless curved staircase which led to the hallway on the highest floor of my parents' palace. The full moon bathed the dark corridor in an eerie glow, and its brilliant light peeked through the translucent beige curtains draped over the windows.

The peaceful sounds of the gentle rain outside mingled with my ragged breath, the echo of my frantic footsteps, and the distant, haunting melody of the palace organ which played somewhere in the depths of the palace.

I was supposed to be alone.

The Follyn royal family nearly eliminated my bloodline from existence. Their crown prince, Altair, acted as the tactician for this massacre. He wielded powerful magical abilities, drawn by enchanted tarot cards and fueled by his insatiable greed. Altair sought to absorb the magical powers my family also gained through these cards.

He succeeded, leaving me as the only remaining survivor.

I recently witnessed the deaths and captures of everyone I loved— my mother; my father; my twin brother, Alphonse; and our caretaker, Xander.

Alongside Altair, Follyn's royal family's assassin, Corvus Noir, wielded the power of two of those tarot cards. He used one of them to unleash a gruesome, deadly plague upon my kingdom's citizens. This villain used his second card's ability to control sound. He mastered it by transforming objects into any instrument he wanted, effortlessly. Tonight, he mocked me by playing the organ in my family's palace ballroom, and using the power of his tarot card, he manipulated the sounds that came from it to track me.

Despite setting a trap for Altair, I clung to the hope that the assassin, the right-hand man to my primary enemy, would not locate me using the organ's sound waves. However, I hoped in vain. Before long, the sound waves rendered me deaf to the timbres of my surroundings, which indicated that Corvus Noir found me. Except, he didn't come after me.

He didn't stop playing.

He let me run.

Perhaps, somehow, the audio vibrations lead his master to me, and the realization of it made me more fearful of my fate and my plan, but I couldn't do anything else for myself.

I was the mouse Altair needed to catch. If he caught me exactly where I lured him into, I could win.

As opposed to Corvus Noir, Altair rarely used the abilities of the cards he possessed. When I witnessed him in battle, he specialized in attacking close-range, and that's exactly what I needed for him to do.

In my study, past the endless curved stairs and past the dark hallway at one of the highest points of the palace, I drew up a ritualistic circle through the entire circumference of the room. My use of invisible ink made things complicated, but I focused on the precision of my hand movements. I prepared everything needed for the ritual as specified by the last card of the enchanted tarot deck—card number twenty-one, The World. For The World to do my bidding, the ritual required a lethal amount of blood to be spilled in the center of the circle by another's hostile hand, along with the card itself.

I was ready to do the last thing I could do for myself.

I targeted the door within my sights, and even though I closed the distance between it and myself with rapid steps, I felt as if everything drifted. Before I laid a hand on the doorknob, the sounds of the organ ceased, and an eerie silence oppressed the ambience.

My intuition alerted me to something behind me.

Using the power from card number one, The Magician, I manipulated the elements. With hand motions, I dragged the rain and flowers from outside towards me, and I circulated the chaos of nature rapidly around me. The water engulfed me like a small rainstorm, and it shielded me from the dagger Altair threw my way.

So much for close-range.

He stood at the opposite end of the hallway, and I didn't have to turn to know he charged towards me, fast.

I flung the door open to my dark study and let the storm of rapid-spinning wind, rain, and flower petals block the entrance. The dance between the razor-like petals and knife-like raindrops formed a formidable barrier. Any attempt by Altair to pass through would mercilessly tear his skin apart. I would have attacked him, but my lack of energy and stamina wouldn't allow me to endure a battle—let alone against two opponents. At the very least, I wanted to use the last bit of my strength to pretend I shielded myself until the very end. My barrier bought me enough time to take my place within the trap I laid out for him.

I positioned myself towards the back of the room, below the center of the circle, and gripped The World. This card granted its wielder power to manipulate time, but it came at the cost of life.

Tears ran down my eyes.

I hated Altair with all of my being. He made the entirety of my life miserable. Because of him, I spent most of my life hidden and afraid. I believed my brother and I could live peacefully if we vanished together. I thought my family and I would be free from anyone's hatred and prejudice, but I was wrong. Altair and his family caught up to us before we had the chance to react in proper defense.

Amidst the chaos of my rainstorm, I discerned the outline of my enemy. He believed that in my desperation to stay alive, I accidentally barricaded myself in a trap. He also knew I would soon deplete my energy. Patience was his strategy.

Moments with my father, Xander, Alphonse, and my mother flashed through my mind. I felt their energies beside me. If my plan worked, I would see them soon.

I recalled the moment I let my mother in on my plan with The World.

Her words lingered in my head: "Remember, honey, place the card in reverse, and think of everyone you love. Your sacrifice will not be in vain. I know it."

With renewed determination, I focused on the circle and the card in my hand. A faint glow emanated from the card, infusing my heart with resolve. As I approached, the circle's energy responded to my presence, poised to activate the moment my blood touched the center.

My surrounding storm faltered, its fury diminishing with each step I took.

Altair's patience ran thin. His silhouette shifted, preparing to break through my barrier. My time was running out. I took a deep breath, steeling myself for my final moments.

I raised the dagger I concealed in my sleeve and pointed it towards the door as all my strength and energy gave out. The blade glinted ominously in the dim light of the room as I held the card in my other hand, positioning it in reverse.

Altair burst through my weakening storm, glaring at me with a high that made him appear to levitate in the dark energy surrounding him. I saw it through the glow and vertical-slit pupils in his blue eyes—resembling an ocean masking itself in the outer beauty of its deep-blue color, but underneath it all, there resided an abysmal depth that swallowed one in an endless darkness.

This devil held a sword in his hand—not that he needed it.

The moment in which we stared each other down seemed eternal. We encountered each other every so often, but after I went into hiding, the man and I never exchanged words in the few instances he caught up with me. We only shared stares filled with passionate hatred.

My expression showed immense hatred, disgust, discontent, distress, and displeasure at the sight of this man, and his eyes reciprocated the emotions. However, something in the depths of his irises wavered. Every time this devil snapped into his realization of hesitation, he did something drastic to hurt me—something to remind us of our opposition and hatred. The hint of his inner conflict vanished almost as soon as it appeared. The first time I perceived it, he killed my twin brother. When I discerned it the second time, he murdered my mother. At first, I thought my eyes saw what I wanted to see—hope that Altair held a hint of humanity in him.

That night, I witnessed his wavering gaze for the third time, but I didn't react. I no longer showed an ounce of empathy. I didn't feel a hint of light or hope for the creature that stood in front of me. Both of us knew, whenever this devil caught up with me, I encountered another tragedy.

Tonight was no different.

He took a step forward. I raised my dagger and charged towards him. I got to the center of the circle when Altair's sword pierced my heart.

Pain exploded through my body, but I held onto consciousness, focusing on the ritual. My blood spilled onto the center of the circle, and the room hummed with an otherworldly energy.

I locked my gaze into the eyes of the devil that ended me until I lacked the energy to keep my head up.

As my head dropped, I witnessed a thick, beautiful, illuminating silver strand as it pierced my chest. I focused the last bit of my sights on its beauty, and I wondered if it came from the murderer's sword, but it couldn't have. A unique sense of serenity accompanied it, and it stretched away from my chest, almost parallel to the sword, but not completely. I just didn't have the strength to look up and follow where it connected to. Not that it mattered—Altair's actions became meaningless, rendering them inconsequential.

I watched as my blood spilled all over the center, and this triggered the ritualistic circle to emit a brightly lit white glow from all of its invisibly written letters and patterns. The circle activated, and time itself wrapped and twisted around us.

The World card, now stained with my blood, pulsed with power.

Altair must have realized he fell into some sort of trap. He immediately pulled out his sword, and in one swift motion, he retreated from the glowing area and observed from the door frame.

In the final moments of my living consciousness, I dropped to the ground with my right palm flat on the floor. A reversed world successfully rested under it.

I felt a sense of peace. I did everything I could. The rest was up to the forces I set in motion. As darkness claimed me, I hoped that my sacrifice would be the key to ending Altair's reign of terror and bringing peace to those I loved.

Everything faded to black.

The Fool

I woke up in Xander's beach house on a cliff which faced one of Aquaenterra's shores—the kingdom neutral to Altair's and mine. Our parents kept my brother and me hidden in this kingdom for most of our lives. I awakened in my new life at seventeen years old—roughly sixteen years before my death.

The overwhelming shakes of anxiety made my breaths shallow and my muscles tense up. Desperation clawed at me, urging me to take action, but I couldn't afford to be impulsive. I attempted to calm myself by remembering that my physical being lived once again.

Sitting up, I ransacked my room for a notebook and a writing tool. With trembling hands, I jotted down events from my past life. My mind wandered through distinct moments in time—the good and the bad. Various scenarios played out in my head—things I should have done differently, things I could do again, and things I needed to watch out for. I mapped out timelines and approximate locations for any enchanted tarot cards. I came up with a variety of plans to push forward and find success.

Every card on the enchanted tarot deck lived up to its name. The World card placed time in the palm of my hand, making the world and its events hang at my mercy. This dismayed Altair, as the card he most desired—card number twenty-one—allowed me to steal his victory. However, the card only survived a single use, and after a successful first use, the card destroyed itself, and its ability ceased to exist.

I gambled with the card's ability because it brought the world back to a random point in time, but I seized a second chance with it—a reset I sincerely appreciated.

The image of Altair's eyes constantly replayed in my mind because something about it bothered me. As I looked into that devil's irises, just before my head became heavy, and I cast my gaze down, the color of his eyes bore a subtle change. They went from their blue hue to something closer to burgundy—much like the blood-sucking vermin Xander hunted. Not that it would surprise me—Altair being a vampire would make him more of a devil than I thought possible.

The events of my future felt like a vivid nightmare, but it all happened. I labeled those events as my past life because, this time around, I aimed to pursue a different path for my future. I couldn't allow myself to forget any of the events from my failed past. This time, I would tread carefully, and I would not hide.

So, I wrote my goals:

1. *Prevent Follyn from seizing my loved ones and my kingdom.*
2. *Establish an alliance with Aquaenterra before Follyn does.*
3. *Defeat Altair using any strategy possible—including gathering intelligence on his weaknesses.*

I needed to move secretly—especially for my third goal. I ran from Altair and hid from his family in my past life because of the severe anxiety I felt when facing them. Therefore, in this life, I vowed to confront them, determined not to let fear paralyze me again. I wanted to infiltrate their lives like a Trojan horse and cause mayhem in Follyn from within. Anything, as long as I kept them away from my home, The Kingdom of Deltrea.

In this life, I vowed to embrace stealth and cunning. I would no longer cower. Instead, I planned to infiltrate Follyn grounds and sow discord from within, but the dilemma remained—how would I achieve that?

After relentless writing, I paused and took another deep breath, allowing the weight of my words to settle. I closed my eyes and delved into the depths of my emotions. A pervasive taint of pure hatred settled in my soul, a dark cloud which seemed to overshadow everything.

Life encompassed a tapestry of beauty, woven with moments of joy and wonder, but negative emotions acted as a veil, preventing me from fully appreciating its magnificence. In my other life, I turned a blind eye to the warmth and kindness of people, and I fixated on the apprehension that arose from encountering the cruelty of others. So, I resolved to try again and tread a different path in this new life.

Once more, I closed my eyes and tuned in to the symphony of sounds around me: from the faintest whispers of the wind to the distant hum of life. I replayed past conversations in my mind. I remembered the moments of fulfillment shared with my loved ones— the laughter and the tears.

In my heart, a kaleidoscope of emotions swirled—genuine happiness, profound sadness, intense curiosity, wholehearted appreciation, and an insatiable desire to explore what my second chance offered. Unfortunately, I never felt this way about myself throughout the entirety of my past life. I didn't realize many others also faced numerous hardships in school. As a result, I kept quiet about unpleasant situations and dealt with them on my own, guided by the whispering voices of fear.

My background and culture didn't help. My kingdom, Deltrea, carried an infamous reputation and history of magic and witches. Vegalia, perceived as the most powerful witch in the world, ruled as a queen in my bloodline. She achieved her power by making a dark deal with the deity of the underworld, Xenoxas. The deity gifted her a tarot deck which brought the magic of the Major Arcana cards to life—the first twenty-two cards on most tarot decks. The knowledge and assistance Vegalia gained from these cards granted her immense abilities.

People widely speculated Vegalia sacrificed a Follyn prince to secure a powerful gift from Xenoxas himself. As a result, the people of Follyn met Vegalia's reign with disdain. They responded by ceasing trade and increasing prices for Deltreans, demonstrating their disgust, disappointment, and disagreement with Deltrean leadership. Shortly afterward, the kingdoms closed their borders to one another. Vegalia's reign triggered a chain reaction of wicked events between Deltrea and Follyn, planting the seeds of permanent rivalry, tension, and hatred which flourished between the royal families of both kingdoms.

When I was an infant, Follynean forces invaded Deltrea. Despite being a small kingdom, fiercely loyal citizens rallied alongside the king and queen—my parents. Follyn's continuous aggression and the resistance from my parents and our people caused such chaos and destruction that Aquaenterra, a neutral neighboring kingdom, intervened.

The royals of Aquaenterra proposed the construction of a neutral town for the children and youths of all three kingdoms—a place where the borders of the three countries converged. This town would feature three major schools: two private boarding schools for children and youths and a university. The royal families established the town intending to foster peace and understanding for future generations. Therefore, they decided not to construct any permanent residences, except for dormitories for students and faculty. Aquaenterra declared they would officially ally with the kingdom that showed most willingness for peace and coexistence.

This proposal offered more than the prospect of genuine peace. It also served as a convenient way for the kingdoms to keep a close eye on each other. After all, everyone wanted information regarding the lost magical cards.

My family wisely remained vigilant, but they showed their commitment to peace by sending me, their six-year-old child, to the children's boarding school. This school, along with the secondary school for grades seven through twelve, were both boarding schools, making all parties involved very reluctant to send their children.

However, integrating new ideals into children, and continuing to nourish those ideas as they grew, proved simple.

Aquaenterra forcibly encouraged each family to enroll their children in the town's schools to set an example and demonstrate their willingness to make things work. Therefore, after my brother and I were born, my parents kept one of us a secret.

Everyone knew that during the talks of forming this neutral town, my mother and the Follyn Queen were both pregnant. Despite my parents' hesitation, when the time came for me to attend the children's school, they cooperated.

Allegedly, Aquaenterra did not have children my age, but the Follyn kingdom had their own six-year-old, Altair Antares.

The highest-ranking royals and officials of all lands sent their children to this school. It reflected the friendly, allied, and often hypocritical features of Follyn, Deltrea, and Aquaenterra.

The school administration, whether through malevolent luck, a sick joke, or an attempt to help Altair and me become accustomed to each other, placed us in the same classroom for three straight years. Even when we stopped having classes together, he made it his mission to terrorize my school life until I left the children's school at ten years old. The other kingdoms disapproved of my parents' decision to keep me from attending the secondary school, so people spread the word of my weak leadership. People spread rumors about the frail princess who often needed to be taken out of school and brought home for weeks at a time. They also talked about my frequent crying, my fear of others, and my constant trips to the infirmary because of illness. These rumors somewhat allowed Aquaenterra to turn a blind eye to my disappearance. They saw me as a sickly princess who needed to be taken care of.

My parents communicated with Aquaenterran royals to voice their intentions of placing me back into the neutral town for university, depending on my physical and mental health. However, in my past life, they never forced me back there, and I never asked. This, perhaps, played a major role in how our lives unfolded. The people were right. I feared returning. In that neutral place, individuals frequently pointed out my grotesque differences from everyone else, and my classmates didn't hesitate to highlight it. I didn't understand why some individuals actively sought weaknesses in others to feel superior, especially when they discerned beautifully unique characteristics in their targets. As a child, I grew up feeling ashamed of myself and my Deltrean bloodline. I felt dirty, weak, and helpless.

Also, my unnatural violet-colored eyes and my corpse-like complexion only added to my sense of alienation.

"Are you going to grow a beak?" The children asked me this question daily.

Aside from the similarities to dark birds, they compared me to the dead or to a witch. Throughout the entirety of my past life, I believed them. My appearance suited my Deltran bloodline.

Contrarily, in this lovely second chance at life, I grew quite proud of it.

When I was ten years old, negative events behind the scenes heightened tensions between Deltrea and Follyn. Speculations arose that a significant number of cards from Vegalia's tarot deck granted all members of the Follyn royal family an ability, which alarmed my parents. They decided my twin brother and I would stay with their secret friend, Xander Von Almont, for safety until we could secure and learn to use an ability. We left Deltrea's capital for Aquaenterra's shores.

It was time for me to show new confidence and leadership. People needed to know me, and I had to form friendships and gain allies. Despite my intimidation, I needed to change from my past self and face my traumas, enemies, and responsibilities in my kingdom.

Six of Cups

"I'm surprised you came out without a disguise and without Xander." Alphonse played relaxing melodies on his kalimba as we journeyed into the nearest town. "I used to tell you to stop being paranoid, but now I'm anxious about it. Are you sure it's okay for you to be out and about?"

"Well, you're always out and about." I grinned at him.

"Mother and father kept me a secret. People aren't exactly aware a Deltrean prince exists."

I lifted my eyebrows. "Yeah, and I think we should keep that going for as long as possible—even when we return."

His eyes widened. "We're going to return?"

I nodded. "Soon. I'm done hiding."

"Whoa. What pulled the trigger on the sudden change of heart?"

"Death."

Alphonse stopped in his tracks. "Did someone die?"

"I want to avoid death for a long time if I can. Don't you?"

"Well, yes. That's why we're out here, so I don't think our parents or Xander approve of us going back to Deltrea."

"We agreed to go back after each of us secured a card. Xander will get one soon, and the only way we'll secure a second one *is* by going back."

"Lyra? Is everything okay? Did you somehow come across some information?"

I nodded and turned to face him with a smile. After I awakened in my new life last week, I looked for my twin brother—my very best friend. I hugged him as I cried and sobbed with emotions mixed with happiness, relief, and gratitude. In my past life, I mourned him in despair and sorrowful thoughts which forced me to accept he ceased to exist.

I snickered. "Tomorrow, when Xander returns from his mission, I am going to ask him to extend our daily combat and sword-fighting training sessions for the next seven months." I couldn't waste another day sitting around in a mess of thoughts.

My brother groaned. "The training is heavy enough as it is. I already train five days a week. We agreed you only had to do three because of all the concoctions you prepare for us and Xander's journeys. You got little sleep when you worked all five days, remember?"

"He's going to have to stop going on missions until after we leave."

"Are you stupid? The only time we get a break is when he leaves. Just join me for the other two days and choose not to sleep. Damn."

I shook my head. "Alphie, we must do it. We need to remember what we're up against."

"Lyra, we're not exactly at war."

"Yet. But, it will happen."

"I think you're overthinking things."

I shook my head. "We need to be ready for anything. Think about it, we're still living in hiding."

Alphonse remained quiet.

"After we complete our training for the day, I'm going to dedicate my evenings to train an ability."

My brother's eyes widened. "What do you mean, an ability? Getting one soon is all just your positive speculation, Lyra. We can't make any plans without the goods."

"I'm confident Xander succeeded in his mission. He's going to return with a tarot card."

"Hmm," my brother hummed in thought. "You've always said hope brings disappointment." Alphonse paused again; this time, he turned to face me with a suspicious expression. "What makes you so sure this time?"

I shrugged. "We got to manifest the positive."

We walked in silence. Then, he said, "Did you see the news I left on the table?"

"The one where Follyn royals execute a man in possession of a forbidden ability? Yes, I did." The media wrote many similar headlines throughout the entirety of my life. The Follyn royals conducted public executions, and in my past life, when Altair took charge of those public executions, he made an example of one of my own.

I shook my head at the disturbing thought.

In the past, fear and anxiety petrified me when I read those articles. They reminded everyone of the harshness and viciousness of the Follyn royal family, and Altair grew into the perfect fit to continue their tyrannical legacy.

"That family is another step ahead of us." My brother's expression looked thoughtful.

I believe the Follyneans make these articles public to inflict fear and hint that they have gained new abilities. However, I didn't want Alphonse to dwell on it, so I changed the subject. "For now, all we can do is go down to the town near here and browse the All Hallows' Eve shops."

Alphonse loved the haunting holiday. I wanted to enjoy it with him once before life became too... real.

He cracked a smile. "Does that mean you're joining me in the celebrations this year?"

"Well, what are you planning to do this year?" I asked my brother.

"Many Aquaenterrans have massive parties. I know because I used to go with Syrena, and we hopped from party to party in our costumes."

I stopped in my tracks.

Syrena? That's right. He met her during our time in Aquaenterra.

"You shouldn't be too careless, Alphie."

"We did nothing wrong. I had fun." He gave me a mischievous grin.

Ahh, yes. I understood his grin well, and with quick facial-analysis, I got the impression this brat had already made moves on Syrena. In my past life, I remained ignorant of the significance and power of this woman, but today, I knew an acquaintanceship with her held crucial importance.

I reciprocated my brother's grin. "Well, this time, I'll be joining your all's party hopping. Syrena sounds nice."

"I don't know about that, Lyra. Syrena's gone. Once she started university, she only comes here during the summer breaks."

Damn it, I thought.

He continued, "Also, the events are in three days, and you don't have a single costume."

"We'll find something."

He chuckled. "Xander's going to be so mad."

*****

"Oh, look at this, Elle!" Alphonse pointed to a witch's hat. "The one who created these hats must have thought of you!" he joked.

We avoided saying my real name in public, so he and Xander called me Elle—the initial of my first name. I grew my hair and stripped its dark color to give it a rose gold hue—the tips of its straight length fell past my lower back. I formulated an herbal potion I used as a regular eye drop solution. By applying one drop in each eye, I successfully eliminated the violet pigment for a minimum of twelve consecutive hours. My eyes took on an incandescent, dark gray tone—like those from a newborn's eyes.

I smiled at him. "You may be right, I should go full witch this All Hallows' Eve."

"Some of this stuff's *really* creepy," my brother said.

"I need to buy ingredients to reverse the rose-gold pigmentation on my hair," I muttered aloud.

"What? Why?"

"Well, right before we go back home, and I mean our actual home, I'm going to change my hair back, and I'm going to stop taking my eye drops."

Alphonse stopped paying attention to me as he got distracted while looking at all the items. "Look at this!" He pointed to a round, black rug which looked like a ritualistic circle. "Do you ever think these patterns are based on a Xenolian circle?" he whispered.

I shrugged.

My brother's body twitched with surprise after a creepy, skull-faced, black-cloaked figure convulsed and laughed manically—a shop worker did an excellent job at staying still until we passed right by him.

Alphonse laughed at the spectacle, and I snickered at him. He shook his head between laughs and trotted away from the aisle. With a harsh wave of his arm, he said, "I'll be back. I'm going to the men's room."

"Damn it, Alphie," I whispered as I shook my head. I hated when he left me alone, but I figured I would catch up to him once I browsed through the herbs in the store.

A whole little section of beautiful masks stood in front of me—half masks, full-face masks, and jester masks. Jester masks. My eyes flashed back to an unpleasant memory of Altair and his posse from when we attended the children's school. I shook my head.

Next to the masks, a row on the shelf displayed lovely, shiny velvet cloaks with smooth, spacious hoods. I mentally pieced together an improvisational last-minute outfit for the All Hallows' Eve celebrations. I picked a black velvet cloak and combined it with a black mask decorated with glittered-pink accents. The cute, simple outfit matched my rose-gold hair nicely, and I loved masks. Hiding my face always gave me a sense of comfort.

My eyes fell upon the fake bloodsucker fangs for sale, and I remembered the flash of burgundy hue which swirled over Altair's blue eyes on the night he murdered me. Might I have imagined it? Could it have been my blood falling into my eyes that skewed my vision? I shook my head. Perhaps, the transformation happened in his recent future.

I contemplated the thought as I walked out of the aisle with my materials in hand. As I scanned the store for the men's room, I recognized someone with a familiar yet intimidating presence, and he had just entered the store.

It was Altair Antares.

My body shook impulsively. Not a fortnight ago, this devil thrusted his sword into my heart. For that lengthy second, I tried breathing normally, but my subconscious knew better—the freshness of my mental wound did not allow me to face him.

The moment I noticed his gaze fixated on me, I turned around, praying he focused on more pressing concerns than a curiosity towards an unknown woman.

"Hehehehehe!" The same worker that startled Alphonse astonished me now, too—almost as if he laughed at my fear or mocked my cowardice. Even worse, this grim-reaper gave away my position.

"You just *had* to get me, huh?" My voice came out in a hissed whisper.

The worker gave a dumb laugh, and I blocked out his voice as he said something. I nodded dismissively as I walked away in a panicked haste and paced towards the next aisles.

When I put comfortable enough distance between Altair and me, I came up with the bright idea of putting on the cloak and mask I thought about purchasing. To the store employees, I looked like a customer trying on a cloak or an employee from the haunted mansion across the street. After all, many of the employees from there came to this store for food, snacks, and breaks.

I put on the items and walked to the next aisle in my disguise. A tingling, anxious sensation enveloped me, so I fast-walked as I looked behind me.

"Whoa!" Firm hands grabbed a hold of my arms as I bumped into the owner of the voice.

"I'm sorr-" I looked up to face him, and my eyes locked into ocean blue eyes.

I faced the devil who took my life away.

Impulsively, I faced the floor, and his hands slowly slid off my arms.

"It's fine." His delicately deep voice made him volumes more intimidating.

At first, I kept my head down, hoping he wouldn't recognize the girl he tormented as a child. I trusted my appearance to hide me enough to walk away unnoticed, but reminders of my determination to be different in this life filled my mind. Looking into this devil's eyes had the potential to push me a small step forward. Therefore, I persuaded myself to find the courage to hold his sapphire gaze on mine.

Unlike in my past life, his ocean-like gaze didn't hold hostility. They penetrated my eyes with a playful curiosity—a look I never imagined I would see plastered on Altair Antares' face.

I gave him a firm nod. Intending to take advantage of the silence between us, I started walking past him.

"Er, wait." I stopped in my tracks, but I did not turn to face him. This overwhelming encounter disoriented my nerves. Before facing him again, I needed to control my expression. To begin with, this marked the first time in our adult lives where we exchanged words.

It felt odd, to say the least.

If fear or hatred showed in my gestures, this devil would sense something off about me. Worse yet, I accompanied my hidden twin.

"Are you okay? It was a pretty hard bump." The odd, unfamiliar, soothing tone of his voice took me aback.

"I, uh," I swallowed before I nodded. "All good." Despite my consciousness attempting to keep me focused on sounding normal, my voice took a timid, low, breathy tone.

"Do you work here?" he asked.

"Not in this store, no," I murmured, and I hoped he didn't hear the slight shake of my voice.

He tilted his head in confusion as he eyed my outfit from top to bottom.

My brain tried to come up with a believable lie in a few seconds.

"Nearby," I added, but right after the word came out, I realized it may not have been the brightest idea. Because I took a second too long to answer, I might have already looked suspicious. Also, my answer may have opened a door to more questions from him, and I did not want to talk anymore. With that thought, my next words came out fast, and I said them as I paced away, "I'm already late, so bye! Have a good one!"

"Wait." The blood-sucking demon grasped the back of my cloak.

I stopped and faced him. My threatening gaze pierced his blue irises, but to my surprise, they returned a look I never perceived in them before. Again, nothing about Altair Antares' eyes appeared threatening. Instead of the usual hatred, these showed a curious mix of suspicion and interest.

"What's your name?" he asked.

"Look what I bought!" Alphonse waved a harmonica before playing a few notes—as if he'd never seen one before. He kept at least two at Xander's.

My anxiety increased, but this time, for my brother's sake.

Then, he directed his body towards Altair. "What's this? You made a new friend?"

Altair eyed my brother suspiciously.

I interfered, "We sort of… accidentally bumped into each other."

"Oof. No wonder you all are awkwardly quiet. You all okay?" Alphonse looked to and from Altair and me.

"Yes, she just seemed rushed." Altair's deep voice surrounded my ambience.

"Oh, did you think I left?" Alphonse asked, but before I responded, he added, "What the hell is this?"

My brother reached towards my hoodie and pulled it down.

"Yes, that's why I was looking for you," I spoke fast and interrupted any further unnecessary comments he would've made, and I hoped he caught the urgency in my voice. However, before I could add to my statement any further, Altair spoke.

"She told me she worked around here." His inconspicuous probing for answers startled me. I became more on-edge, so before my brother responded, I rapidly interjected.

"Yes, and we actually have to return to the haunted mansion! We only came to buy snacks, and I haven't even gotten those! We're already so late!" I paced away from the aisle again.

"Sorry about the bump, and thank you for checking up on me!" I waved behind me as I practically ran out and left a dumbfounded Altair standing behind me.

A sense of relief washed over me as I left the aisle and saw the checkout counter just fifteen feet away. I grabbed a few snacks from the nearby shelves and paid for them, along with my new outfit. I kept my disguise on to avoid suspicion since I *supposedly* needed to return to work. If Altair suspected my true identity, removing my costume would only confirm it.

How upsetting. I wouldn't have known Altair visited Aquaenterra because I never got out of Xander's house or its proximity in my past life. I stayed up on that cliff studying herbs, making concoctions, and doing many useless things!

What in the world did Altair want in Aquaenterra during this time period? Even in my past life, I never heard of any noteworthy events, but if I didn't know better, he sought another card.

Also, now that Altair loitered around this island, I needed to lie completely low until Xander completed his mission.

"So much for celebrating All Hallows' Eve this year." I murmured.

"That guy was Altair?" Alphonse's face showed surprise.

"Yes!"

"What the hell is he doing *here*?"

"We can only guess."

"We have to send word to Xander. Do you think he recognized you?"

"I don't know. If he did, I don't think he would have admitted to it. If he found the Deltrean princess, it'd be wise for him to feign ignorance and be watchful. I guess we'll find out whether he recognized me soon enough. This guy sends in his vultures to lurk and observe."

"Corvus Noir."

"Exactly, so we will not go through with fun plans. Not even you, Alphie. If you bump into him in any of those parties-"

"He will question me or have me followed."

"Yeah, if he got curious about me, I wouldn't put it past him."

As my consciousness took me through flashbacks of my past life and my childhood with Altair, a particular event came to mind. Altair charmed and captivated everyone during our time at the children's school, but unfortunately, he also bullied me.

My innocent naïve-self wanted to befriend him. My parents prohibited any kind of interaction with the Follyn prince, but they told me to watch him closely. He must have received similar instructions from his family because he also paid a lot of attention to me. We often caught each other staring. While this made him intimidating, I also developed a growing curiosity, and I wanted to show him I meant no harm.

One day, I felt daring. Students who completed their assignments for the day sat cross-legged on the classroom's cute, colorfully creative alphabet rug for playtime. Despite the teacher's attempts to keep Altair and me apart, I sat next to him when she focused on helping a classmate complete his assignment. If I got caught playing with Altair, I could innocently tell the truth: I wanted to share the bright-colored building-blocks with him.

I figured the kind action ensured I wouldn't get in too much trouble. Regardless, my subconscious deemed any troubles worthy if it meant he and I could become friends.

Altair froze when I sat next to him, and he gave me a look of distrust. I didn't blame him—we belonged to enemy families. Anyone would doubt of my intentions, but I aimed to show him my friendliness.

I turned to him with a wide smile, stretched my legs, and pointed to my new shiny black shoes. The cute flats looked adorable, with their large plum-colored velvet bow on the front.

"Do you like my shoes?" I asked.

He stared without saying a word.

I continued. "My mama sent me these shoes yesterday. She said they'd make me look cute!"

I looked towards his silent expression and hoped to receive some kind of positive response. To my surprise, he responded with a remark made in disgust.

"You look like a witch."

People in Follyn insulted others by calling them witches, but it seemed hypocritical since their royalty sought a magical deck of tarot cards gifted to a Deltrean *witch*.

"Lyra looks like a witch!" Roselia, another classmate, repeated aloud. Her voice dripped with mockery and amusement.

Why'd it have to be Roselia to hear his negative remark? I thought.

My fellow Follynean classmates, driven by Altair's remark, dubbed me "the witch girl" for the rest of my time in school, highlighting the snobbish and prideful nature of my peers.

The wise Deltrean children kept themselves separate from the ruthless Follynean kids. If the Deltreans saw me get bullied, fear kept them from stepping in to help, and I didn't blame them for their reasonable responses. If I, their own princess, didn't defend myself against the Prince of Follyn and his group, I understood the Deltrean children's lack of confidence and disappointment in me. Even at that age, I knew I meant to lead. I understood a certain responsibility rested on my shoulders, and the circumstances made me lose confidence in myself from a young age.

From that point on, Altair's torment began in school. I learned to keep my distance from him, but my initial approach to him opened the gates of his mischief.

Altair became leader of a posse, which hunted me down relentlessly during playtime. I always saved myself by keeping near the teacher's side.

"The witch girl" possessed a more solid meaning with my appearance in the mix. My classmates viewed me as the creepy princess without a normal color in her eyes.

When I turned ten, our school hosted an All Hallows' Eve masquerade festival during school hours. They wanted to avoid "scary" costumes that might upset some parents, especially considering our rocky territorial relationships. The school staff feared an arise of problems caused by anything offensive.

Therefore, I wore one of my magnificent ball gowns. I didn't take a mask. Instead, I sought to buy the most beautiful mask at the festival. Booths sold countless wonderful ones, and sure enough, I found it—a black mask with black and purple floral-patterned glitter outlining it. The mask featured metallic floral patterns stretching from around the eyes past the outer corners, with glossy gradient shades of plum purple and cerulean blues. My dress displayed a creamy light pink, so the mask created a contrast, but I didn't care. I wanted the beautiful mask, but I realized I left my coins in one of my classrooms.

I ran inside the empty school while teachers, staff, and students enjoyed themselves at the little festival outside.

When I arrived at the classroom, I hurried to a little treasure chest designated to me—the teacher assigned one to each child. In it, we placed our bags, books, and miscellaneous belongings. I kneeled in front of the chest with my name on it, but before I retrieved my bag, Altair and his friends, Roselia and Adrian, creeped up behind me.

Before I got myself up from the floor, a pair of hands pushed my shoulders down while someone sprayed my dress in dark liquid. My screams echoed through the room as I fought against the little devils.

"Keep her quiet, Ian!" The command came from Altair's voice. "I don't want the teachers to hear."

Another hand covered my mouth.

I kept my eyes shut.

"Pass me the purple one!" The discernable amusement echoed in Roselia's voice.

I continued to struggle and cry out, but I kept my eyes shut.

They placed a mask over my face.

Adrian's disdainful laugh echoed in the classroom. "Now she's a jester!"

"Let's tell everyone to come see!" Roselia's voice retreated as she put distance between us.

"No!" Altair exclaimed. "The teachers will find out what we're up to."

"She's Deltrean, Altair. They won't take her side!"

"We still need to be careful."

Contrary to what they believed, I felt blessed to have the mask hide my face. It concealed the tears rolling down my cheek and allowed me to maintain a composed appearance.

"My parents," I breathed.

"What?" Altair responded.

"My parents were right. You and your family are bad people. You'll be a king no one likes!" Despite not being able to see him, I sensed Altair's seething anger.

The sound of Roselia's chuckle reached my ears. "I like Altair," she said.

As someone grabbed my arms, they forcefully dragged me somewhere. I struggled against them.

"Help me put the jester in the closet!" Altair yelled.

Suddenly, I found myself in a tight, muffled space. For the first time in my life, I experienced being completely enveloped in physical and mental darkness.

The jester's meaning shattered my spirit. To these Follynean kids—to Altair—I embodied a joke of a Deltrean princess. Even my fellow Deltreans feared his posse. How could they not? Altair targeted their princess, and he triumphed.

"You better say we had a fun spray-painting game!" Adrian called out from outside the closet.

"Yeah, or we're going to come back for more every day." Roselia added.

"We'll come unlock her when everyone's gone." Altair's voice grew distant in my ears.

I remember the screaming, banging, and crying. With a swift motion, I yanked off the mask and focused on it—the only thing visible in that tenebrous room—an old-fashioned jester. It resembled the sad face drama icon. Little bells adorned it. I tossed it to the side in all my frustration, and I hugged my knees and dug my face into them, and I cried, and I cried.

After what felt like an eternity in that somber room, the jingling bells from the mask interrupted my sobs. At first, I thought I imagined it or accidentally kicked it, but it alerted me enough to stop my sobbing. When my eyes adjusted to the dark, I differentiated the blacker outlines of its face and figure, smiling back at me.

When I took my eyes off it, I placed my head back down between my legs. I didn't want to see it or face the surrounding darkness. I stayed silent, too gripped by fear to let the tears flow.

Each footstep, creak, and distant voice made me hyper-alert. As I listened, I realized they all came from outside the classroom. I kept my legs pressed against my body and stayed a safe distance from the mask to avoid disturbing it.

Just as I slightly relaxed, the bells jingled again. I remained frozen in my position as my face grew pale.

A chill ran up my body during the eternal moment of silence.

Again, the mask produced a light jingle, and I screamed again—more than a cry—my screams carried the terror in my heart.

Altair, hearing the change in my cries for help, opened the door and dragged me out when he saw me paralyzed in my fetal position. The jingles and my screams stopped.

Despite not lifting my head, I sensed Altair kneeling in front of me.

I remained seated, fully expecting him to inflict more pain or mock me, but he didn't, and his entourage did not accompany him. He simply sat in front of me, staring for several silent seconds, but I never looked up to face him. I feared his hateful glare.

Finally, he got up, and he closed the closet door. He opened the classroom windows to let the sun in. Then, he slowly turned towards the classroom exit, and his footsteps retreated.

"I'm gonna tell." I whispered as I peeked up at him.

Altair's footsteps paused, but he did not turn to face me.

I should not have said that. I should've done the deed without warning him I'd do it. Beads of sweat dripped down in dreadful anticipation. Many thoughts raced through my mind at the same time: Would he lock me up again? Would I be in the dark for more time? Would he bring his group back? Were they lying in wait outside the classroom? Even worse, we both knew the gravity of the situation if I mentioned something to my parents. Things were as tense with our families as it was. Would I be causing war or chaos if I said something?

Altair said nothing. He didn't turn back to face me with his intimidating glare. Instead, he walked away silently, but there seemed to be an unusual weight on his back. His head and his small shoulders seemed downcast as opposed to the confident Altair that always held his head high. When I finally got up from the floor, I saw a big white box at the entrance of the classroom. It had my name on it, and it was not there before. Upon opening it, I discovered a beautiful pink dress. The one I wore at the moment had a lighter color.

When I removed the garment from the box, a small bracelet containing a royal blue crystal charm shaped like a pinecone fell out. These Follynean pieces of jewelry used different colors to convey different meanings. Royal blue signified an apology.

That afternoon, something felt different. His presence comforted me. For once, he refrained from displaying any hostility. This might explain why I continued to have hope in him, especially when I detected the hint of hesitation in his eyes during our future encounters.

However, Altair's increasing cruelty and cleverness made him a dangerous little boy, so I did not rule out the possibility that he prepared this to avoid trouble. Regardless, he stopped bothering me after that day. Not that it mattered. I went into hiding with Alphonse and Xander shortly after the incident.

"I guess it's a good thing we have our vulture, too." My brother's voice interrupted my flashback.

"What vulture might this be?" Xander's deep voice came from behind us.

The Magician

"You," Alphonse said with a laugh.

"Training's going to be brutal this week, huh?" Xander said with an irritated grin on his face.

Xander grabbed the top of my brother's head and pushed it down.

I chuckled. "That's what you get for calling him a vulture."

Alphonse let out a small groan. "Say something to make your presence known. You're always walking in like a ninja."

Xander Von Almont stood tall and muscular. His golden tanned skin complimented his big brown eyes and his wavy, milk-chocolate colored hair which fell past his shoulders. The thirty-year-old man typically wore a faded-brown coat, white button-up shirts, brown or faded-black pants, brown boots, and a faded-brown cowboy hat. With a taste for simplicity, he found solace in merging with the natural world, be it the bark, dirt, or surrounding nature.

If people ever witnessed the delicacy and color of Xander's living space, they would have felt more comfortable approaching him.

Xander maintained his house with meticulous organization and cleanliness. Knowing his attention to detail, I understood how his cozy home provided a perfect cover. If anyone investigated this house, they would never believe the ruthless Xander Von Almont lived here.

Outsiders saw Xander as a hurricane-like man. Even though Xander reserved his true appearance for missions regarding my family, many never got to witness the scratchy-bearded, gruff appearance he used in public. When signs of Xander's presence appeared in villages across the kingdoms, it caused commotion, rumors, and uproar among the citizens. People could only guess to describe him as a sharp, agile, observant, multi-talented man who seldom spoke. Word-of-mouth is how Xander got his fame. He gained a reputation as the enigmatic bounty hunter who pursued criminals and supernatural beings, instilling fear in those who couldn't fathom his prowess against demonic entities.

Some people suspected he used Vegalian tarot cards to track down criminals who encountered these cards and used, bought, or sold them illegally without reporting them to the royal families. Others speculated he was a dark creature himself. Questions about his loyalties arose, with rumors circulating that he worked for any human who paid for his services, showing no loyalty to anyone. However, some believed Xander's loyalty lay with Follyn.

This first speculation held true—Deltrea granted Xander special permission to wield card number fourteen, Temperance. As such, when a royal family granted an ability to a royal retainer, they became immune from facing criminal law.

My family relied on Xander as our undercover bodyguard, and my father trusted him as his right-hand man. Alphonse and I stayed hidden while he carried out bounty missions, maintaining a neutral facade to avoid raising suspicion about his loyalties. Therefore, Xander cautiously visited Deltrea, staying in the area just as long as he did in other kingdoms. My transformative herbs and concoctions further enhanced his dexterity in disguises, which helped him conceal his true identity during infiltration missions and secret travels.

People felt intimidated by him, but they admired and respected him. He conveniently built a diverse reputation.

Before Alphonse and I went into hiding with Xander, my father gifted him Temperance. He thought it wise for our most loyal retainer to have one, especially since Alphonse and I would be under his wing. It was a sensible call—Follyn had the same idea with Corvus Noir.

With Xander at our side, they weren't the only ones with a knight on the board.

Xander accepted the abilities Temperance offered, and I couldn't picture anyone wielding it better than him.

Xander lived in a humble home on a small cliff of Aquaenterra—dangerously close to the Follynean border. He hid us in plain sight.

He served as the perfect temporary caretaker, but our stay with him extended beyond temporary in our past lives. Altair murdered my brother before we ever returned to Deltrea. Therefore, Alphonse never lived at home as an adult, and I only returned to Deltrea near the end of my life. I planned to avoid repeating that mistake. Xander Von Almont protected my family until he drew his very last breath.

"Lyra believes you succeeded." My brother interrupted my stream of thoughts.

"He did." I confirmed Alphonse's declaration.

Xander lifted an eyebrow. "You're making quite the confident statement."

My gaze remained fixed on him. "I know I'm right. I had a good feeling about this mission."

"Hmm," Xander scratched his beard. "What are you concocting now?" he asked.

"An elixir that will change my hair back to its original color."

He observed me, noticing my unusual behavior. "Isn't it going to be harder to stay hidden?"

"I'll spread this on my hair the day we return to Deltrea."

This time, he gave no response, but I sensed his curious gaze on me as he shuffled behind me. He likely laid out the spoils from his journey, as he usually did when he returned from a bounty hunt.

"Yeah, I know. She's been a little weird. She accompanied me to the town," Alphonse added as he walked towards his room.

He lay on his creaky bed, playing his harmonica. Xander and my brother loved music, but Alphonse couldn't seem to go about his day without playing something. Whether it was a piano, guitar, ukulele, or a handheld instrument, he always held something in his hands—

even while interacting with others. While he usually favored his little kalimba, today he opted for his new harmonica.

His door remained opened to continue to listen in and chime in on the conversation—another thing he often did.

"Is that so?" Xander appeared to speak his thoughts aloud to himself.

"We encountered Altair Antares!" my brother called out from his room.

At this, Xander's movements froze.

"You should have mentioned this *detail* right when I arrived."

Alphonse feigned cluelessness as he played a lively melody in the background, and I didn't offer a reply.

"You didn't send word?" Xander's serious tone contradicted the ambience my brother created.

"What if the pigeon didn't find you? That would have been delicate information." I replied.

"We have codes for a reason." Xander's annoyance brought about his no-nonsense and matter-of-fact remarks.

I replied. "I don't think it would have reached you; you would've been on your way back as our encounter with that devil just happened this morning."

Xander's brown eyes locked onto mine. "Did he see you?"

"Yes."

"Did he know it was you?"

"I don't know."

"How do you know it was him?"

"I would never forget his face," I said this as Altair's features flashed across my mind—all the times we encountered one another, all the times he hurt one of mine, and the time he murdered me.

"Have you sent word to the king and queen?"

"No."

"Lyra." He sighed, annoyed. Xander sounded like my father when he interrogated others.

When I remained silent, he added, "Did the brat talk to you?"

"Wait! Xander, I will tell you everything, but first, you should know something."

He stared at me, his eyes fixed, waiting.

"I *know* you succeeded."

"I did. I got my hands on one of them."

The music stopped. My brother got up from his bed—only to bring his body frame into view.

"Wait, what?" My brother walked towards Xander with an astonished expression.

I grinned. Yes, he did. In the past, we decided I would take this card because Alphonse remained a secret to the world. I aimed to hasten the process this time since I knew the time and location of another card.

"Xander, I'd like for us to extend our training for the next seven months."

"Why seven months?"

"Because after that, I will have one month to settle in Deltrea and prepare for the upcoming school year."

Poor Xander received his fill of surprises today.

"That's not the deal I made with your parents, Lyra."

I nodded. "I know. We all require a skill before we can go back, but surely, you understand that locating a single card takes years. Only twenty-two cards exist, and it's uncertain if the Follyneans and Aquaenterrans have half of them. Searching the kingdoms for these cards is tough; they could be anywhere."

"Why the sudden urge to go back?" Alphonse asked with concerned curiosity in his expression.

"Don't you want to go home?" I looked into my brother's honey-brown eyes, but his gaze dropped in a thoughtful gaze after a second—something he did when he found himself unsure of how to respond.

Xander shook his head. "It's not safe."

"Well, our parents promised the other kingdoms I would return for the university years."

"If the kingdoms have anything to say about it, we'll listen. Until then-"

I interjected. "What if I told you we could have another card in our hands by the next All Hallows' Eve?"

Xander shifted his weight from one foot to the other. "Did you somehow come across some information?"

I tilted my head to the side and shrugged. "Somewhat. Yes."

"Explain."

"You wouldn't believe me if I told you."

Xander pierced me with his gaze. He never pried, but he definitely contemplated something. Finally, he let out a frustrated sigh.

"Lyra, you're going to have to give me more than that. I can't exactly take you all back without following through with my part of the deal. If the Follyneans have as many cards as we predict they do, you all are not safe in Deltrea—much less in that neutral town."

"The card will be here, in Aquaenterra. However, it will be near the town of neutrality."

"Then we will be there until then."

I shook my head. "Contacting the card requires a specific text found only at the university."

My statement only revealed half the truth. If I could pretend to gather information at the university, it would be easier to persuade Xander and my parents. However, a merchant with the text would simply pass by the Aquaenterran entrance to the university.

Both my brother and Xander wore grave expressions on their faces. Obtaining card location information proved challenging. Their reactions showed a mix of wonder, questioning whether I truly knew the details or went insane.

"You know, Lyra," my brother broke the silence. "If you want to return, we can explore alternative methods to persuade our parents, but inventing something like this? They won't believe-"

"Do you doubt me, Alphie? Really?"

"Okay. Well, allow me to rephrase my question. How did you come across this information?"

"I..." I paused. The story of my past life would undoubtedly provoke Xander, my father, and possibly my brother into becoming impulsively hostile.

"I dreamed of it."

Xander and Alphonse appeared flabbergasted.

I wanted to be honest with them, but some cards peeked into a person's mind. Therefore, to ensure everyone's safety, I alone carried the burden of knowing about our past lives. Instead, I told them that, a few days ago, I experienced a prophetic dream and woke up ready to face everything. I shared enough to gain their faith in my actions, but not enough to spark conflicts.

Truthfully, my family and I gained all the information on that card's location in my past life, but we arrived at the locale too late. The Follyneans got to it first.

When Xander and Alphonse said nothing, I continued speaking. "I dreamed of your success today, too, Xander. The card which currently rests in your pocket is card number one, The Magician."

Xander's eyes widened, and his expression paled.

"Is that true, Xander?" Alphonse asked.

Xander sighed. "Are you sure you're ready to go back?"

"Positive, and it should also be sufficient time to master manipulating my first ability."

Xander raised his dark eyebrows. "I thought the cards terrified you."

"I have no choice, Xander."

"Hmm." Xander took out the card and handed it to me.

Welcome back to my life, I thought as I looked at the card.

The enchanted tarot cards could stand upright. Silver edges outlined all the ones I encountered, and translucent shades of purple, blue, and crimson adorned their backdrops. An inner and an outer black border interrupted cards' illustrations and spills of color. Silver embossed letters read the cards' names.

Even though the cards resembled fine glass, people could fold them, set them on fire, and do absolutely anything else one could think of to destroy them, but they always looked new. Not a single scratch, crease, or tear flawed these cards.

"Did you test the card's legitimacy, Xander?" my brother asked.

"I did."

"Let's take a look, then," I said.

I placed the card at the center of a piece of parchment because these cards exposed another neat feature when placed on it. All the instructions on how one could permanently possess the card's ability appeared in silver-lined glowing letters on the blank paper.

Together, Xander, Alphonse, and I watched as lines of text and shapes appeared around the card.

A moving circle appeared at the top center of the page—each tarot card revealed unique patterns on the outlines of their circles.

The card itself showcased a shimmering Roman numeral I on its top center. In its bottom center, it read, "The Magician."

A shut eye rested below the card's number. All cards displayed this eye. A shut eye indicated the card was dormant and unowned. When the eye opened, it signified that the card had responded to the person who awakened it through its corresponding ritual.

An open eye could only shut with the death of its card's master, causing the card to lie dormant until a new, worthy master awakened it once more.

"What ingredients and actions are required for you to complete the ritual?" my brother asked.

Xander raised an eyebrow. "She must confront four fears. One for each element."

That's why it took me so long to awaken it the first time.

"That won't be a problem." My tone reflected my confidence.

"I mean, she kind of already encountered Altair. Does that count?"

A slight smirk formed on my lips. I've faced the death of all my loved ones. I've faced my enemy. I've faced failure, and I've faced death itself. I used to fear much more than this, too.

I moved the table where the card and the parchment sat.

"A dream, huh?" Xander's low voice echoed through the room.

I nodded. "A dream which also sent me the message that I needed to go back to Deltrea, and I needed to start university in the neutral town—where I will gain many allies."

"Hmm." Xander often let out a single, low hum as he listened, immersing himself in doubts, thoughts, and questions.

"Do you think our parents will agree to us returning?" Alphonse murmured his question, just loud enough to be heard.

"Whether or not they agree, I will go back. Our future depends on it."

"Hey," Xander finally spoke, but his tone took a dark undertone, so I interrupted him before he lectured me or questioned me further.

"The card, Xander! Right now, I need solitude. I must focus, and I need all the space in our living room." I expelled the two sizable males from the premises. "You can trust me. I will only take a few minutes."

"Wait, do you even have everything? There are some ingredients in there that-"

Xander interrupted Alphonse, "Lyra, it also requires a bunny, apart from the fact that slaying one is something you'll never do-" I ignored my brother and walked towards Xander.

"I have everything. Xander, please. You all need to step out for a bit."

"Wait, but what about facing your other fears?" Alphonse asked, but Xander dragged him out with him.

Xander faced me. "If this works, you owe me an explanation."

My brother yelled from outside the house, "What the hell, man? Our conversation wasn't over!"

I nodded. "We have a lot to talk about."

Xander gave me a hard stare, but he said nothing more. He walked out and closed the door behind him, but I still heard Alphonse's muffled complaining.

"Do you think she's possessed? She was a different person just last week. Oh! She's been weird ever since she woke up in tears and hugged me the other day. You should've seen her!"

My brother's voice trailed off as I focused on the new task in front of me.

After I made sufficient space in the living area, I drew the ritualistic circle on the floor, following the specific symbols, letters, and shapes as instructed by the card. This process began the unification with the card, serving as a welcoming and an opening.

I copied the design exactly as it appeared on the parchment. Once completed, I sat at its center and placed the card and parchment in front of me, facing me.

Before my brother woke up that morning, I prepared a little jar of mixed ingredients needed for the ritual, and I caught a beautiful little bunny.

I took out a box which contained the bunny I caught that morning, a dominantly gray-furred lionhead whose irises reflected a deep dark brown over big black pupils.

I extended my hand to caress the little thing.

"The card said nothing about slaying a bunny," I muttered to myself.

In my past life, I wasted many months without mastering The Magician's ability because I doubted my worth. Every time I attempted the ritual, it never worked. The circle never glowed, and to my dismay, the bunny I slayed never resurrected. I made an unfortunate mistake.

The ritual needed a live bunny.

The parchment contained a chant that the card's potential possessor must read once, marking the first declaration of partnership between card and master.

I read it aloud:

With elements that bend to thy command
Thou blend'st Fire, Water, Earth, and Wind at hand.
I present to thee this vessel of mine,
Imbue my soul with magic so divine.

Let wrath unfold with Fire's fierce desire,
Let Water's untamed dominion inspire.
Bring forth the storm with fury unconfined,
As elements obey my will and mind.

Commune with the calming peace of the Earth

And Wind, serene, doth whisper of its worth.
In peaceful harmony, these powers blend
To shape the world where natural forces mend.

Lend me thy power till death doth us part.
Trickster, arise, and show thy cunning art!

The Magician accepted the ingredients, and the bunny's eyes glowed along with the circle's glowing shades of purple, blue, and silver, which engulfed my surroundings.

As the eye on the card opened, I grinned instinctively as it peered back at me.

To my knowledge, only this card sought to control another creature. The card and bunny emitted a radiant glow, as bright as the circle, capable of blinding any onlooker. Despite the card and ingredients disappearing, the bunny remained. The little animal became a vessel for The Magician. Their spirits merged, with the bunny's heart becoming The Magician's new dwelling. Even if anyone tried to kill it, the bunny remained immortal until my death.

He made for a cute little companion. When it needed to remain hidden for me, it could shapeshift from its bunny form into a little ball of light at will, and the tiny ball of light would hide and live in one of my pieces of jewelry—preferably something I wear every day.

"Hello, Benjamin." When The Magician took on the bunny form, I named him Benjamin in my past life.

The little bunny scratched its ear, and it looked at me as if it didn't have a care in the world, but I knew he understood *everything.*

I took out the bracelet Altair gave me as a child. Throughout my past life, I refrained from adding any additional charms to it, and I never wore it either. This time, I intended to imbue his gift with powers which would ultimately bring about his downfall. I gestured to the lone blue pine cone charm.

Benjamin understood, and he shapeshifted into a little ball of light that faded into the charm, and he sealed himself in.

The Magician lent me his power once again.

Xander, Alphonse, and I trained as a team.

"When we arrive at Deltrea, it'd be wise to be in the eyes of the public all the time. False evidence and rumors could circulate if we're caught alone." In my past life, this is how Follyn framed my family and gained Aquaenterra's allegiance.

"You are overly confident we're returning soon." My brother replied to me with skepticism.

"Whether or not your return to Deltrea comes soon, Lyra's right. If we get caught alone in foreign territories, we run a greater risk," Xander added as he observed Alphonse and me.

Xander was a brutal coach, but he significantly increased our combat skills and knowledge. He grew up in the servants' quarters of my parents' palace. Noticing his capabilities, my parents provided him with an education from the royal family tutors. He eagerly pursued this knowledge, often saying he would teach for the Deltrean royal family. That became his plan—a prodigious teacher intending to educate the future prince and princess of the kingdom.

My parents altered the extent of his plan when they sent Alphonse and me away with Xander to go into hiding. Xander became our teacher and taught my brother and me everything throughout the years. I excelled in sign language, history, herbs, and medicines while my brother excelled in archery, fencing, and music. I mixed herbs and created new concoctions better, while Alphonse picked up sounds and rhythms skillfully. He and Xander shared a passion for music. I loved it too, but Xander and Alphonse dedicated themselves to learning almost every instrument they got their hands on. Now, with their help, I filled the gaps in everything I lacked in combat.

"Imagine if Altair would've remembered you?" my brother asked as he blocked my sword with his.

"We might need to change locations soon, just in case the Follyn Prince loiters around," Xander added.

I shot Xander a frustrated look. "There's no need to change locations. We're fine. Our next destination is home, anyway."

My brother swiftly dodged another one of my attacks and spoke as if he faced no challenge. "What will we do when we return, though? What if nothing improves and tension lingers?"

"Well, first, we need to possess tarot cards."

I rolled my eyes at Xander's stubbornness.

He remained unconvinced with my plan, but after a few back-and-forth coded letters between my parents and me, we reached an agreement: I could enroll in Crescencia University—the school of higher education in the small college-town of Crescencia—the town developed to be neutral grounds for citizens of all kingdoms. However, I could only attend school for one year, and if I could not secure a card in the upcoming school year, I would go back to hiding with my brother and Xander.

"It took you years to find a card for Lyra, Xander, and it was only your second find. I don't mean it in a bad way, either. We understand finding a card is brutal, but if you let me join your journeys, we probably would've obtained a third one."

"You're a hidden prince, Alph. We can't risk it."

"If we're home before All Hallows' Eve, and I attend the academy, we'll be within reach of a new card. That one will be Alphie's."

Xander and Alphonse ceased all of their movements at my words.

"You have another prophetic dream?" Xander asked sarcastically. He doubted my story but didn't press for details, even though he struggled between trusting me and his hunch, which told him I hid something. The latter irritated him, but I simply shrugged at his comment.

"Been having those a lot lately, huh?" my brother asked. As opposed to Xander, Alphonse genuinely believed me.

I nodded. "We'll get you that card when the time is right, Alphie."

"As for assisting me through my journeys, Alph," Xander lit up a cigar. "Questing cards is important, but tense situations always end up exploding, so keep yourself safe and stay alive, so one day, you can come out of hiding, and you can be home openly. You know, for yourself and for your people."

"That's right. No more running, and for our second goal, we must aim to secure Aquaenterra's allegiance."

Alphonse looked at me with a surprised expression.

Xander gave me his default, unreadable, hard stare, which analyzed how my personality changed from one day to the next.

"How do you expect to do that?" Xander lifted his eyebrow.

"The university. I'll begin with the new generation of Aquaenterrans attending school."

"I mean, I have a few friends here, too."

"It's different, Alph. You're a secret prince. Also, there's a difference between making friends while in hiding and making friends while facing the world in a neutral ground where there are eyes of every kingdom all around you."

Xander gave a small nod in agreement as he blew a puff of smoke away from Alphonse and me. "You're right, but also remember Lyra, leaving grade school made you light up again. Are you sure you're ready to go back?"

Alphonse and Xander indirectly referred to my traumatic childhood experiences in Crescencia, but after facing death, I believed I could overcome a new round of school and face a fresh path. Therefore, I nodded in response to their observing eyes. "I should have gone back a long time ago."

"That's the thing. Maybe we've waited too long. By now, Altair Antares might have the upper hand there, don't you think?" my brother interjected.

I cringed at the demon's name. "If he's anything like his childhood self, he sticks to Follyneans. People remain loyal to him out of fear. So, even if he holds the upper hand, I will change that."

As far as I knew, he did not associate himself with many Aquaenterrans until later in his lifetime.

"Hmm." Xander continued smoking.

He started smoking more often than he did in my past life. Recognizing the potential stress it could cause the poor man, I opted to conceal my third goal. Both Xander and my family would likely struggle to accept it, and I expected it would be the most challenging one for me to achieve. I aimed to get Altair Antares to question his loyalty to the twisted ways of his own kingdom. I wanted to end him— whether through his death or by betraying him after gaining his trust and friendship.

In this life, I awakened wiser and much more mentally and physically fit to defend myself and my kingdom. Despite that, I felt psychologically unprepared to return, but I pushed myself. My future would remain doomed if I didn't conquer my fear. Since I witnessed the destruction of The World in my past life, this new beginning gave me my last opportunity.

*****

Every other night, after Xander and Alphonse slept, I sneaked away from the house to enjoy walks in Aquaenterran territory with Benjamin. Occasionally, I used this time of night to train my ability and build my stamina. I walked about a mile to the shore and basked in the beautiful melodies of the waves.

As the night fell heavier upon the earth, my mind buzzed with many potential plans to trap Altair.

Soon after I began my way back, a sinking sensation hit my stomach.

Someone watched me.

Impulsively, I glanced at Benjamin, who gave me a wary look. The best thing about our partnership was that The Magician synchronized with my thoughts and feelings. He always understood exactly what I wanted.

I bent down to pick up a wooden stick and acted as though I cleaned it. With my thoughts, I used The Magician's ability to carve a message into it.

The wood divided to form the letters I wanted. It bent, curved, and engraved the word *HIDE* according to the soft dictations of my fingers.

"Fetch, boy!" I threw the stick, pretending to play with the bunny.

Take it to Xander, I commanded the little animal with my thoughts.

Benjamin hopped away with my message. Feigning annoyance after losing sight of him, I pretended to follow Benjamin into Aquaenterra's palm forest.

Beads of sweat ran down my face, not from exhaustion, but from nerves and fear. I ran from the shore to the forest for about fifteen minutes, in the opposite direction from Xander's house—I hoped to give him and Alphonse enough time to evacuate and hide.

"Benjamin!" I yelled as I ran, pretending to be unaware of my stalker's presence. I hoped Xander and Alphonse heard me, but I knew it was a long shot.

I entered the forest and followed the lanterns which lined the sides to its dimly lit trail.

"Benjamin, please come out!" I wondered what took the stalker so long, but I figured he waited to see if I would walk further into the forest, too.

Snap! I jumped at the sound, only to look down and spot Benjamin.

Good, I thought. *If Benjamin's back with me, Xander and Alphonse should have gotten somewhere safe.*

"There you are, baby!" I picked up the bunny and kissed his little head.

My excitement faded when Benjamin jumped out of my arms to face something behind me. I turned and followed my bunny's gaze to a figure ahead of us in the distance.

A dark silhouette faced me.

The full moon's glow glistened above him, highlighting the entity's characteristics and enabling me to perceive him clearly. Dread overtook my entire body when I recognized the outline of the long, beaked mask on the entity's face. The black hood worn by the figure cast a shadow over the yellow glow emanating from the mask's eyes.

My mind processed the ominous silhouette, and my heart raced as I locked eyes with Corvus Noir's foreboding presence.

The assassin's long black cloak, with its ripped and tattered ends, stood out unmistakably. His black scarf billowed in the wind, and though I couldn't see his exact garments beyond the outlines, I vividly recalled his distinctive attire.

Like Altair Antares, Corvus Noir always wore his default black attire—fitting for a phantom of the night. Even though I couldn't see him clearly, I recognized his black shirt tucked into his black trousers, which were tucked into short, pointed boots.

His plague mask symbolized the essence of his sinister power, granted by card number thirteen, Death.

In my past life, people believed that sightings of this masked figure brought bad omens. People from all kingdoms believed that those who saw him wouldn't live to experience the sunrise. The spectators that Corvus Noir spared watched their entire families and villages fall to the plague he brought to Deltrean villages.

Through his silhouette, I watched as he pulled a small thin wand out of his cloak, and in the blink of an eye, he transformed it into the scythe where he stored his card's ability—a sight which I unfortunately recognized.

The appearance of the tightly gripped scythe in his left hand filled everyone who witnessed it with an overwhelming sense of dread. When Corvus Noir struck a victim with it, the victim did not die immediately. Instead, a mark appeared on the chest of the victim—an eerie, black, circular clock largely inked right above the victim's heart. The clock's black circular outline resembled the reptilian pattern of a snake. Victims of this mark heard the ticking seconds of this clock in their inner ears—a tick which grew louder and louder as death neared and their pain worsened.

The short hand moved as the hours progressed, but the long hand of the clock never moved from twelve. Those with the clock-mark faced certain death within the next twelve hours—all while suffering through a painful disease.

Now, I confronted this entity—much earlier on in this life than in my past life. The assassin looked down at me; he wanted me to spot him. He wanted me to be afraid.

The unwelcome fear consumed me.

Corvus Noir took on a threatening stance. I remained frozen, contemplating my next move. For a moment, neither of us budged as we waited to observe and analyze each other's first action.

I stood ready to fight or defend myself, my intention clear in my eyes. When a person fell under the influence of a card's ability, their irises glowed according to their color, and the pupils became slits—much like a snake's. Therefore, my eyes made it evident that I possessed an ability.

Suddenly, Corvus Noir spun the scythe in a swift circular-vertical motion. The staff of the scythe stretched into a long, thin shadow, reaching the lantern nearest to the tree where the assassin stood. The blade of the scythe absorbed the lantern's flames, as if it consumed all light it touched.

I swallowed hard, but I didn't move. I recognized this evil being all too well, and flashbacks surged through my mind as I examined his threatening stance. The freshest memory weighed on me—the sounds of the organ he played on the night Altair murdered me.

With single-handed ease, Corvus Noir spun the scythe in the same motion as before. This time, the scythe stretched into the shadows, moving a little closer to me. The blade extinguished another lantern upon contact.

I let out a quick breath.

This entity roamed at night, causing mayhem, and people speculated the assassin harnessed greater power in darkness. In my past life, I encountered him only under the cover of night—except for one time. We met in a lit-up area; he seemed the most human then, but even that turned out to be a trap.

Tonight, he gave the impression he wanted to leave me in darkness.

Another swing, another lantern extinguished.

Then another.

He swung faster, and his darkness began to engulf my surroundings.

While he could see in the dark, I needed light. My next telepathic command to Benjamin was stern and clear as I glanced at the remaining lanterns lighting the forest path.

Swallow.

At my thought, the little bunny hoped towards the lantern closest to us and inhaled the flames in one quick movement. His little body glowed in shades of red, yellow, orange, and blue.

He ran back into my arms, and we strayed from the path as Benjamin became our only source of light.

I gritted my teeth. As I sensed Corvus Noir chasing me, I blindly sprinted through the forest. I turned back to locate my stalker, but to my horror, he was nowhere to be seen. Instead, I faced only pitch-black darkness.

An icy breeze rushed past me, and my alerted glare followed it, landing on the menacing curve of the assassin's blade, which gleamed ominously in front of me. I crouched and somersaulted underneath it. Rising, I turned back to see the scythe pointed at me, but he remained still in our eerie ambience. His yellow reptilian eyes glowed with a sinister light in the darkness, but a glint of playfulness communicated that he had no intention of hurting me or killing me. Instead, he taunted me, reveling in my fear. His presence presented Follyn's message: They knew my whereabouts.

With each deliberate step I took backwards, Corvus Noir mirrored my every movement.

"What is it, Noir? Surely, you're not here to murder me." I snickered. "It'd be a very impulsive mistake, and you know it."

While I sensed he didn't plan to murder me that night, I couldn't be too sure of his impulsivity.

My words bought me a precious second. My grin and comment threw him off balance. Hesitation flickered in his reptilian eyes. He might have wondered how I confidently identified him as Corvus Noir. During this time frame, he was just starting to build his infamy, or perhaps he expected to confront the cowardly Lyra everyone remembered.

I seized the moment to send my telepathic command to Benjamin. He opened his little mouth and unleashed flames like a dragon, successfully setting a chunk of the surrounding palms ablaze.

I focused all my strength on my energies and the power of The Magician. With waves of my hands, I moved and tangled the trees around me as Benjamin spread his flames, creating sounds and movements in the opposite direction of where I stood. I hoped to confuse the assassin lurking behind me.

Manipulating abilities in multiple ways simultaneously demanded skill and more energy. It felt like playing the piano with both hands at an expert level. In a sense, my mind needed to be divided with careful attention and precision: one side commanded the vessel The Magician rested in, and the other directed my own self to manipulate more of The Magician's ability. This process drained me, but practice in my past life improved my current proficiency. My brain, not yet accustomed to the stretch in my new timeline, still remembered the motions.

I created a tangled mess of trees in many directions, setting them ablaze and manipulating them to form a maze.

After distancing myself from the assassin, I performed a quick hand movement, splitting trees open while keeping the flames at bay. I swiftly took cover inside them and maneuvered them to enclose me tightly.

I tried to silence my breathing.

The area became quiet.

Too quiet.

I spent the entire night hidden inside that tree, hoping my enemy wouldn't discover me.

*****

The sun rose, yet my fear prevented me from venturing out of my twisted, tangled trees.

"Lyra!?" Tears welled up in my eyes when Xander's worried tone reached my ears.

"Xander." I wanted to cry out the name, but I only whispered.

"Lyra!?" My brother accompanied him.

With a swish of Benjamin's feet, the tree made a small opening for me.

As soon as I got out of the opening, my legs gave out, and the bunny and I collapsed onto the ground.

"Lyra!" Xander ran toward me, and in a swift movement, he carried me in his arms.

"Hold on, Lyra. We're getting out of here."

"How did you find me?"

"I noticed the mess of trees. I knew that was you."

"They found us," I murmured.

"It's okay. We're going home to Deltrea."

"We are probably still being watched."

"I checked the vicinity. We're fine, for now."

"Lyra!" Alphonse hugged me. "After I received your message, I kept telling Xander we needed to come help you!"

"You haven't possessed an ability. He needed to stay with you in case they went after you, too."

"That's exactly what I said. I knew you'd have it under control."

My eyes widened. It meant a lot that Xander believed me capable enough to hold my own.

"Thanks."

"Was it Altair?" Alphonse asked.

"Corvus Noir."

My brother gasped.

Xander rubbed a hand down his face—a gesture he often made when stressed, but today, he looked more than stressed; he looked guilty.

"Xander," I start. "His skills in disguise, stealth, and combat rival yours. You have no fault whatsoever. He caught us off-guard."

He shook his head. "Do you think you have enough energy to make an underground tunnel for us? If we can put some distance from the house without the risk of being seen, we-"

Xander paused when he looked at my sickened reaction. My face probably looked green.

"Okay." Xander placed a hand on my head. "All the more reason we must go now."

We returned to Xander's home. He and Alphonse grabbed necessities and packed them on to the backs of our horses.

In my past life, this demon gained the ability to manipulate music and sound. This entity showed ambition, deadly intent, and loyalty to the Follynean royals. He became deranged and served as Altair's right hand, just as Xander served my family. The Follyneans eventually gained two other loyal followers who posed serious threats to my family, but none were as threatening as Corvus Noir.

Even then, I couldn't deny that the frightening encounter came at a perfect moment. The blessing in disguise served as the cue to go home.

*****

The familiar bubbling of anxiety in the pit of my stomach increased the moment we reached Deltrea, and it only worsened as the first day of school drew closer.

Just as I planned, I took one month to settle in, and then, I made my public appearance by returning to the town of neutrality which I desperately fled from.

I spread thick liquid on my hair to remove my pink dye.

School began at the start of August, but I didn't attend until two weeks later. I walked nearly five miles from the main Deltrean fort to the path leading into the neutral town of Crescencia, which led straight to Crescencia University.

I woke up early and wanted to be one of the first students to arrive, fearing the stares I might attract if I walked in after a crowd gathered.

Since a 'lonely' walk put me at risk, my father told Xander to follow me closely and stay disguised. No one, including myself, could spot him. I couldn't tell if he cloaked himself as a student, a cafe employee, or a professor—no visible clues revealed his role. However, knowing he watched over me reassured my anxious mind.

I took the lavender-colored brick path from Deltrea to Crescencia, which headed towards the university's belt, a thick walkway surrounding the school and stretching for another mile. Three branches—north, south, and west—extended from this belt.

As I glanced back towards the south, I saw the trail leading to Deltrea, my kingdom. The north path led to Follyn, and the west path directed me to Aquaenterra, where the school's main entrance stood. Rows of trees, native to their respective kingdoms, lined each major path. Blue spruce trees towered from Follyn, blue jacaranda trees adorned Deltrea's path, and tall palm trees framed Aquaenterra's path. Cherry blossom trees dominated the rest of this neutral town, symbolizing the start of a new school year and promising a vibrant future.

Students lounged around the belt, drawn by the attractions.

As I walked the path towards the university grounds, I realized Crescencia had expanded since my childhood. The abundance of new buildings left me awestruck.

The west side of town greeted visitors with most of Crescencia's shops and restaurants.

To the south, the children's school and the secondary school stood prominently. Both schools matched in size and included their own dormitories within their grounds.

The north part of town held the town's massive gardens, which also served as Crescencia's festival grounds. The different setups and displays always transformed the land into the most beautiful events. At the center of the gardens stood a large, black-bricked clock tower. The silver roman numerals shimmered brightly under the rays of the sun, and the clock tower echoed its powerful voice throughout the entire town every hour.

The dormitories occupied the east side of town. A black-bricked building housed the university students. On the opposite side of those dormitories, a smaller building provided apartments for staff, workers, and professors. No outside routes led into the east side because a gate blocked access. One could only reach it through the town's internal paths or the university's belt. This area bordered Deltrea and Follyn.

The campus featured a dozen buildings: four connected through the university's belt and eight smaller ones within the grounds. The north, south, and west paths led directly to three of the four major outer buildings. The west trail from Aquaenterra ended at the front stairs of Crescencia University's first major building. Two tall pillars flanked the stairs, connected by an arch displaying the large, silver name of the university. Students ascended three layers of five sets of stairs to reach the main entrance—Crescencia Student Hall.

On the far north of the university, facing the beautiful festival grounds, stood Crescencia University's massive library—Cygnus

Library. The Orion Training Grounds highlighted the east, featuring a gymnasium and surrounding fields which faced the dormitories.

I continued walking my trail, past the school which harbored gloomy childhood memories, until I reached Crescencia's fourth major building, the Crescencia Student Guidance Center.

Under the school's name, it said, "Building Unity and Peace Among All." I scoffed. Even though this town stood as the only neutral ground between the three territories, I experienced such division as a child. In truth, the three kingdoms intended to use the neutral territory to monitor one another while showcasing civility. With Crescencia, they kept each other close, hoping to gather any available information regarding Vegalia's cards.

The town lay open for all to exploit.

*****

I stood in front of the door of my empty classroom for a solid minute before I found the courage to reach towards the handle and let myself in.

I faced the classroom wall, where four massive windows lined up side by side. The pleasant outside-view stretched out from the third floor. The paired desks lined the classroom, and the chalkboard and professor's desk sat to my right at the front of the room.

Posters displaying maps and significant dates adorned the room. The scent of the school lingered in the air. It had been years since I last smelled it—a mixture of paper, books, school supplies, and wood.

A sense of relief settled in my belly when I realized I arrived first. However, uncertainty clouded my mind about where to sit, since I didn't know which desks remained unclaimed.

Ultimately, I settled for a desk in the last row, hoping to go unnoticed.

"So, I asked him if he could come, but he said he doesn't step foot into those places." The clear voice of a girl echoed outside the classroom.

My heart raced.

To avoid possible incoming interactions, I thought it'd be best to pretend to be asleep, so I put my head down and faced the direction of the windows.

The click of the door thundered inside my ears.

"He's afraid of the dumbest things." The second voice belonged to a young man. Its deep timbre sounded familiar.

"Wait." The first voice interrupted him. "Who's that?"

A pause.

The first voice continued, "I don't think there's anyone in school with hair like hers. I would've noticed."

"Yeah. It's captivating." The deep voice responded.

A gasp.

Then, the first voice answered. "Does her hair have a shade of blue where the sun is hitting it, or is it just me?"

"That prick, Altair, has black hair. Do you think it's one of his sisters?" I flinched at Altair's mention.

"No, his sisters graduated a long time ago, and his is just... super black. Hers is a beautiful dark. It looks blue when you look at it from the correct angles."

"Oh! You know what? The Deltrean king has signature black-blue hair color."

For a moment, all grew quiet again.

The girl broke the silence in a whisper. "Do you think it's the hidden princess?"

"It's possible," he replied.

"Should we wake her?"

My anxiety bubbled inside my stomach.

"I think so. That way, she's not surprised when the bell rings and sees everyone here. Also, I think we have to. That seat is where-"

The girl gasped. "You're right!"

I listened to their approaching footsteps. Then, I felt a light tap on my shoulder. Slowly, I picked my face up and confronted the two people in front of me.

The first girl stood short, with brown eyes and olive skin. She exuded cuteness, her symmetrically oval face free of a widow's peak.

Her brown hair, parted in the middle, fell in loose curls just above her shoulder. Her lavender tie created a flowing effect as it freely drifted over her plum-colored uniform shirt. She neatly tucked the shirt into the black uniform skirt, which appeared shorter than the school accepted, and she walked on long, shiny black boots.

I couldn't describe my emotions at that moment. The last time I encountered her in my past life, she cried and sobbed on forest grounds; her arms grasped Altair's legs, and she screamed and begged for him to spare my brother's life.

"Not him! Please, he's got nothing to do with the Deltreans!"

"Hi! Sorry to wake you," the girl said this behind a white-teethed smile, interrupting my flashback.

"Whoa." The boy next to her, tall and slim with sandy-beige skin and dark brown eyes, looked at me in shock.

"Robin! Don't be rude!" The girl gave him a light slap across his stomach as if to scold him.

"No! I didn't mean it in a bad way. It's just... you really have nice eyes." He blushed as he pulled on the tips of his short, platinum blonde hair, which complimented his dark brows. His timid reaction unparalleled his messy-fitted uniform. His lavender-colored tie drooped over the plum-colored button-up, which rested untucked over his black slacks.

He donned flat black sneakers with white accents—those that remained in style for ages.

The girl called him Robin. I met him in my past life, too—on opposing sides of battle.

Robin Ravoux rose to become Follyn's knight commander alongside a woman named Sabrina Daeryn. Despite the title, he grappled with his loyalty to his kingdom. We shared a single proper conversation in our past lives, where he revealed his uninfluenced beliefs and how they cast burdensome doubts about his commitment to Follyn. As a result, he played a small part in the butterfly effect that led to my successful trapping of Altair with The World. Before I caught Altair, I learned Robin paid a heavy price for his actions.

Funny, he said the same words about my eyes the very first time we spoke back then.

"Thank you," I said in a low tone.

If I aligned myself with him from the start, I could support and contribute to his growth as a great man with an unwavering commitment to fairness and justice. Recognizing the scarcity of individuals like him in the world, I felt a strong desire to assist *him* this time around. I owed him a better future—a happy one.

"You're Lyra? The Deltrean princess?" the girl asked.

I didn't need to ask what gave me away. My jet-black hair characterized the Deltrean royal bloodline. People often discussed the abnormality of my violet-colored eyes. Some believed I was the reincarnation of Vegalia. Others claimed my appearance embodied a cursed manifestation from the wickedness behind my bloodline.

I looked down to hide my eyes.

"We're so sorry! We don't mean to be rude." The girl sounded remorseful.

"I didn't mean to make you uncomfortable, Princess Lyra. I'm sorry."

I shook my head. "You've done nothing wrong, and, err, Robin? Thank you, really. I've always hated my eyes," I muttered.

"You hate foolishly." He gave me a smile. Back then, his eyes carried a burdensome sadness, and he never smiled—except once, when he aided me, he flashed a smile which held a glimmer of life and rebellion. Today, genuine contentment emanated from his grin, and his eyes reflected a child-like light. His features held an innocence I had only glimpsed during his confessional monologue in our past lives.

"He's right, princess. You're really beautiful!" The girl interjected. "Oh! I'm Syrena, by the way, and as you caught, this is Robin. We're pleased to meet you." They gave me a small bow.

Everyone knew the girl standing in front of me as Syrena Garcia. However, about nine years later, just before her wedding with Altair, the revelation of her real name, Syrena de Cervantes—the surname of the Aquaenterran royal family—spread through the kingdoms.

Syrena and Altair's marriage united Aquaenterra and Follyn, and it officially marked the beginning of Deltrea's destruction.

Like Alphonse, Syrena kept her identity a secret. As the younger of two siblings, her family assigned her to watch over Altair Antares and me, in case I returned to society.

Meeting her early in my new life gave me a favorable start in Crescencia. I needed to seize the opportunity and charm her to become her friend. If I turned her against Altair from the start, it already meant a victory on my side.

I gave them a small, nervous smile. "It's nice to meet you, too. Please, drop all formalities. I am simply Lyra."

As more of our classmates shuffled into the classroom, they directed curious glances my way. Despite my best efforts to block out the commotion, I overheard conversations about me, and as I expected, it did not take a genius to deduce my identity. I focused on Syrena and Robin, which made my classmates hesitant to interrupt.

Finally, the disorder settled down with the thundering vocals of the clock tower's bell; it marked the start of a new hour and the commencement of class.

"Would you look at that? My class is lively this morning." The professor's amused, sarcastic tone and loud, authoritative voice broke the noise, shifting the environment into a peaceful silence. He spoke with a lovely Aquaenterran accent.

The classroom instructor took long strides towards the front desk. He held a thick, loose book in one hand, which probably did not fit in the burgundy satchel he wore.

He stood taller than me, and he showed a good physical build; one would guess he trained and weight-lifted every day.

He wore a tucked white button-up shirt beneath a long-sleeved light blue V-neck sweater. His neat blue satin tie peeked out, and his shiny brown shoes stood out below his khaki slacks. Kindness radiated from his hazel eyes, and a scratchy beard framed his easy-going smile. He appeared young, perhaps in his late forties, though stray white hairs dominated his black hair.

The professor took his black-framed glasses out of his satchel and put them on.

"For the next five minutes, I'm going to ask every one of you to write a synopsis of yesterday's assigned reading."

Everyone shuffled around for paper and a writing utensil.

"We had homework?" Robin's desk partner whispered to him.

"Yes—on the philosophies of ancient Ghanro civilizations."

The dejected student covered his face with his hand.

Xander's teachings filled my mind with images and words, and I knew exactly what to write. As everyone got their materials out and became distracted, the professor whispered to me.

"Lyra." He held his hand out to me. "I am Dr. Andres Diestro. I want to extend a formal welcome to you."

A bead of sweat ran down my face when I recalled his name. In my past life, we did not know each other, but a few years before I died, I heard the Follyn royal family executed him.

I shook his hand.

"Oh! Dr. Diestro!" Syrena yell-whispered to him. "Can Lyra be my seat partner? People already sit where she's at, and I don't have a-"

"Ah, that's right. Go ahead, Lyra. Syrena will be an excellent guide and an exceptional friend."

We sat towards the back of the room. Johann and Robin sat in front of us, and a pair of empty desks remained next to us.

From everyone in the classroom, I only recognized Adrian, whose features remained the same. He sat in front of the room next to a boy named David. His short, ash-colored hair featured a smooth gradient fade at the sides. Although his hair on top looked messy, it appeared intentionally styled. He donned his uniform with complete disregard, casually and loosely. Adrian's scowl remained unchanged—his emerald green eyes still pierced the soul with hatred. His warm beige skin tone still reddened with anger at the sight of me.

"So," I whispered to Syrena. "Is Altair Antares still a student here?"

Syrena made a foul face. "You don't have to worry about that human waste. He rarely ever comes to school."

I chuckled, "I take it you don't like him very much."

She shook her head. "He's snobby and unapproachable."

"Hmm," I nodded.

I wondered if she said that because of my identity as the Deltrean princess. I questioned if she pretended to dislike him to fit in with me, or if she genuinely disliked him at that point in her life.

Despite my negative feelings towards the guy, I made a conscious effort to show kindness. Even though I felt the urge to speak ill of him, I restrained myself. Convincing Syrena of my innocence increased the likelihood of gaining her friendship and alliance. To strengthen an alliance with her, I needed to have Alphonse enroll—at least for the second semester.

First, I needed to secure an ability for him.

CHAPTER EIGHT

The Devil

Even though I had classes with Adrian and Roselia, I found my first week pleasant. Their hostile glares didn't bother me because new companions enriched my life, and my old enemies kept their distance.

Altair Antares remained absent from the university. I never inquired about that devil, but my classmates mentioned him occasionally, speculating he stayed away because of odd trainings.

Although this should've alarmed me, I found it reassuring and wished for him to stay away longer because his absence gave me the chance to win people over to my side. Despite the various backgrounds of my classmates—Deltrean, Aquaenterran, or Follynean—the ambience in my classes held a sense of unity, which made me enjoy school. I grew close to Syrena and Robin faster than I expected. We synchronized with ease, and we formed a fulfilling connection that blossomed with true fondness.

The following week began as usual. Robin lingered around Syrena's desk and mine, fully captivating my focus. As we spent the entire morning engrossed in conversation.

"Oh, you're back." Adrian's voice caught my attention.

Robin spoke next. "Lyra? Do you want to come get a coffee with me before class starts? We should arrive back in time if we leave now."

"Ah, yes."

My body stiffened.

I sensed burning eyes on my back, and a sinking feeling settled in my chest, but I ignored it. Instead, I gathered my little purse. I got up from my desk and walked behind Robin towards the entrance. I stopped in my tracks when I locked eyes with the person Adrian spoke to, and I did not avert my glare.

In front of me stood a tall boy with beautifully wavy coal-black hair. The soft, lazy tips of his hair peeked out from the back of his long neck. At first glance, his body appeared slender, but closer inspection revealed surprising fitness and definition. He wore a loosely tied lavender satin tie over his untucked plum button-up and black slacks. A black sweater vest lay over his shirt, and like Robin, he sported flat black sneakers that dominated the current trends.

Robin lingered by the door. His expression shifted into a look of realization as he turned and directed a look of alarm at Syrena.

I didn't turn to look at Syrena. I kept my eyes on the monster, afraid he would hurt me if I looked away.

The class grew quieter by the millisecond, which allowed me to make the inference that our classmates remembered the conflict between the two of us.

"We should go before it gets too late." Syrena appeared at my side. I didn't even hear her rise from her desk.

On my free side, Robin went and grabbed my wrist. "Let's go."

I walked past Altair without bringing down my glare, and I walked out of the classroom with my friends at my sides.

We paced towards Crescencia Café, the library's coffee shop.

"Lyra," I glanced at Syrena. She continued, "Are you okay?"

"Yes." My voice sounded hoarse. "I'll be okay."

"You gave him a death glare, and he looked so amused!" Syrena shook her head as she continued, "What an obnoxious guy!"

"Do you want to talk about it?" Robin asked.

"After class. We can talk." I nodded.

Syrena interjected. "Let's get the coffee. It'll be weird to return to class without it."

CHAPTER NINE

Page of Cups

The clock tower's bell rang as we reentered the classroom. To my horror, Altair's desk sat next to mine—the seat I took when I first entered the classroom. He didn't have a seat partner, likely because the professor arranged for him to sit alone, given his negative influence on others.

Altair kept his body and face turned away from me, angled towards the windows.

I faced forward to retain my engagement on the professor, but my consciousness kept my attention on my peripheral vision as I wrote notes.

Now and then, Altair made subtle movements.

When I sensed him glancing in my direction, I resisted the urge to look at him and confirm my suspicion.

At some point, my peripheral vision caught him lowering his head, as if he planned to sleep through class. I took advantage of the opportunity and gave in to the temptation to glance at him. Sure enough, Altair had his head down, but he faced me. To make matters worse, his eyes were open, and he stared right at me.

I flinched the instant our eyes locked; his sapphire gaze froze me in place.

I whipped my head away, trying to focus on Dr. Diestro as he paced around, explaining ancient history, but my efforts proved futile.

My heart pounded with anxious curiosity, fueled by the whirlwind of questions swirling in my mind.

I rested my elbows on my desk and intercepted my hands together. Then, I placed them near my nose. I made it a habit of putting lavender oil on my hands every morning as the scent helped me calm my stress and anxiety.

The meaning behind Altair's blatant observation weighed on my shoulders. Realizing it was more of a gaze than a glare, I became more tempted to look his way and confirm his gestures, so after a deep, discreet breath of soothing lavender, I turned to face him again.

His head remained down, now facing forward, but he must've sensed my movement because he turned to meet my eyes once again.

Summoning all my willpower, I fought to control the anxiety shakes creeping up my skin, and I refused to look away. I aimed to return the hateful glare he often gave me as a child. I didn't want him to know I still feared him. Instead, I wanted to show him I could stand my ground. Yet, the situation confirmed my initial observation—a softness settled in his gaze. A completely different Altair Antares stared back at me, devoid of the one who ended me in my previous life.

In my past life, whenever Altair and I met, I glimpsed moments of hesitation and inner conflict in him. However, his cruelty and disgust overshadowed these glimpses of humanity. This time, the usual cruelty in his eyes was absent. A different sort of inner conflict brewed in his unfamiliar expression—a mix of various sentiments that made me feel different. The softened gaze that held my eyes caused my hatred to falter.

I frowned as a response, but I kept my eye contact.

He turned back to his desk and lifted his head, revealing that it rested on a notebook. Altair slipped a hand into his pocket and pulled out a pen.

As he wrote in his notebook, I faced the front again, pondering what occupied him since he seemed too disinterested in the lesson to be taking notes.

Not a minute had passed when I sensed his intense gaze burning into me once again.

His eyes met me without a trace of malice or animosity. A flicker of something unfamiliar sparked in his eyes, instantly turning my cheeks a rosy shade. It sent a pleasant shiver through my body, hinting at danger because of its addictive potential.

I shook my head as alarm bells rang in my mind.

I met his eyes with stubborn hostility, but he didn't reciprocate it. Instead, his eyes signaled to something below him, on his desk. He pointed to the bottom corner of a page in his open notebook. That corner displayed a written message.

Altair slid it further to the edge of his desk for me to read.

For a moment, I debated on whether I should look away without humoring him, but suspicion and anxiety gripped me as I considered the note's message, fearing a written threat.

If it contained a threat, I would counter with one of my own.

I frowned at him with my hateful, distrustful glare, but he simply signaled again.

The absence of hostility in his eyes intrigued me, leading me to succumb to my overwhelming sense of curiosity. Compelled by this, I took a peek at the paper; it read:

Welcome back

I stared at him, my eyes widening with surprise and suspicion. This time, he looked away first, leaving me to question whether I should reply.

I chose silence.

First, I needed to observe his behavior. I pondered the meaning behind the note and convinced myself he didn't mean it. I couldn't be sure, but it seemed possible he mocked me or intended the note as a twisted, sarcastic welcome. Perhaps he aimed to drop my guard and crush my spirit, a move that made sense because if I saw an opening to get him to drop his guard around me, I would seize the opportunity for the same reason.

"Altair!" Dr. Diestro's voice interrupted my flood of over-thoughts. "Since you kept your head down throughout most of my lecture, come up here and summarize three key points for your classmates."

Altair sighed, but he rose from his desk.

"C'mon kid, prove me wrong." Dr. Diestro gave Altair a piece of chalk.

"Lyra, are you okay? What happened? You kept turning to face Altair." Syrena whispered to me.

"How does the professor find the courage to taunt crazy boy?" I whispered back, ignoring her initial question.

"He's like that with everyone. He pushes for responsibility. It's one thing that makes him such a good professor, don't you think?" Syrena sighed. She showed clear googly eyes for Dr. Diestro.

I observed Altair's oddly neat, pointy, and thin handwriting. He made swift strokes with the chalk.

Altair's soft demeanor probably stemmed from us being only eighteen, which eased my tensions and anxiety. In a way, he remained a blank slate, and I needed to leverage that to my advantage.

The clock tower bell rang.

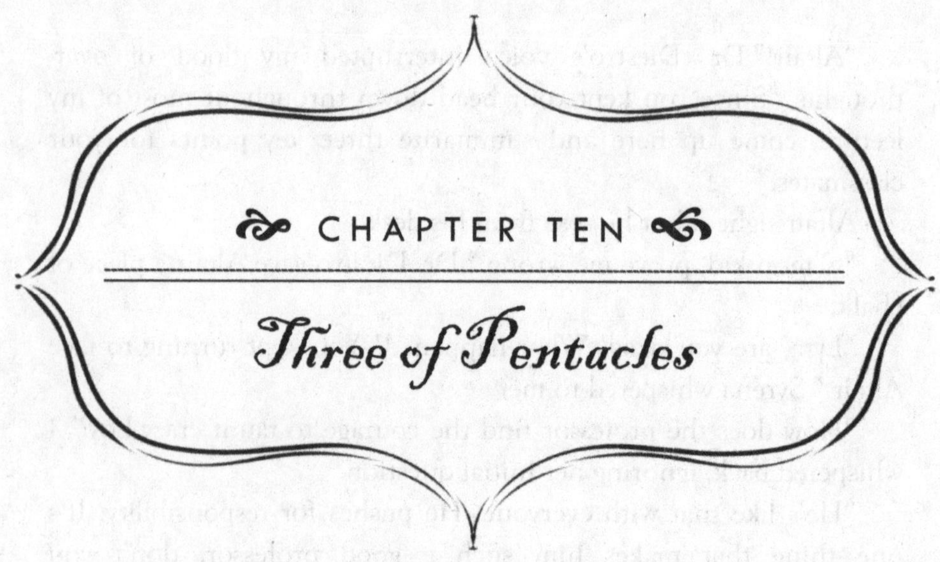

CHAPTER TEN

Three of Pentacles

After classes concluded for the day, I met with Syrena, Robin, and a few of our other classmates, Anya, Johann, and Kalix, on the third floor of the library. A large sitting room on that floor allowed for conversation and lounging.

Robin began, "How are you holding up?"

"I'm okay, guys. Thank you." I flashed a smile.

"Ugh, it doesn't help that you're alone in Professor C-Rod's class with him," Anya added.

Our mathematics professor, Mr. Cesar Rodriguez, preferred to be called C-Rod. He leveled with his students, taught enthusiastically, and he always smiled with kindness. His authenticity and empathy showed he attempted to understand everyone who worked with him.

Laurie, his sister, taught my arts class for the semester. Altair also had that class with me, and thankfully, Robin and Syrena did, too. Ms. Rod meant business. She mirrored her brother's genuine approach to understanding her students, but she pushed us harder to explore our creative strengths and limits. Her dedication and sense of responsibility often placed stress on her shoulders, yet she always gave us her best. The classroom decorations reflected her personality and an abundance of creative learning. I truly enjoyed her class.

I shrugged. "With the professors that manage the classes I have with Altair, I feel quite safe, to be honest."

Syrena spoke softly, "We-" She hesitated. "We know what happened between you and Altair when you attended the children's school together."

I nodded. "There's also the matter of the family and kingdom rivalry."

Even though people knew about the obvious enmity, they chose not to mention it. I was thankful for that, too. Hearing about my past was difficult, and I feared others perceived me as weak because of it.

"Wait!" Anya put her hands up in a *stop* gesture. "You don't have to talk about this if you don't want to!"

"Yeah, we know things are different now." Robin interjected.

"But we also know it doesn't help that you have him for like... three out of the five classes!" Syrena exclaimed.

"Altair and them always sit next to our lunch table, too, but did you see how they didn't turn to look at us today?" Anya asked.

"They only talk to us because of Robin and Kalix," Johann said.

"What? That's not true. There's a difference between being friends and simply getting along," Kalix replied.

"What the hell's the difference?" Johann asked.

"We're not friends with Altair, per se, but we get along with him," Kalix said. "Except Johann, he's open about not being able to stand them, and he's constantly arguing with Altair and Ian."

"Well, out of respect to Lyra, we should keep a distance," Syrena said.

"No, absolutely not," I interjected. "Do as you always do. Regardless of whether you talk to him, I consider you my friends, and that will not change."

Everyone eyed each other in astonished silence, which meant my response caused a stir in their heads, whether they realized it or not. In truth, I *barely* obtained friendships, and while I wanted their loyalty, forcing things never yielded favorable results. Force left an unpleasant taste. It bred doubt. Therefore, my patience, restraint, and display of pure kindness worked like reverse psychology, drawing people to my side, yet these thoughts caused me a lot of inner turmoil.

I didn't want to be a dishonest person to my new friends, but my actions desperately aimed to secure a better future.

"It's very admirable for you to think that way, Lyra." Robin interjected.

The seed of guilt greeted my consciousness. If it meant anything, I truly liked them and the friendships.

"A respectable leader, indeed. I agree with Syrena, though. I can't with Antares." Johann made the remark with indifference.

Kalix expressed annoyance, "Uy, here we go again."

"Antares looks down on everyone," Johann added.

Oddly enough, I still couldn't wrap my head around it. Eighteen-year-old Altair somewhat contrasted with the Altair that murdered me.

Kalix responded, "I mean, he exudes an intimidating presence, yes."

Except, *intimidating* didn't quite capture the essence of his presence. His aura emitted an eerie, unsettling supernatural energy, which carried a dark and captivating allure reminiscent to vampires. Even though the natural instinct avoided them, people still followed and admired them.

"I kind of feel dread when I look at him, and when he talks," Anya replied.

"He rarely talks, though. He's a no-nonsense kind of guy. One who doesn't talk for the sake of it," Kalix responded.

"Yeah, but he does... observe. It's... I can't quite describe it," Robin said.

"Unsettling?" I asked.

"Yes! That's the word. Unsettling."

Kalix shrugged. "He's not exactly hostile, and he keeps to himself. I respect the guy."

"Kalix, just because you're Follynean doesn't mean you can deny the guy is an unapproachable bastard who's probably greedy for abilities. I don't trust him," Syrena interjected.

"I mean, the royals have always been clear about possessing those dark things. It shouldn't be a surprise. He's setting the tone for his rule, any-"

"Wait, wait," I interrupted Robin. "Kalix is Follynean?" I asked.

The group got quiet.

Johann spoke first. "The Follyneans are not *all* bad. Just look at Robin."

Kalix arched an eyebrow and gave Johann an unsure smile. "I don't know if I should take offense to that."

"He means it in a good way, Kalix. I mean, you have all of the Follynean lunatics—beginning with your crown prince and his cult." Syrena rolled her eyes.

"And Vegalia wasn't a lunatic?" Kalix's tone dripped with playful sarcasm, but he glanced towards me and added, "No offense, Lyra."

"I don't mind. I am aware of Vegalia's... irrationalities." A smile spread across my face.

"Is that a bad thing?" Robin asked.

"What?" I asked.

"I mean, is it uncomfortable for you to hang around with Follyneans?" A melancholy gaze flashed through Robin's eyes. Though we'd gotten quite close, he never mentioned his nationality. Not that it mattered; I already knew.

"Hmm," I thought about my response for a second. "No, it isn't. The friendship we're developing means a lot to me, and I genuinely like all of you guys. I want to continue nurturing this." I meant it, but I needed to do more—I needed to lie, manipulate, and exploit the positive image they held of me to gain their alliance. Their perception of Altair already fueled the beginning of my plans.

I continued, "In fact, I'm interested in knowing your guys' feelings. Are you all okay? Hanging out with me—I mean... under the circumstances." I locked eyes with Kalix.

They all talked at once. "Of course!"

Kalix's voice drowned out everyone else's. "You're pretty cool, Lyra. Sure, you may be the princess of the opposing country, but we can be normal humans without sides in this place. Isn't that why we're here?"

I always believed that to be a front, but I said, "Yes, it is. It's my goal, too. That's why I haven't asked about anyone's nationalities. It doesn't matter to me."

The group gave me soft smiles, but Johann shook his head. "That's all well and all, but it's not a wise thing to do, Lyra. I think knowing everyone's nationalities is important."

"Do you doubt us or something, Johann?" Kalix asked.

"Where in the world is the trust, my friend?" Anya's quirky voice popped up from her naturally smiling face.

"What? Why? What the hell difference would that make? Robin!" Syrena pointed at Johann. "Tell him something."

"Well, I actually agree with Johann on this matter." Robin paused, as if he gathered his thoughts into words. "See, we can be the best of friends, and we can lean on one another and depend on one another while we're in a peaceful situation, but these things come to the test when big things happen between our kingdoms."

"Well, what about loyalty and respect for these friendships we've created? Aren't these forces stronger than a person's nationality?" Syrena's disappointment tinted her tone.

I understood each of their arguments. Those thoughts plagued me from the moment I made friends at this place. Sometimes, I got so caught up in the comfortable moments that I forgot my objective, but it strengthened my resolve to make my companions loyal to *me*. My mission remained personal, strictly against Altair and his family.

For now, I agreed with Robin, but...

"The circumstances can go both ways." Realizing I spoke my thoughts aloud, I elaborated. "It comes down to what the person in question values more—loyalty and respect for their friendships or loyalty and respect for their kingdoms. I have faith that if the time ever comes to make that choice, you will all do what is right for you. For now, our hearts align through this academic journey, and that is more than enough for me."

The group remained quiet. Thoughtful expressions filled their faces.

"Regarding the thing you asked about, Syrena," I sighed. "Yes, I have scars and trauma because of Altair Antares. I went away to regain my strength and better myself. Despite my efforts and time, I was not ready to face the world as I expected. I pushed myself to excel. In fact, I thank you all because your friendship and welcome made this new journey for me so much easier. I know I have to face *that guy* every day, but I also know I will not let him hurt me again. I refuse to be his victim ever again."

"You have me now!" Syrena put her arm over my shoulders.

Robin gave me a bright smile. "And me."

"You have all of us," Johann gestured to our group.

Aquaenterrans, Follyneans, and Deltreans alike. It was heart-warming. I cherished my time with them, hoping to nurture my friendships and build alliances. Yet, I also reminded myself to stay vigilant.

At that moment, a balance between both options seemed perfect for me.

Altair and his posse favored a Crescencia Dining Hall table neighboring the one my group preferred. I glanced at Altair and caught him looking at me.

Even though we avoided each other, our eyes met... a lot.

Whenever I glanced at him and we locked eyes, we looked away in an impulsive rush that accompanied the wave of embarrassment from being caught staring. In those moments of quick reflection and recovery from sheepishness, I'd find my courage and meet his eyes again, glaring at him to convey my frustration.

Altair always met my eyes again, too, but he never glared back. His eyes softened, showing understanding and interest; the darkness behind them had vanished.

This odd communication through eye contact became a daily occurrence, and we often stared at each other until I looked away—I was always the first to shy away. Fear crept over me for being so daring, but another emotion lingered in the air when we stared at each other—one I couldn't quite name or pinpoint because of my unfamiliarity with it. This new emotion made me nervous, and its presence caused a weight of confusion and a hint of sweetness in my soul. It swallowed the anger, spite, and all other negative things I felt for Altair, but the sensation overwhelmed me. It invaded my thoughts, and I always looked away from Altair to quiet the warm, internal bubbling which made me hyperaware of his presence.

Regardless, this pattern of glances and stares at one another persisted, and when it happened among our groups of friends, I tried my best to be more discreet about the eye contact. However, as the days passed, I struggled to avert my eyes from Altair. I justified this by telling myself I needed to keep tabs on him and be cautious in his presence.

Then, I reflected: What did I hope to gain from these glances? What caused my sudden fixation on locking gazes with the man who orchestrated my downfall in a previous existence? Why did my eyes look for him? Why did I want to see him?

At first, I hoped to intimidate him and show him I could face him. I aimed to prove I could maintain eye contact, unlike when I was a child, but instead of fearing his gaze, I felt drawn to it. These moments fostered a silent, forbidden, and mysterious understanding between us, thrilling me with their intensity, yet despite sitting across from each other in Dr. Diestro's class, we never spoke a word to one another.

*****

All Hallows' Eve approached, so on Tuesday, September 1st, the Aquaenterran royals set up a haunted mansion in an old, little vacation home they frequently visited before Cresencia became neutral ground. They restricted access to the mansion, occasionally using it to host events like this one.

During one of our lunch breaks, Johann, Robin, Syrena, and I agreed to meet at the entrance of the haunted mansion after school that Friday—the same week of opening night.

As the week progressed, circulating rumors warned us about the eventful hauntings inside the mansion. This year, the place showcased real cursed objects instead of the usual actors and decorations. Enthused classmates gossiped about the paranormal activity they experienced inside the location.

I stopped in front of the haunted mansion's entrance and bought tickets for my group before a line formed. The few students waiting around the area probably stood there for the same reasons I did—waiting for their respective possies to assemble.

"Do you want to buy a talisman?" The girl at the booth said.

"No, thanks." I already had all the spiritual protection I needed.

"Suit yourself," she said as she handed me the tickets with a shrug.

I took a quick glance around the area to check for any sign of my friends, but Altair's sapphire eyes caught my gaze.

He walked towards me.

"We only let in one group of five at a time." The girl from the ticket booth spoke to a large group of students buying tickets.

"It's just two more of us!" A boy responded to her, and more from his group interjected, but I did not turn toward the commotion. I kept my eyes on Altair as I moved between the ticket booth and the arguing students. Panicking, I handed a ticket back to the girl at the booth and said, "I'm fine going in now."

"Er, I wouldn't recommend-"

I faced her. I do not know what look dominated my eyes, but she stopped talking. Instead, she went to open the door for me.

Groans and protests from the group of seven resounded behind us.

"Make arrangements that'll work between your group first!" The girl from the booth replied to them.

As I stepped foot into the dark place, the girl grabbed my arm. "If you're going in alone, at least take this." She held out a black-stone bracelet with five protective charms dangling from it.

"Thank you." I put it on and went right into the eerie darkness as the door shut away the light behind me.

Looking at Altair from a distance was one thing, but talking seemed daunting.

I wasn't ready.

Determined to hide out in that haunted mansion for a while, I decided to apologize to my friends later for going in without them.

As I ventured further, I noticed the event organizers added makeshift cardboard walls to guide onlookers through the haunted mansion. My footsteps and breathing echoed in the silence. The hallway remained dark but not pitch-black. I scoffed at the unnecessary faint, glowing white arrows painted on the walls because the cardboard walls left no other path.

My only way was forward.

After a few moments, I reached a large wooden door, which greeted me with a loud creak as I opened it.

Stepping forward, I faced an extensive set of descending stairs. Two lit torches on each side of the wall provided the only light, illuminating the top of the stairs and revealing a dark descent before me.

As expected, the journey began through the basement.

For a moment, I considered releasing Benjamin and having him swallow the surrounding fires, so he could act as my personal lantern, but I shook my head. I didn't want to risk revealing my ability and how it worked.

People avoided Altair because they suspected he possessed terrifying abilities. He instilled fear and intimidation in people. Unlike him, I sought to form alliances based on positive emotions. Gaining loyalty proved challenging, but it endured, and it revealed true strength. I couldn't afford to push people away, so instead of using The Magician, I reminded myself that I only witnessed the spectacles of a town's haunted mansion. Facing the attraction still seemed better than facing Altair alone.

I went down, down, down to the rhythm of the sound of my breath. My tapping footsteps echoed against each concrete step.

Heavy, damaged souls plagued the air with pain, maliciousness, anger, and profound sadness. I sensed their troubled presences as I descended the steps.

My ears prickled at a low, muffled, baritone hum. I froze, straining to confirm that my ears didn't deceive me. The hum abruptly ceased, plunging everything into an unsettling silence.

My eyes darted around the darkness as I reminded myself that noises and voices would be common on the brief journey through the mansion, but a slow dread washed over me as I moved forward into the eerie, pitch-black area. Fear crept up my spine—not because of the dark. I couldn't pinpoint it, but something more than the darkness perturbed me. Perhaps it was a primal fear stemming from my near-confrontation with Altair, or the dread that he might follow me into the mansion. I had no choice but to rush toward the exit. Shaking off the negative emotions, I pushed forward until my feet touched the bottom step.

I faced a faint red light illuminating a large, captivating painting at the end of the first hallway in the basement. The painting depicted a handsome man with shoulder-length caramel-colored hair, dressed in formal attire, and seated elegantly in an extravagant golden chair. He rested one hand above his crossed legs, while the other held open a black hardcover book without a title, picture, or symbol. Judging by the white-teethed grin on his face and the warm flush across his cheeks, he seemed to enjoy the content. His eyes sparkled with innocence, interest, and curiosity as he fixed them on the pages. To the right of his seat, an enormous bouquet of brightly colored dahlias stood in a golden vase on a golden-outlined glass end table beside the chair.

The artwork evoked something abnormal, making me feel apprehensive instead of relaxed.

I noticed subtle changes in the painting's details as I got closer, so I stopped to observe it properly. I stared at the portrait for a long moment, but nothing changed, making me wonder if my mind played tricks on me. However, the artwork's attributes seemed different from when I first saw them. The dahlias beside the man in the image were darker. They lacked vibrancy, and they didn't stand as tall.

What I mistook for a warm expression on his face actually turned out to be a frown. I finally noticed a faint engraving on the book he held, but it remained unclear.

My mind tried to reason with what I looked at. When I first laid eyes on the artwork, I stood far from it, walking in darkness. The red light above it guided me towards the painting, possibly skewing my perspective from a distance.

Seeing no more abnormalities, I resumed my walk towards it. I figured that moving closer might help me distinguish its features better, but my sinking feeling worsened as I neared the painting.

I walked forward in a slower pace.

Little goosebumps crept up my arms as I confirmed that each step towards it promised a new grotesque addition to the overall image.

Flames now encircled the bottom of the chair.

After another cautious step forward, blood dripped from his hands, staining the engraving on the book and turning the cover's symbol into a vibrant burgundy. Now, it stood out: a two-headed serpent forming a circle, each head facing the other with open mouths, ready to consume. Wings pointed downward rested on each side of the serpent. This symbolized a Xenolian emblem, representing the dark evils of the world.

The deliberate paint strokes and color blends captured a haunting, evil essence in the portrait.

I questioned my sanity, especially as blood pooled under his feet.

As I moved closer, the flames in the painting rose higher, encircling the man in the chair. The golden chair became covered in black soot and bloodstains. His beautiful smile twisted into a toothless grin. Beside him, the dahlias blazed and blackened.

I increased my pace, hoping to conclude my encounter with the image, and I watched the rapid transition of how his mouth suddenly formed a large "O," and how his eyes shot up from the book to look at me in terror.

For a moment, this eye contact caused me to pause in my tracks again. I stood only a few feet away from it, keeping my peripheral focused on the corner to turn into the next hallway. As much as my senses dreaded it, I needed to pass by the image at a close distance.

My heart pounded as I took a swift breath during that pause, and with a sudden surge of adrenaline, I paced forward again.

Hollowed eye sockets shattered our eye contact.

The once handsome man transformed into a grotesque, sightless creature emitting bone-chilling screams.

"Argh!"

I turned as a man's loud, muffled scream erupted at my side—a guttural sound of desperate fear and suffering.

Then, another scream pierced the air behind me.

A third scream followed immediately, significantly louder, coming from in front of me.

This time, it didn't fade away. It surrounded me.

If anything, it appeared as if it came from the man inside the painting.

I took a quick breath, and I kept my eyes on it as I paced past it and away from that hallway—leaving the red glow of light behind me.

Knight of Cups

A new, long cardboard hallway lay ahead of me, and I followed it to my next destination. A dim light glowed at the end of the hallway to the left wall. I paced towards it, frequently glancing back to monitor my surroundings.

As I distanced myself from the painting, the screams faded away.

A deafening silence enveloped the area, leaving an eerie stillness in its wake.

I continued through the second hallway until I reached the dim light and faced the large door that it illuminated. The door seemed out of place in the mansion's grandeur, suggesting it belonged to the improvisatory cardboard. Considering this entry existed on purpose, I guessed another cursed object awaited inside.

Before I pushed the door open, the same baritone hum that first welcomed me into the mansion's basement echoed through the ambience again.

The muffled humming came from a man, and a distinct gut feeling warned me he intended to hurt me. Unease, discomfort, and instinctual fear bubbled in the pit of my stomach, and it didn't help that this hum sounded louder than it did the first time I caught it.

My self-doubt and fear grew too strong to ignore, so I turned back to the hallway behind me, intending to retrace my steps. Instead, I faced a black mass sitting on a large, extravagant, shimmering, golden chair at the end of the hallway. Darkness enveloped the area, but a red light stretched to the corner, revealing the entity. The man from the painting manifested into the real world, perceiving my intentions.

He sat there, threatening and waiting.

With this obstacle blocking my path, turning back became impossible.

I stood in my place, frozen and careful to keep my eyes on it. Sounds of disturbed little bells came from it.

The familiar terrifying sounds forced me to take a cautious glance at his hands. The entity no longer held a book as he did in the painting. Instead, a little jester doll rested in his hands, and the mask it wore matched the one which haunted me in the dark classroom closet when I was a child.

The mask's hollowed eyes, mischievous smile, and floral patterns brought back the frightening memories and emotions of my childhood.

With an aggressive scoot forward of his chair, the entity caused the doll to twitch violently in rhythm.

The action compelled me to grab the makeshift door handle and rush inside the new room in a panic. I hurried forward, desperate to reach the mansion's exit.

Rushing footsteps sounded close behind me, prompting me to run in random directions through what felt like an endless, dark maze. For all I knew, one of the entities haunting this place followed me— the humming man, the painting's protagonist, an unseen evil, or worse, whatever devil possessed the jester.

My heart raced as heavy, dragging steps and rattling chains blended with the rapid running behind me. Both sounds drew closer, amplifying my fear.

My dread and desperation to find a way out increased with every dead-end I came across in the pitch-black maze.

Before I could react, the lighter, brisk steps stopped behind me, and firm hands gripped my waist.

My fists flew behind me, striking something solid. The unknown entity seized my wrists to stop me from inflicting further harm.

"Whoa! Hey. Calm down. It's just me." A man whispered—his voice was familiar, but it was also too soft for me to identify.

His large, icy hands moved from my wrists and found my hand. "Let's go."

"Robin?" I questioned.

He kept his firm hand in mine but remained quiet.

I yanked my hand away. Even though I couldn't make him out in the darkness, I sensed the man in front of me was the one I initially ran from.

"I've been meaning to talk to you," he said.

His low voice sounded clearer.

I did not respond.

He sighed. "I will not mess with you. I'm not a child anymore."

"I don't believe you. You've always been cruel."

"The circumstances are different."

"No, there's no exc-"

The heavy, slower-paced footsteps and dragging chains in the distance silenced me again.

"One of your friends?" I asked, annoyed.

"Mnn, not one you'd like to meet."

I scoffed—so much for not messing with me. "If you're going to threaten me, be straight about it."

"It's not a threat; it's a warning." He grazed his fingers against my hand, and I smacked them away.

"I don't want to touch you either, Celestia, but if we walk separately, we *will* continuously end up in different directions, and getting out of here will take life."

"You located me quickly enough."

"I know my way around. You don't, and it's you the entity will target."

"I'm not taking your hand, Antares."

"My sleeve, then."

His voice carried a slight sense of urgency. The heavy, dragging footsteps drew closer. I hesitated before inching my hand forward to catch his sleeve.

Altair guided us through the dark maze. The obscurity made me cautious, but a part of me felt safe. His energy didn't feel evil, at least for the moment. His calm aura contrasted the energies of the entities that haunted me so far. More than that, his presence felt *real*.

Alive.

In several instances, Altair stopped and struck the walls of our path to find a way, and I clung to the end of the sleeve which linked us together.

Finally, he pushed a door open, and the faint light that came from the inside revealed a set of ascending, curved stairs.

My gaze rose to behold the captivating man in front of me. As if sharing the same thought, he turned and eyed me with his sapphire irises. My intense concentration on him caused me to overlook the eerie stillness which enveloped our surroundings.

Only a moment later, Altair broke eye contact to focus on something behind me.

"What?" I asked.

Before Altair responded, loud, rapid rattling closed in behind me. I turned and faced the entity. It charged towards me on all fours, dragging loose, broken chains behind it while shackles bound its hands and feet. No piece of clothing covered up its oily, yellow-beige body. Despite the creature's lack of a face, it knew exactly where I stood.

Altair tugged at my arm and pulled me towards him while his other hand slammed the door shut behind us.

We exchanged grave looks; our eye contact confirmed we witnessed the same thing.

He released me gently, and after a silent mutual agreement, he ascended the creaking steps. I followed him closely, the air thick with an unspoken dread.

Torches lit up the stairs. Altair climbed slowly, constantly glancing behind him—perhaps wary of me.

When he arrived at the door at the top of the stairs, he held it open for me, and extended his hand to me, but I did not take it. Instead, I averted my gaze from it and walked past the open door and past Altair to walk into a study. Despite the heavy hues of gray outside, the unevenly boarded windows allowed enough soft daylight to light up the room.

"I see. The stairs we just climbed were a passageway from the basement," I said my thoughts aloud.

"Indeed." Altair replied.

We made a beeline for the door to exit the study, hoping it would lead us to the next hallway.

Altair reached for the door knob. "It's locked from the outside."

I twisted the knob to confirm and found that the door would not open. Of course, haunted houses were never easy.

I sighed as I turned to face Altair. "I'm assuming we need to find a key?"

My violet eyes locked onto his. Neither of us looked away, and for that moment, we took the other in and examined one another's irises in the close distance between us.

Altair nodded.

I strolled along the perimeter of the area, admiring the elegant decorations in the glass displays. I wondered where a good hiding place for the key would be. Each detail I observed sparked ideas for the perfect hiding spot.

"I wonder where they got these cursed items. They're not good." I spoke.

"They're borrowed." Altair responded.

"From where?"

"Regnum Noctis."

Of course, it didn't come as a surprise. Whispers circulated about Regnum Noctis, suggesting that its displays housed a remarkable array of cursed artefacts. Spirits and demonic entities near Vegalia's unclaimed tarot cards tainted these items. When those cards roamed loose and without a master, they attracted many spirits. Regnum Noctis carried a reputation for being dark and eerie—much like the post-Vegalian generations of Follynean royalty.

"What was the cursed item in the maze we just came through?"

"Shackles once used in a torture chamber. They hung inside the entrance door to the maze."

"That thing... Would it have hurt me?"

Altair stayed quiet.

I continued. "Is it that aggressive with everyone who comes in?"

Altair shook his head. "The entities are not guarding any cards, so they don't manifest at full force. Everyone else hears noises, the chains, voices, but... *you* are a descendant of Vegalia, and that already makes you *their* enemy."

Unfortunately, he spoke the truth; I remained silent.

"Second, you are a card possessor."

"What makes you so sure?" I inquired.

Altair looked into my eyes. "Card possessors manifest powerful energy by nature, and these beings can feed off it. Otherwise, they wouldn't have been able to be as violent."

Again, I didn't respond. If I lied or acted naïve about having an ability, I wouldn't fool him.

Instead, I told my brain to focus on getting out of there, so I walked toward the desk in that large room. Its surface displayed three pages of handwritten correspondence. A transparent, protective glass covered them.

"Are they equally aggressive towards you and your loved ones?"

"No."

"Ah, I assume they like their living arrangement in Regnum Noctis," I said sarcastically.

"Yes."

"Hmm," I hummed. I already knew getting information out of him would be excruciatingly difficult.

I studied the first written note for any clues to the key, but I only made out a few distinguishable letters in a sea of inked symbols.

The journal entry beside it was also a bit difficult to read, but I could distinguish the writing. The author painstakingly recreated a phrase in various styles, sizes, and letterings, making subtle alterations in the phrases with each repetition, resulting in a chilling entry.

People believe that an identity within me is a defect to my being, but he is not a defect. He has been me all along. They believe, they say, they whisper that an identity within me is a defect, a flaw, a crack in my being. But he is not a defect. NO, NO, NO. He is me. He has always been me. I don't believe that an identity within me is a defect to my being. He's been me all along. They think he is a defect. But he is me. He is me. He is me. He is not a defect. He is not a defect. He is me. He is a defect in my soul. He is a defect in my soul. He is me. He is me. He is a defect in my soul. I have a defect in my soul.

It went on and on and on.

The writer of the third entry composed sentences which made no sense and contained many scrambled words. For a moment, I believed the jottings to be codes or clues which would help us locate the key—if deciphered correctly.

Different people wrote them. The penmanship lacked consistency. Each letter displayed uniquely distinguishable characteristics, yet the energy radiating from these messages contained an eerie similarity. They emanated feelings of creepiness, sadness, anger, and fear.

"Did you find something?" Altair's voice drew my attention away from these writings. He stared at the armchair near the fireplace with a confused look on his face.

"Diary entries, it seems."

"Hmm," he hummed. "Letters written by the insane."

"I see." My attention shifted back to them. "I'll read through them. Perhaps, they'll contain infor—"

"I'd advise against it," Altair interrupted my words. "Those are there to distract us. If you look at those for too long, and if we're in here too long, we'll end up writing one of those ourselves—at least until staff unlocks our area."

I redirected my gaze towards Altair, who I caught watching the same leather seat near the fireplace with a concerned expression.

"You keep looking over at that chair."

Altair sighed. "I don't mean to alarm you, but I'm almost positive one of our dolls is supposed to be displayed sitting on that chair."

I looked from him to the chair and back.

"One with a jester mask?" I asked.

Altair nodded.

"The same jester mask you locked me in the closet with when we were children?"

"Yes." Altair spoke in a low voice.

We eyed each other quietly for a moment. Then, Altair continued, "You saw it."

I nodded.

"Hmm," Altair hummed, again. "He probably remembers you."

I scoffed, but I said nothing. Instead, I turned my attention to the bookcase after I watched him go through the bricks from the fireplace.

I went through book-by-book, and I opened them to see if anything flew out from the inside.

"Why did you come in here alone?" Altair asked.

"Isn't it obvious?"

Altair studied me in silence as he felt the fireplace around for an irregularity. "Because I walked toward you?"

I nodded in response.

"I saw you buy tickets, and I wanted to warn you against coming here, even with others. Also," Altair paused. He averted his eyes from mine and rose one of his hands to his beautiful, silky, dark hair to scratch the back of his head. A hint of sheepishness flickered in his demeanor. "I've been wanting to talk, but you're always surrounded by others."

This devil presented such a human emotion, which left me speechless. I couldn't understand his desire to communicate. Child Altair made me cry at first glance. Past-adult Altair tried to kill me on sight and succeeded. This one wanted to talk to me.

"I see." I couldn't offer him more of a reply.

Altair nodded once in response.

"What did you want to talk about?" I asked.

The same muffled, distant humming that followed me throughout the mansion interrupted our conversation.

My eyes widened. Then, I placed my pointer finger near my ear and gave the finger a wave to signal at Altair to listen.

He nodded in agreement; he heard it, too.

"These things are abnormally active," he said under his breath.

"What is that?" I whispered, but my voice carried loud enough to silence the threatening humming.

"The humming comes from an entity attached to a wooden box sealed in wax. Therefore, it can't hurt you, but the negative energy that oozes out of it is enough to cause a bit of alarm."

I raised an eyebrow. "A *bit* of alarm?"

When Altair didn't respond, I continued. "I wonder why they allowed such dangerous items to be placed here."

"Well, it is a haunted attraction. Also, the entrance has a warning sign."

"Contrary to human actors, there's a *real* danger here."

"They're usually more withdrawn around new people—especially groups."

I said nothing. Rather, I sped up my pace by looking for any clues of the key through the insides of books.

"Even with the warning and the rumors, you walked in alone."

I kept my focus on the books, and I responded with a nonchalant nod to show Altair I would not give him further insight on my feelings, but instead of dropping the subject, he pressed further and asked, "You wanted to avoid me that badly?"

From the corner of my eye, I noticed him watching my reaction. I pursed my lips and raised my eyebrows in his direction.

I flipped open another book. This one kept its pages intact but featured a hollowed-out center with a neat, ornate key inside. A single sentence appeared on the brown tag attached to the key.

"Hey!" I called out to Altair, took the key out, and showed it to him as I read the tag aloud: "After you unlock the door, please put me back where you found me."

"That was easier than I thought," Altair muttered.

My eyes darted toward the lounge chair when I spotted movement through my peripheral.

I locked eyes with the jester doll. It sat neat and still in the chair, as if it relaxed there the whole time.

"Look." I whispered.

At my alarmed tone, Altair walked forward to place the chair in his line of sight.

When he saw the doll, he smiled. "There's the little villain."

"We should get out of here." I made my way towards the door.

"Right." Altair's footsteps echoed behind me. "If it helps, you don't have to worry about this one doing anything to harm you. This one's loyal to *me*."

I gave Altair a suspicious glance. "And the other one wasn't?"

Altair shook his head. "It won't hurt me, but it is loyal to my father."

"Ah, I see." I gave him a knowing, sarcastic smile. "So, he's under the orders of killing a Deltrean on command."

"Vegalia's bloodline, actually."

I rolled my eyes, but kept silent and focused on the task at hand. With a swift motion, I got the door open.

"I got it." Altair held out his large hand, and I placed the key in his palm. As he walked towards the shelf to return it, I marveled at his wide back and broad shoulders.

He differed from the Altair I knew as a child and the adult Altair I often encountered in my past life. Instead of adopting a defensive stance, he exuded confidence. His expression, usually a default frown, now showed caution and distance, but not enough to hide his interest in our situation. His gaze maintained the same hesitant look I had only caught glimpses of back then. Ultimately, eighteen-year-old Altair possessed a curious innocence that later transformed into contempt, hatred, distrust, and dark ambition as he grew older.

At that moment, something clicked. If I prevented Altair from developing in such a sinister way, made his hesitant expression permanent, and wove my way into his life, I could win. If I also succeeded in my other goals, the Follyneans wouldn't stand a chance.

Altair met my eyes, pulling me from my scheming thoughts. He caught me eyeing him.

I averted my gaze and focused on his hands as he slammed the book with the key shut. Then, I directed my eyes to my feet.

His footsteps grew closer. "Ready?"

I did not need to look up to see he stopped in front of me—his shadow loomed over mine from the floor.

I nodded in response.

Altair guided us to the end of the new hallway, which split into two paths. If we turned right, we would explore more of the haunted mansion upstairs, but if we turned left...

"If we take this path, we head to one of the mansion's exits." He gestured to the path on the left.

Altair glanced at the right path, which led to the next set of stairs. "I could guide us through the rest of it, but-" He glanced at me. "I'm sure you're ready to head out."

His voice contained a hint of daring expectation—as if he subliminally challenged me to complete the rest of the journey with him.

I wanted to do it.

The current Altair sparked my curiosity, and it made me feel strange—something about the situation attracted me, making me want to take the long way out.

The unfamiliar and conflicting cognizance was unlike anything I ever experienced, but my subconscious reminded me of the wrong and forbidden nature of my situation, suppressing the sensation.

Perhaps the sentiment sparked because we spoke, or maybe because, for the first time, being alone together didn't feel so bad. Quite the contrary, the feeling was strange and intriguing.

Maybe the feelings arose because I relied on Altair's partnership at that moment. It felt like taboo because he represented a terrible memory and was the subject of my revenge, but it was nothing more complicated than that.

I shook my head in response. My pride outweighed my curiosity, so I also wanted to reject him. I planned to create more opportunities to crack his walls—especially when I controlled my feelings better.

"It's time to go," I said.

I took the path on the left until I arrived at the mansion's large back doors. Enough daylight peeked in through the unevenly covered windows, which allowed me to see the ornate black outline on the glossy wooden door.

Altair grabbed the handle before I did, and he held the door open for me.

"Thanks," I said as I walked past him and into the beautiful gardens of the little Aquaenterran mansion.

The garden pathway allowed three people to walk comfortably side-by-side. Altair and I strolled in silence. Daylight refused to hide behind the gray clouds, illuminating the bright colored flowers outlining our path.

My suspicions about Altair's vampirism resurfaced, making me wonder if it afflicted him later in life. Sunlight didn't harm him. He seemed normal. Still, I couldn't ignore the strange, eerie energy surrounding him and his attractive fruity scent mixed with pine. What in the world did he get himself into in the future? Did I misperceive the burgundy tint consuming his blue irises?

Two university students sat on a weathered wooden bench near the garden's golden gates. The vibrant blooms of various flowers filled the air with a sweet fragrance, mingling with the earthy scent of freshly cut grass. They glanced in our direction, their eyes widening in surprise. A young woman raised her hand and signaled to her companion to notify the employee at the entrance that the haunted mansion awaited the next group of thrill-seekers. He complied, his astonished gaze lingering on Altair and me as he darted around the corner of the mansion and disappeared from sight.

"I'm surprised he didn't bump into anything."

"Hmm?" I turned my gaze from the boy who had vanished, and I focused on Altair.

"She's been watching us," Altair smirked.

I glanced at the girl by the garden gates—she appeared to be engrossed in a book, but just as Altair said, she kept stealing glances in our direction.

Something occurred to me.

"If they follow a turn-based system for entering the house, how did they allow you entry before I finished?"

"Simple persuasion."

I eyed Altair with suspicion. "So, she just let you in? Funny. I'm almost sure she knew I was..."

"Avoiding me?"

"Keeping my distance." I corrected.

Altair and I walked the scenic garden path back to the entrance of the haunted mansion, where we suddenly realized people in line gawked at us. A sea of bewildered expressions stared at Altair and me as I searched for my friends.

"Lyra!" I turned to the sound of Syrena's voice in the distance.

Robin stood next to her. His face dropped when he saw me walking alongside Altair.

Syrena paced towards us and got in-between Altair and me.

"You okay, Lyra?" She glared at Altair as she said this.

"All is fine." I gave her a single nod and a friendly smile.

"Did he force you in there?" she asked.

Before anyone replied, Altair impatiently interjected, "Okay, well, I'll leave her to you all." He turned to face me. "Until later, Celestia."

I responded with a short, firm wave of two of my fingers. Again, without looking at him.

I could not look at him.

A combination of disappointment and confusion washed through me as our time together ended, particularly because he turned out to be quite nice.

Robin interrupted my conflicted thoughts. "So, I'm curious about how that happened. You and Altair in there, you know? I mean, the history between you all, the cold-shoulder you have been giving each other all month-"

"Did you both enter *together*... like... on purpose?" Syrena cut him off.

I wondered if she tested me. Fortunately, Syrena didn't like Altair yet. She already saw me as someone to protect, but I needed to show I trusted her. So, I decided I wouldn't lie about the simplest things.

I shook my head. "No, of course not. I went in there to *avoid* Altair. I didn't mean to enter without you guys."

"So, Altair deliberately followed you inside?" Robin asked.

I shrugged. My friends' perplexed expressions mirrored my confusion.

Altair plotted something. Thinking otherwise would be naïve. I constantly reminded myself of his malice since our troubled childhood. I witnessed his clear path to wickedness, and my gut feeling gnawed at me with suspicions about his ties to vampirism. So, why did I doubt his inevitable villainy?

"Did something happen in there, Lyra?" Robin asked.

I sighed and placed a hand on my forehead as I shook my head. "I'm not quite welcome by the dead."

King of Wands

On the Monday that followed, Altair entered the classroom, and we glanced at each other as usual. I offered him a small smile this time, and his eyes widened in response—another whole unfamiliar expression of beautiful surprise. A hint of victory and revitalization flooded me upon witnessing it.

Dr. Diestro drowned out everyone's voice.

"Alright, class. There are exactly twenty pieces of paper in this little container."

He held up a small black box.

"In this container, there are two of each number: two ones, two twos, two threes, and so on. If you draw the number seven, look for the other person in the class who also drew the number seven. That person will be your partner for our next project."

"Why can't we pick our partners, sir?"

Ignoring Brandon's question, Dr. Diestro continued, "Over the next two weeks, you and your partner must complete a historical research paper."

"How long does it need to be?" Another classmate asked.

"Once everyone's settled, I'll hand out the requirements and the rubric. After you get a number, don't open it. We'll open them together." Dr. Diestro began going around class with the black box.

After everyone held a folded piece of paper with them, the professor finally instructed us to open them.

"I got eight," whispered Robin.

"I'm one." Johann eyed Robin with a mocking grin. "I'm always number one."

Syrena directed her words at me. "Nine! What'd you get, Lyra?"

I looked at my paper, but before I said anything, Dr. Diestro gave the next set of directions. "Find your partners and make arrangements to sit beside each other from now on."

"Who got two?" David, the one next to Adrian, yelled.

Everyone began shuffling around the room.

"We're not together, Lyra?" Syrena asked, disappointed.

I shook my head. "I got seven," I said, looking down at my paper.

"It seems we're together for this one." Upon turning back towards the familiar voice behind me, I found myself face to face with Altair.

My eyes dropped from his blue eyes towards his hand. He held out the little piece of unfolded paper. Sure enough, it read "7."

"Hmm, I guess that means I won the lottery," I sarcastically muttered as I gave Altair an annoyed look.

He snickered in response.

Syrena gaped at us. "Do you want to switch, Lyra?" She glared at Altair.

No, that'd be a terrible idea. I couldn't have these two get close, I thought.

"I'll be okay." I directed my gaze to Altair, who gathered his things to move into Syrena's desk.

"Oh, don't worry about it. *I'll* move. The window seats are the best," I added.

Dr. Diestro drowned out the class. "Alright, get to your new seats and decide whether to research history in Follyn, Deltrea, or Aquaenterra. Keep it to our side of the world; we'll focus on the other side next semester. You can also write about the influence of gods and artifacts in our history."

The professor passed out the paper containing the requirements and the rubric.

He continued, "My lectures will proceed as usual, but I'll give you the last fifteen minutes of each class to plan meetings, discuss doubts, address concerns, and work on your papers. I expect you to meet outside of class as well. Don't throw something together the night before it's due. If I have any doubts, I'll ask you to present it, so cite your sources."

The silence between Altair and me brought a new sense of anxiety where awkwardness and light tension filled our space. Though the haunted mansion broke some of the barrier between us, my mind still raced with possible ways to approach him and topics to discuss.

I decided that sticking to conversations about the assignment was the best course of action, but I also knew that such a strict line might prevent any breakthroughs. If anything, this forceful partnership gave me the opportunity to trojan horse my way into his life, yet maintaining a pretense of distance seemed like an ideal place to start. I would see if that's what he wanted, or if he would try to close the gap.

My mind ran in circles.

I sighed and willed my mind to speak.

"I like to get things done early. Once we decide what to do, I'll get started."

His blue eyes pierced into mine. "Do you think of me as foolish or incompetent, Celestia?"

"*Unfavorable...* to work with."

He nodded. "If you're not comfortable, we can ask to switch."

I shook my head. "It's fine. Honestly, I just want to get this done quickly and effectively."

He gave a nod. "Okay. What do you want to write about?"

I shot him a skeptical look, but before I responded, he said, "You should know, I will not do the history of Deltrea."

I frowned at him. "I will not work on the history of Follyn."

Altair narrowed his gaze. Then, he shifted his focus to our classmates, causing the classroom to fall silent.

I turned and caught our nearby classmates pretending to look elsewhere.

"Both of you, let's go take a walk." Dr. Diestro ushered us outside the classroom.

He shut the door behind us.

"I intended to separate you immediately after seeing you partnered up, but I believe you should seize this opportunity to deliver an outstanding paper. This is the first time in our modern world that the future leaders of Follyn and Deltrea collaborate on something. Synchronizing your ideas can significantly enhance your skills and communication as future leaders. You are both old enough to practice making sound decisions and *judgments*." He specifically looked at Altair as he emphasized that last word.

Dr. Diestro continued, "Now, I ask you both, future king and future queen, is this going to be a problem?"

"No, sir." Altair, towering over the professor, kept his gaze down and maintained intense eye contact. Despite Dr. Diestro's shorter stature, the professor met his look with confidence.

I shook my head.

He continued, "Lyra, if you're uncomfortable, let me know. I will instantly make a switch."

*****

Before leaving class, Altair handed me a piece of paper. After he left, I opened the little folded note.

7AM tomorrow, Crescencia Cafe

An odd disturbance stirred in my chest, and I couldn't pinpoint if it stemmed from anger, fear, or...

A sweet curiosity.

I reached Crescencia Café around fifteen minutes before seven. The place stood empty, except for one staff member.

I ordered a minty lavender tea and settled myself into an isolated booth in the corner of the little cafe. Just in case a few souls arrived, I wanted to be isolated enough for a decent talk between my *partner* and me.

As I waited, I took occasional sips of my stirring hot tea, and I read—just to put my soul, my heart, and my mind at ease.

Movement in my peripheral interrupted my reading. An attractive scent of coffee accompanied it.

"Good morning," I said to Altair, putting my book aside.

He nodded my way, clearly not a morning person, and he took a whiff of the air.

"What is that?" he asked.

"Lavender mint tea." I took a sip.

He smirked. "Did you need a stress-relief tea just to see me?"

"Yes, I did, actually." With a touch of sarcasm, I sniffed my tea for emphasis, keeping my eyes on his.

A small laugh escaped through his nose. "It smells nice."

"Have you ever tried it before?"

He shook his head. "I've only ever had chamomile and peppermint."

My eyes widened. "That's it?"

He nodded with a small smile on his face.

"Would you like to try it?" I scooted my teacup and saucer toward him.

He hesitated.

Again, I gave a small laugh through my nose. "*You* may need it more than I do."

He gave a small chuckle. "A sip for a sip?"

I eyed his coffee; it smelled amazing—an aromatic scent of chocolate drifted into my nostrils along with a hint of something I couldn't quite make out.

"Sure," I said as I eyed his drink curiously.

We grabbed each other's cups and slowly raised them to our lips.

The hazelnut notes hit my tastebuds with prominence. Slightly sweeter than my usual drinks, it captivated me from the first sip.

"This is lovely," I voiced.

Altair gave a nod. "Yours is, too."

"Deliciously floral, isn't it?" I said, playfully.

"I never would've thought," he played along.

I smiled.

As we slid our cups back to one another, I said, "On a serious note, I never would've thought you had a dominant sweet tooth."

Altair smiled. "What did you think, then? Black coffee kind of guy?"

I nodded, staring into his blue irises, and for a moment, we stayed that way—eyeing one another in silence. Then, as usual, I averted my eyes, and they fell on my teacup—exactly where Altair drank from. Sweet bubbling stirred in the pit of my stomach when I realized the indirect, familiar contact which came with sipping from the same cup as someone else. The action flowed so easily and naturally that it blurred the enemy line between us. I felt shy. Conflicting emotions stirred inside me—how could a tiny action like that affect me so much? Heat surged through my face, and I swore my thoughts showed in the blush of my cheeks. I hoped he didn't notice.

To focus on the purpose of our visit, I initiated the assignment discussion. "Instead of focusing solely on the history of one country, what if we explore the history of our collaboration—like the peace treaty and the creation of a school to unite all?"

Altair's expression looked thoughtful. "It's a little too in the modern times, don't you think? It could put wounds out in the open."

"The wounds have been out in the open, but no one addresses them. There's blind hatred and ignorance because of lack of communication."

"Yes, but," he sighed.

Then, he said his following words with a slow cautiousness. "I don't think you're foolish enough to really believe this school unites us. This academy is just a front."

He wanted to lay out the obvious. He probably aimed for no-nonsense in our academic partnership, and his tone didn't sound hostile, yet the idea of him seeing right through me made me defensive.

"A front for what, Antares?"

"You know what I mean." His tone sounded monotonous, bored. True to my expectations, he intended to be direct. He saw past my façade. I didn't want him to discard any form of communication because he suspected me of instigating something. I needed to convince him of my naivety and unwavering kindness, so I increased my efforts. "No, I don't know. Not everyone thinks the way you do."

"Interesting. What do you suppose I think?" His tone remained serious, but I detected a hint of curiosity in it.

My eyes demonstrated a growing frustration, but I said nothing.

Altair continued sarcastically. "Please, do tell. You seem to know my mind quite well."

"Well," I shrugged. "I understand what many people think of the treaty and our academy—it's a front, it doesn't work, and it's only preventing the inevitable, but I don't agree with any of it."

He gazed into my eyes, assessing the honesty of my thoughts.

I continued, "This," I gestured to the area with my eyes, "It *has* done something good, hasn't it? It's not just a simple front. I mean, *you and I* are here. Two opposing sides are sitting in a cafe together. *This* means something. It's an advance in the right direction—a slow one, but a move forward nonetheless."

Altair glanced towards the window and exhaled. I couldn't read his expression, but something about it gave me a glimmer of hope that he believed in my innocent persona.

I pushed further. "It's not just me who thinks that. Dr. Diestro gave us an insight into his thoughts on this, too, and I strongly believe he is right. *We* could get something started."

Seconds passed us by, and Altair kept that distant look in his eyes as he stared out the window.

Finally, he opened his lips. "I see."

I gave him a puzzled expression, but I remained quiet as I anticipated his next words.

"The little girl who wanted to bond through shoes is still there. How disappointing." Altair narrowed his gaze at me.

I almost smiled. It seems I got him. However, in the same millisecond, the weight of his words sunk in, and they struck a nerve.

"What did you expect? A vengeful or cowardly woman influenced by your every move?"

I didn't need to act to show my annoyance with him. He probably expected to find the helpless, insecure, weak, anxious person from our childhood. I let trauma follow me into adulthood. That negativity, paired with my paralyzing fear of Altair, his family, and Corvus Noir, caused me to fail miserably. Regrettably, I let my family down and didn't meet my own expectations. If it weren't for The World, my story would've been finished.

"I *do* influence you, little princess. I acknowledge that you're not vengeful or cowardly, but you remain naïve. You haven't grown or seen the ways of our world."

I gritted my teeth. A part of me wanted to laugh in his face and reveal that I lived a second life with the help of The World, but I bit my tongue.

My time would come.

Even though this man killed me once before, I no longer felt the same fear because, in a way, I survived his terror.

I held the upper hand.

For now, I didn't bother to hide my exasperated expression. "You haven't changed much, either. You're still an arrogant *little prince.*" I returned his nickname right back to him. If he bit me, I would reciprocate.

Altair clenched his jaw. "I could say the same thing about you—acting self-righteous when we both know you must have a hidden agenda in there somewhere. Unless you really are naïve, which would only prove how your father's judgement backfired when he kept you locked up."

Despite him striking another chord, I attempted to maintain a calm demeanor. "I don't think your disappointment compares to mine. I thought *you'd* grown, and *you'd* have some humanity—like the actions you demonstrated at the haunted mansion."

"That *is* me. *All* of this is me. I have no reason to be insincere with you. We both know where we stand."

Right, we stand at a mutual, necessary distance. If we get along in the neutral grounds, even a bit, it's only momentary, but beyond those walls, we still sought each other's blood.

"Yes, I see. You're perfectly clear to me; you're still that insecure little bully-boy who's afraid of a pleasant change." I shook my head.

"Go on. Let it all out." Even though he spoke seriously, I felt insulted. My pride sensed mockery, but my reason and intuition recognized his genuineness, and I hated it. I loathed his tone because it didn't match what I wanted. I didn't want to "let things out." Part of me wanted to show him he shouldn't trifle with me. That same part wanted to make him regret and repent for all the trauma he caused me. I wanted to inflict damage on him, too. I wanted him to be intimidated by me and my name.

Contrary to what I wanted, things didn't turn out so bad—the haunted mansion thing happened, and we exchanged secret gazes. In fact, a tiny part of me believed maybe a truce wouldn't be so bad, but our current altercation crushed that belief. I foolishly forgot I dealt with my infuriating, murderous enemy, yet I couldn't figure out why I felt so conflicted and captivated.

Facing him again proved so difficult. His presence, his words, and his personality took an effect on me, and I suspected he realized it.

"Face the realities of our world and our politics, and this is what it's like, Celestia. It's vicious, and people voice their counter-arguments."

"I've heard people can't even have a counter-argument in Follyn." I hissed at him.

His expression formed a small smirk, but he composed himself immediately.

Altair held back his authentic expressions. He didn't want me to read him.

He kept his pointed, narrowed gaze at me when he said his next words. "My kingdom is fine. We must be doing something right. After all, it's not me Corvus Noir is after."

I couldn't hide the surprise in my expression. "You seem to be very *aware*."

My comment came across as an indirect accusation. After all, my family knew the assassin worked for the Follynean royals, and I would have been foolish to believe Altair knew nothing about it.

"It's no secret to those of us with watchful eyes," he replied.

Of course, he taunted me with a vague response.

"Watchful eyes?" I scoffed. "Is that all it is? I thought you had no reason to be insincere with me, Antares."

Again, he clenched his jaw in response.

Upon emptying my tea, I slid the cup towards the middle of the table. I picked up my belongings and got up to leave. "I'll see you in class."

As I passed by his seat, he spoke in a low tone. "Be realistic and keep your eyes open."

"I am." I contacted his sapphire irises again. "I know your family sent him."

"Who knows?" He shrugged.

His response upset me more than it scared me. My spark of abhorrence reignited. Altair disappointed me, but I felt even more disappointed in myself for letting his attractive face make me hesitate and doubt my goals.

I sighed in frustration as I left the café. When I hit the fresh air outside, I took a deep breath to calm my irritation.

Determined to complete this project with Altair as my partner, I reminded myself to project an "I believe in peace and unity" front to earn his trust. For now, I resorted to cooling down and trying again later. I needed to get used to Altair's aura and presence to stop feeling so overwhelmed by him. More importantly, I needed to learn to stop taking things personally. Allowing him or his remarks to affect me would already be a losing battle.

I sighed again.

I figured I could take things day-by-day with him. A part of him believed I acted naïve, but the part that didn't buy into my innocence needed some stubborn persuasion. That way, I could lower his guard a bit. Once I convinced Altair of my gentle-driven nature, manipulating him might become easier, but I did not want to appear weak, either. I needed to be kind without raising suspicions. Most importantly, I had to win Altair's incapable-of-loving heart if I got the chance. If I infiltrated his heart, I would become his weakness.

This last idea seemed tough and a bit of a long shot. Love didn't come easy, especially to a person like Altair Antares.

Then, the question of that devil's abilities and how many he possessed arose. I knew he acted like some kind of bloodsucker, but I still couldn't determine how he connected to the vampires Xander hunted. The ones Xander hunted couldn't be out during the day; the sun's rays immediately incinerated them, but Altair remained fine in the sun.

Altair's unknown power must have caused this.

My head hurt. I still needed to understand so much.

Ugly insecurities in the back of my mind bubbled up in my thoughts—if everything played out as it did in my past life, Altair would possess several deadly abilities. Then, Corvus Noir, Altair's sisters, and his parents presented whole other forces I had to deal with.

My brain constantly thought, schemed, and speculated—remaining in that state daily. I couldn't find a single moment of meditative silence.

Determined to brighten up, I focused on what I could control. During the Crescencia Fall Festival, one card would fall within my sights, but afterwards, another long wait for news loomed.

I couldn't afford that time.

I already made major changes. For starters, I formed new friendships—something I never experienced in my past life because I hid. More importantly, I secured Syrena's friendship. While I moved a step closer to my goals, the finish line remained far.

Cards in Follyn eluded me, and I needed to do whatever it took to thwart Altair's success. If necessary, I would swallow my pride and propose a loveless political marriage. Not only would the idea align with my rightfully driven persona, but unfortunately, deep in my subconscious, I knew what needed to be done in order for a Deltrean royal to infiltrate Follyn legally without causing a war or bringing any kind of danger to my family, my people, or myself.

I needed to prevent him from marrying Syrena, anyway.

Since Altair and I made no progress that morning, I decided to write a rough draft and let Altair handle it however he wanted. Also, I sensed that starting the paper without him would irritate him, and the thought brought me bliss. So, I took a quick trip to the library before class.

Few people livened up the library that morning, but as I ascended to the higher floors, the areas grew lonelier and quieter. When I reached the fifth floor, the historical section of the library, I stood alone among the dusty, least-borrowed books. I spent at least half an hour skimming through the contents of the tomes with promising titles and borrowing those which synchronized with my ideas.

Upon looking at a higher section of one of the endless shelves, a title caught my eye: *The Birth of Xenolian Abilities*. Talking about the abilities wasn't exactly taboo. While the tarot cards caused conflict among all the territories, this book seemed a suitable place to begin. However, another book caught my interest: *Xenolian Vampires*, which was placed a few rows above the one I originally noticed.

I extended my arm, straining my fingertips to reach it, but I fell short by a whole foot.

A beautiful hand, with delicate veins and the graceful familiarity of a pianist, extended from behind me, reaching for the same book. A black and silver ring adorned the hand, its beauty enhanced by a black obsidian stone. I saw that hand this morning holding a cup of excessively sweet coffee—no mistake.

I turned toward the person I least wanted to see.

Altair's blue eyes pierced mine.

I broke my gaze and reached towards the book in his hand, but instead of giving it to me, he yanked it away from my sight and glanced through the title. Altair raised an eyebrow and smirked.

"Interested in vampires, are we?" he asked, his tone teasing. "What exactly are you hoping to find in this book, Celestia?"

"I'm curious about the legends," I said it with a nonchalant shrug, trying to hide why I *really* wanted to learn more.

I reached for the book again. This time, I successfully yanked it from him. "For our paper, I'm going to write my piece. You can tear it and start it all over again, or you can write the second half."

Altair laughed through his nose. "Fair enough." He spoke in a low and playful tone.

I continued, "Also, I find it to be in poor taste to follow someone around and creep up from behind them."

This time, he laughed out loud. "Stubborn and narcissistic. Who's following who?"

I raised an eyebrow at him. "I'm obviously minding my own business. *You* have a knack for following me. You followed me into the haunted mansion."

Altair sighed. "Again, with the mansion."

I shrugged, took a last book, and descended towards the book-checkout desk on the first floor. Altair followed behind me.

"I only ran into you here. See, I also meant to look through this area and have at least one source for our paper. We got nothing done this morning."

"I wonder who's to blame for that," I said sarcastically.

I continued, "I mean, why are you even talking to me? Clearly, you have some strong negative feelings about me, and frankly, you bragged about your dog coming after me. I-"

I shook my head, and I turned my back to him as I waved my hand away in frustration.

"You're right," Altair started. "I was out of line earlier. It was unnecessary to bring that up."

I nodded.

"I'm sorry."

Surprised, I turned to face him. Upon seeing his serious expression, I gave him a small nod. We never got along, but at least, this terrifying man apologized.

"So, why didn't you want to take the long route of the mansion with me?" he asked.

For a split second, I froze, but I composed myself. "Isn't it obvious? I was expecting to go through it with... friends."

Altair smirked.

"I don't understand what's funny." I muttered.

"Instead of making excuses or lying about your feelings, have you ever thought of simply not answering questions?"

I turned to face him. "You know nothing about me or my feelings."

"That's not true." This time, he spoke in a mocking tone. "I know you don't like me very much."

"I'm not going to sugarcoat it. I dislike you." I turned back towards the checkout desk – it was finally in sight.

"The feeling is mutual," he said from behind me. I faced him again to observe his expression. Altair's smug smirk remained plastered on his face.

I didn't believe him. His gaze held a mysterious allure, even if he seemed unsure about his own emotions.

"And yet, here you are—grinning whilst in my company." I snickered at him.

Altair let out a laugh, but before he said anything, I paced towards the checkout area, and I directed my next words at the librarian. "Just these three books, please."

Altair stood beside me now. "It's your innocent, stubbornly righteous ideas, naïve, attention-seeking personality."

"The reason you're still here?" I asked in nonchalant sarcasm.

"No," he scoffed. "The reason the feeling is mutual."

"You know, I never understood why. I did nothing to bring that upon myself." I shook my head and continued, "Not like it matters now. When the cruel, egotistical little prince with a corrupt sense of justice makes indirect, prejudiced comments, I can't even feel offended."

I hit a nerve. Altair glared at me; his jaw clenched. Funny, the librarian didn't hush us. It's possible she felt intimidated by Altair or shocked by the argument between the Prince of Follyn and the Princess of Deltrea. I didn't know—I didn't see her expression. I challenged Altair with my stare, and I didn't back down.

"Thank you," Altair said to the librarian. He took the books from her, too—all while he kept his eyes on mine.

I held out my hands so he could hand me the books, but he did not. Instead, he tucked the books in one of his arms and walked forward toward the library's exit.

"Hey, those are under my name!" I motioned to grab them, but he moved them to the other arm before I got them.

"They're heavy. We're heading to the same place, anyway."

"Oh, so now you're helping me?" I mocked.

I got in front of him and took the three heavy tomes from him. Altair glared in annoyance but stayed silent, remaining beside me.

Pride swelled within me, preventing me from accepting his help. I questioned his intentions. He claimed to dislike me, yet he extended a hand—one that felt genuine, devoid of disgust or hatred. Instead, curiosity flickered in his eyes—curiosity he seemed cautious of, one he struggled to resist yet eagerly entertained. Strangely, I understood it, as I felt the same way, which added to my frustration and inner conflict.

During the walk to class, I fell behind. However, I maintained my pace until Altair matched his steps to mine, irritating me further because I refused to show any gratitude for his considerate gestures.

Silence, tension, and awkwardness enveloped our walk. We exchanged no words. In that moment, I believed our destiny mirrored that of our families—to remain enemies, unable to get along.

"You know," Altair finally broke our silence, "You talk a lot of garbage for someone who looks at me a lot."

I stopped in my tracks. "Clearly, you can't distinguish between a simple look and a glare."

"No, I've seen you glare at me. It's not as often as your gazes." He smirked again.

My heart raced. I didn't think he would confront me about it. I turned away to hide my reddening face and continued forward with our walk.

"You started it." I muttered.

He shook his head. "Your eyes have always freaked me out."

"You're a man without taste. I love my eyes." I lied. "Your comment doesn't surprise me, either. People like you wouldn't know how to admire beauty."

Altair smirked in a way I already found familiar. "People like me?"

I nodded.

"You completely misread me, Celestia. That's exactly *it*. They're so beautiful; it's freaky," he said.

I faced him. He returned my eye contact. Again, my face grew redder and redder, and I didn't realize it until Altair's expression transitioned to that of surprise.

I turned away. It would do me no good for him to know he made me blush, so I walked past him.

Altair caught up in only a couple of swift motions, and he took the books off my hands.

"Stop being stubborn, Celestia."

"I really don't need your help, Antares."

He turned to face me. "Altair."

I narrowed my eyes at him. "I will reciprocate your way of communicating. If you want me to call you by your name, you must first call me mine."

"Okay." Altair gazed at me intently, his eyes softening as he spoke my name. "Lyra."

Goosebumps prickled my skin once again.

We reached our first block's building without realizing it, and before we entered, more students crowded the area. They directed their puzzled stares at Altair and me, causing some to bump into each other in their distracted trances.

"We should head inside." I hastened my pace and reached for the door handle of the building's entrance.

"Lyra." Altair called out from behind me.

I turned towards him. "What?"

"My name."

"Altair," I said with a grin.

He moved toward me, and his actions seemed subconscious.

"Lyra!" Robin called out to me as he placed himself between Altair and me.

Altair's eyes shifted to irritation as he stared at my friend's back. They radiated hostility, and I sincerely thought Altair would lash out at Robin with disrespectful words, but my rival kept his jaw clenched.

"Let's walk together," Robin said as he motioned a hand towards the classroom door.

I looked at Altair and noticed he shifted his focus toward me, too—as if he also anticipated my response.

"Altair and I will catch up. Thank you, though."

At the mention of his name, Altair's eyes slightly widened.

Robin hesitated. He gave a firm nod, and without turning behind him to acknowledge Altair, he took his leave.

*****

Dr. Diestro's class began. I sat next to Altair as expected. I heard him scribbling in his notebook, but he didn't take notes. Instead, he doodled—circles within circles, and a plethora of eyes in various shapes and sizes. They all looked unsettling, except for the one he focused on when I glanced at him. Even through the drawing, it captivated the viewer.

I looked at my paper and moved my pen to follow Altair's doodling lead. I thought of the season—a pleasantly fresh autumn. Bright colors among the trees, bare branches without an abundance of leaves, and the darkness of the upcoming All Hallows' Eve moved my pen. In one corner of my paper, I drew a short trail of pumpkins—some with faces, some with shapes, some with nothing. In another corner, I drew a tree with branches stretched bare, except for a few leftover leaves that held on by a thread. This doodling created the distraction I needed to keep my mind off my mysterious rival sitting next to me.

When the last fifteen minutes arrived, Altair and I each grabbed one of the three books I picked out and skimmed through them.

We sat in silence. I scribbled away, and I tabbed promising chapters.

"Considering we're both hot-headed, we should meet in a private study room next time." Altair spoke without picking his head up from the book he read from.

I nodded. "When would be best?"

"Hmm, let's give ourselves until the end of the week. I liked your idea. We'll each write half—our points-of-view, so to say. Then, we can…" He trailed off.

"Find potential solutions to the issues, together," I said, playing my I-want-peace role.

He shrugged.

I rolled my eyes.

"Oh, and Lyra?"

Altair's mention of my name made me blush, but I feigned nonchalance by keeping my focus in placing my belongings into my book bag.

"Yeah?"

He leaned in towards my ear. "I really am… sorry."

The clock tower bell rang.

I turned to face him, but before I said anything, he rose from his desk, and I watched him leave.

For the rest of the day, I read through *The Birth of Xenolian Abilities* and *The Deltrean Avarice*. A Deltrean wrote the first book. A Follynean wrote the second one, and while it presented a negative perspective of my ancestors and my people, I aimed to understand their hatred and grasp why our rivals viewed things as they did.

What points did they get right? What issues could I counter with an effective solution?

After some research, I wrote notes summarizing important details and the progression of events:

> *During Vegalia Celestia's reign, conspiracy theories and sinister coincidences surrounded her. Known as a cruel leader, she executed many people, including her own husbands. Mysterious murders and strange deaths plagued the time period, ceasing only after Vegalia's death. Royals and civilians from Deltrea, Follyn, and Aquaenterra believed she orchestrated the deaths, conducting countless sacrifices to gain an audience with Xenoxas, the king of the underworld, who would grant her powerful abilities through tarot cards.*
>
> *Deaths ranged from realistic nightmares to gruesome illnesses, particularly affecting men. Medics were especially intrigued by the Mark-of-Death phenomenon—where victims awakened with a mysterious black-inked clock mark on their bodies. Apart from the infernal ticking in their heads, the patients described a stinging and burning pain where the*

ink rested. As the day progressed, the pain intensified as the ink spread throughout every vein in their infected bodies. By the next sunrise, their bodies were unrecognizable, charred from the inside out, as the venom suffocated and burned them.

At first, people thought some sort of pestilence caused the deaths, but the disease didn't spread, and the victims appeared random. Men, in particular, suffered throughout the realms, while women rarely fell victim to this horrific mark of death.

Despite the lack of a concrete cause, one thing remained certain. One chrysanthemum, one white lily, and one marigold tied in a black ribbon always appeared on top of the dead corpses. It seemed like a signature of sorts.

When people discovered that most of these men had lustfully pursued Vegalia, they grew suspicious. Their suspicions were confirmed when the youngest Prince of Follyn and Vegalia's husband, the King of Deltrea, both caught the mysterious illness and died before the next sunrise. On top of their cadavers, people found a combination of one chrysanthemum, one white lily, and one marigold.

Tensions among the kingdoms rose, and rumors spread about Vegalia potentially passing her abilities to her bloodline, which threatened the surrounding territories due to the dark magic's evil source. If Deltrean royals inherited such power throughout the centuries, the world risked falling under the demands of a wicked Deltrean rule.

A prophecy regarding Vegalia caused Xenoxas to become concerned about his partnership with her. He tried to reclaim the cards he had loaned her to strip her of her abilities. In a desperate bid to keep her power, she hid in the light, away from her benefactor's reach. There, Vegalia used her wind manipulation abilities to scatter the cards throughout Deltrea.

Deltrean researcher, Dr. Aries Cunala, reported that cards from Vegalia's deck also appeared in Follyn and Aquaenterran territory. She had three theories:

The first theory claimed Xenoxas led people from other territories into Deltrea to find the cards.

The second theory suggested Xenoxas granted the royalty of Follyn with complete knowledge of Vegalia's abilities and their whereabouts. In doing so, he would have achieved revenge on Vegalia, and he would have played a successful part in causing humanity to hate and obliterate itself.

The third theory introduced the existence of occult creatures in our world. Before Vegalia's abilities, people considered vampires mere superstitions and stories of paranoia. After Vegalia, the belief in their presence grew with an increase in deaths, where victims always bore punctures in their necks—as if a snake sucked them dry. Theory number three stated Xenoxas controlled these creatures—demonic puppets drinking human blood for life, energy, and nutrients to exist in the land of the living and carry out his misdeeds.

I sighed in disappointment. I already knew everything I wrote, but I couldn't expect new knowledge from open history.

Even before she possessed the tarot cards, Vegalia broke through portals separating the physical realm from the underworld and the spirit realm. Otherworldly creatures followed suit—myths of vampires, shapeshifters, demons, phantoms, and reapers became historical facts.

Vegalia needed to be stopped. She terrified the world.

Witches always existed, but society shunned them. After Vegalia's legacy, hostility towards witches grew. Town leaders became paranoid of their own citizens. Neighbors grew suspicious of one another. Kingdom monarchs faced lingering anxiety, wondering how many tarot cards their enemies possessed.

To move on from Vegalia's ways, modern Deltrean leaders avoided anything questionable. They vowed to their people that Vegalian tarot cards would remain unused unless their usage defended Deltrea and its people.

Contrary to the cruel and unmerciful reputations of the current Follynean royals—Dante, Desdemona, Altair, and his two older sisters, Solaris and Luna—my parents showed mercy, and their compassionate nature earned them a loyal following. My parents built up my kingdom's morale, and they established a strong sense of respect and admiration. Citizens did not fear giving their lives for the continued prosperity of Deltrea.

My parents never boasted about our tarot cards, so everyone assumed we had a fair share. Therefore, Aquaenterra refrained from opposing Deltrea because they couldn't determine whether we possessed terrifying occult riches from Vegalia's diaries. They believed

Vegalia left much behind for Deltrea, allowing it to keep many secrets within its palace walls, and since some cards invoked unknown, fearsome abilities, no one dared to risk war and death.

Ghanro, a distant kingdom, underestimated us. My teenage father and my grandmother obliterated them as easily as taking a bite of their favorite meal. Deltrea's threat made greedy leaders halt all plans to invade it.

Follyn's confidence arose from their ample resources to defeat us, but their ignorance of Deltrea's extensive knowledge prevented reckless actions. Follyn knew their best course of action was to partner with Aquaenterra.

Aquaenterra monitored closely, intending to ally with the side where victory seemed imminent. If they allied with Follyn, Aquaenterra planned to invade and share Deltrean knowledge. If they allied with Deltrea, they would defeat Follyn and seize its stolen knowledge.

My shame in facing my people, my dread of Altair and his family, and my anxiety crumbled the tower of respect and stability my parents reestablished in Deltrea. Although they never blamed me, I witnessed Fear puppeteer the destruction and waste of beautiful life in my past.

The stressful thoughts that plagued me most of my life continued their invasive circulation in my head: I longed to uncover the secrets within Follyn's walls, but gaining that knowledge peacefully would not come easy. I sought new information to aid my success, but the journey to such goals presented many obstacles.

My impatience increased by the day—another encroaching emotion I couldn't fall prey to if I expected things to go my way.

I sighed as another burdening thought looped through my mind— the fact that vampires *existed*. I usually shoved thoughts of these entities to the back of my mind while Xander eliminated countless numbers of them.

Thanks to Xander's protection, my brother and I avoided encountering these creatures. On the night of my assassination, I noticed a slight burgundy tint spread in Altair's eyes—just like those creatures. I suspected him, yet I doubted myself because even before this lifetime, I saw him out during the day. I doubted my suspicions on all sides.

Follyn and Altair held secrets and intentions, which made me restless. Altair's mysterious mind intrigued me; understanding his thoughts would provide insight into certain matters, and I *wanted* to know him.

Did he lust for power as much as Vegalia? If so, did this thirst shape him into the devil I recognized?

If I knew, I could understand. If I could understand, I could prepare a concrete strategy.

I hated to admit it, but in the current timeline, he displayed a certain kindness which brewed deep in his soul. If intentional, he let it bubble up more often than not. Altair's eyes revealed an ongoing internal battle, making me suspect that his treatment of me played a significant role in it.

Our interactions sparked hope that I could change his point of view.

Seven of Wands

I scoured through *Xenolian Vampires* after finishing my project notes. Otherwise, I would have overanalyzed the information instead of focusing on my assignment. Unfortunately, most of the book's contents provided knowledge I already knew.

The wicked demon, Xenoxas, unleashed a sinister curse upon certain humans, condemning them to a twisted eternal life in the realm of the living. He referred to this maleficence as his divine blessing. Our world referred to them as vampires.

As with all *divine blessings* tainted by evil, one must pay a heavy price. Xenoxas not only used these vampires as his spies, knights, and lackeys, but their cursed existence demanded a dark tribute. To live in death, they had to take life.

Vampires sustained their existence in the human world by drinking the crimson elixir flowing through the living. Like everyone else, they aged, but they defied time's cruel effects by savoring fresh blood. The vermillion essence rejuvenated their bodies, making them appear at their most refined and attractive, while mending their wounds with a mysterious potency. With the absence of thirst, their strength surged and their speed intensified. Without this life-giving fluid, they revealed their true age, their frailty laid bare, and an emptiness gnawed at their core. They craved it, and a vicious thirst accompanied monstrous withdrawal symptoms, making resistance to this lifetime addiction impossible.

The nocturnal beings, unable to bear the scorching radiance of the sun, dwelled in eternal darkness, forever bound to the comforting embrace of shadows.

Their alluring presence possessed an enchanting charm, yet it also emitted an unspoken warning, dissuading others from drawing too close.

The exact nature of Altair Antares remained unknown, but I sensed something other than human.

I couldn't quite identify it.

*****

The school days proceeded normally for the rest of the week. Eye contact with Altair became more interactive. I stuck my tongue out when I caught him looking, and when he didn't flash an amused smile, he returned the gesture. Sometimes, we challenged each other. We stared until one of us smiled and looked away. This time, I had a few wins.

Our classmates loved eavesdropping on Altair and me during the fifteen minutes of project independence in Dr. Diestro's class, so we talked little about the project. We read and wrote our own thing, occasionally asking each other questions. Sometimes, we wrote quick inside notes to each other—including little faces sticking their tongues out.

That Friday, I left Altair my notebook so he could go through my ideas more thoroughly and organize his.

*****

I sat in the library drinking a tea with rosehips and chamomile while I worked on assignments for my other classes. From a library window, I admired the orange hues in the sky.

The thought of my father's worry made me sigh. On Fridays, I traveled a long way to reach my parents' palace, so I had to leave soon.

That night, I'd arrive late.

An eerie emptiness followed me from the library and outside to the paths of the school. Everyone left, venturing into the college town, abandoning the school and dorms for a lively night. In contrast, I enjoyed the peace brought by the lifeless university grounds, so I took an evening walk among them before my departure.

I kept my gaze down in thought as I walked past the dormitories.

In the otherwise silent ambience, the crunching sounds of brown leaves at my feet blended with the soft sounds of the cool autumn winds which caressed my face.

A sudden feeling of someone watching me interrupted the tranquility.

I followed the sensation, and my eyes led me to look above me, to the windows of the dorms on the highest floor.

From his open window, Altair locked eyes with me, anticipating a connection. With my gaze on him, I turned towards the path which led straight to his building, and I stopped in front of its main entrance. A mischievous little smirk appeared on his face—one I reciprocated.

I broke eye contact to look for a nearby rock, and when I located one about the size of my fist, my smile widened.

I took out a marker and wrote a message on it:

What's got you so captivated?

I scanned the area to ensure it remained clear. I considered hiding my ability, but I assumed Corvus Noir already informed the Follyn royals on its details. After confirming Altair stood as my only audience, I gazed up at him. My eyes glowed, and my pupils turned into slits. My little charm monster, Benjamin, glowed as his bright essence emerged from the charm, transforming into his full bunny self as he manifested on the ground.

Altair's smirk remained plastered on his face—as if he expected my next move.

At my mental command, Benjamin unleashed a powerful gust with his back legs, which launched my rock like a flying arrow.

I intended for the rock to halt just an inch from Altair's face, hoping to make him flinch.

To my astonishment, he effortlessly snatched it out of the air.

I kept my eyes on him as he wrote something on the rock, and when he finished, he threw the rock straight-down, away from me. He probably wanted to make sure it wouldn't hit me.

Sweet flutters filled my stomach as I picked up the rock and read his message:

Come up.

I looked up and faced Altair's impish expression. He turned and walked away from his window, giving me the privacy to make a choice.

I gripped the rock in my hand as I glanced through the message again. With it, I made my way towards Altair's dorm.

*****

Nerves bubbled up in the pit of my stomach when I stood in front of his door.

I didn't knock.

I feared my nervousness would become apparent with the way I knocked, so instead, I rapidly tapped my fingernails on his door.

A tiny door window above my eye level decorated the door. I didn't peek through it, but I knew Altair saw me. So, I stuck my tongue out and made faces, hoping to annoy him with my presence. Altair chuckled past the door.

As the door opened, I put on my best smile and pretended I made no such grotesque faces at his window.

"Charming as ever, aren't you?" I gazed at the man who disturbed my peace of mind.

"Always."

He opened the door wide for me and made a gesture with his hand to welcome me inside, but my nerves kept me rooted to my spot. My eyes darted around the inside of his large dorm. Contrary to my expectations, Altair Antares lived in a humble, comfortable area rather than a lavish copy of a castle chamber. A modestly sized bed occupied one corner of the room. While it may comfortably fit two people, the bed couldn't compare to a castle bed's extravagance. If anything, it reminded me of the one I slept in while I stayed at Xander's home.

A few thin, black shelves lined one of his walls. The compact kitchen featured a small table which may accommodate two individuals. It seemed Altair never imagined receiving more than one guest.

"Do you need a verbal invitation?" Altair interrupted my observations of his room.

I scoffed. "What do I look like? A Xenolian creature?"

I stepped inside and walked around freely as I admired his living space.

"I'm a little surprised you made the journey up here," he said behind me.

"I came to bring you back your gift." I held up the rock we threw to one another and shook it playfully. "You dropped it out the window like some fool."

"Are you here to find a suitable place for it?" he asked as he walked toward me.

I placed the rock on his shelf. "Yup. Right here at eye level. I hope it reminds you of me and gives you headaches." I grinned at him.

"Great." Altair eyed me as I skimmed through his treasures. "Do you want something to drink? Coffee? Water? Tea?"

"What tea are you offering?"

"Ahh, I have... chamomile and peppermint."

"I'll take peppermint, please."

I walked about the room, taking in every detail.

Altair had already prepared hot water, and I couldn't decide whether I felt amused or flattered, or if I read too much into the action. He must've figured I *would* come up.

"It's not odd for you—living away from your castle or your family's hotel to come live here?"

"Not at all. Large living spaces are suffocating. Why do you ask?"

"Your extravagant lifestyle seemed to suit your preferences."

"I see. You thought me a snob."

"I did."

Altair shook his head. "What about you? Would you ever consider living in such a tiny room?"

"I would." I wished for my own dorm, but my father would never allow it.

He placed our tea cups on his coffee table—right beside my notebook, which lay open on top of the table as well. I followed him over and sat on the black sofa adjacent to the elegant glass table.

"So, what are you still doing here?" he asked.

"Studying. Researching. And, you? Don't you go to Follyn or Regnum Noctis on the weekends?"

He shrugged. "Regnum Noctis is loud, and home is far."

"I see... I'm curious because... everyone seemed surprised you started showing up at school."

Altair remained silent beside me.

"You left to train some sort of ability, didn't you?" I asked.

"Well, what about you?" He returned the question back to me. "You can't expect me to believe the Deltrean king and queen allowed their daughter to return defenseless."

I smirked. "You *would* be foolish to believe I am defenseless."

"Oho. That's a bold statement, but you're right. Your little bunny is quite the opponent."

I chuckled. His unfamiliar playful tone synchronized with mine.

He continued, "I meant it as in... you're here because you must've *mastered* handling an ability."

I shook my head. "It's not just about forbidden abilities. I'm here because I trained my body and sharpened my skills. I faced my traumas." Despite my smile, Altair flinched and averted his gaze when I mentioned *traumas*. Shame settled in his expression, and I figured my comment unintentionally hit him in the chest.

We fell into silence once again. I met his gaze, and he reciprocated my expression with his—a complex reading rested in his eyes. I didn't know how to interpret it. As someone who often over-thought, I worried Altair still harbored a deep hatred for me, stemming from our childhood animosity and ingrained prejudices. Yet, for once, we actually got along, and I sensed that his struggle with negative emotions mirrored mine.

I pointed to my notebook. "Did you read my notes?"

"I did."

"And? What did you think?"

Altair cleared his throat. "Vegalia committed a lot of questionable actions."

"She did, didn't she?" I said, almost to myself. "So, let me ask you this: In your eyes... did Vegalia win?"

"No, I don't think she won."

"Neither do I."

"We seem to agree on one thing."

A scream in the distance interrupted our curious conversation. At once, Altair and I rose from our seats, but before we looked outside his window, the scream ended abruptly.

We peeked out the window and spotted the source of the scream. In the distance, a person latched onto a girl's throat. The scene looked intimate but felt *wrong*, more like a bloodsucker quenching his thirst.

Realizing this, Altair remarked, "Looks like a comrade is getting a late-night meal."

I shook my head at his indifference. "Altair, that could be a classma-"

A bright, blinding light interrupted my words. My arm instinctively shielded my eyes from it.

Altair swiftly moved away from the window, groaning in pain. He clenched his hands into fists and placed them firmly over his eyes.

What? Did that hurt him? I thought

"Altair, are you okay?"

"I'm fine." His words came out through gritted teeth.

I hissed in pain when I felt a burning sensation on my arm. When I looked at it, I noticed the intense, dark red hue resembling a severe sunburn.

We found ourselves in a conundrum. The radiance lasted a single second. I could not piece together how I ended up burned and why Altair also seemed hurt.

From the window, I observed the scene.

If the light hurt Altair and me from this distance, it must have disintegrated the bloodsucker because I couldn't see him anywhere. However, the girl remained at the scene. She lay unconscious, likely from blood loss. Oddly enough, our professor, Dr. Diestro, appeared at the scene, too.

"You okay?" Altair asked through gritted teeth.

I let out a soft gasp as I put two and two together. I already knew Dr. Diestro had an ability, but I didn't know which one.

Now, as I watched him carry the girl's limp body to safety, I was certain.

Altair remained unaffected by the sun, but Dr. Diestro's scorching light burned him like a normal vampire under sunlight, revealing our professor's possession of the power of card number nineteen, The Sun.

I closed Altair's curtains, but he noticed and yanked them from me. Despite my struggle, he pulled so hard that they came off.

I peeked out again, hoping Dr. Diestro had left before Altair saw him. Unfortunately, the professor disappeared just after Altair caught a glimpse of him.

Leave it to a teacher to care more about his students than his own safety. His concern for discretion vanished when he saw the girl in the arms of a predator.

I couldn't let Altair hurt him.

I faced my opponent. Severe burns marred his face, and his eyes appeared bloodshot.

He glared at me.

He knew why I closed the curtains.

Altair paced towards his door, but I dashed behind him and grabbed his wrist before he grew near it. He made no comment, but I felt his anger seething through his being.

"You *will not* do anything to hurt him! He is our teacher. We all love him!"

"That's your verdict, Deltrean leader?" His tone sounded irate.

He continued, "How disappointing."

"*You're* disappointing! How could such dark thoughts cross your mind?"

"It's the only way," he said.

I shook my head.

"What do you propose, then, Lyra? There's no alternative to depriving him of his abilities. The user needs to die."

"We can question him. We can make him aware we will monitor him and his use of-"

"Absolutely not! Not just anybody can possess those abilities."

"He isn't just anybody; he is a good person!"

"I see. Deltreans let any interloper possess such dangerous abilities. How irresponsible."

"Why should we have everything? Because we're royals?"

"Because it keeps our world functioning. There is order, and we prevent chaos from erupting by keeping this insane situation under control."

"You think we're keeping it under control when royals may possess all the ones they encounter? That brings chaos regardless."

I've seen it!

I've *lived* it!

I desperately wished I could tell him how power and abilities corrupted him in our past lives.

Altair gave a small laugh through his nose. "Let's not forget your ancestor put the entire world in this situation."

I remained silent. The world would never let me forget, nor would I let myself forget. These messy situations existed because of my bloodline. I knew the fact better than anyone.

"That's not something I'll ever deny." I whispered. "But, explain to me this: You are against anyone, except royals, getting the abilities of Vegalia's Tarot Cards. However, you Follynean royals are also okay with Corvus Noir having such a horrific ability." My stomach churned as I said the assassin's name aloud.

Altair's jaw clenched.

I got him.

I continued, "If what you're saying is true for Follyn, where only royals can possess abilities, then is he one of you? One of the Antares siblings? Perhaps, one of your paren-"

"Corvus Noir," he started, "is a Follynean loyal—a deranged fanatic, if you will. He's no different from what Xander Von Almont is to Deltrea."

I gasped.

"We know a lot more than you think, Lyra."

My eyes stung. Hearing Altair blatantly confirm his link to the assassin suffocated me—a feeling that worsened when he mentioned Xander.

I pushed Altair away from me.

"Are you going to send him after our professor?"

"Corvus Noir is under my father's order, and I have to inform him about what I saw. Who knows? Noir might bring him to us alive for another public trial."

"If you send that murder after Dr. Diestro, I will fight him myself."

His jaw clenched again. "You'll only end up dead."

I shook my head. "You underestimate me, Altair. I've faced him before. You should know this."

"You're frustratingly stubborn!" He threw his arm in my direction.

"Then, don't tell your father!" I raised my voice.

"You will not influence my decisions." He snapped. "And, you have no say in Follyn's judgement, either."

"A Follynean royal attacking an Aquaenterran professor on neutral grounds means war. Considering the circumstances, I may even end up with immense support at my side."

My declaration caught Altair off guard.

Altair closed the short distance between us. His footsteps were heavy, irate, but I didn't move from my spot.

He spoke in a low and hoarse tone. "So, as soon as Dr. Diestro becomes involved, your dormant bravery, defiance, and voice slips out."

"He's twice the man you'll ever be." I snapped.

Again, Altair faced the door, taking swift steps toward it.

"Where are you going?" I panicked. "Those like us, burdened with abilities and forced leadership, should not harm those who protect. Too much evil exists in this world, Altair. You're looking in the wrong direction."

Altair shook his head. "I'm still going to talk to him."

I grabbed Altair by his arm. "Leave him be."

"Let go, Lyra. I don't want to hurt you." Altair glared at me.

"I don't want to hurt you, either."

I couldn't hold him back. Altair escaped from my grip and moved forward.

"You can't leave looking like that!" It appeared he disregarded his charred condition, yet despite my reminder, he kept walking towards his door.

As a final resort to stop him, I broke one of the glass teacups and gripped a shard. Pressing it against my skin, I impulsively chose a spot where the wound wouldn't show—just below my shoulder and above my breast. I made a small incision, causing blood to drip.

A thin trail of blood trickled down, down, down—enough to trigger a blood-sucker's cravings. I gambled on a gut feeling, almost certain the crown prince of Follyn was a vampire. There was no other reason for his exposed skin to become so burned, so charred. We both faced the same scene, yet my arm only ended up with a bad sunburn.

Altair paused right as he cracked opened the door, and I *knew* he caught the scent of my open wound.

Altair closed the door with weighted force, pressing his palms against it. He didn't face me, but I heard his sharp breathing. With the way he held himself, I believed he became engaged in an internal conflict—probably battling against attacking me for my blood.

I took a step forward.

"Don't! Don't. Get. Closer." Altair struggled for words.

Altair turned to face me. He pressed his back against the door, but his eyes held a predatory desire. His sharp fangs, ready to pierce into flesh, targeted me as the only candidate in his path.

"You're gonna... have to use your ability to get out... of this one, little Lyra."

I hesitated. His evident self-restraint and his determination to resist himself made me unwilling to abandon him—not in that condition. I didn't want to risk Altair harming others or himself.

I felt a drop fall to the floor.

It took Altair one swift motion until I found myself in his arms. One of his arms held the small of my back, and his other hand held my head, and a burgundy hue claimed his irises.

"Control yourself, Altair." I whimpered, but I knew it wouldn't work to reason with an injured vampire who just smelled an open wound.

Altair gripped at the sleeve of my dress and pulled it down to reveal the skin beneath my shoulder. His cold fangs pierced my open wound. Oddly enough, the pain quickly faded and transitioned into sweet feelings of desire and pleasure.

The compelling power of a vampire's bite was frightening, but once people became trapped in it, they welcomed it. It was dangerous, like everything that surrounded Altair Antares.

I tightened the grip of my hands on his shoulders as I let out a pleasure-filled sigh. Altair continued to feed on my blood, and I gripped him against my exposed skin; I didn't want him to stop.

Altair reciprocated my grasp by tightening his arms around me. One arm stretched diagonally from my lower back towards the top of my back. His other arm gripped onto my waist, and I held on to him for dear life.

For a moment, I found the voice of my consciousness. Even though my physical being didn't want to leave, my mind rang with urgency.

My eyes glowed at the thought. In my confusion, I instructed the bunny to consume the liquids scattered throughout the room.

It took immense mental strength to resist the allure of the addicting sensation, but I overcame it by forming a small but powerful offensive shield with the bit of liquids I had gathered. The forceful, rapid friction of the swirling water focused on Altair's vampire fangs, keeping them from piercing my skin and effectively separating us.

Unfortunately, Altair's draining of my blood and the use of my ability left me weak. It didn't take long before I was completely out of energy.

My barrier weakened, losing water by the second as it splattered between Altair and me. I struggled to keep the water flowing smoothly until a single thin, rapid stream separated us.

I looked into Altair's dazed eyes, but he didn't hold my gaze. As the intoxication from my blood faded from his expression, he turned away, revealing a conflicted and ashamed look on his face.

The burns on his appearance had disappeared.

He looked like himself again, and his eyes took on his normal sapphire hue to them.

That's right. Blood not only satisfied a vampire's thirst, it healed them.

My legs gave out. As I sunk to the floor, Altair lifted me and kept me steady. In a final attempt to get away from him, I grabbed his arms and pushed him away, but my fight held no more force.

My eyelids grew heavy.

*****

I woke up in Altair's bed and scrambled to gather my belongings, remembering I needed to head home. I looked around and spotted Altair sleeping on his sofa.

Relief washed over me. Altair didn't leave me alone. He didn't run.

Disappointment in my lack of self-control filled my mind. Why was I happy he stayed? Fury should have consumed me at his impulsiveness. Terror should have gripped me, but it didn't. I didn't feel threatened. Instead, before I succumbed to drowsiness, I saw his remorseful expression. Altair couldn't contain himself. The scent of fresh blood made it brutal for vampires to ignore it—especially when they were hurt.

Questions flooded my mind. I couldn't fathom why Altair wasn't completely affected by the typical traits and weaknesses of vampires.

I eyed his sleeping figure from my distance.

My actions must have caught him off-guard.

He and the Follyneans kept his vampiric nature a secret, and they hid it well. Pandemonium would erupt if people learned that the next ruler of Follyn was a Xenolian creature. The sensitive situation favored my goals, but I needed concrete evidence, and at the moment, I couldn't prove my bite mark came from him. At least, the incriminating nature of this revelation may compel him to remain silent about Dr. Diestro.

I got up from the bed and gathered my belongings—including my notebook. I ripped out one of its blank pages and wrote a letter for Altair.

> *Dear Altair,*
>
> *Please don't hurt our teacher. Without his help or encouragement, our current situation would probably be different. Despite any rooted hatred, we've been doing okay, haven't we?*
>
> *For now, I need some space. Tonight was… a lot.*
>
> *Thank you for inviting me and letting me recover.*
>
> *Sincerely,*
> *Lyra*

King of Swords

I barely settled at home for ten minutes before my father summoned me. His fit and muscular frame came into view as I opened the door to his study. He wore his black-rimmed reading glasses, his gaze focused on the documents in his hand, but he didn't sit at his desk. He paced throughout the room, as he often did, when stress overwhelmed him.

"Lyra." His voice sounded concerned. Before he continued speaking, he put his documents on his desk and he made a gesture for me to sit.

I complied. If he felt annoyed, or worse, upset, this conversation would be quick. He would interrogate, throwing questions and comments one after another. To prevent him from probing into my hesitations or investigating my matters further, I needed to answer as quickly as he asked.

"Before we let you enter the university again, what did we discuss? Keep your distance from the Antares boy."

Xander reported everything to my father, but I wasn't sure if he saw me enter and exit the dorms. If he had, he hid it. Otherwise, my father would have ordered me to pack my bags and leave the university, disrupting my plans. Instead, he simply repeated his warning, indicating that only a lecture awaited me.

The good thing about my father was that he didn't yell or raise his voice, but the sternness and hint of annoyance in his tone were enough to intimidate anyone. He was a no-nonsense kind of man, and his actions, body language, and direct questions and comments demonstrated this.

"We ended up together for a partner project."

"You couldn't have asked for a change?"

"We agreed we'd work together."

"Did he put you up to it?"

"I *chose* to work with him."

"Have you forgotten our history with the Follynean royals?"

"I have not."

"Did you forget what he put you through?" My father referred to the events of the children's school.

"He's different now, father."

He looked down at me in silence. Honestly, my answer surprised *me*. I remembered everything Altair Antares did to my family, and my father remained unaware of the evil Altair managed in our past lives, yet I stood by my words. Something different about Altair made him not as unlikeable as I expected, and as much as I loved my family, their passionate opposition to Altair and his family severely threatened my goal of winning Altair's heart. Planting the seed of Altair's redemption seemed ideal.

My father sighed as he poured himself a drink. In times of stress, he always prepared a glass with two fingers of cognac.

He sat cross-legged on the sofa, which directly faced me. He eyed his drink as he moved the glass in circular motions near his nose.

"Different." He emphasized, as if to himself.

"Give him the benefit of the doubt! He-"

"I don't want to hear it." My father put up his pointer-finger and waved no as he took a small sip.

"He is cooperating with the assignment and-"

"By all means, tell me all about him." Now he spoke sarcastically, but I continued speaking over him, drowning out his voice.

"I'm keeping my guard up with him, and I'm learning how to defend my voice, and-"

The door to the study opened.

"Oh, good, your mother's here. My dear, please talk to your daughter. She thinks the Antares boy is *different*."

My mother's face immediately shifted to alarm.

"Mama, he's exaggerating a little-"

"And 'he's cooperating with the assignment.'" My father quoted me, but he added an emphasis on my words, as if they meant more than they really did.

"That's because that's *all* it is. We were-"

"They had a date at the library's coffee shop." Ah, there it was— the news that stressed him out, but it made me wonder why Xander left out the fact he saw me leave the dorms, and again, I wondered if he witnessed me go in. Perhaps he trusted my actions, but his loyalty to my father must have compelled him to say *something*, at least. Yet, he didn't.

"It was strictly business!" I corrected my father.

My mother interjected, "Okay, okay. Wait a minute. You're both talking over one another again. Honey," she sat beside me and put one of her arms around my back; she placed her free hand on my arm. "What's this about going on a date with *that* boy?"

"Mama, it wasn't a date. We-"

"It seems they walk to class together, too."

My mother turned to my father. "Why doesn't Xander interject?"

"The situations don't seem hostile," my father said.

I spoke again. "That's because they aren't hostile. We shouldn't expect Xander to blow his cover on such a minor situation I chose to be in."

"Yes, but honey, the Prince of Follyn is *very* dangerous." My mother's face demonstrated concern.

"All men are vicious, Lyra, and that Antares boy is the worst of them." My father spoke in a matter-of-fact tone. He took another sip of his drink.

"The situation is not, at all, what you all are making it out to be," I said.

"Something about an assignment. I understand." My mother's smile always comforted me.

"You understand she's working closely with that Antares boy?" My father now directed his annoyed tone at her.

"Well, of course, darling. I understand Lyra may want to grow a tolerance of the vibrations and energies the boy gives off. If it's only an assignment, let's trust she will keep it to that. Strictly business, as she said, right?" She softly brushed my hair with her fingertips as she directed the last bit of her sentence to me.

"Do we all not..." My father removed his glasses, pressed his fingers to his eyes, and faced my mom and me again. "...remember the Follyneans placed a target on Lyra's back with Corvus Noir?"

"Well," My mother began, "Perhaps this is Lyra's chance to observe and listen closely. He's unintentionally bound to give off information."

"We shouldn't expose Lyra to that."

"Why not, Father?" I asked. "I'm eighteen years old, and I have no allies. I haven't built a strong reputation, and I've been on the run most of my life. How else can I expect to lead alongside my brother? I must begin somewhere! Our own people will come to doubt us!"

My father remained silent. Then, he directed his gaze to my mother. "What does your intuition say?"

My mother possessed a heightened sense of intuition, a trait inherited from the ability she got from The High Priestess, the second card of Vegalia's tarot cards. My intuition didn't match a fraction of hers. I needed to connect with myself through a lot of meditation, but my flood of over thoughts and inability to silence my restless mind kept this part of me dormant.

My mother smiled. "Our baby is going to be okay." She continued to brush my hair with her fingers.

"Is the assignment really all it was?" My father made an obvious gesture to my mother, communicating whether she should use her power on me. My mother's ability also granted her telepathic communication and mind reading, but it came at a painful cost to the victim and a massive amount of energy for the user.

Therefore, my father's signal alarmed me.

I gasped. "Father! What are you implying she do?"

"Darling," my mother said calmly. "I am not invading our daughter's thoughts."

"That is too far! What in the world did Xander tell you? Surely, there must be a misunderstanding!" I dreaded my father's reaction if he discovered I spent time in Altair's dorm. If he learned about Altair's vampirism and that Altair bit me and drank my blood that night, my father would hunt him down.

"The way you're defending the Antares boy, along with your frequent encounters with him, could put you at risk. As a matter of fact, it could put us all at risk."

"I am handling it!"

"My sweet loves," my mother interjected again. "Stop it. Darling, you and I both know we will not invade her mind. Also, Xander sticks around for a bit on the perimeter of the academy. He must've seen them both from a distance; I trust our Lyra is careful with her words."

My father downed the rest of his cognac and set the empty glass on his desk. "I suppose I have no choice. For now, I trust you will be careful-"

"Of course, I will."

"Let me finish." The seriousness in his tone sent a chill down my spine. "I trust you will not drop your guard and reveal nothing of importance."

*****

I looked at the scar from Altair's bite in the mirror. I should have felt repulsed, and I should have pushed Altair away immediately. Yet, I continuously tried to block the thoughts that made me recognize the sweetly suffocating pleasure that ran through my body after he pierced my skin. I wanted to explore and indulge in the feelings even more. Fluttering emotions enveloped me as I remembered the addicting sensations of when he pulled down the sleeve of my dress, when his mouth's invasive allure brushed my skin, when his teeth possessively penetrated my skin, and when his dominating hold gripped me. Despite my efforts to ignore these memories, the passions circulated in my head.

My mother interrupted my thoughts by knocking on my bedroom door.

I sighed for the millionth time that night as I sat up in bed when my mother entered the room.

My mother grabbed a brush and a ribbon from my dresser, then sat beside me and began brushing and braiding my long hair.

I loved it when she did my hair. Her comforting actions and loving words were my greatest joys in life. I avoided falling into deep depression because she stayed with me for most of my life—until I obtained The World. That's when I lost her.

I held my mother's hand as a throbbing knot formed in my throat, and I pushed the painful thoughts of her loss away.

"What is it, honey?"

I shook my head.

"Your mood shifted. I felt it." She gently ran the brush through my long hair.

"I just missed you. You know? All these years... with Xander... I missed home."

My mother hugged me. "You do not know how much your father and I missed you both, too. The days held a sad intensity, and some days, I did not want to leave the bed. I just wanted to sleep the days away. I wanted my babies, but I did not want you at risk."

My mother began braiding my hair. "You've grown strong, and so, so beautiful, my Lyra. You came home with a new sense of bravery, which tramples the anxiety that once dominated you."

I smiled.

"It seems Altair Antares sees your beauty, too."

I blushed at my mother's mention of his name. "It's nothing like that. He just likes to... argue."

"Still?"

I nodded. "Well, sometimes... I'm the one that starts them."

My mother gave a light-hearted laugh. "Well, if you say that's all it is, then..."

"That's all it is." I confirm.

"Look, I did not want to alarm your father, but I sense a peculiar interest in your energy for the Prince of Follyn." My mother lightly pinched my cheeks. "And this cute little blush gives you away."

"I'm just interested in the things that move and shape Altair's twisted ideas."

"Altair, hmm?" My mother frowned. "And how do you see his personality nowadays? I'm assuming a little better, considering your demeanor and the *frequent encounters*."

I blushed again. "He's not as bad as I thought he'd be."

Altair didn't want to hurt me last night. He didn't want to reveal his secret, either. I took advantage of the knowledge I gathered. I took advantage of his burned *condition*, and it made me feel a little guilty.

When my mother said nothing in response, I covered my face and continued spilling my thoughts. "He is unbelievably frustrating and handsome, and there's a kind side to him which I've only seen glimpses of, and I hate it so much because he's not supposed to be kind. Altair's not supposed to be any of those things." He's supposed to be ugly and cruel, and I wished I would have seen joy in his eyes when he bit me—anything evil—anything to push me away. Instead, conflict raged. He visibly struggled, and it must have taken every ounce of reasoning to keep himself from taking more of my blood after I blacked out.

I sighed, but I remained silent. I did not want my mother to worry about the foolish, passing emotions I felt for Altair Antares.

"I see." My mother tied a ribbon to hold my braid in place.

Before she got up to leave, she parted with a word of caution: "I second what your father said. Don't forget who you are dealing with while you work with him."

I nodded.

"Okay." My mother kissed my forehead. "Goodnight, honey."

*****

After the talk with my mom, I finally threw myself back on my bed, and once again, invasive thoughts about Altair attacked my mind when I eyed my notebook.

I only thought of my last encounter with him. Along with the attraction, I felt shame. First, I failed to defend myself the way I always swore I would, especially with him. Second, as much as I hated to admit it, I wanted to see him at that moment. Now, I worried whether he saw right through my emotions. If he caught the sound of my heart or a dumb look in my eyes, I feared he would laugh at me forever.

I sighed and opened my notebook, intending to skim through the notes Altair read. I felt oddly self-conscious of my handwriting, despite it being quite neat.

To my surprise, extra notes appeared on the sides of my own notes. I gasped upon recognizing Altair's thin, pointy handwriting.

He wrote little remarks and comments on my thoughts. Some of them added to my ideas, some of them agreed with what I wrote, and other comments presented a different point of view.

I turned to the next blank page. Instead, I found a note from Altair written on it.

Lyra,

I've been meaning to ask, but I guess... in my shame... I've been avoiding the subject all together.

I'll get straight to it—is there a part of you that fears me for what I've done to you?

I sucked in a breath.

How could I respond to Altair's message? Ironically, he wrote this before he bit me. He wrote this with our hostile exchanges as children in mind, yet it posed such a powerful, significant question in the current moment.

I sat on my bed and stared at Altair's writing in absentmindedness.

My brother's rhythmic knocking brought me back to reality. It seemed my whole family wanted to talk that night.

Alphonse poked his head in and whispered, "What happened?"

A slight smile was plastered on his face when he said this, so I knew he came for the gossip.

I sighed, "Not now, Alph."

He let out a little gasp as he walked into my room. "What's that?"

Impulsively, I closed my notebook. "It's my homework. What do you want? I'm busy."

"Damn, alright, then. It's not my fault that Father upset you," he muttered under his breath as he closed the door to my room.

I opened my notebook and flipped the pages until I arrived at Altair's message once again.

I considered different responses, including denying his statement. Instead, I decided to confront his question with the truth. After all, I didn't have to face it in person. I also preferred the way he addressed this issue because I could think about my response clearly and without pressure.

Yes.

Altair and I moved forward, but our relationship couldn't progress because of rivalry, uncertainties, and lack of communication about our childhood. Truth was necessary in this circumstance, even if I could only start with a single, powerful word that stated the hard reality for both of us.

I feared bringing up our childhood past together, too, because addressing this delicate topic within the uncertainty of our affiliation might take Altair and me a few steps back. For now, I could only offer him a simple but truthful answer. I didn't need to bring up resentment or worsen matters by insulting him.

The next move belonged to him.

Four of Cups

I didn't stress too much about any potential awkwardness between Altair and me because he was absent. At first, I felt relieved, but an underlying dullness pervaded the entire day. With his absence, a certain emotion went missing, and I didn't quite like it. I sensed an incompleteness, but I struggled to put it into words.

Thick gray clouds hovered above the school grounds. The bleak day brought a bitter cold and a persistent drizzle which soaked the area.

The following day, a thin cloud of fog enveloped the ambience, and it appeared more concentrated on the school grounds.

Every day thereafter, the fog thickened until it completely obscured the school.

October was off to a hollow start.

*****

The second week of Altair's absence weighed heavier with each passing day. My confusion deepened, and my irritation grew more noticeably uncomfortable. The persistent blinding fog around the school worsened my mood. Altair took the days' clarities with him.

Annoyance, agitation, and anxiety intensified, yet part of me longed to see him.

I sighed.

I wondered if he avoided me because he bit me or didn't want to face the professor. Maybe both.

Was I a relevant enough reason?

Perhaps Altair trained a new ability.

Another gloomy week unfolded as my thoughts piled up with various conclusions about Altair's absence.

*****

"Adrian, I want to talk to you." I caught him after one of our classes earlier that week.

A hint of astonishment flashed in his initial reaction, but he quickly replaced it with a mix of distance and distrust.

"It's Ian, and I want nothing more than the opposite of what you want."

He walked away before I said anything else.

I followed him, but he moved fast, and he prevented me from reaching him by entering the sea of fog outside the building.

Throughout the rest of the week, I pursued Ian for information at every opportunity—unless Roselia accompanied him.

On the second hollow Friday of the month, he seemed fed up enough with my attempts to talk to him.

"You're stubborn," he said, facing me with a firm tone and holding himself with contempt.

He stood tall, matching Altair's height, and his honey-hued eyes looked down on me with hatred and prejudice, just like when we were children. However, as he locked eyes with me, I noticed something new—curiosity.

Perfect. That's what I wanted. If I kept that bit of curiosity fed and engaged, I could get a few minutes of his time.

"Altair told me the same thing."

Ian narrowed his eyes. Perhaps he didn't like that I referred to Altair by his first name—it felt daring, intimate, and in a way, authoritative—entitled. After all, to them, I represented the enemy.

"What do you want, Celestia?" His tone came out dry, but his curious eyes betrayed him with an underlying glint of interest.

"Where is Altair?"

"I thought you knew better than to ask *me* about Altair." Ian glared daggers at me.

"I had to try."

He scoffed. "Why? Were you actually expecting me to give you a response?"

"Would you at least give this to him for me?"

Ian's glare moved down towards the envelope in my hand. Inside it, I placed a letter I wrote earlier that week. It read:

Dear Altair,

If I'm what keeps you away, I guess I can claim a small victory.

For the sake of the odd relationship we shared, I hope that wherever you are, you're well, happy, and not causing trouble or hardship to the innocent.

Love,
Lyra

While writing the letter, I contemplated whether to sign it as *sincerely* or simply sign with my name.

I chose *love*. The word carried a sense of irony—one that a Deltrean royal never spoke or wrote to a Follynean royal. Perhaps it contained a hint of sarcasm, but it possessed enough power to get an enemy thinking. The word carried the strength to bring hope into a situation, even when used in deceit.

A mischievous smile spread across my face as I closed and signed my letter. I hoped the bait would lure Altair back, but reaching him was tricky. Knowing Roselia's feelings for him, I doubted she would deliver it for me.

Ian was my only hope.

He gazed at the neat black envelope, sealed with red wax depicting a teacup seal.

He shook his head. "I haven't seen him either, Celestia."

"I know you might get hold of him. Please?" I softened my voice, and I pleaded with my gaze.

"It's important. There's information in here Altair *must* know about."

Ian scratched his head and sighed in frustration, contemplating it for a moment. Then, he yanked the letter from my hands and walked off with it.

With my back turned to him, and no one to see me, I let my little victorious smirk make its appearance.

Friday was a win.

The fog on the school grounds diminished—just a little.

Two of Pentacles

The third Monday morning without Altair arrived, and I couldn't muster the energy to wake up and greet the middles of October.

I got up sluggishly, and for the first time, I arrived late to campus.

At least, the fog diminished.

The skies cleared up.

Later that evening, I watched the sunset from the library windows as I absentmindedly made my way outside, towards the back of the building—the festival grounds. The area became a sanctuary for me. Even with the decorations, the area remained abandoned, except for the haunted mansion. Despite its loveliness, everyone retreated indoors to nearby cafes, restaurants, and buildings, particularly at night.

A tiny forest lined with organized cherry blossom trees stretched along a pathway which divided into sections surrounding the grassy areas where booths set up during the festivals.

In the deepening indigo darkness of the skies, I positioned myself where no one saw me through the library windows. I moved closer to the gated border of the festival grounds, which seperated the university from Follyn territory.

I sat against the center of one of the tallest cherry blossom trees in one of the furthest, darkest corners of the grounds, and I closed my eyes.

Despite my conflicted emotions, the pleasant area emanated a peaceful ambience.

*****

Movement rustled beside me as I drifted off, but I didn't open my eyes. My consciousness continued to bathe in the tranquilities of my surroundings.

Much to my surprise, I felt a light tap on my cheek, which transitioned into a delicate caress as it fell from my face.

The energy in front of me carried no hostility or negativity. I felt a familiar sense of fulfillment—one I had missed for days.

"Lyra." The soft voice of the man I waited weeks to see made my heart race, but I kept my eyes closed. I frowned, pretending I wanted to be left alone.

A light laugh slipped through his nose. "Lyra."

Once more, a gentle tap graced my cheek.

I slowly opened my eyes and faced Altair sitting beside me.

"Whoa. Look at those pretty eyebrows, all scrunched up."

I stared at him in silence.

He ran a hand through his silky black hair and sighed, deep in thought.

"How are you... er, feeling?" He pointed below his neck to indicate what he meant.

My monotonous expression did not change. I kept my eyes on him without saying a word.

"You really are mad." He looked at me with remorse in his eyes.

"You threaten our teacher. You take a bite out of me. You leave me to stress about a research paper that is due this week. Then, you have the audacity to disappear for two weeks instead of facing me. What did you expect? You expect me to welcome you back or something?"

"I apologize," he paused. "For attacking you, and for disappearing. Truthfully, I thought you would have preferred me away for a while."

Again, I said nothing as my eyes pierced his.

"As for our professor, I thought about what you said," he sighed. "No harm will come to him. I will do nothing against him, and I'll keep it all... confidential. I hope that much gives you a peace of mind, for the time being."

"How can I be sure you're telling me the truth?"

Altair shrugged. "Time. I will not ask you to trust me—just that you wait and see for yourself."

"Hmm," I lifted an eyebrow.

"The great Altair Antares apologizes to the Princess of Deltrea. Isn't it the second time you do it?"

Altair remained quiet.

I continued, "So, you *do* have a heart, and you *know* you've done wrong. What happened to Altair Antares, who declared me and mine enemies without batting an eye?"

Altair kept his gaze on me, but his expression looked conflicted.

"What's changed, Altair?"

He let out a deep, weary sigh, the sound escaping his lips like a heavy burden. With a slight slump in his shoulders, he turned away from me, his gaze fixated on the distance.

"I'm assuming you were absent because you were hoping to avoid questions? I'm still going to ask, you know."

He shrugged in response. "Doesn't mean I'll answer anything."

"You owe me answers, Altair."

"What do you want to know, Lyra?" His tone carried frustration.

He continued. "You are aware of my true nature and have the bite mark as evidence. So, what is your exact intention here? Are you trying to get me to admit what you already know? What's the point of that?"

Familiar conflict settled in his eyes, and I realized he sat much too close to me—even closer than our usual seats in class. Despite the calm emotions I showed him, I was a mess inside. My stomach fluttered, a strange sensation which contradicted the expected feeling of revulsion.

I grew comfortable in his presence. His return made me ecstatic. I wanted to hug him and rest my head on his shoulder in order to ease his conflicted expression, but my pride, my dignity, and my sense of reason refused. While I wanted him to trust me and let his guard down with me, the flawed offensive tactic would also make my heart ache. A genuine vulnerability emerged in that moment, untainted by our pretenses, hypocrisies, and falsehoods. Therefore, I remained still and silent beside him. Just this once, I wanted to let the moment be.

Finally, he spoke. "I understand your curiosity about many things. Among those, I assume you want to know why the sun doesn't affect me."

I nodded, never averting my gaze from his sapphire eyes.

I thought it related to a tarot; he definitely stood out from a vampire, but he shared similarities, too. For starters, the sunlight didn't affect him, and I witnessed him drink and eat human foods, too.

Contrary to Altair, vampires supplemented with blood—everything else held no appeal and neither satisfied, nourished, nor replenished them. Much like predatory animals, they hunted and saw clearly in the darkness. They possessed greater strength than the average human, but not to an unstoppable degree. Their keen senses and hunting skills made them dangerous and powerful. If they fed properly, age did not touch these timeless creatures. Some speculated that Xeno implanted the vampiric disease for personal agendas, but many questions lingered about the existence of these entities—and they did not stand alone among the abnormalities. Demons, reapers, shapeshifters, and even ghosts all followed Xeno's dark commands.

Despite this, Altair did not possess most of the typical vampire characteristics.

"The sun does not affect me because I am... human."

This caught me off-guard.

Altair kept his eyes in the distance. "While I am stronger than the average human, I am not stronger than the average vampire."

I waited for more information, but nothing came.

Finally, I tried asking him a question. "How... does that... happen?"

Altair took a deep breath and shrugged. When he didn't offer a response, I tried a different question. "Do you... actually enjoy eating... normal food?"

"Of course. I crave sweets in the same way, and when blood and coffee scents mix, I usually choose the coffee."

"How were you able to control your thirst as a child?"

"Unlike vampires, blood doesn't bother me unless I'm thirsty or injured. I can control myself even after going without blood for several days. Scents of blood were never overwhelming."

"Vampire eyes turn into shades of burgundy to crimson when they're... thirsty. Do yours turn burgundy?"

"They do."

I knew it. "Your eyes were their color that night. You weren't thirsty, yet I could've sworn I saw them change when you..."

"When my body needs to heal from a painful injury, it thirsts for blood—much like a vampire's hunger when they haven't fed properly. However, there's another factor at play with *you*, Lyra. Something grows and gnaws at me the... *closer* we get. With you and my need for healing combined, I attacked without control. I'm not trying to justify my actions. I was irresponsible, and I am sorry."

Yes, the first reason aligned with my expectations, but the part about *me* thrust me into a bewilderment—one I knew would spark a dangerous conversation if I dared to ask.

"You apologize for your irresponsibility, but you don't apologize for hurting me?"

"Both." Altair corrected.

Altair stayed silent once more, avoiding eye contact with me and the scenery. He looked down at the grass, and his expression remained serious.

Again, I pushed for an answer to my initial question. "What happened to the Altair Antares who declared me an enemy?"

Despite everything he shared and all my questions, nothing visibly bothered him as much as this one.

Altair shook his head. "Who knows?"

After figuring out he would only offer me that response, I pressed him differently. "Who are you *really*, Altair?"

He sighed in resignation.

"It's quite the conundrum for me as well."

I nodded in understanding. Then, I voiced another thought. "Why didn't you... attack me as a child?"

"What are you talking about? The extent to which I hurt you is something I haven't completely forgiven myself for."

I shook my head. "I mean... why didn't you drain my blood and fulfill your desires to end me?"

Altair shrugged. "I didn't *want* to end you," he sighed. "And I had to be careful not to make any mistakes. This... me... it's a secret, Lyra. My ambitions and my father's approval outweigh my desires. But you've made it difficult for me." Altair looked at me with the familiar, conflicted eyes.

He spoke the truth. A vampire in Follyn's royal family would bring destruction because people hunted and detested vampires the most. With Altair's human traits, both vampires and humans might see him as an abomination. Speculations would be scandalous. People would suspect either the king or queen is a vampire, or that Follyn named an illegitimate child as their crown prince.

Altair continued, "I didn't want to hurt you when we were kids. It's strange to say now, but I held on to a hatred I didn't understand. When we first met, your smile charmed me. You brought light and laughter that didn't exist at home, and I thought that's why we hated Deltreans. Our classmates liked you, and I grew jealous. I envied you and everyone who talked to you freely, so I aimed to isolate you. If I couldn't have your friendship, I didn't want anyone to. I never understood why. I couldn't grasp why a part of me wanted to be friends with you despite the hatred. When I confessed this to my father, he said it was because you were a witch, and... I believed him. Then, he said..." Altair paused.

"My father said he would kill me if I slipped up and became friends with the Deltrean princess. He had no need for a weak prince in his castle," he snickered.

"Fathers may say things like that to scare us into being careful, but I'm sure you knew he didn't mean it."

Altair let out a dry laugh. "No. No, my father meant it, and I knew it."

CHAPTER TWENTY-ONE

Two of Cups

I see. I don't blame you.

My gaze lingered on the new words Altair left in my notebook. I slid it onto his desk earlier that day before leaving class, and today, it returned to my possession. Things felt odd after our interaction behind the library, but neither of us mentioned it. I pressed my thumbnail to my lips, struggling to resist the urge to bite it.

We formed a plan to meet after classes to write our paper, and this agitated my chaotic feelings. I missed him when he was absent, and when he was present, my eyes searched for him. Each time I saw him, my heart raced. The more time we spent together, the more a strange, dominant warmth blossomed inside me—something I couldn't name or understand.

I sighed at the thought.

Truth and vulnerability on paper seemed like a good idea. Writing to each other made communication easier.

Therefore, I wrote my response:

I won't deny we've made odd, yet constructive, progress in how we interact. However, that only makes things more... confusing for me.

I question the authenticity of our interactions because of our personal history and the tense history between our families. I can't shake the unsettling thought—when will little-devil-Altair reappear in my life?

I avoided mentioning his non-human condition because of its sensitivity, especially in writing.

While contemplating whether to add anything to my response, Syrena's voice interrupted my thoughts.

"Ooh, what's that?"

I turned to face her; Robin and Johann stood beside her.

I shut my book. "Notes."

"I could've sworn I saw Altair's writing." Johann eyed me suspiciously.

I chuckled. "They're notes. We're working on the paper together, remember?"

Robin looked at Johann incredulously. "How do you know what his writing looks like?"

"It's easily distinguishable. It's enviously intimidating, neat, and aggressive at the same time. I've tried to mimic his writing."

Syrena blocked out their conversation. "Are you coming to the school's Fall Festival with us, Lyra?"

I pursed my lips.

"C'mon, let's all four of us go! It'll be fun!"

"Nah, I hate celebrations of demons and witches." Johann chimed in.

"Alright, then the three of *us*." Syrena made a circular motion with her finger between Robin, herself, and me, while looking at Johann with an annoyed expression.

"You know, it's ironic you feel that way, Johann. I mean, you're Deltrean. Witches and demons are a part of your all's history." Robin interjected.

"We've come a long way. Where we strive to become better, you Follyneans continue to–"

"Okay," I interjected before it became another debate.

"I will go with you guys." I nodded.

Johann groaned.

I laughed. "Well, Johann, how about we meet at the entrance of the fort, and we come to the festival grounds together?"

He nodded. "Why don't we do that every day? Walking with some good company is always nice."

"Sounds good." I grinned at Johann, but when I eyed Robin, his expression turned grim.

Before we continued the conversation, the school clock tower bell rang.

It was time to meet with Altair at the library.

*****

When Altair arrived, I led us to the reception desk to ask for a study room.

"Is that necessary?" Altair asked.

"Yes. People stare a lot when we're together. They become quiet. They eavesdrop."

"You care too much about what other people think."

"Qualities of a good leader."

Altair chuckled. "Qualities of a *weak* leader."

Ah, there he is—back to his usual self. As irritating as he could be, I missed that side of him.

"Altair, it's important to care, especially when you're going to lead your kingdom in the future." Something in his demeanor softened, though I couldn't figure out why.

I shook my head and muttered, "You're incredibly ignorant," as I unlocked the door to our study room.

"Enlighten me, then. Why do you care so much?" he asked.

I opened the door to a small yet elegant study. Chalkboards lined the side walls, and a large desk sat in the middle, surrounded by four chairs. Instead of a wall, the opposite side featured a large window spanning the room's entire length. The study room occupied the library's uppermost floor, promising a pleasant view, though the curtains covered it.

"We're going to discuss each other's notes, writings, histories, and kingdoms. These are things others shouldn't hear because rumors and panic could spread." I responded to Altair while we began unloading our materials onto the desk.

"If such a situation arises, we could address it together. It might lead to something good; don't you think? Anyway, I think we're *already* causing quite the stir." Altair's little smug smirk, highlighting the lovely dimples on his face, made me irritated.

He sat in the chair next to mine. By now, it was probably a habit, but it still made me self-conscious.

I hated to admit he made a valid point, but my approach still made more sense. "It just seems reckless."

He nodded. "You're right. It is, and a study room *is* a good idea. If you didn't get one, I would have done it."

I gave him a puzzled expression. "You're agreeing with me? Wait, so what was the point of-"

He interrupted. "I used this instance as an excuse to point out how you *do* care too much about what others think."

I gave him a dry laugh. "We're right back to where we started." I shook my head and continued, "You're one of those who enjoys arguing for the sake of it, huh?"

Altair shrugged. "Just with you."

"I doubt that."

"No, really. I don't talk much to others."

I noticed. "Why is that? You're too good for the world, Antares?"

Altair's grin awakened his cute dimples, and despite the hint of mischief which came with their appearance, I ardently wanted to touch them.

"Do *you* think I'm too good?"

I shrugged. "Not better than anybody else."

Altair nodded with a satisfied expression. "Fair, enough."

I blushed at my slip-up. To bring down his ego, I should have said something that emphasized he behaved like a devil, but I didn't consider my response.

"You didn't answer my question." I insisted.

"You answered it for me. Didn't you?"

I gave him a puzzled expression, but before I asked anything, he continued, "You do that a lot. You ask me things about myself, and then, you answer them for me."

"I answer them based on everything I know about you."

"You seem to study me a lot."

"Oh, so I *was* right. You think you're better than the world. Figures."

"Are you done speculating?"

I sighed, but I said nothing. Instead, I focused on taking out my materials while avoiding looking over in his direction.

Why did he have to smell so intoxicatingly attractive?

"I don't think I'm better than everybody else." He spoke lowly. "My social group is enough."

I turned to him and contacted beautiful sapphire eyes. The initial closeness surprised me, and I think it took him aback, too. I broke our eye contact when I looked down at my hands and sighed. "There's nothing wrong with expanding it a bit, you know?"

"People avoid me, and I respect it. I understand the circumstances."

"Well, have you ever wanted to connect with more people?"

Altair shook his head. "Too many uncertainties come with new connections."

"Everything comes with uncertainty, don't you think?" I looked up at him, and again, my eyes gazed into blue irises which examined me with perplexity—one which turned into soft hesitation with every second we quietly kept eye contact with one another.

I broke the connection again when I turned towards our materials. "We should get started. You left me to work on this *alone* for two weeks, and it's already due this Friday."

"We'll bring it together just fine." Altair made a welcoming gesture toward his notes as I glanced at them.

I focused on the paper to keep my mind from overthinking every moment with this man and read the first page of Altair's notes.

Initially, people felt uncertain towards Vegalia because of her peasant background. To survive, she took on various jobs, some of them controversial. As a seamstress, doll-maker, herbalist, and fortune-teller, she navigated through different roles. Selling her body, however, led men to become obsessed with her, including the youngest Prince of Follyn and the King of Deltrea, who eventually married her. Later, Vegalia revealed her witchcraft abilities through her enchanted tarot cards, and rumors of her wicked methods turned society against her.

Deltrean researcher Samara Stein theorized Vegalia tried to destroy the cards because they led to her downfall and lunacy. When destroying them proved difficult, she scattered the cards throughout Deltrea. As a result, Deltrea guarded its borders closely. In her desperate attempt to rid herself of the cards, she unintentionally scattered some in neighboring kingdoms, like Follyn and Aquaenterra.

Tensions persisted, but the kingdoms eventually signed a treaty, allowing all parties to search for Vegalia's tarot cards in their territories. Citizens who found a card handed it over to their kingdom's royal family.

Deltrean history books often avoided mentioning Vegalia's negative ambitions. They celebrated her *positives and how she placed protection around Deltrea, which survived constant invasion attempts. Various territories tried to claim Deltrea, hoping to find an abundance of Vegalia's knowledge.*

Ultimately, outside Deltrea, people saw Vegalia as a witch rather than a priestess, royal healer, or mage responsible for safeguarding her people. Anyone who defended her actions faced imprisonment and torture if captured by the enemy.

My parents and ancestors struggled to uncover Vegalia's history. Many speculated that Follyn's forces somehow seized it. Altair's notes only revealed surface-level information. If he knew more, he kept it hidden.

"Wow. You actually did your part." I looked at him, impressed, as I leafed through two more pages of context and solid resources he used in his notes.

He flashed me with his captivating half-smile. "Of course."

"Although, I don't quite agree with Samara Stein's theory on why Vegalia tried to destroy the cards."

Altair stared at me in anticipation of my next set of words. I explained, "Vegalia's relentless pursuit of her dark ambitions inflicted immense damage to humanity and the kingdoms. Many believed she spiraled into lunacy, but I reject that notion. She fully understood her actions and did what she deemed necessary."

"You're harsher than me."

I shrugged. "Dark ambitions destroy people. They darken one's aura and corrupt one's soul. I don't attribute her actions to lunacy. She embraced evil and thrived on it, becoming the world's greatest villain of her time, devoid of empathy yet fully aware of her downfall. Her pride took a hit, so she deliberately scattered her cards across Deltrea, hoping her bloodline would find them and continue her sinister legacy. Unfortunately, subsequent rulers upheld contrasting principles."

If he knew how much of a devil he would become, my words would have struck his pride, too.

"So, the Deltrean leaders after her didn't actively seek cards?" I almost smiled at Altair's question.

A truthful response benefits the enemy. After all, Follyn only held back from attacking because they believed we possessed more than we actually did. Unfortunately, we did not.

"They did." I offered a vague truth. Deltrea actively quested cards, but we often failed. Clues led us to dead ends, citizens obtained and moved cards, and spies from other territories crossed borders and beat us to some cards. Many factors made it difficult for Deltrea to possess these things.

"People believe Vegalia once possessed all cards, but if that were the case, Vegalia would have stayed in power without issue. Don't you think?"

I couldn't determine whether he tried to gain information out of me or simply sought my perspective—or both. Truthfully, I always questioned the same thing, and I always wondered why she did not just use The World.

Instead, I said, "Well, not only did she upset everyone in society, but she offended her benefactor, Xeno. Going up against the entity who taught you his basics is probably no easy feat."

"How do you know the cards were just his basics?"

"It's just a theory." I shrugged.

I brought our attention back to his paper and penned necessary edits. "I'm going to change *enemy* to *Follyneans* in your last sentence."

"What's the difference?" Altair added with a smirk.

"It's important to be specific." I took the verbal jab at him, too.

"Hmm." Altair didn't press further. He probably figured I would offer nothing more on Vegalia, Xeno, and the cards. After all, if we continued to speak about these things, we might leak information. Our talk carried significant risk.

"It seems we agree on Vegalia's darkness. The alignment between my piece and yours seems to work." I grabbed my pen and put my notes and his next to each other as I started writing in edits. As I did this, I subconsciously murmured my next words, as if I said them to myself, "We need to make it flow and transition."

Altair said nothing, but through my peripheral, I noticed he watched me intently. I pretended not to acknowledge him as I kept my focus on penning deletions, additions, comments, questions, and revisions on our notes.

All the while, his gaze didn't budge.

When I felt a blush creep up my cheeks, I spoke again to break his entranced state.

"Where did you get this information from?"

For a moment, he remained silent, as if it took him a minute to register my words. "I mentioned her name in the beginning."

His voice came so close to my ears that it sent a rush of goosebumps through my body. My heart palpitated in excitement.

Again, the red glow attacked my cheeks, and I knew if I turned to face Altair, I would become just as entranced as he was.

I desperately wanted to shake off the intrusive emotions that raided my being. Despite their addictive attraction, an alarming sensation in my consciousness warned me they worked against my favor.

"Right. I don't recognize the researcher." Contrary to how I felt, I responded with nonchalance.

Altair shrugged. "That's why I didn't quote it directly. I remembered the information from a book I read back home."

"Interesting." I eyed him, and he met my gaze with an enticing, challenging look. I wondered if he purposely made that comment, implying he read extensively on Vegalia's knowledge and owned books from researchers and authors unknown to me. Rumors suggested that Follynean royals received Vegalia's journals and details directly from Xeno.

I continued. "You seem invested in the details of my ancestry, Altair."

The playful look in his eyes faded, leaving only enticement.

I flinched as the invasive emotions coursed through my body with a brighter intensity.

"What?" I asked.

"You always call me by my name when I annoy you."

I scoffed. "You annoy me all the time."

"You're a lot nicer on paper."

"I've written one word to you."

"Hmm," Altair hummed and grabbed my notebook from the desk.

I gave a small gasp when he opened it.

After taking a glance at my new response, he said, "It's more than one word. Looks like I'm in for a treat." He gave me his charming half smile, which made me melt.

"Were you done writing it?" he asked.

I nodded.

The seductive look within his sapphire eyes held me in place, and I no longer found the strength to break my contact with them.

The enchanting lines of his irises arrested my gaze before flicking to my lips.

I followed his lead.

Altair's beautiful face drew closer.

An alluring force pulled me towards him, even after I closed my eyes.

Forbidden sensations overwhelmed me—a sweetness I longed to indulge in, which intensified when Altair's nose gently brushed mine. My heart leap with each breath until I felt the slight touch of his lips.

Knock, knock, knock.

Altair and I pulled away from each other as far as we could, staring at one another in astonished perplexity.

"Is this room being used?" Dread overshadowed every other emotion when the voice behind the door sounded too much like Xander's.

"Hello?" He called out again—just before we heard the jingle of keys.

"Yes!" Altair called out.

The keys on the other side of the door went silent.

"As we said, there are no rooms available on this floor." His voice sounded low and muffled, as if he spoke to someone outside instead of us.

I sighed, but I couldn't face Altair. I don't think he could face me, either, because for the rest of that session, we kept our eyes on our task and completed it expeditiously.

As I left the university, I heard heavy footsteps behind me. Xander followed closely.

"Your father is going to be furious."

I continued walking. "He's furious about everything I do lately."

"Of course. Everything you do lately involves Altair Antares."

"Don't exaggerate, Xander! Whose fault is it that my father and I are constantly at each other's throats?" I retorted.

"You walked out of the library with the Prince of Follyn. Almost everyone in the academy was gone for the day. What were you two doing?"

"What makes you think I was with him? I could've been studying on my own and bumped into him. The library is enormous!"

"You've never been one to lie to me, Lyra."

I paused in my tracks. I purposefully lied. Xander and I knew he had checked on Altair and me in the study room. Still, I wanted to upset him for interfering. I wanted to hurt him for doubting me. Yet, his timing was perfect. Without Xander's interference, I would have sunk deeper into a confusing mix of emotions.

I sighed in resignation. "Yes, Xander, I spent the evening alone with him in a study room. We worked on our paper. Don't you trust me?" Guilt planted a seed in my heart as I included the last phrase. I did something which made *me* doubt the trust I held in *myself*—I kissed

Altair Antares. Or rather, I *almost* kissed him. A brush didn't quite qualify as a kiss, but it confirmed our intentions.

"I trust *you*, Lyra. It's him I don't trust."

"Don't you understand what boundaries are?" I responded.

Don't I? My consciousness took constant jabs at me.

"He's up to something, Lyra. You're forgetting to be cauti-"

"Xander! I'm okay. If I'm not within Deltrean borders, I'm at the university!"

"Follyneans have illegally crossed through the borders, Lyra. Are you that naïve or are you feigning ignorance? I *know* I taught you better."

He sounded like Altair, but he spoke the truth. I couldn't grasp the liberty I craved because of the surrounding dangers. Still, I yearned for that freedom to achieve my goals of befriending Altair, impeding his marriage to Syrena, and securing Aquaenterra as an ally. Even though it was wrong, I lashed out at Xander. Being watched or followed limited me. Sometimes, I wanted to risk my safety for a taste of that freedom, believing it would also help me untangle the turbulent emotions and identify their causes.

I sighed.

If I could bring Altair to my side, I would achieve certain victory and end the terrors of Follyn and Corvus Noir. Xander knew I embraced a newfound purpose, but he didn't trust me, and it stung—especially because, as much as I hated to admit it, he was right.

To top it all off, he told my father everything, putting me at risk of my father pulling me out of school. I couldn't afford that conflict with my parents. Such a thing would only distract us from the genuine threats beyond Deltrea's walls.

"You know, you have a reputation for being one of the most feared bounty hunters in our territories, yet here you are, wasting your time protecting me and being my bodyguard. Isn't that exhausting? Doesn't it impede your freedoms?"

It was true. Xander's reputation and successful missions attracted many loyal friends and allies, including those who declared their longtime alliance to him.

He remained silent.

I continued, "You taught me a lot. I can handle myself."

Still no answer, but I listened to his heavy footsteps behind me.

"Even in a knight's uniform, you risk recognition. We're in Deltrean territory, but as you've mentioned, spies can be anywhere. Take your reports, for example. They are very thorough, especially when you're out of sight," I said, sarcasm dripped from my tone.

"I'm disappointed in you, Lyra," he spoke his final words before his footsteps faded, leaving me to walk my path alone again.

*****

"Nice to see you finally make an appearance," my father spoke with sarcasm, his eyes seething with fury.

The king and queen rarely stayed at a Deltrean fort, but my questionable actions brought them to the quarters reserved for them.

My father appeared calm as he read a book on the mansion's balcony inside the fort, but I knew he was worried. When he saw me, he retreated to his private chamber, but I knew he'd be inside the front doors upon my entering.

I was right.

"Do I need to hear an update from you or from Xander?" he asked.

"Father, I was studying in the library." I walked past him toward my mother, who followed behind him.

"You're missing the point. What must I do to make it clear? Corvus Noir. Sound familiar?" He followed behind me.

The assassin's name sent shivers down my spine, but I never admitted it to my parents. I hoped that showing a strong face would ease their worries.

"Lyra," my father said sternly.

"Honey," my mother grabbed my hands and whispered, "don't disrespect your father." Concern filled her voice. She pleaded with me. I could tell she, too, was worried.

"I'm going to have them change your schedule."

"You're exaggerating!"

"These people purposely put you two in the same classes, and I didn't step in because you assured me you could handle it, but-"

"I have *been* handling it, and I think they're doing that to test us, and we're doing *fine*. Nothing is wrong. He's not a kid anymore; Altair knows how to be civil."

My father's jaw clenched at my mention of Altair's name.

Alphonse appeared near the stairway and diverted our conversation to a different matter. "Father is concerned because there've been mysterious murders around our kingdom, Lyra."

My jaw dropped at my brother's appearance. "How could you bring him here? He's not supposed to-"

"He came as Xander's apprentice," my mother said.

"Mother, are you listening to yourself? You're this family's voice of reason. Am I the only one who sees Alphie's presence as a risk?"

"I insisted on coming, Lyra," my brother added.

"You didn't even listen to what he said, did you?" my father asked.

For a moment, I remained silent. When my brain registered my brother's initial words, I asked, "Murders!"

Alphonse nodded. "Two of our knights were buried alive. Only their arms and hands stuck out of the dirt. We suspect Corvus Noir did this."

This event occurred in my past life, too. A series of murders took place; I wasn't in Deltrea when they happened, but they marked the beginning of Follyn's covert hostility and provocation. Their aim was for us to slip up, declare war, and look bad to our own citizens and the Aquaenterrans. However, it occurred much too soon in this timeline.

"Noir has Death, and the card is as grotesque as it's described in historical records."

"Maybe it also buries people alive," my brother shrugged.

I shook my head. "His ability spreads disease." One he spread *after* Follyn and Aquaenterra declared Deltrea an enemy. "This was... someone else."

I was almost certain Altair possessed this horrendous ability.

My father studied my face. He saw the fear flash through it. More than that, my heart sank. A plethora of thoughts attacked my mind, stressing me and worrying me to the point of feeling sick.

I sat down as I held my head.

"You know something," my father said.

"When did the murders take place?" I asked.

"The first one happened around the time you had that date with the Prince of Follyn. The second one happened this past week," my father added.

"I've been going home every weekend. None of you told me anything?"

"Well, an additional issue fell into our hands. Your concerning acquaintanceship with-"

"Father, we're talking about the lives of people."

"And I'm talking about *my* daughter dealing with the same man who is part of this evil cause."

I replayed moments between Altair and me. I scanned my memories for his absent days and tried to align them with the murders.

"Did they happen near the fort?"

"Near home," my mother said.

My father nodded. "If they happened around here, you'd be long gone, Lyra."

"Surely, the Follyneans know I'm *here*."

"It's probably a message directly for us, my dear." My mother glanced at my father.

Altair lived in Cresencia Dorms. It wouldn't surprise me if he left the university every night to cause silent mayhem by illegally crossing the Deltrean border. However, home was far. The first murder happened while Altair was in Crescencia all week, so it couldn't have been him. If the second murder took place last week, it couldn't have been him either, as he was returning from Follyn, which is in the opposite direction.

Altair might not have gained this burial card yet. If anything, these incidents might put the current possessor in Altair's sights. Present-day Altair still needed to grow into the destructive devil I recognized. I shook my head at the unpleasant thought. I figured that another explanation must exist, one that didn't involve him at all.

"What do you know, Lyra?" my father asked, again.

"I don't think it's Corvus Noir."

"We know that, but what makes you think the Follyneans haven't allowed him a second ability?" he replied.

Alphonse interjected, "With the way he successfully sneaks past Xander and everybody, it has to be him, Lyra."

Or Altair.

I shook my head. "You're right, but for now, I'm sure that's the only ability he has."

Corvus Noir obtained a second card in the past—one which did not come into his clutches until a few years before my life ended. Now, it's the card I wanted for my brother.

My father eyed me intently. "How do you know this?"

"Did *he* tell you something?" my mother asked, referring to Altair.

"I've gained a bit of information through my interactions with... *schoolmates*."

My family stared at me as they waited for me to elaborate, but I said nothing further.

"Lyra," my mom started, "We do not want this to become public knowledge. We want to prevent battles, or worse, *civil* battles, to break out. School would be unsafe for all kingdoms. I'm certain the Follyneans want the opportunity to say we are not keeping the peace."

"I understand." I felt ashamed of myself for getting carried away with that devil.

"So, this could be *anyone*." My father sighed as he ran a hand through his black hair.

"That's clever. Who's to say the knights' murderer is under the orders of the Follyn royal family? The Follyneans can argue that the assassin is acting on his own." I nodded in agreement with my brother's response.

"Investigate is all we can do for now, my sweet loves. We don't know who we're dealing with, and the power behind this person may be Follynean royalty, so we need to tread carefully." My mother whispered, keeping her eyes on me. I knew exactly what she meant. We couldn't rule *anyone* out.

"Therefore, stay careful and be responsible," my father paused. "I trust Xander to ensure you arrive home alive and safe, but I refuse to endure that anxiety again. Next time you fail to come home before dark, I will be in the school's square myself."

My father poured cognac into a glass. "Do what you need to do for your coursework, but leave it at that. Otherwise, stay away from the boy."

*****

"My intuition battles with unease, honey. You left something out about your interaction with that boy today, didn't you?" My mother raised her eyebrows.

I sat on my bed and placed a pillow on my lap. I played with it as I faced the second interrogation of the night. Considering the sharpness of my mother's intuition, I knew she would catch on to my feelings and intentions.

"Of course not, Mama. You feel that way because two knights were murdered," I muttered.

"I'm talking about your growing familiarity with the Prince of Follyn."

"You've never been around him in person. You can't sense his energies if he's never been around you."

She smiled. "You're quite defensive."

I laughed through my nose. "That *was* defensive, wasn't it?"

"I'm sure if I could have sensed your vibrations clearly when you were a child, I would have caught on to his malicious acts sooner."

"He's different now, Mama," I sighed, disappointed in myself, as I insistently defended him like a fool.

"I know, honey. I see it." She pointed to my face. "I see it in your eyes, and I feel the energies emanating from your being, your heart, and your mind. There is so much confusion. What's there to be confused about?"

I looked down. "He's not super... unlikeable."

She nodded. "I was afraid of that."

I looked at her, waiting for her to elaborate.

"There's a glow in your heart, and I know you feel it."

I blushed.

"It's even stronger today, my baby." My mom caressed my face. "What did he do? Did he try something? Did he kiss you?"

I kept my gaze down on my hands, and I shook my head.

"He didn't."

My mother sighed. "I need to get that boy in front of me and find out what he's really thinking."

"I wish I had your intuition, Mama." A light chuckle escaped my lips.

"You do, my baby. You're just not as in-touch with it as I am."

I gave my mother a doubtful look, but I said nothing.

"You do." She insisted. "Honor it. Listen to it. Try it. What does your intuition say about Altair Antares?"

I shook my head, but then, I stayed still, and I allowed myself to *feel*. I closed my eyes and took a deep breath.

"There's something dark. It's deep, internal, and it keeps me at a distance, but it doesn't compare to everything which draws me in. Every other part of my soul feels that he's... good, and as much as I want to shake off any positive emotions, they're becoming much harder to ignore." I sighed again.

My mother nodded. "Some people are good at wearing invisible masks to hide their hidden agendas and hypocrisy, especially leaders who have an ambition for power."

"See, I don't get any of those feelings from him." Oddly enough, I never got them in my past life, either.

"Some people are incredibly talented at deceit that it becomes simple to ignore your internal insight, or they shine with such a false light that dulls the intuition."

"You think he's like that?" I asked.

"You need to be cautious. You might be dealing with a man who will mock your loyalty and use you as a pawn for his ambitions. Seeing my beautiful girl in the grasp of a man who won't love her would feel like a fate worse than death. So, please, I beg of you—be conscious of your feelings and control them. Most importantly, Lyra, do what it takes to keep yourself from falling in love with the Prince of Follyn."

CHAPTER TWENTY-THREE

Queen of Swords

My mother's warning and the knights' murders weighed on me all morning. I sat next to Altair, resisting the urge to glance his way, even when I felt his eyes on me. He probably thought I kept my distance because of the almost-kiss.

The clock tower chimed, and I blurted goodbye to Altair without looking back. I stood up and followed Syrena to the library for our thirty-minute break.

Syrena caught up on reading for her next class while I pretended to review my notes. Truthfully, Altair left my notebook on my desk that morning, and I anxiously flipped through the pages. Despite my efforts to stay composed, warmth and relief flooded my core when I saw a new response.

If it means anything... you must know, our interactions are entertaining.

I sighed and read the words over and over again. Conflicting emotions stirred within me as part of me lamented his insistence on viewing us as enemies, yet he spoke the truth. It was a shame that our circumstances locked us into such opposing roles. Disappointment overwhelmed me when he made no mention of our closeness last night. Perhaps he felt the same way about how I treated him that morning.

He was a better person than I expected, but the deaths of the Deltrean knights also made me reconsider the notion.

I sighed again. His abnormal handsomeness didn't help.

I wrote my response:

I'm not really sure what to tell you. Why haven't you brought this up when we're together?

"Syrena," I started.

"Hmm," she looked up from her book.

"Have you ever-"

She raised an eyebrow.

"Er, never mind."

She gasped and closed her book. "Lyra, you can't just start a conversation and leave a person hanging. Just say it. What's wrong?"

"I just... feel weird, sometimes."

Syrena gave me a puzzled look.

I continued. "Well... like... What's it called when you start paying attention to someone and then, you find yourself feeling...?" I shook my head. "I don't know; I can't quite describe it."

Her eyes lit up. "You have a crush?"

"No!"

"Is it Robin?"

I shook my head.

"Are you sure? Because... I'm rooting for you guys! Oh, wait! You talk to Johann a lot! Is it Johann?"

"No, Syrena-"

"Do we know the person?"

I averted my eyes.

She gasped. "Is it someone we *don't* talk to often?"

I shrugged. "Look, I can't exactly call it a crush; I don't even know what that feels like."

"Do you feel jittery nerves all over your body when you speak to them?"

Perhaps my blushed face stood out more than I thought because her mouth gaped open.

"Do you like to look at them?" she asked.

Yes, but I refused to admit it.

"This isn't about Altair Antares, is it?" she continued.

I firmly shook my head in protest.

Syrena's eyes widened. "That was too aggressive, Lyra. It's him isn't-"

"No! Syrena, I could never!"

Did it matter to her?

I wondered whether I should test the waters and agree, or if that would put me at risk of losing her friendship. It occurred to me she might see my "crush" on Altair as a threat.

So, I denied it again. "With Altair... I could never."

"You both look at each other a lot."

"I keep my eyes on him in hopes I'll survive another day." When Altair first returned to Crescencia, this was true, but I soon realized that looking at him didn't *just* attract me; it healed my soul. I hated it, and I loved it so much.

"Well, that sucks for Altair, then."

I gave her a perplexed expression.

"The guy can never keep his eyes off you. He's started following you around a lot, too. Haven't you noticed? It didn't surprise me he followed you all the way into the haunted mansion, either."

I shook my head. "I cannot trust him. If he's really following me, he's up to something."

Syrena shook her head. "No, Lyra. I used to monitor Altair myself. At first, I planned to jump in and crush him if he tried to hurt you like before. But, seeing him grow so attracted to you took me by surprise, so I let him be. Then, Robin told me to pay attention to Altair during lunch hour. Altair gave no one a second glance back then, but now, he's always scanning the crowd, and when you appear, his gaze fixes on you. We've noticed that outside of lunch hour, he walks towards you whenever he spots you. The day of the haunted mansion, we didn't see you walk in, but we saw him walk in. And, on the days he's here at school, we can't reach you anymore because he's always ahead of us."

"I'm sorry." I looked down.

She put her hand above mine. "No, Lyra. That's not your fault. What I'm trying to tell you is that Altair's got a serious, forbidden case of infatuation."

I met her teasing smile with a worried expression. "I'm a future Deltrean leader. He's up to something, Syrena. There is no other explanation."

"Altair Antares has always been self-centered, only caring about himself and his Follyneans. It's ironic to see him so smitten with the Princess of Deltrea! It must feel like a strike to his groin!" She gave a heartfelt laugh.

I shook my head, but before I said anything, Syrena added, "I mean, just today, Altair couldn't keep his eyes off you. I swear, every time I looked over, his eyes were glued to you, and it wasn't hostile at all! Lyra, what have you done to him? His parents would freak out if they saw the way he looked at you."

Searching her words for signs of hostility and warnings about Altair, I found myself gripped by fear for the opposite reason. Her words seeped into my mind, making me believe they might weaken my resolve.

"You're looking too much into something that is not there. It's not existent. Altair and I are incompatible and everything is against us—even our own selves."

"I don't think so, and unfortunately, you can't help who you fall in love with." She shrugged. "I *almost* want to root for him, but I *really* don't like the guy, and I hate that he already takes you from Robin and me."

I chuckled. "If it makes you feel any better, I don't believe myself capable of crushing on *him*."

Syrena's teasing smile widened. "That's what he gets for being a mean little boy."

"But how would you know when that feeling hits you?"

"You just *do*."

"Do you like anyone here?" I asked.

Syrena's gaze faded away—into something far away. "No, but I've... had *feelings* for someone."

"If you don't mind my asking, what happened?"

"I never told him how I felt."

"You don't see him anymore?"

Syrena shook her head. "I liked him for a long time, and I saw him every time I spent my summer and holidays back home. Life felt the most fun and fulfilling when I was with him." A look of longing filled her eyes.

"Do you plan on telling him sometime?"

She sighed. "Recently, I received heart-breaking news. The guy... he left a letter with my caretaker. He left... for good."

"Just like that?"

"Just like that," she nodded.

That must have been Alphonse. Stupid, stupid Alphonse. I burned with curiosity to ask him what he put in the letter, but as much as I wanted to reveal everything I knew, I resisted. Alphonse would impulsively enroll in the academy before I actually needed him here.

First, I needed to plan everything out. Syrena's information helped immensely. My brother had the potential to play a crucial role in preventing the unification between Syrena and Altair, but I needed him to step in sooner than expected, and I had to ensure he wouldn't mess it up.

I had to convince my parents to let him enroll for the spring semester in January. I didn't want to wait that long, but I embraced patience as a powerful ally and fought against impulsivity like a great enemy.

The sound of the university's clock tower chimes resonated throughout the school grounds.

It was time for the next class.

Knight of Wands

A knock at the door interrupted the start of class.

It swung open to reveal my beloved ash-brown haired brother, Alphonse, wearing the university uniform and a backpack.

"Hi," he directed his words towards the professor. "I'm Alphonse Forté. I'm a new student."

He used his undercover surname—the one he went by in Aquaenterra.

I eyed Syrena during my brother's semi-private exchange with the professor. Both of her hands covered her mouth, and her eyes expressed astonishment with a hint of worry.

I didn't blame her.

I felt the same way.

This must have been my father's doing. He sent Alphonse to keep a closer eye on me because I rebelliously hung around Altair and all.

Altair, sitting a few seats in front of me in class, glanced from me to Alphonse—not a good sign. His reaction alarmed me, but I feigned ignorance of it.

Alphonse took a seat near me, but he didn't speak to anyone. If he noticed me, he spotted Syrena since she sat right next to me.

His unusual silence surprised me, given his outgoing and friendly nature. Then again, first days of school carried similar weight on everyone's shoulders—awkward and nerve-wracking. Since Alphonse had never attended school before, the experience must have been overwhelming—especially if he saw Syrena.

I didn't quite understand what happened between them, but Syrena's spirits sank, and she turned her face away from my brother.

Moreover, if Altair remembered Alphonse from Aquaenterra and recognized me as the pink-haired girl who accompanied him, we needed to acknowledge our *acquaintanceship*. I couldn't risk a major slip-up.

*****

After the clock tower bell signaled lunch, I gathered my things, discreetly dropped my notebook on an empty desk near Altair's, and headed straight to my brother.

"Alphie!"

He turned, wide-eyed. I caught him by surprise. He probably didn't expect me to approach him directly.

I grinned at him and hugged him. When I brought him close enough towards me, I whispered in his ear. "Go along with it."

"Elle!?"

"Yes! It's me! I can't believe you're here! How did it happen? Tell me all about it!"

"*You're* Elle?" Syrena interjected. She looked worried.

"Er, well-" I pretended Alphonse didn't know my real name.

"Syrena!" My brother's face lit up.

Syrena skewered her mouth and didn't make eye contact with him, but she gave him a simple wave.

"I'll wait for you at our table, *Lyra*." Syrena's upset tone became apparent with the way she emphasized my real name.

"Sure," I called out and pretended not to notice.

After inconspicuously scooping up my notebook, Altair loitered with Ian outside the classroom door, as if he tried to observe or listen in on Alphonse and me.

"Alphie, walk with me to Crescencia Dining Hall. We have a lot to catch up on." I grabbed my brother by his sleeve to drag him out of

❧ 184 ❧

Altair's earshot before he said anything unnecessary. "And if you need someone to show you around, I'll be happy to do it."

My brother let me drag him out, catching on to the two men loitering about. He must have remembered Altair Antares' face because his next question followed my whims and schemes. "Wait. Why did Syrena call you Lyra?"

I froze and suppressed a smile because if I laughed, he would, too. "Elle is the name I went by in Aquaenterra."

I faced him with my eyes cast down, hoping to look ashamed.

My brother's brown eyes widened. "So, your name *isn't* Elle?"

I shook my head, "My name-"

"Her name is Lyra," Altair interrupted. He looked like a dog marking his territory.

Ian, Roselia, and Altair walked near us. Considering we all headed to the same place, it made sense, but Altair timed it that way. He wanted to listen in on our conversation. Lucky for me, Alphonse understood his role.

I raised an eyebrow and cast a glare in his direction. Altair pretended not to notice, and he directed his attention and conversation back to his posse.

"Lyra. Like... The Princess of Deltrea?" My brother acted dumbfounded.

I nodded, careful not to smile.

"Wow. You're completely different here, huh? You're almost unrecognizable."

I smiled, "I'm still me, friend. You're not mad at me, are you? I'm so sorry."

Alphonse shook his head. "Nah, I understand. I won't hold it against you. You're important to me." He shrugged. "If anything, I'm honestly glad we'll be in school together. Life in Aquaenterra was no fun without you."

Altair's glare fixated on us.

My brother and I took a seat with Syrena, Robin, and Johann. I sat between Syrena and Alphonse, so they wouldn't have to look at each other.

Altair and his group sat at the table next to us.

"Hey Lyra! You're already friends with the new guy? You're fast," Johann commented.

"You say it like it's a bad thing," Syrena said.

"Oh! No, I didn't mean it in a bad way. I just meant it's easy for her to make new friends because she is very approachable, and she's friendly."

"And, she's fair," Robin interjected.

"Qualities of a good leader," my brother grinned.

"Yes, sir!" Johann said.

I wanted to turn and look at Altair with a smug expression—considering this discussion came up between us yesterday.

"They've been friends for a long time," Syrena interjected.

I nodded. "Since childhood, basically."

"Whoa! How did you know that, Syrena?" Johann asked.

"Er, I also-" she began.

"Syrena and I have also been friends for a while," Alphonse interrupted.

Syrena raised her eyebrows, but she remained silent.

"She and I hung out every summer for a few years," he paused. "I had to leave Aquaenterra behind and move closer to the academy because my family pushed for me to enroll here. I just never thought I'd bump into both of them here—especially El- er, I mean, Lyra."

"I see. Did you hang out with Lyra during the summers, too?" Robin asked.

"No. She always kept to herself. It took a while to befriend her as kids. When I did, we hung out almost every day."

"Wait, so Lyra, did you and Syrena know each other back then, too?" Robin's tone carried curiosity.

I shook my head. "I-"

Syrena interrupted, "I always asked Alphonse to invite Lyra to come out with us, but she never wanted to. As Alphonse mentioned, she remained reserved."

Johann's and Robin's eyes widened. "I can't imagine our Lyra being so reserved," Johann said.

"Neither can I," Syrena murmured.

Her foul mood leaked from her aura. She probably didn't quite like me as Elle.

I smiled nervously. "I hadn't found the courage to face my fears and traumas. One day I woke up, I looked in the mirror, and I was ready to face the day. I asked Alphonse to invite you to hang with us, Syrena, but he told me you weren't in Aquaenterra this past All Hallows' Eve. When I found my courage, I really wanted to meet you."

A melancholic smile graced Syrena's lips, her eyes betraying a subtle sadness.

Anxious thoughts plagued my mind, and I desperately wished my previous identity as Elle wouldn't hinder my current situation. Then, the question of what happened between my brother and Syrena lingered. She avoided him, but Alphonse seemed fine. Somewhat.

If a misunderstanding existed between them, especially one caused by me, I needed to resolve it.

My brother appeared serious. Maybe he just tried to keep up an act.

"I'm thinking I need a lighter color on my hair. Dark colors on a girl are *disgusting!*" Roselia's loud voice drew our attention.

Subconsciously, we all turned to her conversation with Altair and Ian, who appeared apathetic and oblivious to our eavesdropping.

Tsk, Alphonse sucked on his teeth. He knew she threw the indirect comment at me, and it visibly bothered him.

Altair smirked. "Well, you know, as long as it's not *pink*."

Alphonse and I faced each other in surprise.

Altair definitely remembered.

Roselia skewered her face. "I like pink. Why not pink?"

"Yeah, what's wrong with pink?" Alphonse chimed in.

This got Altair's attention. He eyed my brother with a hostile glare, and Alphonse responded with an expression glossed in entertainment.

"Mind your business, Forté," Altair said, unbothered.

Alphonse ignored him. "My girl, Lyra, pulled off a damn cute pink-hair look throughout her time in Aquaenterra." He turned to me and loudly said, "That's why I didn't recognize you."

"*Your* girl?" Altair glared. His defensive reaction astonished me, but it fed my brother's devious taunts.

"Yeah. My girl. The best friend of my life." My brother hit his chest with an open hand and rubbed it.

Next to me, Syrena shuffled out of the table. "I'm going to take off, guys. I'll see you all later."

My brother's face dropped when his attention turned towards Syrena. He sighed as she walked away.

"What's wrong with her?" Robin asked.

Johann shrugged. "Roselia and Altair kind of annoy her. That's probably why she left."

Before the situation escalated any further, I grabbed Alphonse by the arm. "Let's go, Alph." I turned to Johann and Robin. "We're taking off, too. I'd like to show the new guy around."

My brother and I paced out of the dining hall.

"You're going to have to tone it down, Alph," I whispered. "People might get the wrong idea about us!"

"I really don't care what other people think. They're not living my life for me. Why would their opinions be relevant?" Alphonse sounded annoyed. "And it was fun to stick the knife into Antares."

I shook my head and chuckled. "You stuck it and twisted it."

"Lyra," Altair followed us out.

My brother's eyes lit up—not in a good way. He looked ready to zap Altair alive.

"You know, you look very familiar," Alphonse said, pretending he didn't remember him. "I've seen you before somewhere, haven't I?"

"You've got poor memory, Forté. Even I recognized Lyra in her pink hair at the time—just as easily as I recognized her in her natural color," he smirked.

My eyes widened. I wore a different hair color *and* eye color. He shouldn't have known my identity. I figured he bluffed to provoke my brother.

"So, who are you?" Alphonse asked, bored.

"Altair Antares." Altair lifted an eyebrow. His expression radiated readiness for a challenge. He knew the load and the power which came with his name, and at the moment, it looked like he wanted to put Alphonse in his place.

Unfortunately for him, my brother simply nodded. Then, he looked to and from Altair and me.

"I see. The Deltrea and Follyn leaders are in the same room. Now, I understand why you threw indirect comments about pink hair."

Altair clenched his jaw, but instead of playing into Alphonse's comments any further, Altair turned to me. "Lyra, I need to talk to you."

I shook my head, "Not now, Altair."

"What? You actually talk to this guy, Lyra?" my brother asked.

I panicked. Alphonse was at the university to spy for my father. I needed to douse the flames before Altair gave out more unnecessary information.

"We worked on a project together, Alphie. Nothing more."

"Is that so!" Altair furrowed his brows.

"Yes, Altair," I insisted.

"We sit next to each other in our first class, Lyra."

My brother's expression flashed surprise before it settled into concern.

Contrarily, Altair looked victorious again.

I shook my head, "Alph, there's no need to get any kind of wrong idea here-"

"Is it not the truth, Lyra?" Altair asked.

"What are you telling me, Antares? Speak clearly," Alphonse remarked.

"Contrary to what you believe at the moment, it's actually quite normal to see Lyra and me together." Altair's implication that we shared a connection startled me, and the possibility of Alphonse alarming my parents with misconstrued information unsettled me.

"Are you saying that Lyra's your... girlf-"

"No, no. We're just friends, Alphie. There's nothing for you to worry about." I didn't know how Altair perceived my statement, but he stared at me hard.

"Why would he concern himself with worry about our relationship, Lyra?"

My jaw tightened. "*What* relationship, Altair? You're the one constantly reminding me we're enemies."

"Ah, now I remember," Alphonse started. "You're the one from that All Hallows' Eve store last year; the one Lyra ran away from."

I faced my brother with an incredulous look. "I'm done with this conversation. Either follow me or don't, Alph." I walked away.

Altair called out behind us. "Oh, and I must agree with you on one thing, Forté. She looked cute in pink."

I meant to direct a glare in Altair's direction, but I messed it up when I blushed.

He continued, "But, I must say, she looks sexy in her natural color. Its darkness suits my palette."

I turned away and walked in the opposite direction from where Altair stood. He made me unfathomably upset, yet a single stupid comment made my heart palpitate.

"What a jerk," I muttered.

"Why does Antares look like he's got some kind of possession of you? What's going on?"

His questions clearly stemmed from Altair's provocative and misleading remarks. With a shake of my head, I signaled my refusal to engage further. "We'll talk later, Alph."

Before he gave my parents inaccurate information about my "relationship" with Altair Antares, I just hoped he would give me the opportunity to explain.

CHAPTER TWENTY-FIVE

Five of Wands

Altair slid my notebook onto my desk right before class started. We interacted minimally, especially with Alphonse around—I made an effort to avoid Altair and pretended we had brief communication.

Dr. Diestro walked in to class right as the clock tower bell rang.

"Good morning, everyone!" He took one look at everyone's quiet, sleepy eyes and continued speaking through a grin. "It's nice to see you all in such lively spirits. As you know, the Fall Festival takes place on the 30th and 31st, and the decorations around the area aren't ready. Therefore, I volunteered our class to help with the set-ups once a week."

This got my classmates to chatter.

Dr. Diestro continued, "Now, settle down. There will be other classes providing assistance. My class is going to stick to one section. As long as you're helping, you'll get credit for today."

We made our way towards the Crescencia Festival Grounds.

The lovely, chilly breeze blew, but my uniform coat provided enough warmth to keep me comfortable outside.

"Syrena," Alphonse started. "Do you want to go to the Fall Festival together?"

Syrena eyed him. Then, she eyed me. "Lyra? Are you going, too?"

Robin chimed in, "Didn't we all agree to meet up there?"

I nodded. "We did, didn't we? I'll be there."

Large white and orange pumpkins adorned the festival grounds. A poster persuading people to paint pumpkins lay on the ground, waiting to be decorated. As I reached for a paintbrush, my brother reached for the same one.

Through laughs, we fought for it by yanking it from one another.

"If you don't let go, I swear I'm going to paint your face." I laughed.

Alphonse responded by dipping one of his fingers on the orange paint. "You want some?"

He aimed for my face, but I dodged his little attack.

"Wow," Elizabeth, one of our classmates, said as she stared at us.

"What?" I asked.

"You all are very close, huh?"

Alphonse and I looked at each other.

Of course, we're twins. I thought, and an unwelcome little smirk appeared on my face.

"I think Lyra found her soulmate," David said.

My brother and I looked at each other and made disgusted faces. I stuck my tongue out and scrunched my eyebrows. Alphonse twisted his face in revulsion, but it made both of us laugh.

"She's my best friend, boy. If anything, a soul *sister*. Don't be confusing and twisting a healthy friendship between two people."

"A guy and a girl cannot be friends," Roselia retorted.

"You can if you all aren't toxic," my brother replied.

"You've been in the academy less than a month, and there are already rumors about you everywhere, Girlfriend Snatcher," she grinned at the nickname my brother had gained throughout school.

"Okay. What's your point, Rosabitch?"

Roselia's mouth gaped opened. She lifted her middle finger up at Alphonse, and he returned it right back.

"You're mad because I see right through you," he added with a little smirk on his face.

"You're mad because Lyra doesn't give you enough attention," she replied.

"From where I'm standing, it looks like *you're* the one who's all bitter that I don't give *you* enough attention. You've got it now. What do you want?"

Roselia made a face. "No, keep facing your beloved, Lyra. With your reputation, you'll get what you're looking for with her."

"Rose," Altair's voice carried an air of authority and seriousness.

He glared at Alphonse, but my brother wouldn't back down. Whenever Alphonse encountered Altair's posse, he wore a permanent scowl that conveyed annoyance. "Antares, if you have something to say, spit it out and stop dancing around it. Damn. You vultures are all the same."

"What do you mean by 'vultures' Forté?" Ian retorted.

"Obviously, the shoe fits you perfectly, too, Aiden," Alphonse grinned.

People around us gasped and laughed after my brother got Ian's name wrong.

"It's Adrian. You still don't catch people's names? What an idiot," Roselia added.

"See, I really don't care. That's how much of an impression he has on me."

Ian looked bothered. "Answer the question, Aqen! If you're talking about Follyneans being vultures, then-"

"Goddamn, man," Alphonse became more visibly annoyed. "This isn't about Follyneans. Are you that dense, or are you trying to create mass division? What's your game here?"

"What is *your* game here, Forté?" Altair interjected.

"Mind your business, Antares."

At this, Altair paced towards my brother. Impulsively, I ran and placed myself a few feet in front of him. Altair stopped in his tracks, a conflicted look in his eyes.

My brother grabbed my shoulders and placed himself in front of me. Altair's jaw clenched.

"Alphie," I grabbed his arm, hoping to get his attention. This needed to stop before it got any worse.

Robin stepped in. "We know what you meant, Alphonse. Ian can't manipulate us to think otherwise."

"You call yourself a Follynean, Robin?" Ian spat out.

Infuriated, I chimed in, "There you go again, Ian—bringing up the nationalities."

Roselia retorted, "It *is* about nationalities, Celestia. It's *always* about nationalities."

"Sounds like a personal problem, girl," my brother interjected.

"I don't know where you're getting nationalities from, Roselia. Vultures feast on the weak. You think that because Alphie's the new guy, he's just going to keep his mouth shut and take what you're telling him?" I asked.

"I don't want to hear any explanations from you, Celestia," she replied.

I snickered, "Why not? Is it difficult to hear just how wicked you are?"

Roselia shook her head with a smug grin.

I continued, "I see what you're doing. I understand perfectly. You're trying to put Alphonse through the same hell you put me through when I was a child."

Silence.

Roselia snickered, "Of course not. It was different with you, Celestia. I was upset for Deltrea. You make such a weak leader that your kingdom is already on a time-"

"Rose!" Altair glared at Roselia.

I glanced between the three of them, wondering what she intended to say. They schemed something, but instead of losing my cool, I smiled. In this life, I held the upper hand. I stood braver, and my brother stood by my side. I bit my tongue to resist the urge to reveal that he held the title of Crown Prince of Deltrea.

Instead, I just said, "You're right. It was different with me. While I refrained from any negative actions towards anyone, you underestimated Alphie. He won't keep his mouth shut about personal injustices."

"Celestia," Ian turned toward me. "If you don't show your friend his place-"

"Ey, tell me straight. What're you going to do, Aiden?" My brother extended his arms.

Ian mirrored Altair's steps and paced towards Alphonse, but before he walked further than five feet, Altair jumped in and grabbed Ian by his back. "Control yourself."

I didn't realize that, once more, I placed myself between my brother and Ian until Alphonse, yet again, grabbed my shoulders and put me behind him without removing his expression from Ian.

Altair intimidated people with his serious glare, but my brother caused others to cower upon seeing his infuriated grin. He looked maniacal—as if some evil spirit possessed him. Above his grin, Alphonse's glare showed a determination to eliminate.

I loved that about my brother. Even without a card, he faced any challenge and fought against threats to those he loved.

"Antares, keep your dog on a leash before he hurts someone," my brother said.

"Alph!" I grabbed him by the shoulders and faced him.

Everyone remained quiet in the tense environment.

"It's you that's asking to get hurt if Lyra doesn't learn how to control *you*," Altair remarked.

Again, my defensive-sister instinct kicked in. I stepped in front of my brother, as if to shield him from Altair's glare—a death stare that I mirrored right back at him.

"You threaten him, you threaten me, Antares." My words took him aback. He glanced between Alphonse and me, searching for a reason behind my protective stance.

Being left in wonder is one of the worst things. It breeds a flood of over thoughts, which can mentally drain a person. I wanted Altair to make several speculations, hoping that one of them would entertain the possibility of Alphonse being a Deltrean royal. If he did, he would realize he made a massive mistake in threatening my brother.

"And me." Robin stood by our side.

"Me too." Syrena inched closer to us.

Johann said nothing, but he confidently walked to our side as well.

At that, the class moved and divided into sides until Dr. Diestro's voice froze everybody in place.

"Really, guys? I couldn't leave my class of young *adults* alone for five minutes without risking everyone getting into an argument?" He exhaled. "I don't want to hear a single word—from anybody—or we will go back into our classroom and work on a new research project. Altair! Lyra! Let's take a short walk. Everyone else, continue with the decorations."

Pairs of eyes bore into my back as Altair and I approached Dr. Diestro.

He walked with us about fifteen feet from the festival grounds, keeping the class in our field of vision.

"I called you both out because I've seen you work well together. I trust you can explain what happened while I was gone."

I fixed my gaze on the ground. Altair faced our teacher and didn't direct a single glance at me. He *couldn't* look at me. I sensed his anger mixed with a hint of regret, likely from a small fragment of... affection?

Maybe he cared a bit. Perhaps he grew a *little* possessive, which explained his irrational hatred for Alphonse.

Syrena's observations about us made me think. Would he care if he saw me upset?

Confirming his level of concern would mark a significant turn for me. I could grasp onto that hint of care and nurture it, but first, I needed to test it.

I kept my eyes on my shiny, knee-length boots. I crossed my arms around my chest, pretending to close myself off, and I purposely breathed deeply and shakily.

Altair looked towards me, but I kept my face down.

"Lyra, is everything okay?" the professor asked.

"C- Can I go to the infirmary?" I delivered a quiet, turbulent tone.

"Of course." As soon as my professor confirmed, I walked fast—away from the festival grounds.

In my thoughts, I gave Dr. Diestro a personal, silent apology for putting up an act. A wave of sadness washed over me during the confrontation, but Altair's reactions gave me a sense of control.

"Altair! Where do you think you're-"

"The restroom!" Altair's voice sounded closer than I expected.

Instead of walking fast, I ran.

"Lyra, wait!"

I needed fake tears, and fast. As I ran, I covered my face with my hands. While the action fit my fake-distraught image, I also did it to hide the change in my eyes as I used my ability to force water out of them.

When Altair gripped my shoulder, I stopped using my ability. He spun me around to face him, and I looked at him with tear-filled eyes.

"Can't you let me be angry in peace, Altair? Does it amuse you that you can still do this to me? Are you satis-"

"No! No, I-" As if driven by impulse, Altair's hands rose towards my tear-filled cheeks, but just before he touched me, he drew back and closed his hands into fists.

"I just wanted to make sure you were okay. I-"

"I'll be fine, Altair. Just go."

His eyes brimmed with questions and uncertainty. He probably wondered why I fiercely defended Alphonse. Part of me hoped his conflicted expression stemmed from inner turmoil, questioning why he followed me to the infirmary.

Instead of insisting, Altair nodded and let me go.

*****

I picked up my bag and materials from Dr. Diestro's class before heading to the infirmary. Once there, I took out my notebook and read Altair's response as I lay on a bed.

I haven't brought it up because it might reopen some wounds I caused, and I'm worried it might mess up our...

unusual affiliation. I didn't want to make you feel awkward by bringing it up in person, either.

Here, you can think it over and decide if you want to reply or not.

His response made me sit up.

Did he speak genuinely, or did he plot something?

I let out a guilt-filled sigh and kept my reply simple, avoiding any mention of Alphonse or today.

Is that why you didn't speak to me the first weeks you returned? Because of my wounds? Or was it the prejudiced hatred?

With that, I closed the notebook. Now, I needed to decide when I would feel *unbothered* enough to return it to him.

Altair and I didn't speak at all, even during Dr. Diestro's class, where we sat next to each other.

The morning after our altercation at the school's festival grounds, I pushed the notebook towards Altair at the chime of the clock tower. He seemed taken aback by my action, but I figured I needed to pursue some form of communication if I wanted to advance towards my goals.

Also, I *wanted* to interact.

I *wanted* to know him.

We exchanged our notebook with a voracious addiction.

*****

Both.

I'm a prideful being, and you made me feel shame—a feeling I had long buried.

I blocked you out.

I'm assuming that another reason for that block was because we're "enemies by default."

That's right. The torches will be passed down to us soon, and our kingdoms are in conflict. Our roles demand action for our realms, even if it means standing against each other. Think about it. Beyond politics and our responsibilities over our subjects, you and I still don't see eye to eye on many things. This might be the most peace we'll ever have.

I know what it means, Altair. I know what we face, but I think it can be different between us.

It's naïve to think that way, Lyra. There's too much blood between our kingdoms, too much dark history between our realms, and too much tension between our people. These are things we can't ignore.

We can face our conflicts differently, Altair. Our families have never spoken to each other. There's a blind hatred that causes them to act violently. Our prejudice was established before we were born, but you and I have moved beyond aggression to communication. Doesn't that mean something?

Think about the last time we spoke. I wouldn't exactly call that moving beyond aggression to communication.

Sometimes, things get worse before they get better, right? Wouldn't you call these messages to each other communication?

Yes, but I made you cry last time. I'm going to be straight with you—I can't guarantee it won't happen again. There's an integrated, unavoidable rivalry between us, so it's probably best we keep our distance.

I cried in anger. You can be so infuriating to deal with—especially in public. When we're alone, you're more relaxed. I see a better side of you. I understand you better.
If we build on that, I know we can at least make a friendship work.

Lyra, I left a physical scar on your body.

And despite everything, I still interact with you and have explained why I hold on to our unusual relationship. Now, I'm curious—why do you continue to correspond with me, Altair?

I get a glimpse into the mind of the Princess of Deltrea.

Is that the only reason you talk to me?

Well, you said it yourself; you understand better. I do, too.

It doesn't explain your constant gazes at me. You stare a lot.

You stare a lot, too.

If you're going to look at me, I'm going to look, too. I have to remain cautious.

Ah, so you stare at me because you're on the defensive? How funny. I haven't seen "caution" in your eyes in weeks.

You've been staring at my beauty so much that it's dulled your readings on people's expressions.

I see. You're not clueless about your effect on people. It's irritating, and it's always thrown me off, but can you blame me? It's human nature to be drawn to beauty.

I know. I'm partly at fault for the same thing. You do such cruel things with that handsome face. It's loathsome.

Next to this statement, I drew a face with its tongue out. I added hearts for eyes, but I placed X's inside each heart.

In all seriousness, I stare because it's important to keep a close eye on you, and I know it's mutual. Sometimes, you glare—a glare hinting at hatred towards me, and I get it, but it's unfortunate.

There you go again, making assumptions.

When I first saw you at the university, I wanted to approach you but didn't know how, so I just stared, contemplating my approach. Whenever you came within my sights, I found myself observing you. When you weren't around, I caught myself looking for you. When you held my gaze, I saw it as progress—a silent, private form of communication. I can't quite describe it. Odd, isn't it?

When you smiled at Robin, I realized I had never seen you smile before. I thought you were incapable of smiling, and I blamed myself for it. It's nice, your smile. It made me more determined to approach you.
So, you think I'm handsome.

Of course, I do. It's difficult, isn't it—having such a beautiful rival?

I sketched a face with eyes looking downward at the reader. I added big eyelashes to it and a cocky smile.

One with mesmerizing violet eyes. You have no idea.

I do, actually. I have this frustrating, handsome rival with the most beautiful sapphire eyes.
You know, I have a concoction that strips eye color for hours. It'll make the rivalry easier for you if you use it, too.

Nah.

Okay, then…

I miss you, Lyra.

I miss you, too.

You've been distant with me… ever since that night at the library. You showed up at school the next day, looking exhausted, like sleep never found you. I thought about asking if you were okay, but I didn't want to trouble you.

I just… didn't sleep well that night.

To be honest with you, I didn't, either.

Why?

I think we both know the answer to that.

Altair, it's best that it didn't happen.

I know.

I've been meaning to ask… Why did you approach me at the haunted mansion?

*****

After school one day, Altair found me in a deserted area near the library. Since then, we met there to exchange the notebook without speaking to one another.

I always walked away first.

This time, he spoke before I walked past him.

"Lyra, can we talk?" Altair pleaded.

His longing gaze urged me to accept, and his soft voice tempted me to declare my shared desires. Still, I couldn't abandon my goals. I needed to keep my emotions in check. For now, I could only offer him my writing until I figured out my feelings, but I couldn't decide if Altair's vulnerability in his writing helped my case, as his words stirred a tempest of bittersweet and conflicting emotions within me.

"The notebook is sufficient. I must go." I dismissed him.

"The festival is tomorrow," he blurted.

"Won't you be in Regnum Noctis?" I returned.

"That depends."

"On what?"

"Will you be here tomorrow?"

I nodded.

He continued, "Will you talk to me tomorrow if I come by?"

"If you find me, sure."

Altair wanted to talk, and so did I. Realizing how this threat fed the turbulence in my feelings, I needed to set boundaries. Maybe he aimed to manipulate my emotions, just as I planned to play with his.

Except, in this reality, Altair caused unwelcome fluttery feelings with a single glance.

I shook my head, trying to dispel the intrusive thoughts. Falling victim to my cunning plan would be a foolish mistake. I aimed to put up an act as a naïve, innocent woman falling into forbidden love with him, not to *actually* end up infatuated.

If I became Altair's weakness, he might find himself unable to harm me. He wouldn't hurt my family either. The idea seemed plausible, but I also knew him as an evil man incapable of love.

I needed to ensnare him, not the other way around, yet I couldn't deny that the distance between us stung. With our separation, Syrena's words rang true. Before Alphonse joined the university, I *embraced* Altair's company.

Sighing, I reminded myself not to lose sight of my goal despite his beauty, kindness, vulnerability, and the insights I had gathered about him.

I missed him.

*****

Shaking my head to scatter invasive thoughts, I found a lonely area in the library's fourth floor. Before taking out any of my books or assignments, I anxiously checked Altair's response.

I wanted to reach out, but I couldn't until that day.

You smiled, and you weren't surrounded by others.

Suddenly, I found myself in the mansion, searching for

you. I understood why you hid, but I couldn't stop myself from trying to talk to you.

I thought I could maintain my distance, but I couldn't.

Then, I felt your warmth, and you spoke to me, thinking I was Robin. I don't fully understand it myself, but I wanted that normalcy with you.

It's just... it's never been simple between us.

I understood his perspective, but I didn't know how to respond. He couldn't claim he wanted normalcy with me after trying to kiss me that night at the library; normal friendships don't include *that*.

Why did you try to kiss me?

I regretted my message and lazily scratched over it before closing our notebook.

Our exchanges stirred my heart.

Unable to focus, I left my notebook on the table and reclined on the sofa. I figured a quick mental break would help me get Altair off my mind and begin a new response with a clearer head. I'd also erase all traces of what I wrote.

To my dismay, I drifted into a deep slumber.

*****

My heavy eyelids fluttered open at the chimes of the clock tower.

Lost in thought, I flipped open the pages of Altair's and my notebook.

To my utter shock, I found a response under my scratched message.

He must have caught me asleep and checked the notebook!

My heart raced at his new reply.

Did you want me to?

Three of Cups

Dark circles framed my eyes on the morning of The Fall Festival.

Alphonse, Xander, and I secured our first real chance at obtaining an enchanted tarot card, but I spent the night tossing and turning. First, if the tarot mission failed, I faced the risk of being sent back into hiding. Second, I couldn't come up with a response to Altair's last message. I struggled to push his intrusions out of my mind, but questions flooded my thoughts, making me nervous and more confused about our situation.

Despite all the thoughts, I didn't give Altair the true, one-word answer to his question: Yes. Instead, I offered another less-complicated, honest response.

> *A kiss is powerful.*
> *A kiss is sacred.*
> *A kiss blurs the boundary, drawing us into a complex abyss of entanglement.*
> *It is a boundary we should not cross.*

A kiss would crumble my resolve.

If I had a grip on my emotions with Altair, I could spare a kiss for the sake of my goal, but I still lacked the mental strength to fool him.

For now, I could only end our forbidden, flirtatious conversation with a passage that snapped us back to reality.

I focused on my outfit—tradition dictated wearing a costume on All Hallows' Eve, so I chose one that embraced the infamous witchcraft Deltrea practiced. I laced up black, pointed boots over black and plum striped leggings, and I wore a plum-colored corset over a short black-lace dress. A thick, elegant, black hooded robe completed the look. I would find comfort in the night's coolness.

Also, I successfully made my bag for tonight look like a broom. Thin bamboo and palm tree fibers, neatly straight and brushed downward, decorated the entire bag's fabric. Three strands of black yarn stretched across the center. The fibers hung below the bottom of the bag. I used light-brown leather to create the handle.

I was Lyra, the witch.

Just as much as I wanted to own up to the controversies of my kingdom, I wanted to look my best, so I hyper-focused on my face, and hair. I packed a few more little necessities and returned to the mirror to add final touches to my appearance.

My brother entered my room and took over my mirror. "Wow. A political statement. I love it!"

"Alph, don't you have your own room to get ready in?"

He smiled. "Yeah. Hey, at what time did you want to meet up with Xander?"

"Ahh, ten tonight."

"At what time are you heading over to the festival?"

"Around six or seven."

"Hmm, okay."

"What?" I asked as I focused on my hair.

"We're only going to be there for a little while, then."

"Yeah, why?"

"Just."

I figured he wanted to spend more time with Syrena.

I sighed and stopped my beauty process when I paid attention to my brother's reflection in my mirror.

"What are you?" I giggled. "You look like a magician."

As he put on a red bow tie, he responded, "Yeah, I wanted to keep it simple. I got the idea from you." He grinned. "Syrena is going to be my costume partner."

I gave him a puzzled expression. "When did you all agree on that?"

This past week, Syrena used to go home to Aquaenterra for the All Hallows' Eve celebrations, and we were costume partners every year. When I asked her to do it again with me this year, she initially rejected the idea, but I convinced her—especially when I suggested I be the magician and she be the rabbit." He grinned. "I guess she thought it was a cute idea.

"You all barely talk." My expression remained confused.

"I know, but she'll come through."

"If you don't mind my asking, what happened between you guys?"

My brother shook his head. "I left a letter I shouldn't have left, but I like to think we're mending our friendship."

"Do you have feelings for her?" I asked.

Alphonse sighed, "I mean, yes, but you know me, Lyra. I like my freedom, and I'm only going to end up hurting her if we cross that line. Our friendship would become irreparable."

"You're telling me." I muttered.

"What?"

"Nothing. I mean, what are you afraid of, Alph? What makes you think you'll devolve into a friendship if you take that big step forward with her? She's a pretty damn good person."

"She is." He took a quick glance in my direction and added, "You're going to make Antares wish he wasn't the Prince of Follyn."

*****

We arrived at the festival grounds separately.

A massive line stood outside the haunted mansion, despite being up all month. A massive corn box laid beside it. Alphonse played in it with Syrena. I shook my head, a little laugh escape through my nose. He embodied such a playful, devil-may-care attitude, so seeing him dive into the corn box like an eight-year-old didn't surprise me. How he convinced Syrena to join him was beyond me, but at least they laughed wholeheartedly, genuinely looking like they were having the most fun.

They didn't notice me, so I kept walking and looked around to find Robin and Johann.

I passed a large area where some of my classmates painted or carved pumpkins. Next to that, a small hay maze dominated a chunk of the festival grounds. They stacked the hay up high, making it easy to get lost, even in the small space.

Towards the center of the festival grounds, countless booths offered mini-games, items, and food for purchase. Instead of heading there, I continued walking along the perimeter and discovered an area where students played checkers. The checkerboards, large enough to hold small pumpkins in each square, featured white pumpkins on one side and orange pumpkins on the other.

I lingered for a few seconds as I admired the boards and watched one student annihilate his companion.

A sinking feeling gripped me.

I sensed a gaze on me, so I looked around and faced an entity which resembled Corvus Noir. He wore a plague doctor's mask, and his clothing appeared entirely black. His long black cloak, much like Noir's, included a loose hoodie over his head.

The figure faced me directly but made no motion.

To confirm my suspicion, I slipped into the hay maze and glanced behind me. While others noticed the creepiness of his costume, they seemed oblivious to the fact that he followed me.

Upon entering the maze, I made various turns in an attempt to lose him, but the more I paced through it, the more I felt as though I endlessly circled the same area.

I gasped when I hit my first dead end. With no way forward, I turned back.

Giggles and voices, coming from unseen people, reverberated near me, and I hoped they would distract my pursuer as much as they distracted me.

To my dismay, I hit a second dead end. The giggles echoed, hitting me at the right times—as if they mocked my attempts to escape or laughed at my failure to find the correct path out.

I turned back, retracing my steps through the area. This time, I froze as Corvus Noir strode past the path I walked through.

I exhaled, relieved he didn't see me. I headed in the opposite direction from where he went.

Then, I hit my third dead end.

I sighed in frustration as I looked at the mountain of hay in front of me. Just then, I heard slow footsteps coming up behind me.

My heart accelerated. I could not afford a battle. I couldn't risk classmates seeing my ability. Even worse, I couldn't risk losing any energy because I needed it for my mission that night.

The footsteps approached me cautiously, and I took advantage of their pace. My eyes took on their glow. I didn't intend on attacking, but if I needed to use the dirt below me to shield myself and run, I would.

The footsteps grew louder.

When I turned to confront my opponent, my eyes contacted sapphire eyes.

"Whoa! It's just *me!*" Altair took a step back.

I closed my eyes and willed my ability back to sleep.

"Do you want me to leave?"

I ignored his question. Instead, I opened my eyes and looked around us like a lunatic. Tall stacks of hay surrounded us. I saw no signs of Corvus Noir. I saw no signs of other people.

Distant laughs reached our ears once again.

"Lyra, talk to me." Altair approached me.

Without making a single motion, I simply looked him straight in his eyes. The hostility I held in them caused him to pause in his steps.

I observed his outfit. No school uniform. He didn't exactly dress up in a costume, either, but he wore all black—almost like he simply came as himself, elegant. Attractive.

I shook my head and approached him. I circled him, searching for a place in his outfit to hide a pointed mask, and comparing his attire to the assassin's.

His clothing matched the black of the creature that followed me, but his outfit differed. Altair wore a trench coat over a black button-up shirt, while Noir wore a hooded cloak like mine. Corvus Noir had long, jester-like boots with upward points, but Altair's boots were normal, polished leather. Unlike the assassin, Altair didn't wear a scarf. I saw the lovely, long length of his neck.

For a moment, I sighed in relief, but then, I remembered who gave Corvus Noir the orders, and my guard took over again.

"Open your coat, Altair."

"Why?"

"Because you will not make a fool out of me. Show me what's in the pockets." My hostile gaze and my commanding tone made Altair respond with a single nod.

He opened his coat.

In an impulse, I closed my distance between the two of us, and I dug into his pockets.

Altair let out a nervous breath. I figured it was because I felt into one of his inner coat pockets, and I found what I wanted to find.

"I knew it!" Again, I confronted his sapphires with antagonism. I didn't need to feel more of the item's texture. My certainty was absolute. Altair toyed with me, but when I took out the mask from his pocket, I realized...

I was wrong.

This mask didn't belong to Corvus Noir. Altair's mask glowed blood red, unlike the assassin's black mask. Its beak was smaller. Where Noir's mask looked menacing, Altair's mask exuded elegance, like something from a masquerade—a fitting accessory for the Crown Prince of Follyn.

I sighed as I gazed at the mask. Then, I scanned the open exits again and wondered if escaping without being seen by Corvus Noir would be in vain. After all, his master already stood with me.

"Lyra, talk to me," Altair repeated.

I shook my head. "If you have an ounce of respect for the relationship we're building, you'll tell me the truth."

Altair clenched his jaw, concern and conflict clouded his eyes. "What do you want to know?"

"Why did you send your dog to come after me?"

Altair shook his head. "Lyra-"

"I swear, if you say you do not know what I'm talking about, you and I will never speak to each other again."

Another moment passed, but Altair said nothing. He kept his eyes on mine, but for the first time, I saw a flash of fear in them.

I shrugged. "You know what? I'll make it easy for the two of us."

I shoved his mask to his chest. As he caught it, I walked past him, but before I put much distance between us, Altair grabbed my arm.

I tried to shake him off, but he didn't budge.

"I'm not letting you go, Lyra."

My eyes took on their glow. "Do you want to start something, Antares?"

"Attack me all you want. I'm not letting you out of my sight until you explain what happened."

"Why are you pretending you have no idea who I am talking about? Your dog, Antares! Your serial murder who's got his eyes on me!"

"If you're talking about Noir-"

"Of course, I'm talking about Noir!"

At my words, Altair's expression shifted to alarm. Just as I did, he scanned the exits of the hay-hall.

"How do you know it was... him?"

"I felt it." I felt the dread.

"Hmm."

"You don't believe that's who I saw?" If he said no, I'd be determined to prove him wrong.

Instead, Altair nodded. "I was supposed to wear this at Regnum Noctis today."

With that comment, I knew what Altair implied. Noir was there to keep watch—on me *and* their prince.

Fair enough.

All Hallows' Eve celebrations were important in Follyn. During the day, they conducted executions and celebrations and the annual Regnum Noctis Masquerade filled the night. With that thought, I relaxed a little. I eased my eyes. A new realization dawned—it wasn't time for either royal family to witness us being questionably... close.

"I'm letting go, but please, don't run away," he said.

I nodded.

Altair put on the red mask he carried. Granted, he was not completely recognizable, but...

"Your hair stands out."

I took off my cloak and passed it to him. "Wear the hood."

"What about you?" he asked.

"The Plague already knows I'm here, but from your reaction, *you* haven't encountered him. It probably won't do either of us any good if we're seen together."

"Right." After Altair followed my directions, he held out his hand to me.

"Let's stay together. At least until we get out of the maze, we don't want to separate and encounter him alone."

I eyed Altair in suspicion, but those sapphire eyes behind the red mask held a sincere look.

Reluctantly, I placed my hand in his. A sense of instantaneous delight and regret traveled with the palpitations of my heart and the sweet flood of red which pooled in my cheeks.

We walked through the maze in silence, side-by-side.

"You know, instead of seeking help or running to populated areas, you have the bad habit of isolating yourself in questionable places."

"Why do you follow me?"

"Why do you run?"

"Why do you side with me?"

Altair turned to face me. "What do you mean?"

"I'm able to get out of dangerous situations alone, you know? I've done it all my life. And, if I get hurt, wouldn't that be points for you and yours? Why are you so... *okay* with making my life a little easier? I mean, as kids, you did everything you could to make my life harder. What's different?"

"I grew up, Lyra."

I eyed him, confused. "But that doesn't change what you're always reminding me we are. So, *why* do you side with me?" I insisted.

"Who knows?" Altair stopped in his tracks.

I looked ahead and noticed we had exited the maze.

Silence enveloped us.

Though I should have let go of his hand, we lingered, fingers entwined, savoring the stillness of the moment.

"Lyra!" Robin and Johann appeared behind us from the maze as well.

I let go of Altair's hand, and his demeanor changed—his expression darkened.

Robin wore black rubber gloves and some sort of black safety goggles around his neck. A long white lab coat draped over a white button up and black slacks.

"What are you supposed to be? Some sort of scientist?" I smiled at him.

"Yeah," he nodded.

"And I'm supposed to be his zombified abomination," replied Johann.

"See, when we heard Alphonse and Syrena were going to come in paired costumes, we thought it'd be fun to do it, too."

"So, ah, who're you with, Lyra?" Robin asked.

"Oh, er-" Right before I came up with a white lie, Altair faced them and lifted his mask up so they could catch a glimpse of his face.

"Altair?" Robin and Johann looked dumbfounded.

"Nice to see those eyes aren't just decorations." Altair smirked.

As if his comment wasn't enough, he took my hand again and guided me back towards the academy.

"Altair! That was unnecessary."

"I thought we were trying to avoid coming into contact with Noir," he remarked.

"I thought *you* were trying to avoid you being *seen*."

"Noir is the only one I'm avoiding."

"I'm only letting you take me from my friends to make sure you put enough distance between yourself and them. And we need to talk. I need to make something clear."

Altair and I walked until we arrived at a secluded part of the university.

"We're far enough, Altair."

Altair removed his mask. "Why do you care about those guys so much?"

"For the same reasons you care about Ian and Roselia."

He sighed. "There are *many* flies swarming around you."

I shot Altair a puzzled look. "What? Are you comparing my friends to flies?"

"I am."

I gave a small laugh through my nose. "Funny. Out of all my friends, you and I spend the most time together. I guess that makes you the biggest buzzing fly of them all." I grinned at him.

"Am I, really? We kept our distance from each other for *over a week.*"

"Well, how was I supposed to react, Altair?" I shook my head.

Altair sighed, but he held his silence.

"Why are you even here with *me*? All we do is fight."

Altair walked closer to me. "I came here because you said we would finally talk if I found you, and... I found you."

I returned Altair's sigh while I looked into his intoxicatingly blue eyes. "And what was the point of doing something like that? What in the world would possess you to be absent from your family's celebrations for a chance of finding me—your enemy?"

Again, no response.

"Tell me the truth. What am I to you, Altair?" I continued.

"You know the answer to that, Lyra."

"No. I *thought* I knew. I thought we were enemies. Then, with how we interact, I thought we were friends. Since birth, our families engraved our oppositions into our brains, but I think we've evolved away from that idea."

Altair shook his head.

"Altair, forget the impossibilities and focus on what *is*."

"No. We're having fun. We're playing the role of the disobedient children, and it's thrilling."

I frowned. "That makes no sense. Why would this be thrilling?"

"Because we know all odds are against us—beginning with our families, and we know that in the future, it will not be like *this* between us."

"How do you know that?"

"Ever since your ancestor did what she did, things have been this way, Lyra. It's not something we can run from. It's reality. This–" He gestured towards the university. "It's a distraction."

I shook my head. "I don't believe that, and I don't believe you're even sure of what you're saying anymore. We're already making positive changes. Why would you want to create an unnecessary setback between us?"

Altair didn't respond.

I sighed. "I must get back. They're probably wondering where I've gone."

"Really?" Altair gave a cynical chuckle. "Which one of them are you talking about? The pair we just ran into, or the guy swimming in corn?"

"Alphie is twice the man you'll ever be."

Altair clenched his jaw. "You seem to think that way about every man in your life who isn't me."

When I said nothing, he slowly closed the space between us.

I didn't back away. Instead, I met his glare with my own.

"He and Johann and Robin are flies swarming over a Deltrean with abnormal eyes and crow-colored hair." He snickered. "I mean, what color is it? Is it black? Is it blue?"

I shook my head in disgust and walked away from him.

"Lyra," He called out, but I walked onward.

Altair grabbed my hand and gently tugged, redirecting my gaze towards him. I obeyed, ready to engage in an argument, but his eyes betrayed a sense of remorse.

"I didn't mean it." He pleaded.

This is exactly how I wanted him—a conflicted man who struggled to keep his composure and contradicted his words on impulse. Yet, why did I feel a hint of guilt and understanding?

"You're still Altair, my little bully-boy. Unfortunately for you, I know better, and I'm confident about my appearance. You can't manipulate me or belittle me anymore, Prince of Follyn."

"Lyra?" Upon hearing my brother's voice, I shook off Altair's hand, and I backed away from him. Surprisingly enough, my brother accompanied Roselia.

"Altair?" Roselia's expression carried suspicion and betrayal.

Altair cleared his throat. "You done playing with corn?"

"Yeah, actually. I still feel some up my ass. Want to help me get it?" Alphonse turned his back to Altair.

"Where's Syrena?" I changed the subject before they went at it again.

"She ran off. I was wondering if you could help me look for her." Alphonse turned his attention back to me, his eyes signaling that it was time to go.

"Of course!" I responded.

"Altair, we've been looking for you, too." Roselia tugged on his arm, but he kept his gaze on me, silently pleading for me to stay. I pretended not to notice.

Instead, I waved a hand at my brother. "C'mon, let's get out of here."

We took the path on the university's westside to enter Aquaenterra.

CHAPTER TWENTY-NINE

Eight of Swords

Alphonse and I arrived at the path leading to Aquaenterra's stretch of forest. Although Aquaenterra controlled less than a tenth of the forest, which mostly lay in Follyn territory, it still felt like they owned a significant portion due to its immense size.

The area welcomed people—especially on All Hallows' Eve.

I asked Xander to handle three tasks before our arrival. First, he needed to keep people away from our search area. Second, he needed to ensure no one followed my brother and me. Third, he needed to acquire something from a merchant who recently passed through the Aquaenterran land which neighbored Crescencia.

I told Xander to light a small bonfire at our meeting point if he succeeded in all his tasks. Sure enough, he came through, and Alphonse and I stopped our long hike right in front of that bonfire. Onlookers saw the distant fire as a typical All Hallows' Eve ritual, and people always avoided those because they connected to Xeno and his underworld.

Seconds after Alphonse and I arrived, I heard a thud behind me— as if someone jumped down from the trees. Neither my brother nor I turned to verify.

We knew who appeared behind us.

"How did you get rid of the people here, Xander?" I kept my eyes on the beautiful fire.

"I let a blood-sucker loose."

"Hmm," I nodded.

"Did you get him back?" my brother asked.

"Of course."

"The Temperance restraints are nothing to mess with, huh?" Alphonse asked.

"Benjamin," I called out.

The Magician flowed out of my bracelet and took its bunny form as I summoned it. "Light the way for us, my boy."

The bunny swallowed the flames from the bonfire and walked ahead of us as my mind directed it. The path diverted, twisting and turning until pitch-black darkness engulfed us. Brightness only came from the light stored within the little body of The Magician.

"Lyra," Alphonse whispered. "Are you sure your energy won't drain out?"

"I'll be fine."

"We could just carry torches," my brother suggested.

"No, the entities holding the card we seek are drawn to pitch-black darkness, but The Magician will attract them. To them, the light Benjamin emits is enchanted because it's held in his body with other-worldly power."

"You mean their master's power? Xeno?"

I shrugged, "Something like that, yeah."

"I see, so they'll keep themselves hidden from man-made light, and if we light up torches, we'll fail the mission before we even begin."

"Exactly. Like this, they'll show themselves when we arrive." I responded.

"Would it help if I brought out Temperance?" Xander asked.

I shook my head. "Save every ounce of energy, Xander. There may be a lot of entities that will need to be restrained with your ability."

"What if we get stuck in the darkness?" my brother asked.

"I won't let that happen."

"Lyra, are you sure about this?" Xander's tone hinted concern.

"Yeah, what if you feel drained before we arrive?" Alphonse added.

"Precisely." Xander replied. "I'm not risking either of your lives. If it's too dangerous, I'm carrying you both out of the situation."

"We have to see it through, Xander. If we don't, mark my words— The Follyneans *will* get that card, and they *will* give it to Corvus Noir," I said.

Xander remained silent. He knew I wouldn't give him any more answers to how I got my knowledge.

"I still disagree with your brother's presence," he muttered.

"I can hold my own," Alphonse said.

"Considering the card is integrated into its setting, Alph might need to be present to transition the card into his spirit. It may be brutal or even impossible to remove it otherwise. It's been dormant for too long and has heavily adapted to where it rests. Think of it like a gravestone: when first placed, it's polished and new. But after a hundred years of neglect, it becomes part of the earth, hidden by dirt and grass."

Xander nodded. "Same with a medium. If ghosts find out you can see or talk to them, they'll get excited; they'll be active. The reaction's the same when they sense a card user."

"Ahh, Lyra is like the medium. She's announcing to the devils she owns a card by using Benjamin as a torch."

"Exactly. And we need to draw out the demons to know we're closer to the card," Xander responded.

"Have you ever encountered something like this, Xander?" my brother asked.

Xander shook his head. "It's easier to obtain the cards when they're used to shifting from possessor to possessor. They're not in one place long enough for entity infestations or integration into their resting place."

"Right. Like the ones that belong to Mother and Father... those were just passed down upon our grandparents' deaths."

"Yes." Xander responded. "Those were sweet and easy possessions."

"Did you bring the item from the merchant?" I asked Xander, and he handed me a leather tube. An old piece of parchment rested inside it. I opened it carefully with both of my hands near Benjamin's light.

"Xeno's Sonata." I read the title aloud, and I clutched the original sheet music that would awaken the card we aimed to gain.

"What a creepy item," I heard Alphonse behind me. "It has a very dark weight on it—like it really gives me the chills just to look at it."

I grinned. "People say the notes came to Vegalia in a dream."

"Supposedly, Xeno does that to talented musicians—particularly Follyn ones. Right?" Alphonse asked.

I shrugged.

Xander studied it. "Look at the notes on the thing."

I lightly grazed my finger over one note. "Look at the color. Doesn't it look like someone composed it in blood?"

"Yeah, and if you're reading the notes themselves... it's a melody that'll sound anything far from lighthearted." Xander replied.

"Yeah, I see what you mean," Alphonse added. "It already sounds creepy in my head. I can see evil having fun with this piece." He twitched to shake off his chills.

"I'm glad Xander taught you how to play then, Alph." He would need that skill to awaken this card's loyalty.

I continued, "C'mon, we need to get there soon. The location should be visible by midnight—on the first minute of October 31st. If we don't hurry, we have to wait until next year."

It took us six years to even have all the information we needed for it in our past lives, and even like that, the Follyneans found the card right before we did.

After hiking forward a few more minutes, the temperature heavily dropped.

The area darkened.

Xander, Alphonse, and I locked arms to stay together as we walked, with Xander on my left and Alphonse on my right.

Benjamin's light battled the darkness, guiding and attracting us.

Xander stayed silent, but his watchful eyes during the hike revealed his suspicion. I sensed he believed I deceived Altair to gather information, but he also questioned if today's mission stemmed from the dubious knowledge I gained from my *prophetic dreams*.

*****

The three of us walked for about an hour in soft conversation before we heard a muffled piano playing in the distance.

My brother gasped, "Guys, do you hear that?"

I smirked. "Yes, that's the one. We must listen closely and follow its melody."

From the clues I gathered in my past life, the first sign appeared—the piano playing deep in the dark forest unveiled the source of the enchanted tarot card.

My brother groaned. "I've heard of this urban legend, though. If you follow the sound of the piano, it takes over your mind. You go crazy, you get lost in the forest, and all you hear are the loud sounds of its melody ringing in your ears. Those that made it out of the land's proximity survived to tell the tale. Others just never came out."

"It's more than an urban legend," I started. "The sound of the piano is the first sign that we're on the right path. The louder it gets, the closer we are. Some say that those who die in this forest while listening to the piano's melody become another soul attached to the forest, with no choice but to befriend the devils that lurk in it."

Xander added, "Considering how many ghosts this place has, and how it's a Xenolian ability we're to attain here, that's probably true. That's why the locals are terrified of this forest. They only stick to its entrance for All Hallows' Eve."

"With that bloodsucker you released on them, they won't even get to enjoy the thrill of the entrance," Alphonse laughed through his nose. Then, he gasped. "The melody changed."

"You're right; it's gotten much louder," I confirmed.

The initial lament morphed into a creepy, energetic melody.

An antique set of piano lungs played the muffled, haunting tone, which moved around the atmosphere of the eerie forest. The forest winds hushed, and the rustling of leaves became absent, as if the surrounding musical notes intimidated nature's sounds. The piano's malevolence carried out its will.

We drew nearer, and the melody grew louder. Its eerie notes weaved into the depths of my mind until the sound became too much for my consciousness to handle, overwhelming my thoughts and making it difficult to think straight. The dark forest around us only added to the disorientation, with no one and nothing visible except for Benjamin's fading light—just bright enough to make a dent in the darkness.

Desperate for better clarity, I willed Benjamin to hop on my shoulder. His light allowed the three of us to keep track of each other's expressions, but the piano's melody continued to dominate our senses, filling our heads with its relentless tune.

I turned to Xander. He sweated profusely. Like me, he probably felt the thoughts of his mind fade away into nothing but the wicked musical notes.

I pulled Xander's and Alphonse's locked arms closer to me as I shuffled through my bag and took out three pairs of earplugs. "Here."

My brother groaned, "You had these, yet-"

He seemed to have lost his train of thought.

"Better?"

"Somewhat," Xander said, but his expression looked pained. I think mine did, too.

Alphonse seemed to struggle as well. He closed his eyes tightly and tried to breathe normally.

"Can you keep a single thought going, Alph?" I asked.

He nodded. "A bit."

Maintaining a concrete thought grew challenging with every step forward. Our mental fights against the tune further weakened our streams of consciousness.

The darkness in the forest faded into a shade of red, and the more we approached the loud cries of the piano, the redder the forest got. It looked as if we crossed a portal to the underworld.

The cold bit our bones. Instead of the fresh air of fall, this chill stung the skin. It cut deeper than winter's bitter temperatures, yet no ice appeared. No snow fell.

With every blink, the forest's crimson darkness intensified. Part of me felt grateful for the unnerving red light that painted the environment because it lifted the darkness enough to let me see my partners' faces.

I kept a tight hold on Xander and Alphonse. If any of my ear plugs came loose, I risked succumbing to the melody that drove one to insanity.

The three of us stood in silence, our voices stifled by an overwhelming absence of thoughts. Even if we conjured words, the solemnity of the piano's melody swallowed them. Devoid of sound, our surroundings became a void, save for the piercing notes that emanated from the vocals of the distant instrument, haunting our ears and penetrating our souls.

I tried to focus on my breathing.

Ritual, I managed a thought.

I grunted in pain. "Benjamin!"

Before I could think of why I wanted Benjamin, I kept getting distracted by the muffled piano melody resounding in my ears.

"Did you-"

Alphonse yelled the words, but he didn't finish his sentence.

Wind! I commanded The Magician with my thoughts.

Benjamin released the fire in his body to control the wind, creating a barrier for Xander, Alphonse, and me. The little bunny ran around us in circles, manipulating the breeze to encircle us aggressively. The relentless gusts disrupted the sound, helping us regain our senses. Even as the wind whipped around us, we caught fleeting glimpses of the sinister silhouette darting between trees.

"Whoa!" Alphonse exclaimed. I finally heard him better.

"Did you get a look at that thing's face?" Xander asked.

I studied my mentor's expression and noticed a hint of fright— something I'd never seen on his face before.

Temperance

The humanoid figure emerged from the trees, dancing to the piano's haunting melody in the background. With each move, the figure progressed closer to us, and its graceful ballet transitioned into a macabre dance. Its movements became stiff yet unnaturally flexible, as if it stood on broken bones that realigned with every step. Occasionally, the entity lagged, repeating an abrupt spin or an eerie bodily shift, as if stuck in a disorganized loop.

The few thin strands of hair clinging to its mostly bald head hung lifeless and dry, like those of a corpse's, swaying with each unsettling movement.

Its face was the most haunting part of the scene. Deep red gashes carved through its features, splitting the skin in gruesome patterns. The foreboding red glow of the surroundings reflected off the intact patches of its pallid, decayed flesh. A large, pointy grin stretched across its face, as if someone had carved upward cuts into its cheeks to widen the smile. Instead of ordinary teeth, it revealed sharp, shimmering white, triangular ones. The dim red light reflected off them, adding an ominous glow to its menacing grin.

Wait, was it the crimson of the environment? Or was the redness in its teeth something more sinister? I thought.

No eyelids covered its eye sockets, and no eyeballs filled them. Empty, black spaces replaced where eyes should have been. Its nose jutted out long and pointy, with large nostrils flaring. As it danced towards us, it randomly pointed its nose up and sniffed the air before it continued to dance straight in our direction.

Oh, I see what it's doing. I thought.

The thing couldn't see, and the piano probably drowned out any noise for that thing. Therefore, it relied on its sense of scent.

Crack. Crack. Crack. As it drew nearer, the unsettling crack of its bones echoed with each twisted dance move. The menacing sound of its bones breaking merged with the piano's melody, creating a haunting composition.

"We should split," Xander said.

"It's smelling us, isn't it?" Alphonse made a disgusted face.

I nodded. "Who knows how much time it's lived under the sounds of that piano? That thing is also deaf."

"Alph, you're staying with Lyra!" Xander exclaimed. Then, he directed his sight to me. "Lyra?"

"I got it!" I gave him a look that told him to be careful as he unlocked his arm from mine.

Xander ran away from Alphonse and me, and we ran in the opposite direction. I needed more energy to have The Magician cover a larger distance with wind. Besides deflecting some sound away from us, I used wind to direct the thing towards Xander, but my action seemed to make it angry.

It stopped dancing, and it faced my brother and me as if it could see us.

It knew exactly where we stood.

Alphonse and I advanced slowly, away from the creature, but its face followed our every move.

Xander's eyes took on a glow, and his pupils became vertical slits—like a snake's. He prepared to wield Temperance.

As if the thing sensed danger, it got on all fours and ran straight towards my brother and me—bones crackling with every move.

"Go!" I yelled at Alphonse, and we ran forward through the crimson path.

The creature's shuffling grew louder as it closed in behind us. While running, I turned and disintegrated a dead tree into thousands of sharp pieces. Using my ability and all the mental force I could muster, I launched these pieces at high speed towards the creature—all without distracting Benjamin from using wind to soften the piano sounds for Alphonse, Xander, and me—though Xander received the least help since he was far away.

A shrieking cry erupted from the creature, surpassing the sound of the piano as thousands of pieces of wood stabbed its body. Slowed and weakened by the attack, it struggled against the black, foggy chains belonging to the Temperance.

Xander would handle the rest.

"Lyra." I turned toward the sound of my brother's voice and saw a large, abandoned place in the distance. Nature disoriented the building, but it looked like a large pub with two floors.

"It's there; it has to be."

Alphonse and I ran toward it, but the closer we got to the place, the louder the piano's vocals grew. At some point, I couldn't even recall why I ran towards the crumbling building. Perhaps my legs acted on instinct. Perhaps my subconscious remembered where I needed to go.

As my survival instinct desperately used the winds to keep the piano's melody from distorting my consciousness, the disorienting tune seemed to hook onto the nerves of my brain.

Upon bursting through the front doors, the piano's melody ceased.

All sounds stopped.

All grew silent.

Alphonse and I collapsed onto the floor, catching our breath, gathering our thoughts, and remembering our circumstances.

C'mon. Xander trained you for these things. I thought to myself.

I picked myself up and offered a hand to my brother. As he took it, I glanced behind me for any signs of threats or Xander. Instead, I faced the entrance doors we had just barged through and wondered when and how they had slammed shut behind us.

"Why do you think it stopped?" my brother whispered.

"The card probably senses our presence."

"Is this like a restaurant? In the middle of nowhere?" he asked.

"I guess we'll find out."

I guided our way further inside.

The crimson glow from outside seeped into the opulent restaurant, casting eerie shadows across the massive bar at its center. Beside the bar, a grand piano stood like a silent sentinel.

The second floor overlooked the entire first floor. I figured it must have been some exclusive high-class bar at some point.

A colossal, shattered chandelier dangled precariously from the ceiling; its loose fragments swayed with life.

The area appeared decayed; the frail floor looked ready to collapse. Spider webs clung to every corner. Thick layers of dust coated the ancient, discolored piano; it looked exactly as it sounded—old. Hollow.

"What do you think played that thing?" my brother asked quietly.

"The card that rests inside the piano."

"How do you know the card is in there?"

"It's the only thing that would explain the piano's deafening power. The card has been without a possessor for so long that it's learned to take care of itself."

I trudged toward the culprit of our struggles and observed it from a safe distance. "Alph?"

"Yeah?"

"Did Xander ever teach you how to clean the inside of a grand piano?"

Alphonse nodded.

"Good. Start removing pieces." I took out some cleaning tools from my bag—including a brush, a metal rod, and a piece of cloth. "The card *has* to be inside. While you look for it, clean the piano. Be very gentle with it."

Despite the coldness of the room, beads of sweat trickled down my brother's face.

"You seem nervous," I muttered as I drew the ritualistic circle.

"I can take care of defeating people when I must, but these things are unpredictable, and they're not as fragile as humans."

"Indeed. Many make the misconception humans are scarier than these things, but both can be equally terrifying."

Upon a brief glance in my direction, my brother asked, "How do you know what the circle looks like?"

"The ritualistic circles all have the same layout on the outside. The inside is a little different for each one, so once I'm done preparing the outer part of the circle, I'll need the card to fill in the figures, letters, numbers, symbols, and shapes that correspond to the inside of its circle."

"Don't you need ingredients for some of these cards? What if you don't have them?"

"All you need is what I asked you to bring and the sheet music I asked Xander to get."

Alphonse nodded.

"As I told you when we first planned this mission, this card is too active. Instead of asking for ingredients, it's going to test us. Since it's been living in a piano for so long, when you acquire its partnership, it'll synchronize with your spirit if you have an instrument it can inhabit—just like The Magician resides in the charm of my bracelet."

"You really don't think it'll ask for anything else?"

I shook my head. "I told you to prepare yourself mentally, didn't I? And to practice music."

He nodded. "I did. I practiced a lot while you were away at university—before I joined."

In our past lives, Luna, Altair's older sister, claimed the card was easy to obtain. She described the challenge, stating that the ritual only needed a single instrument and the original copy of "Xeno's Sonata."

Despite our clues, endless research, and exaggerated preparations, the Follyneans got to "Xeno's Sonata" before we did. The Follyn royals juggled more cards than they could manage, and they needed their human weapon to grow stronger to help them destroy everything I loved.

I gritted my teeth.

"Why was yours so easy, Lyra?" My brother distracted me from the unsavory flashbacks.

"We don't know what Xander went through to obtain it. He investigated and gathered all the information before fighting whatever he needed to fight to get it. I did the simple part. Also, all cards require different things. As Xander said, some cards are easier to possess than others—especially if they haven't been dormant for long."

"Poor Xander. He never talks about his fights, huh?"

I shook my head. "Be sure to concentrate. One wrong move could cost your arm, Alph."

The piano just caused us hearing damage, so we knew it was alive with the card. It silently sat in wait like a Venus flytrap. If Alph mishandled it, the piano would bite off his arm. He needed to tame the dormant card.

"I know you know what you're doing, Lyra, but can't I just take the card and complete the ritual somewhere else? Do you really think we'll have to fight our way out of here?" my brother whispered in the eerie silence of the unsettling red darkness.

"This card is tricky to possess because it's been dormant for so long. It has adapted without a partner and grown too powerful, perhaps too comfortable. It won't just let us walk away with it. As you saw earlier, evil spirits protect it."

In my past life, I concluded that claiming the card required a brutal musical challenge.

Tonight, even if I saw an opportunity, I doubted my strength could save us all, and I was unsure of Xander's remaining energy.

The risk was ominous, as this card could transform an inanimate object into something deadly.

Mostly, cards *wanted* someone to possess them; they wanted to be awakened but were very picky about who they considered worthy. If someone carried a card without awakening it for *too long*, it attracted bad luck and unwanted attention—the card carrier with a dormant card usually ended up developing a sort of fruity-apple scent, too.

"You would think a dormant card wouldn't cause so much noise," Alphonse said.

"When they're dormant for a long time, they'll wreak a bit of havoc with the setting they're limited to—as you just witnessed. When they have possessors, they unleash their full potential; the card's eye is open and focused to align with its possessor's goals and mind."

"I see," he paused. "I got it." His tone sounded incredulous.

My brother observed the card between his fingers. Unlike the rest of the place, the card looked brand new and intact.

I placed a piece of parchment on the bar and positioned the card on top of it.

Finally, card number twenty is ours. I thought.

"Judgement," Xander read the text aloud.

"Damn it, Xander. I hate it when you do that. Make yourself known," Alphonse retorted.

A sinister grin spread across my face as I read the ritual's requirements.

"Well, what do you know? Luna wasn't lying," I murmured to myself.

The ritual required my brother to choose an instrument and play "Xeno's Sonata" as long as the instrument could be adapted to the sheet music. A perfectly good piano sat in front of my brother and, fortunately, he played skillfully.

Despite the song's difficulty, he needed to play it flawlessly from start to finish to awaken the card.

"Luna? Antares?" It took Xander's reply for me to realize I said my thoughts aloud.

I changed the subject. "What did you do with our little dancing friend?"

"It's stubborn. It's still being held by my restraints." Sure enough, his eyes were still slit pupils.

"Alphie, did you bring your old kalimba like I asked?"

"Yes," he responded.

"Good. Get in the center of the circle along with it."

"I'll be right outside," Xander made his way out.

"No! Xander, wait!" I cried.

The moment he opened the door to exit, clanking noises shuffled behind us, prompting us to turn and face the source.

I blinked, and the surrounding scenery transformed. The red hue remained, but it no longer dominated the dim golden glow that now engulfed the pub.

The torn down, abandoned building now gleamed clean and pristine, with a person stationed behind the bar. He beamed widely while polishing whiskey glasses.

Then, he spoke. "Leaving already? You haven't even had a drink with us!"

Us? I thought.

All I did was blink, and when I opened my eyes, the bar teemed with the liveliness of countless undead souls.

CHAPTER THIRTY-TWO

Seven of Swords

"How about a drink before you go?"

"Err," I glanced at my brother. My stomach knotted.

"Thank you, but it's time for us to go," Alphonse responded.

In a heartbeat, the setting's liveliness died, overtaken by the sinister red hue. In that chilling instant, every entity in the room fell silent, and their eyes locked onto us. Their smiles twisted painfully, stretching wider than humanly possible. Crimson reflections gleamed on what should have been the white of their teeth, just like the unnerving dancer we encountered earlier.

"I'll have a drink!" I yelled.

Again, in the blink of an eye, the setting changed to the golden dominance of the lively, non-hostile environment. People resumed their activities as we faded from their view.

"Excellent choice. I assume the two of you will join us as well?" The bartender referred to Xander and my brother. A relaxed, permanent, unnerving smile rested on his face.

I nodded in their direction—signaling them to go along with it—for the time being.

"I'm eighteen," my brother said.

"We serve anyone capable enough to enter our exclusive club." He poured a whiskey and slid it towards my brother. "This one's got a green apple flavor to it; I trust you'll find it palatable."

My brother looked at his glass before looking at me with uncertainty. I'm sure he hoped he wouldn't get poisoned, but given our circumstances, he sipped cautiously.

"I'll have a glass of your finest wine," Xander said.

His choice puzzled me. I had never heard him ask for wine before.

"My apologies, sir. We don't carry that spirit here." The bartender faced him with his creepy smile. Then, he poured two fingers of bourbon in a glass and slid it towards Xander. "You might quite like this one, however. You look like a fellow who has a taste for exquisite liquor."

Xander took a whiff. Then, he took a sip and raised an eyebrow in approval. "Hints of vanilla."

Next, the bartender concocted a combination of tea, gin, and rose petals in a glass and slid it towards me. "I'm sure you will find this one to be an appropriate fit for your taste pallet."

Like Xander, I took a whiff. The drink's strong floral scent enveloped me.

I let the liquid touch my lips with a small sip. It packed a punch, but as the bartender predicted, I savored it.

"It's got essences of rose," he said.

He observed us through his black irises for a short, quiet moment.

Then, with a voice like a whispering shadow, he spoke again. "We lack a pianist."

We waited in tense silence, anticipating his next words.

The bartender's expression turned expectant; a sinister smile played on his lips. "You see, if we're not entertained soon, we become quite... irate."

The card's trial started.

Xander and I looked at Alphonse.

"Oh?" The bartender followed our gazes and directed his words at my brother. "Will you play for us, sir?"

My brother nodded after taking another sip from his drink. "I'm willing."

"Hmm," the bartender hummed as he refilled Xander's drink.

"You should know, if you take on the task, we expect you to play until midnight tomorrow."

This bartender literally asked my brother to play for almost twenty-four hours.

This place became an urban legend among the locals near Aquaenterra Forest. Years after card number nineteen, Judgement, found its tomb there, a few daring souls ventured into that abandoned part of the forest. People recounted tales of countless devils haunting the area, growing stronger and more numerous.

However, eyewitnesses spoke of a phantom bar coming to life every All Hallows' Eve. We had to time our search perfectly. The card and the bar would remain hidden if we searched on a normal night. Unfortunately, the demons protecting the forest grew stronger and deadlier on October 31st.

We encountered the unique challenge of being stuck until the next day or escaping with our lives. If we didn't escape and Alphonse failed as a pianist, we would join these spirits in their return to the unvirtuous realms of the dead or the underworld.

The bartender's voice interrupted my thoughts. "As a fellow guest, we will keep you well hydrated with our drinks."

He refilled my brother's glass.

The sinking feeling in the pit of my stomach caused me to look around and realize that the ambience held a dominant red hue again. Red-glowing stares of the bar's occupants locked themselves on us.

"Xander," I whispered.

"I know."

Alphonse said nothing. Instead, he got up from the bar and made his way towards the piano. He didn't look around. He didn't look at me or Xander, and despite the distractions, he maintained his focus on the instrument in front of him.

I chased after my brother, and I handed him "Xeno's Sonata."

I had set everything for him to play inside the ritualistic circle, figuring that if he could get the power of Judgement right then, escaping would be easier.

I nodded to him as a signal to begin the ritual.

He nodded and took his seat at the piano. By now, everyone, including the bartender, fixed their glowing red eyes on us. Slowly, the spirits inched closer, but their readiness to strike vanished as soon as Alphonse played the opening note, a single G.

After I blinked, everything had changed back into a non-hostile environment. The bartender's smile didn't waver, and a fellow ghost handed Alphonse another drink.

"On us," he said, with that wide, painful smile on his face.

As Alphonse played "Xeno's Sonata," the bar seemed much more alive.

"That's my favorite melody," one creature said, his comment confirming we dwelled amid devils.

The bartender refilled both Xander's glass and mine.

Xander and I drank quickly, in a trance-like state, as if under a spell.

Alphonse quickened the creepy harmony, and he stumbled on a note.

The ambience became hostile.

The guests' red gazes bore into our souls. Their grins grew wider, and they inched toward us once again.

Whether it was the nerves, or the confines of a reverie, Alphonse downed his drink. The drink seemed to reset the ambience, rejuvenating the room after he finished it.

"Try again," said the bartender.

A woman approached my brother as he started the melody. She smiled with a big-toothy grin and placed another glass of whiskey on the piano. "On us."

Again, the bartender refilled both Xander's drink and mine.

Alphonse flawlessly played the dark melody. When the song demanded faster notes, he kept up with the sheet music. At a certain point, some of the bar guests danced. The ambience became livelier.

My nerves frayed every time I looked at my brother. The melody neared its conclusion. Alphonse only had a few notes left before completing the ritual.

Then, he messed up a note for the second time that night.

Once more, the ambience became hostile.

Alphonse chugged the drink the woman had placed on the piano.

"Try again," the bartender said with his pointy grin.

My brother started playing the song again.

I made eye contact with Xander. With my eyes, I signaled towards my drink. "Did you catch it?" I whispered to him.

He nodded.

Downing the drinks reset the trial, so Alphonse's mistakes came at a cost. My brother risked passing out drunk before he succeeded.

The bartender cleaned glasses behind the bar. He didn't look at us, but that painful smile stayed plastered across his face. If he listened to Xander's and my conversation, he pretended not to.

"Xander, this is getting bad," I slurred my words.

"He must play fluently even under the influence of alcohol. Each drink is another chance to play the song correctly, but the more mistakes he makes, the harder it becomes to play straight."

This time, the hard part of the song came and went without a hiccup.

The bartender refilled Xander's and my drinks.

As the room spun, I realized leaving would be harder than we thought. My eyes grew heavier as I succumbed to my drowsiness.

"Lyra," Xander whispered.

I opened my eyes to the circle's shades of purple, blue, and silver. However, the soft red and golden hues of the lively room muted the silver glow.

Alphonse finished the song.

At Alph's distraction from the piano, the room grew hostile again.

I gasped, "Alph, read the card's chant!"

Hear me, O Judgement! I do summon thee,
From slumber deep, declare our sacred bond.
Inhabit now this vessel, grant to me,
Thy noble power, with music beyond.

As partners bound, our spirits intertwined.

Together, let us fill the slumb'ring earth,
In melodies, our destinies aligned
To welcome growth, reflection, and new birth.

Our hearts shall sing through all our nights and days.
With sound and song, till death doth part our ways.

He gasped, "The card's eye is open."

"Alph, play!" Xander and I yelled at him simultaneously.

He gasped, and he downed the liquid left on top of the piano.

The ambience became lively.

"Try again," the bartender said. Then, he refilled our drinks.

Another woman took her side by Alphonse. "On us," she said.

"Xander," I whispered. "There is no chance we can keep this up for twenty-four hours. We have to go now. Can you use Temperance?"

"Yes, but Alph needs to put his ability into play first. It's a necessary distraction," he whispered.

"Alph?"

Alph kept playing as he turned to give Xander and me a side glance. He smirked, and his eyes started glowing. His pupils took on a vertical slit—snake-like.

The tarot card, Judgement, allowed Alphonse to control the speed of musical sound waves, making them travel either quickly or slowly. They could be deafening screeches, or they could be low hums which invaded one's ear drums long enough to drive one mad.

Alphonse played the piano and let the resounding sound waves linger in the air. At that moment, the three of us realized the ghosts, engrossed in the piano's melody, didn't notice us slipping away.

Our hope faded as the door opened.

The ambience turned hostile, and we ran. Xander slowed down, used Temperance, and let loose countless chains to restrain the abundance of ghosts in the bar. It worked, but the overwhelming volume exhausted him. Regardless, Xander's actions slowed them down.

Alphonse took out his kalimba and played his instrument as he ran. Musical notes and amplified sounds traveled towards the restrained creatures, but it didn't seem to weaken them. I suspected the entities grew accustomed to the loud music and card's essence.

"Save your energy, Alph!"

If I needed to shield us, I would, but I had to conserve my stamina as well.

Xander used his restraints to hold them all off, but as we ran, his sweat poured down profusely.

Xander grunted as Temperance's chains loosened on the creatures.

I used thick layers of dirt to shield us, and Alphonse tried playing his kalimba again. Unlike the first time, it actually worked. The creatures seemed drawn to the melody Alphonse gathered around them, and it slowed them down.

*****

After all the running, draining of energy, and drinking, we reached the dark part of the forest. Almost as if we slipped through a portal, the red hue disappeared from our surroundings in an instant, but I still sensed entities following us.

Alphonse and I stumbled and fell, hindering each other's progress.

With his last ounce of strength, Xander restrained both Alphonse and me. He ran through the pitch-black darkness until the forest path's lights near the entrance became visible.

After we reached the exit of the forest, Xander put us down. It surprised me that Alphonse continued running without falling over.

"Did Antares suspect anything? Did he know you'd been questing this card?" Xander asked.

"I don't think so. He's questing his own *major* card, which caused him to overlook little details on clues for other cards." I slurred my words, but as I ran for my life, I realized I couldn't say some things carelessly.

"How do you know this? Did he tell you?"

"Hanging out with him has proved fruitful, don't you think, Xander? He's had some slip-ups." I grinned, but Xander remained unconvinced.

"I'm glad you taught me how to play, Xander. This would've been impossible otherwise," Alphonse said, stumbling as he slurred his words.

A thought occurred to me. "Xander, why did you ask for wine? I've never heard you ask for it, and I've never even seen you drink it." The way he asked for wine felt like a code, but I needed to be sure.

"In my bounties, I occasionally encounter entities at bars and drink with malevolent beings. One thing I've noticed is that these things avoid wine like the plague."

Alphonse ran towards the Aquaenterran path which led to the university. "I'm going to cut through school to head home. I'm tired."

Xander shook his head. "You can't let anyone see you like that. We're taking the long route."

At Xander's words, Alph took off running towards the university.

"Alph!" Xander and I ran behind him.

Xander tried releasing his restraints again. The foggy, black, shadowy chains came out of his palms, and they stretched towards Alphonse.

"Xander!" I held him as blood poured from his lips. "Your body is giving out. If you overexert yourself and your ability, you'll collapse!"

"Damn brat!" He spat out.

"Don't worry, rest here in Aquaenterra. We'll meet you at home."

He shook his head. "No, Lyra."

"It's dangerous for him to return to that all-night festival in his state! Who knows what might come out of his mouth? I have to go after him!" I dug through my bag and gave Xander a herbal healing concoction.

"Here!" I took off the bottle's cork and put it to his lips so he could drink. It helped him gain a bit of energy back in a matter of minutes. At least, he could get himself up and wobble to a nearby inn where he could sleep until his body restored most of his lost energy.

"I have to go after him, Xander." My eyes pleaded.

Xander gritted his teeth as he nodded. "Then, I'll see you at the palace."

"Thank you for trusting me," I whispered.

I ran to Crescencia University.

*****

My brother wisely navigated the deserted university areas. The festival and celebrations continued until dawn, as expected. Noise and liveliness echoed across the grounds, prompting us to steer clear.

When I reached my brother, I put an arm around his waist to help him walk. "C'mon, Alph."

He yelled, "I freaking love you, Lyra!"

"I know, I know."

In his drunken daze, he hugged me—something he never did otherwise.

I chuckled.

As I hugged my brother, I spotted the two people I wanted to avoid.

Syrena and Altair gave us suspicious looks from a distance and loitered within eyesight of Aquaenterra's entrance. My overanalyzing mind wondered if one of them anticipated our return from Aquaenterra.

I didn't want to alarm my brother, so I simply whispered it back to him. "I love you, too."

At my words, he let go of our hug, only to yell out his thoughts in an area he believed a lonely part of the university.

"We're gonna lead Deltrea together!" He slurred his words as he yelled the statement while facing the direction of the festival grounds.

I grabbed ahold his cheeks to force him to face me. "Stop it, Alph." My anxious heart pounded. There was no way they didn't hear what he said.

"We're gonna do right by our people. Just watch," he said.

A pair of hands with obsidian rings grasped my wrists and removed them from my brother's cheeks.

"Let me go, Altair!"

He spun me towards him. Even through my compromised wrists, I turned towards my brother to make sure he still stood.

Syrena stood by my brother's side. "I got him, Lyra."

"Syrena?" Alphonse's eyes lit up.

"No. I got it." I tugged my hands away from Altair, but my efforts were futile. "Alphie! Alph!" I called out to him, but Syrena had captivated him. He stayed by her side, using her arm for support as they walked. I watched their backs as they left in the opposite direction.

I grew frantic.

"Let. Me. Go!" I faced Altair.

"Let Syrena take care of him."

I aggressively attempted to wriggle out of Altair's grasp. "I want to be with Alphonse right now."

My burdensome worry weighed on my shoulders. What if he elaborated on the reckless comment that came out of his mouth? What if he revealed his true identity to Syrena? What if he told her we're twins? What if he exposed details about our mission earlier?

"Altair!" I halted my motions. "Let me go."

Altair shook his head.

"Let me go."

"No."

"If you don't let me go, I will hurt you."

Altair kept his eyes on mine in silence.

"I will use my ability against you, Altair."

"Someone might see you." He spoke in a low voice, his gaze piercing down at me.

"I'm willing to take that risk."

"I'm not letting you go."

"You're trying my patience."

"Why were you drinking with him, Lyra?"

I evaded his question. "What were you all still doing here? You all are stalking us now?" I tried my best not to slur my words.

Altair grinned, "As if I don't have better things to do."

"Since when are you working closely with Syrena, huh?" I stumbled, but Altair steadied me. "Why are you so angry about leaving her with that guy? That girl's your best friend."

With my wrists locked in his hands, I persistently pushed him with my elbows.

"Let me go."

"What is going on between you and Forté?" Altair sounded frustrated.

I laughed hysterically. This Follynean viewed me as his sole rival in the Deltrean bloodline. Altair bested Alphonse in my past life only because he never gained an ability. This time, I *just* secured one for him. I couldn't help but laugh until my lungs were on the verge of collapsing. Unbeknownst to Altair, I secured another silent victory.

At that moment, I understood my brother's temptation to reveal his true identity as Alphonse Celestia—the crown prince of Deltrea.

My laughter caused me to lose strength in my legs, but when I didn't sink to the floor, I remembered Altair still gripped me.

My eyes glowed. "I warned you, Antares."

"You don't want to do something you're going to regret."

"You're threatening me, Prince of Follyn?"

He shook his head, bent his head down, and whispered to me. "Many will witness your abilities. Is the world prepared for it?"

With all of my strength, I pushed him with my elbows again.

Altair released my arms, and since I had been pushing against him with all my strength, I stumbled forward into his chest. In a swift motion, he bent down, scooped up my legs, and hoisted me over his shoulder.

"You're not going to win, little Lyra, especially in the state you're in."

My body dangled over his shoulder. Even though Altair possessed an abnormal sense of strength, and I couldn't make him budge, something about his possessive hold made me not want to fight against it. The feelings I constantly blocked bubbled up into a swarm of butterflies in my belly.

With a wave of my hand, Benjamin flowed out of my bracelet and took on his bunny form. I hoped the sight of him would help me control my urges.

"Ah, there's your cute companion." Altair mocked me.

"Keep your guard down—like an idiot." As I hung limply over Altair's shoulder, I watched Benjamin follow behind us.

"Won't it tire you out more to keep him active?" Altair asked.

I nodded. "A bit."

When he said nothing further, I broke the silence again. "You have Strength, don't you?"

Altair sighed. "I have a lot of *physical* strength, yes."

"I meant the card."

He remained quiet.

"How?" I asked.

"How what?" he replied.

"How did you find out about him?" I referred to my brother. Naturally, I couldn't resist asking the one question that always bothered me in my past life: Where did I slip up? How did the Follyneans learn about the Prince of Deltrea?

"What are you talking about, Lyra?"

"Back then." How did he discover Alphonse in our past life? Surely, he wouldn't have eliminated him otherwise.

I sighed, knowing Altair couldn't remember our past lives. Even if he could, he wouldn't answer.

If anything, Altair's marriage to Syrena must have led someone to discover my brother's identity. Somehow, he must have linked it. If he never made the familial connection, he must have seen Alphonse as a loyalist to Deltrea, like Xander, and that's why he murdered him.

I balled my hands into fists and pounded Altair's back. "I swear. If you hurt him, I will use the power of The Sun to incinerate you."

I made sure things progressed in my favor. Alphonse possessed an ability, and he needed time to explore its various uses and limitations. Depending on its master's limitations, all cards covered a certain distance, so my brother needed to push himself, measure his endurance, and build his stamina.

In my new life, I vowed to protect my brother, even if it meant giving up my life.

I waited for Altair to respond to my threat. I waited for him to toss me back towards the ground, but he didn't.

Instead, he said, "Unless you plan to eliminate our teacher, you're going to have to do better than that, little Lyra."

Even though I wanted to hit him with my words or The Magician, I couldn't, as I found it more difficult to keep my eyelids open.

CHAPTER THIRTY-FOUR

Two of Wands

My eyes fluttered open to the familiar ceiling of Altair's dorm room.

"Hey, how do you feel?"

Panicked, I sat up at the sound of Altair's voice. He sat on a chair beside the bed where I lay. Xander and my parents would flip if they caught me here.

"I need to go," I said.

"It's four in the morning, closer to five. You've hardly slept and you're barely feeling okay. Sleep it off and walk home when the sun is up."

"No, you don't understand. My father is going to kill me!"

I gasped when I remembered my brother probably didn't make it home, either.

"Does Syrena have a dorm here, too?" I asked.

"The sun comes up soon, Lyra. Just wait. You're not even in a condition stable enough to walk home alone in this darkness."

"I feel fine, Altair." He followed me as I made my way towards his door. Truthfully, I still felt slow and muddled.

Altair stood in front of me as if to block me from the door. I wanted to turn away and hide because I must have looked like a complete mess, still battling the effects of that night's alcohol.

"Play a game with me first," he said.

I looked at him with a puzzled expression. "What?"

"Play a game with me," Altair repeated.

"No, I heard you. It was a rhetorical question." I shook my head. "I just can't believe you're asking me this when you see I'm in such a hurry. Please move."

"If you win, I'll give you anything you want—even the answer to any of your invasive questions," he smirked.

This caught my attention. He dangled an opportunity for me to gather information from him, but if Xander showed up at the Deltrean palace alone, I feared my parents' reaction. Moreover, I feared my brother's intoxicated state of mind and the risk of leaving him out there, hoping he wasn't telling Syrena anything unnecessary.

As if he could read my thoughts, Altair commented on my apprehensive expression. "Forté can take care of himself, and he's with Syrena. Don't you trust her?"

I sighed. "What game did you have in mind?"

"Hmm," His eyes looked throughout his room, and they stopped on his two-tier glass coffee table. Transparent glass formed the table's top. Frosted glass formed the bottom, showcasing a neatly arranged chess board.

"Chess," he said.

"What do you get if you win?"

"The same thing."

I nervously bit my lip. "How do I know you're going to answer truthfully?"

He shrugged. "Can you trust me today?"

I raised an eyebrow. "The man who declares himself my enemy is asking me to trust him."

"I won't lie to you, Lyra. You have my word as a future leader of Follyn."

A leadership which meant nothing more to me than my execution.

"Are you sure you want to go through with the game? If I win, I'm going to ask without holding back," I eyed his reaction.

"What makes you think *I'll* hold back?" He grinned.

"What do you want from me?" I observed his impish expression.

"Who knows?" He spoke in a low voice, lacing his words with mischief.

"Hmm... I don't know, Altair."

"If you don't like the first thing I ask for, I'll let you pass on it and listen to an alternative request. I'll leave it up to you whether you choose to give me the first or the second option."

I admired the beauty of the black-and-white marble chessboard Altair laid out. One side held metallic plum-colored pieces, and the other side had lavender-colored figures.

"Shades of purple, huh?" I lifted an eyebrow.

"Of course, it's my favorite color." Altair looked into my eyes as he said it.

I blushed, "Fine, I'll play. The winning conditions will be the same for you. We'll keep it fair."

As a traditional declaration of an agreement, Altair extended his hand towards me. I gave it a firm shake.

"It's a deal." His handsome grin made me nervous. He seemed confident.

Too confident.

I groaned, "Why does it feel like I just made a deal with the devil?"

Altair laughed hysterically. I've never seen him laugh so much before—especially like that. The cuteness of it bothered me, and it made me more annoyed that the light-hearted expression made him more attractive.

As opposed to what I really thought, I directed a suspicious glare at him. "What's so amusing?"

He laughed harder at my tone.

"You're plotting something evil, aren't you? I fell for a trap, didn't I?" I raised my eyebrow in suspicion.

He shook his head, and his laughter calmed down. "Are you hungry? I have some snacks."

Altair turned to his little kitchen cabinets and took out chocolate covered almonds and tea.

"I thought you lacked a sense of humor. Now, I see it's just weird," I responded.

"What do you want to drink, Lyra?"

I shook my head. "I'm good, thank you."

Despite my rejection, Altair brought us two cups of water and snacks.

"Stay hydrated and eat a bit, at least."

"Thanks," I whispered as I took a sip of my water.

Altair took a dark pawn and a light pawn. He moved his hands behind his back to mix the pieces together. Then, he brought his closed fists forward.

"Choose."

I tapped on his right hand. He held it open to reveal the lavender-colored pawn. "You get the light pieces, little Lyra."

*****

"So, what was that? Did you have some kind of random laughing fit?" I moved the pawn above the queen by two spaces.

"You're just... witty." Altair popped a chocolate-covered almond into his mouth.

"You're making fun of me," I accused.

Altair moved the pawn above his king. "You're overthinking it, Lyra. The way you said that comment; it was funny."

"Hmm," I hummed as I moved one of my bishops.

"People overcomplicate the concept of humor. It just *is*," Altair said as he contemplated his next move.

Altair's eye color looked different—darker—like the blood-sucking creatures Xander hunted. He never slipped up, but a burgundy hue currently replaced his sapphire irises.

"Changing the subject, you should be careful, Altair," I looked into his eyes. I wondered how or why he became careless.

Altair answered my question as if he sensed my thoughts. "I don't have to hide from you."

"It's been days, hasn't it?" Since he fed.

He smirked, "What? Are you afraid?"

Altair moved the pawn above his queen.

I shook my head and willed my ability to awaken. My violet eyes took on a soft, illuminating glow, and my pupils became slits.

I returned his smirk, "If you were to try anything, I'd fight back. In fact, it's you that should be afraid."

"Yeah, you'll have that little bunny of yours wreck me, won't you?" Altair laughed again.

I hated the sight of his carefree laugh because it made the insides of my body run sweet and fluttery—emotions that only caused an internal setback for my goals.

I averted my glued gaze away and focused on the game. His charm served as a successful strategy for distraction.

I moved one of my knights to the center of the board.

"How did you figure it out?" Altair moved one of his pawns.

"Is that sarcasm? Your eyes aren't exactly blue tonight, Altair."

He shook his head, "I'm talking about when you... hurt yourself to stop me from..."

I nodded. The question must have weighed on him since the night we discovered Dr. Diestro wielded The Sun. He likely wondered how I knew about his vampirism and where he might have slipped up, possibly recalling scenarios as far back as our childhood.

"I'll answer that *if* you answer one of mine first." Again, I moved one of my knights.

"That depends on how invasive it is." Altair looked at me with suspicion.

"How are you only a half-human? I've never heard of such a case with vampires. I know shapeshifters *are* humans, but vampires and demons are strictly... Xenolian creatures."

All were human once, but demons didn't hold on to their physical vessel. Vampires did. Vampires blended in with regular humans where demons took on grotesque forms—such as the dancer that guarded Judgement. Demons invited involuntary terror and dread in an ambience, but vampires invited attraction and seduction.

Altair let out a half-smile, "Shapeshifters *are* Xenolian creatures, too."

I nodded. Shapeshifting required monstrous preparations for a twisted ritual.

"You all serve the same evil." The same master.

Altair snickered, "I didn't choose to be *this*, Lyra."

"What does that mean, Altair? How does something like *that* happen?"

I theorized Altair had a twisted tarot ability which allowed him to adopt the curses and blessings of Xenolian entities without inheriting their weaknesses. Alternatively, it was possible he possessed a protective tarot ability, which explained why he never employed enchanted offenses or defenses.

Instead, Altair kept himself healed through blood intake and focused on sword fighting. He relied on his trusted ally, Corvus Noir, to wield the power of cards.

"You haven't won the game, Lyra," he smirked. Again, Altair moved the pawn above the king by one space.

I scoffed. "Why were you at the festival so late? I doubt you were out socializing and engaging in the festivities all night. Were you stalking me?"

Altair let out a dry laugh and shook his head. "I intended to follow Ian to Regnum Noctis, but I noticed Syrena at the gates to Aquaenterra. She told me neither of you had reappeared after leaving. Knowing you, your father's character, and your absence from Deltrea on a Friday night," he paused.

"Ahh, I see. Antares, you were worried about me." I flashed a victorious smile at him.

"*Curious*." Altair corrected. "Well, yeah, perhaps I was quite concerned. I meant to stay for a few minutes, but you and your friend came within our sights before I left."

"Hmm," I hummed.

My triumphant smile vanished as Altair made his move. He strategically placed a pawn to capture one of my bishops. The position of one of *my* pawns made it susceptible to *his* knight's victory.

I could only save one.

Altair continued talking as I contemplated my next move.

"Also, you said you were going to talk to me at the festival. We didn't leave off on good terms, and I... don't want to go back to our lack of communication after today."

"Do you know what you're implying? You seem like you *enjoy* my company."

I made my move—I kept my bishop safe.

Altair's expression suggested his mind was elsewhere, beyond our chess game. When he didn't respond, I spoke my next words, intending to study his reaction.

"We don't have to be physically involved with one another. We can keep it to writing—just as we've been doing all week."

Altair looked up from the game and made eye contact with me. His burgundy eyes pleaded. "Yeah, but it's different... when we limit ourselves to writing."

"What's different?"

Altair frowned, but again, he remained silent as he made his next move.

"Your moments lack color when I'm not in them?" I teased him with a cocky smile.

Altair sighed and shook his head—as if he tried to clear it from invasive thoughts. "What will I do without my little Lyra? Winter break is upon us, and my bleak black-and-white world will not see the vibrance of color." His tone sounded sarcastic under his smug grin.

"For an entire month," I smirked, but the weight of time caused our expressions to fade into seriousness and regret.

While pretending to contemplate my next move, I looked down at the board, distracted in thought. Despite my love for chess, I played with a severe lack of focus because my mind circled around Altair. I couldn't contain the suppressed, overwhelming emotions for this devil; they resurfaced in a continuous rhythm, plaguing my conscious thoughts. Something about him attracted me against every will, every moral, every expectation, and every living cell in my being.

At some point, I became determined to befriend Altair for a beneficial purpose. I desperately needed access to Follyn, so I intended to provoke a political marriage proposal by capturing his heart.

Despite my reluctance, marriage was my only legal option. Infiltrating illegally meant starting a war, which I could not risk. However, something genuine about my developing relationship with Altair surfaced in my heart. The abundance of these new, sweet feelings carried the risk of deep, painful regret.

Altair's presence in my thoughts and in my daily life became too impactful to the core of my being. I looked forward to our encounters. When I refused to talk to him, I felt a rush of excitement as he chased after me. Sweet nerves danced in my stomach as I read his responses in my notebook, and against my will, he always found a way into my thoughts.

The captivating nature of his writings added complexity and depth to my original idea of this devil. Every stubborn action and word he uttered drove my desire to understand him better. His gentle and caring side left me in awe, and his reserved personality garnered admiration. The allure of his blue eyes, dark hair, dimples, mischievous smile, and heartfelt laugh overwhelmed my dark ambitions. My curiosity about his secrets grew.

I realized I had developed an undesired infatuation for Altair Antares, and I fantasized about knowing the feeling of his hands, his face, his skin, his lips.

I craved him so much, and it scared me. Despite knowing that indulging in the sweetness of everything Altair Antares would compromise my future, I couldn't help but give in to temptation.

The time to distance myself weighed on me. I needed to heal from the sweet, aggressive feelings he planted in my heart. I needed to step away from playing with a fire that would burn me to *death*. Yet, following through with that logical reasoning was difficult.

I made my next move and took another one of Altair's pawns.

"I know it's none of my business, but that guy, Forté, seems to be into Syrena. He disregarded you, and he left with her instead of you." I failed to notice Altair staring at me.

I raised an eyebrow. "Your move."

"Why did he declare himself the next Deltrean king?"

I shrugged.

"Why did you tell him you loved him?"

"Because I do. He's important to me." I eliminated one of Altair's bishops from the board.

Altair remained silent as he observed the board. Perhaps he planned out a new strategy.

"He was with you that day, too," Altair said, taking one of my rooks. "Pink."

"How did you know it was me?"

"I figured it out the moment we made eye contact. I second-guessed myself because of your eye color, but your face hadn't changed much. You also looked at me the same way you did when we were kids, with a slight difference."

"Like what?"

Altair shrugged. "I don't know. Your eyes looked at me with a genuine sense of... hatred... but there was also... courage. Or, like... determination?"

"Hmm," I made a new move.

He continued, "Have you been friends with Forté for a long time?"

I grinned, "Yes. He helped me grow from the traumas you put me through."

Altair flinched.

I continued, "Why don't you like him? He's a very cool person."

Altair shook his head as he captured one of my pawns. "I'm... selective."

"Well, Johann, Robin, Syrena, and he are my friends. If you want any kind of friendship or acquaintanceship with me, you can't treat them the way you did at the festival today." I captured his second bishop with my queen.

"Friendship or acquaintanceship, hmm?" Altair's expression looked victorious.

Sweat dripped as I assessed my predicament on the board. Altair had set a trap, and I fell right into it. My move positioned my queen within reach of his knight.

I dreaded his upcoming winner's request.

"I have a better offer for you," Altair said as he removed my queen from the board.

Two of Swords

"Checkmate."

I frowned at Altair's smug declaration. "I understand, so please, get on with your request."

Altair chuckled, but instead of saying anything, he pulled out one of Vegalia's tarot cards.

The card's eye remained closed. It was dormant.

"You were right, Lyra. During my year-long absence from Crescencia, I collected a second card. I found it after I ran into you in Aquaenterra."

"You *really* aren't hiding from me anymore." I eyed him with caution.

"It has proven quite difficult to awaken this card to serve me."

"You must underestimate me if you're showing it to me while its eye is still closed."

Altair shook his head. "I'd be a fool to underestimate you. Also, I wouldn't jeopardize our little peace."

"Then, what are you doing, Altair? Are you trying to show off?"

"You're getting so defensive that you're not letting me get to it."

I waited for him to continue as he stared at the card in his hands.

"Card number six—*The Lovers*. This awakening ritual requires two handlers."

"Ah, I see. You want *my* help in awakening it," I said with a sarcastic smile.

"Precisely," he responded, to my surprise.

My smile faded. "You're making fun of me."

Altair shook his head.

"It wasn't a question. It was a realization." I stood.

As I paced around the room, Altair got up from his seat and reassured me, "Lyra, I'm not making fun of you."

"You say that with your smug smile plastered across your face," I shook my head. "What's the connection between this and your chess victory?" I asked, but I anticipated the direction of this conversation.

Altair walked toward me. I stepped back with each of his steps until the wall behind me stopped me. He closed the space between us.

Altair's burgundy eyes flickered, his smile unchanged. He reveled in the moment. I was a cornered rabbit, trapped between a wall and its predator.

"The ritual requires two handlers," he repeated. "Two handlers with a strong passion for each other."

I laughed through my nose, but Altair interrupted my mockery by closing the space between us.

Instinctively, I raised my hands to his chest to block him. My eyes glowed violet, and my pupils became slits. With my mind, I summoned Benjamin, who appeared as a mist and quickly shapeshifted into his bunny form.

The amused expression in Altair's burgundy eyes faded into a hint of reluctance and softness as he looked down at my slit pupils.

"You really are on the defensive, Lyra. You hate being close to me that much?"

"I do." I lied.

My heart was in danger.

I lost the game, and I promised to give him an answer—anything but a permanent commitment.

Altair made no move to push against me. He made no move to touch me, but his gaze remained attached to mine. My hands relaxed on his chest.

"What is your aim here, Antares? You seem to imply you want for us to be the partnership the card responds to."

"You're correct."

"Why? What is the purpose of you willingly sharing an ability with a Deltrean leader?"

"Aren't you the one who always insists we try something different? I'm asking this of you because I'm willing to commit to... to giving *different* a chance. Look at this as an opportunity."

"There's no way you'd look at that card and think: *Hey, maybe I can share this with my family's enemy.*"

"I contemplated it a lot—especially while I was away for the two weeks. I stayed away to find a new solution, but your letter came. You got the timing right, too. Ian placed it in my hands when I accepted the impossibility of finding any other adequate option."

"It's some kind of sacrificial card, isn't it?"

"It's *nothing* like that."

"I don't understand, Altair. Many potential partners were available, such as Roselia or Ian."

"I'm offering to share an ability with you, yet you're suggesting I share it with someone else?

I shrugged. "Once we graduate, it's possible we'll never cross paths, so why are you persistent in possessing it with me? Can't you understand why I suspect your request?"

"Can you at least see the parchment details?"

"Tell it to me straight, Altair. What do you want from me? I can't help but feel you're trying to get me to fall into some sort of trap, and I refuse to fall for it." Perhaps I fell for it the moment I agreed to the chess game.

"It'll be beneficial for us *both.*"

"See, that's where you lose me. Never in your life have you wanted something that could benefit *me.*"

"You're right."

"So, what's different now, Altair?"

"We are."

I shook my head. "You're flaunting the fact the card is in your possession."

"Lyra, I need your cooperation in this partnership."

"I'd be a fool to awaken another power *you* can possess."

Altair's eyes lost any lighthearted feelings of amusement and took on a darker expression. "You'd be a fool to refuse."

I smirked.

Finally, I witnessed the real Altair Antares—the cruel man who unleashed his hostility when things didn't go his way.

"You're threatening me, Prince of Follyn." It wasn't a question.

Altair clenched his jaw and glared at me, but unfortunately for him, his glare already held a permanent softness which had settled for me. "Are you going back on your word, Deltrean leader?"

I shook my head. "Your request is *extremely* heavy. I'll read the parchment, but I'd also like to listen to an alternative request. It's only reasonable, Altair."

I sighed, "I *will* grant one as promised."

Altair placed the card back into an inner chest pocket of his shirt— away from sight. "This card requires mutual passion. This will only work with you."

Did he know my feelings? Did he see the chance to trap me, just as I planned to do with him? I hoped my expression didn't show my anxiety.

I shook my head, and I attempted to disregard the disappointment in his eyes. Instead, my mind fixated on the vivid memories of the painful moments Altair inflicted on me, both in my previous life and during my childhood. As the memories rushed back, a familiar hatred filled my soul once again.

Regardless, I willed my eyes to return to normal.

No longer in attack mode, I watched as Benjamin refused to return to the hidden confines of the bracelet charm. The little bunny darted around my legs before settling down next to my right foot. Maybe, The Magician intended to console me.

"You've gotten the wrong idea. I could *never* love you, Altair. Therefore, I cannot meet the demands of The Lovers, so please give me a second reasonable option for my loss. Write it in the notebook. Considering I'd like to avoid more misunderstandings, after I fulfill your request, we will never speak again."

I turned to leave, but he grabbed my arm.

"Do you mean that?" The familiar conflict settled in his eyes, tinged with a hint of hurt. As much as I wanted to lie to him—as much as I needed to distract him from my true feelings—I evaded his question.

"I'm done listening to your mockery, Altair. Let me go."

"Please, just... hear me out."

Altair sighed, contemplating his next words for a minute. "Cards are complicated. I don't think it has to be a passionate *love*. You know, I'm just not capable of that emotion, but I can feel the opposite— something we've both felt strongly for each other. It's been ingrained into us by our families since we were born, and it's rooted deep in our minds."

He was right. I once harbored strong hatred for the man. Altair Antares embodied mischief as a boy and cruelty as a man. He would grow capable of creating chaos, committing murder, and causing numerous injustices in his quest for excessive power. His palpable wickedness caused me to doubt if goodness could ever reside within him.

He continued, "Look, I wouldn't want to possess an ability with a Deltrean leader if I had any other choice. The risk is the same for both of us, but it's our only loophole. We can take advantage of the rooted hate in our hearts to awaken it, but it must be soon."

"Why? Is it almost time to pass it on to another member of your family?"

It was only a guess, but his conflicted expression made me think I might be right.

"Be straight with me, Altair," I warned.

"I... thrive on the hate in my heart, but you-" he paused. "You're making it difficult for me to hold on to it."

A warmth spread across my cheeks, but I did my best to ignore it. Altair's words caused the sickly sweetness to run through my body—the addicting, venomous explosion I wanted to distance myself from.

"Well," I licked my lips. "Possessing the card may be ineffective if your hatred is gone."

"Like you... I don't think I lack it. I remember everything you and yours stand for, and I know it's *there*."

Hearing it stung, but in a sense, he spoke the truth. Perhaps a part of me felt the same, yet Altair's request for assistance showed the urgency of the situation and made me question his trust in me. If he intended to lead me into a trap, Altair's potential deception would be a major blow in my internal battle.

For now, I knew two things. One, I wouldn't agree with anything until he showed me the parchment. Second, I wanted to give him a bit of a waiting period, but if Altair spoke the truth, how long could I keep him waiting?

"You haven't given me a concrete reason to consider it." Conflict seized me. Paranoia grasped my mind. I got what I initially wanted, but things *changed*. My feelings shifted.

An immense sense of anxiety took hold of me, realizing how this partnership could affect my heart.

Altair gave a single, firm nod. "First, let's go through the parchment."

Altair took a piece of parchment and placed the card in the center after removing it from his shirt pocket. Luminescent details appeared along with the illustration of the card's circle.

I read through it carefully, hoping I wouldn't be some kind of sacrifice. Instead, what I found set my heart racing.

I read the text aloud:

"'When The Lovers doth behold a potent and prosperous union 'twixt two souls whose hearts are deeply entwined, it shall make itself known. The Lovers grant their favor only unto those pairs whose ardor burneth with fierce passion.'"

I looked up at Altair, noticing his stare on me. "Has it made itself known?"

He shook his head. "I haven't figured that out yet."

"Hmm..." I continued reading. "The ritual requires a blank parchment and two rings. One for each of the possessors. To top it off, we must seal our partnership with... a kiss during the ritual." I scoffed. "This card is odd."

"Most of them are, in a way." Altair glanced at Benjamin.

"It says here the kiss will only awaken the card. While it will see us at its masters, its power will only be revealed with–" I took a quick breath before I summarized the text which appeared in the parchment.

"...With the unification of its masters' minds, bodies, and hearts, The Lovers shall unleash their full strength and power."

This one contained more text than previous cards. Perhaps it was because it required a partnership.

"Not only that, but 'This card's power doth require careful nurturing, lest its vigor be spent and its masters sorely affected by its lack of essence.'" Altair finished reading the text.

This card followed a process. Even after awakening, it required steps to unleash its full potential, and those steps proved less than ideal.

"Altair, I don't think *hatred* even qualifies," I shook my head.

"We can stop after the first kiss. No need to go further. Any power we can gain from it puts us at an advantage, and we don't have to worry about anyone else possessing it. It will be ours... until death."

I nodded as I stared into the emptiness of Altair's room with a blank expression. "You want to trap me within the confines of... marriage, basically."

He continued, "Think about it, Lyra. Are you sure you would rather I have this ability with someone else? Or would you like to give it a shot and manipulate it with me?"

"It's much more than manipulating an ability, Altair. It's a strict bond which will follow us until death. You cannot outsmart the cards. Listen to the materials. Listen to the requirements. This is literally a marriage directed by a powerful, supernatural creature. Unlike any family arrangements or our world's laws, this thing is irreversible."

"Well, Lyra, marriage is only a formality for families like us. Wouldn't this unification be beneficial to us? Can't we do something more solid than our families have ever done?"

I shook my head. "No, it's a life sentence."

I pointed to another detail on the parchment. "For most of the cards, rest is required in order to recharge energy, but physical intimacy is the way to energize *this* ability. Marriage *and* physical intimacy? Between *us*? Then look!"

I quoted another detail aloud, "'To discern their compatibility, the lovers must partake in physical intimacy within the textual presence of this card.'"

I shook my head, "I can't, Altair."

"What are you afraid of, Lyra?"

"I don't want to share physical intimacy with just anyone."

Altair chuckled, "Is that how you see me, Lyra? I'm just anyone?"

"Worse. You're the Prince of Follyn." I raised an eyebrow.

Altair clenched his jaw. "Lyra, if you read the parchment, it says nothing about sex—just physical intimacy. Also, I can respect you waiting for your *special someone*, and we can figure something out when the time comes."

"Being tied down with something powerful and supernatural places an impediment on the chance of receiving the special someone in my life when he makes his appearance."

Altair's jaw remained tense as his gaze fixated on me, his expression unreadable. Feeling the weight of his gaze in our silence, I wondered if he had something to say.

"What?" I asked.

He shook his head as if I had disrupted his thoughts. "Nothing."

"What?" I asked, again.

Altair shook his head, "You said 'when he makes his appearance,' so I'm assuming no one's made one yet?"

I blushed. It bothered me how I only thought of saying *yes* as his face took over my mind.

With a sigh, I looked away from his eyes and gave him a vague response, "No."

Altair nodded, "I see."

Then, he reached out his hand. "We could keep any physical contact to a minimum."

I stared at his hand dubiously. "What are you doing?"

"Hold my hand."

I raised an eyebrow and gave him a suspicious look, but I complied.

I loved how the touch of his hand gave me a sweet, jittery feeling in the pit of my stomach, but for that same reason, I hated what it did to me.

A thin, glowing, silver string appeared from Altair's chest and connected itself to the center of mine.

I gasped.

Altair and I exchanged surprised glances, and I withdrew my hand from his.

The sight was familiar, *too familiar*. That shimmering silver string was the last thing I saw when I died.

Dread filled my face, and my heart raced with fear and anxiety at such a picturesque reminder.

"That... has never happened before." Altair's low words seemed to slip from his lips without his consent.

I remained silent.

An overwhelming number of thoughts filled my mind. The weight of a burdening anxiety settled on my soul, entwining with the fear of falling into a trap concocted by the cruel Altair I remembered.

"Lyra?" His concerned tone made me realize he noticed a change in my demeanor.

I shook my head, attempting to appear as normal as possible, but sweat formed in my temples. Uncontrollable shakes threatened to take over my body, but I willed them to calm down.

I turned my back to Altair and walked around the room to hide any involuntary movements with my busy motions.

"Lyra, talk to me."

Ironically, Altair's soothing voice of concern kept me calm.

I couldn't understand my feelings.

I walked to his bookshelf and pretended to be distracted by the many books there.

In our past lives, Altair married Syrena to gain Aquaenterra's alliance. He probably never possessed The Lovers back then because the illuminating silver string reacted with me when he slipped his sword into my heart.

My thoughts became interrupted when I sensed Altair grow closer to me. He stood behind me, but I didn't turn to face him.

"I know what I ask for in unreasonable, and for that, I apologize. You're right to feel the way you do. I should not have asked. We can forget about the deal." His tone was low, remorseful.

If only he could have been mean.

I wanted the cruel Altair to push me away from my conflicted thoughts and emotions. The horrid devil, Altair Antares, did not make it easy for me to despise, deceive, and ruin him.

"What's my second option?" I kept my attention on the titles of his books.

"...Don't stop talking to me."

The request didn't contain the weight of a permanent commitment, but it was a commitment, nonetheless.

"Once we graduate from Crescencia, keeping up with that request might be as difficult as keeping up with the first one," I said.

Altair remained silent, but I felt his gaze on my back.

I continued, "You've tried awakening The Lovers with someone else?"

"Yes."

"Ian?" I asked in a teasing tone.

"Roselia."

This irked me.

I turned to face him, and as I suspected, he stood dangerously close to me. The desire to indulge in the emotions he stirred dominated my fears. My heart longed to surrender to everything he offered.

At some point, I realized a convergence of profound animosity within me. It made me passionate and fueled my ambitions, and I believed it did the same for him. However, in the present moment, if any hatred persisted, I struggled to recognize it.

So, why did The Lovers react to us? Was it passionate, rooted hatred on his part, and... something else... in mine?

"I'm sure your family expects you to fail in awakening it," I said.

Altair said nothing.

"Why me?" I asked.

"If it works with you, it will have the potential to heal the damage and prejudice between our families and our people."

"I thought you believed that was impossible because of the rooted hatred between you and me—a growing seed which has already caused *too much* damage."

"Well, that's true, too. A dark seed was planted and nurtured within us, and it continues to exist. We keep questioning and doubting each other. But Lyra, your ideas have influenced me a bit. Maybe, given the chance, we could transform that dark seed into something better, or cut it off while it's still young and nurture a new, healthy one together."

Altair scratched his head. "I don't know. I mean, now that we know each other, it seems we have better options for our future."

The uncertainty of that new future made me nervous.

I *knew* the future.

I witnessed the merciless, evil man Altair grew up to be. I mourned the end of everyone and everything I loved. The pain, hopelessness, and despair of my loss and failure washed over me. My heart ached with the weight of defeat.

I knew better.

Therefore, my reason, my resolve, my survival, and my new life would not let me give into this idea of a new future so easily. I held back, even though a bigger part of me didn't want to.

Altair continued, "If we don't start *something*, we'll be stuck in a cycle of uncertainty, prejudice, and hate."

"So, what? Suddenly—you changed your mind? Altair, isn't that a little weird?"

"You're right. If I were in your shoes, I'd probably think the same, but... you inspired me."

I searched his eyes for insincerity, but found nothing. Instead, I faced those eyes of longing and conflict.

"When must you pass the card to another family member?"

"Once summer ends, I'll must pass it on to one of my sisters."

"Why not your parents?"

Altair laughed through his nose. "While they are partners in politics, they lack passion for each other. No matter what they tried, the card refused to respond."

"That's... sad."

"Ironic, isn't it? We're meant to be enemies, yet we received a response with a single touch of hands. That has to mean something."

"A perilous situation for us both, wouldn't you say?"

"What are you afraid of, Lyra?"

"You. I'm terrified of you."

Altair flinched.

"I don't mean the Altair with secret abilities. I don't even mean the part of you that isn't human."

"Then?"

"I'm afraid of your hatred. I am fearful of where it'll lead you. I am terrified of what it'll do to you. It scares me to think of the impact it will have on my family and me. I'm frightened. I'm eminently frightened of forming a connection with you that will make me realize you're the best friend of my *life*, only to turn around and realize I'm the only fool who-"

Altair cut me off by placing his hands on my cheeks. As the card lay in the open and we touched in its presence, the string-link between Altair's chest and mine became visible once again.

"I'm afraid of the same things, Lyra. You don't think I've questioned it, too? What am I supposed to do with the rest of my Deltrean hatred when their princess has become my weakness?"

I inhaled sharply. "Do you have any idea what you're implying, Altair?"

In silence, Altair and I shared a meaningful connection through our eyes. Even then, I anticipated his next words, but they never came.

He left me to wonder.

He left me to analyze the conflicted longing in his eyes.

He left me to overthink his words.

He left me to crave his touch and the mysterious taste of his lips, but worse than any of that, his words dissolved my resolve in distancing myself.

Wonder sparked curiosity and curiosity ignited desire.

Altair's thumb traveled to caress my slightly parted lips.

Perhaps my eyes revealed it. Perhaps my demeanor conveyed it, but I surrendered to the sweetness of his touch and his yearning gaze, and Altair drew closer.

The gentle nudging of our noses sent a delicate shiver through me. Just as I felt Altair's breath against my lips, I sensed his hesitation—a momentary pause filled with unspoken desires and a search for the remnants of our restraint.

Unable to resist the overwhelming temptation, Altair closed the distance between us and gently pressed his velvety lips against mine. The touch sent a rush of warmth through my body, leaving me longing for more.

Our kiss began with a gentle, wary brush of our lips. As Altair's hand slid to my waist, the warmth of his touch seeped through my dress. His other hand found the back of my neck, fingers lightly grazing my skin. In response, I eagerly reciprocated, gripping the back of his head, my fingers intertwining with his silky black hair. My other hand pressed against his torso, fingertips exploring the lines of his chest.

Altair's kiss overwhelmed me, a mix of pleasure and fear. If I didn't pull back, I risked becoming addicted to the sweetness of his lips, the lingering taste of him, the intoxicating euphoria, and the blissful feeling of our possessive embrace. So, I broke away, but before I moved more than a few inches, he closed the distance and resumed our passionate connection. The sensation threatened to consume my heart, soul, and reason.

Our intermingling breaths filled the air.

We tested each other—our limits, our hesitation.

I nibbled on his bottom lip. The small, silent declaration communicated a yearning desire to surpass the realm of gentleness, which pulled us into an insatiable, persistent, and unforgettable kiss.

Seven of Pentacles

Xander caught up with me the moment I stepped off the university grounds.

"I saw you come out of the dormitories."

I smiled, but I didn't turn to face him. "Nice to see you've recovered, too, Xander."

"Alphonse told your parents and I that you both stayed with a girl named Syrena in the dormitories."

I figured my father didn't look for me because either my brother or Xander covered for me.

I sighed in relief. "That's right. You all had nothing to worry about."

"Then, why did he arrive home before you?"

"Girl-time. And the drinks knocked me out. My body and my head still have a dull ache. Weren't you affected?"

Xander ignored my rambling. "I investigated, Lyra. That girl does not reside in the university's dorms."

Shame, I was certain she lived in a dorm, but then, where did my brother stay?

Xander continued, "I found out Altair Antares lives in a dorm. In fact, Follyneans took most of the dorms."

"That's because Follyn Castle is far, very far. It's up in some mountains."

"I don't have time for games, Lyra. Your father asked-"

"He asked you to monitor me, and you have to report what you found out. So, you found out I wasn't with Syrena, yet you waited for me instead of reporting it to my father. Why?"

"I wanted your explanation. Lyra, if he finds out about this, he's going to take you out of school. Is that what you want?"

"Isn't it what you want, too, Xander? I seem to be troublesome lately."

When he didn't respond, I turned to check if he still followed me, but he had vanished.

I felt bad. He did a lot for us, but I needed to move without being questioned.

I sighed into the empty air. "I'm sorry, Xander. I really am. I just need you to trust me a bit."

I hoped he heard my apology.

*****

Upon returning home, I struggled to breathe.

I faced my parents and repeated the same lie I told Xander. Reluctance clouded their faces, especially my mother's, but whatever I said must have matched what Xander and Alphonse told them because they stopped asking questions.

When I arrived at my room, I laid down with my cluster of conflicted emotions and thoughts.

Just as I closed my eyes to shut the world away, my brother barged in.

"Get out," I said.

His eager expression hinted at a readiness for gossip. "Lyra, what happened? What did Mother and Father tell you?"

"You literally left me with Antares in order to go with Syrena, and you want to talk?" I hissed.

My heart embraced my brother's actions and sincerely thanked him, while my sense of reason condemned them and mentally cursed him.

I held my aching head with both hands and groaned.

"It went that bad with the devil, huh?"

I threw a pillow in his direction. "Out."

"What? I just brought you some strawberries, damn."

I rolled my eyes. Sure enough, he still held out the little bowl of strawberries towards me.

I knew he used the little bowl of strawberries as bribery. He wanted to be in my room, and he wanted information. My brother set the bowl down on my nightstand. As if I spoke to the wall, Alphonse stayed in my room and started touching all my little decorations.

"Can you not... touch my things?"

"You know, I covered for you," he started eating the strawberries he claimed to have brought for me.

I shrugged. "Yeah, Xander warned me about what you said. My story matched yours when father asked."

"Were you with Antares this whole time?" My brother whispered.

I nodded.

My brother shook his head, his expression showing he thought I did something daring. "I have no idea what you're doing hanging out with that guy, but I'm just going to trust you know what you're doing."

"Were you also with Syrena all night?"

My brother shrugged. "Not really. She helped me sober up—stayed with me, kept me hydrated, gave me snacks she bought at the festival."

"Where?"

"We found an unlocked classroom."

I raised an eyebrow.

Alphonse smiled sheepishly as he rolled his eyes. "Calm down. It was nothing like that. You're worse. You stayed in the devil's dorm."

My eyes widened. "How do you know?"

"Xander told me. He was furious and debated on whether to confront him or tell our father, but I talked him out of it. I reminded him to trust you."

"What did he say?"

"He trusts *you*. He doesn't trust Altair Antares."

"Well, that's... a given. Did you say anything to Syrena? Anything you shouldn't have?"

"Well, she asked what you and I were to each other."

I covered my mouth with my hands. "Tell me you didn't say anything unnecessary."

"Even in that state, I wouldn't say anything unnecessary."

"You publicly yelled you were the next Deltrean ruler while you were still with me. Don't come telling me-"

"Are you serious? No, I didn't." His expression became thoughtful.

I nodded emphatically, hoping he would admit his wrongs.

"Oh," from the looks of his expression, Alphonse remembered something. "No wonder Syrena asked me what I meant when I said that."

"And what did you tell her?"

"I told her I was just spewing nonsense to annoy Antares."

"What did she say?"

"She asked why I cared so much. I told her you were like a sister to me, and I provoked Antares to test his intentions toward you since... well, you know, family enemies and such."

I frowned. "She used to care, too. I think."

"She does. She said she feels like she's been a terrible friend and should've gotten you to come with us. But I told her Antares wouldn't have allowed it, and he would have won because I was in such a dependent state."

"You're a terrible brother."

"You think so? Damn, I thought I did pretty good today. Seeing as how we're still enrolled in school, and father didn't start a war."

Alphonse popped another strawberry into his mouth. He continued, "You know, I actually remember little of how we arrived back at Crescencia. One moment we were running in the forest, and the next, I was in the dark, empty classroom with Syrena."

"Hmm. Are you sure you said nothing else to her?"

Alphonse nodded. Then, he turned to accuse me, "*You* left with Antares! Are you sure *you* didn't say or do anything stupid?"

"I wasn't as bad as you were. I remember everything. Do you think she bought it? That you see me as your sister?"

"I said it was disturbing for both of us when people got excited about these stupid ideas involving you and me."

"How did she react?"

He shrugged. "She smiled."

I groaned.

Since Syrena faced the same situation as my brother, I feared she might deduce he was a hidden Deltrean prince. If the thought crossed her mind, I hoped she would stay silent.

However, if she started speculating about his secret, I wouldn't just stand by and feign ignorance. After all, I still held *her* secret in my hands.

"Did she ask why you were drunk?" I asked.

"Yeah. I told her I had one too many while fighting with a piano. She just laughed."

My fingers squeezed the ache at the top of my head. "I swear, you can never drink again. You talk too much."

"It's fine. She knows I was just drunk spewing."

I said nothing and focused on massaging the dull ache in my head that grew with my conversation with my brother.

He continued, "She also said Antares had a reputation for being cruel, similar to the King and Queen of Follyn."

I nodded. "We all know this."

"Then, why does it seem like you're forgetting?"

The image of Altair sliding his sword through my heart flashed across my mind. "I haven't forgotten."

I constantly forced myself to remember.

"Syrena mentioned that Antares hid the darkest part of himself when he was outside Follyn, but lately, he seemed softer. She noticed a gentleness in him she had never seen before. He had also been absent often, but recently, he's attended school every day."

I scoffed. "Of course, he'd be coming to school every day. School is intriguing. The fragile Princess of Deltrea who kept herself hidden in fear and weakness is back. His presence at school gives him the opportunity to gain as much insight as he can."

"Yes, we thought that could be a reason, but Syrena also believes Antares softened because you actually made his dead, rotten heart beat fast enough to awaken it with life."

"Well, what do you think?"

"Are you hoping Syrena may be right?" My brother looked serious.

I shook my head. "It'd be ideal. If I can secure his heart, I'd have him in the palm of my hand, don't you think?"

"And you don't think he's trying to do that to *you?*"

I pursed my lips. "Yeah, I guess Altair and I are already battling it out in our own way, huh?"

"That's a tough battle. If you get too caught up in it, you're the one who'll end up hurt."

"You have no faith in me, Alphie."

"It's not that. You have a kind heart, and he doesn't. I'm worried that you'll show genuine care, if you haven't already, and he's going to destroy your feelings."

I smiled at my brother. "You're always the one who has to remind me to not worry about you, but this time, it's me who's laid quite the burden on your shoulders."

"I mean, you stayed with Antares all night."

I sighed, "Yes."

"Why did you stay? Did he hold you hostage or something?"

"No."

"Yeah, I figured he didn't." Alphonse paused. "I've been kind of afraid to ask because I think I know what the answer is going to be."

"Then don't ask."

"You don't have feelings for the Prince of Follyn, do you?" He still asked.

I shook my head, unable to meet my brother's eyes. His concerned tone and probing questions filled me with guilt.

"Alright, well, just be careful. I mean, Syrena and I agree he seems interested in you, but he may be up to something."

"There's no need to worry, brother. I might be up to the same thing he's up to."

If Altair and I weren't mortal enemies, if he hadn't killed me in our past lives, and if we didn't hold such prejudice against each other, could we have been more than friends?

If we built a simple, loving relationship, could we truly depend on one another? Would we have been fiercely loyal to each other? I wondered.

The new week held new challenges and new realities to face—including the kiss.

Then, there was...

The Lovers.

*****

I lay in bed, haunted and conflicted by my shifting emotions, actions, and reality. My night with Altair looped through my mind, a constant reminder of my forbidden act in the history of Follyn and Deltrea. All odds stood against my feelings—including my reasoning, and maybe even Altair—if he turned out to be as malicious as I remembered.

Altair and I kissed, and I couldn't shake the sensation or the addictive fluttering in my body. As I feared, I fell into an inescapable hole. Satisfying my curiosity only left me yearning for more. I hoped the weekend would pass quickly just so I could see Altair again.

I sighed at my hopelessness.

If we united because of The Lovers, I risked plunging into an abyss of infatuation with Altair. However, I couldn't imagine any other favorable outcome. Another ability would be on my side, and by partnering with Altair, I could monitor him closely.

Three rapid taps on my window interrupted the constant clash of conflicting thoughts conquering my overthinking mind. When I drowsily opened my eyes, the taps stopped. Curious, I drew my curtains to find a raven resting on my balcony railing. Its striking golden eyes fixed on me as I came into view, dazzling me with their intensity.

I looked around my room until my eyes landed on the bowl of unfinished strawberries my brother left.

I grabbed a clean, unbitten strawberry from the bowl. Watching the bird, I cracked my window and placed the fruit outside.

A few seconds after I closed my window, the raven hopped toward the treat, trapping it in its beak before flying away.

"I guess you were hungry," I said aloud.

I went to bed that night and thought little of it—until the bird returned the next night and tapped on my window as it waited for me to draw my curtains.

The bell rang, and right on cue, Altair Antares waltzed in. He showed little concern for his university uniform and how he wore it, or maybe he knew his loose tie and untucked shirt still projected a sharp appearance.

I wished he had grown unattractive—a reflection of the vile monster he revealed himself to be in our past lives. Things would have been much easier for me.

Altair's personality didn't repel me. He pursued his goals with conviction, believing in their righteousness—that's where the trouble lay. Political conflicts always boiled down to this.

Altair's charm and his unexpected kindness drew me in, making my attraction to him inevitable. This attraction was a nuisance, obstructing my ability to think with clarity, and diverting me from my goals, but it sparked a sense of hope for a genuine union, making my con feel more like a reality than I had imagined.

Then, I remembered his potential, and I recalled him thrusting his sword through my chest, but my hatred lacked the same intensity. The heavy, abhorrent emotions which once fueled my restless heart belonged to a devil distinct from the Altair Antares standing before me. Painting him as an evil being came easily before I knew him. Understanding him, interacting with him, and seeing him every day complicated everything.

I hated how the few times he smiled, his straight white teeth brightened the room. I loathed his deceitful, conniving smirk. I detested his glare, and the fire ignited inside it. Honestly, he portrayed a cunning, grotesque piece of-

"Good morning to you, too." His voice interrupted my lovely thoughts of him.

"What's got you glaring at me so early?" he asked as he took his seat by the window—right next to me. His tone carried a sense of mockery.

"Seeing your face so early is what puts me in this mood," I muttered.

In response, Altair, like a child, took my journal. He grabbed it with his right hand and scooted it to his far left, the hand furthest from me. A smirk formed on his face.

I responded by taking his pen. A smirk formed on my face, too.

To retaliate, he flipped through the pages of my journal, but nothing occupied the space except the notes he and I exchanged.

*****

I absentmindedly tapped Altair's pen in my left hand.

Suddenly, his large hand came over mine, but he didn't take the pen from me. He gripped my hand and gently caressed my knuckles with his fingers. As if giving me the chance to slip away, he loosened his grip, but I didn't move my hand.

These sweet attacks danced on my heartstrings as a rosy hue pained my cheeks. I took a deep breath, attempting to resist their effect. I had two choices: retreat to shield my heart or mirror his movements and watch his reaction unfold.

Opting for the latter, I played along, hoping to unravel his resolve just as he dismantled mine. My fingers traced delicate patterns over his, and my cheeks burned with a deeper crimson. I couldn't muster the courage to meet his gaze.

Altair sighed deeply.

Our hands loosened and explored each other's touch, causing the pen to slip and fall to the floor.

The sharp impact jolted me back to reality, but when I tried to pull away, Altair clasped my hand and intertwined his fingers with mine.

Our hands stayed locked, savoring the sensation of each other's skin, lost in the tender intimacy of the moment.

*****

"Lyra!" Robin approached Altair and me. "I know it's still about four weeks away, but do you have any plans for the Friday before winter break?"

"Dr. Diestro's final is that day, isn't it?" I asked.

Robin nodded. "After school, I mean."

Altair shuffled through his things behind me. Rather than his usual habit of leaving class promptly, he lingered, possibly cavesdropping.

"Do you have something in mind? I'll follow your plans, my friend," I smiled.

"Well, we could go to a café together. Then, I could walk you to the Deltrean entrance."

Robin seemed nervous and sheepish. This might have been his way of asking me on a date.

Altair cleared his throat behind me. "Just wanted to remind you, Lyra, we agreed to meet that day after school." He waved at me, holding my journal to imply he was taking it.

Before I could protest, he glanced at Robin and gave him a cocky nod. Robin and I watched as Altair walked out of the classroom with a smirk on his face.

Robin's concerned, curious tone broke the silence. "You had plans with Antares, Lyra?"

"Right. Ah, I think so. I mean, we mentioned it some time ago. Not only did I forget about it, but he never brought it up again."

"That's weird. You all argue more than you agree. Is he forcing you?"

"No, we've been trying to communicate and talk things out, I guess. We're working on it."

"Working on what?"

"Er, an acquaintanceship? Or something. I don't know, to be honest with you. Whatever *it* is—I mean, we have to start somewhere, you know?"

"That's... unheard of."

"Modern times, am I right?" I offered an uncomfortable grin, doing my best to sound convincing, but impromptu lying wasn't my forte.

"That's not what I mean, Lyra. Antares has a reputation for cruelty. Are you sure he's not toying with you?"

I sighed, and I didn't meet his eyes. I couldn't. "You know, I want to have faith in a positive future."

Robin gave me a questioning look. "Is that all it is?"

"What do you mean?"

"Well, he looks like he's interested in you, and it looks like you might be reciprocating that interest, but Lyra, we can't trust his intentions."

I gave Robin a reassuring smile and shook my head. "You may not trust his intentions, but do you trust me?"

"Of course, I do."

"I'll be okay, Robin. At least, have a little faith in my judgements, please?"

He nodded.

As we made our way out of the classroom, we froze when we noticed Altair leaning against the wall beside the open door, waiting. His eyes focused on my journal, which he held open in his right hand, and a beautiful, hateful smirk was plastered across his face.

At our presence, Altair shut the book and looked at me with his smirk.

"I forgot to hand this back to you," he said, passing me my journal.

"Thanks."

Robin gave a nod in our direction and walked away.

"You took my journal on purpose," I hissed.

Altair grinned and whispered into my ear, "You're a terrible liar, little Lyra."

"What was the purpose of leaving the classroom if you were just going to eavesdrop openly?"

"I wanted to see what he'd say the moment he believed I was out of earshot."

I shook my head as I faced his victorious grin.

"What was the purpose of that?"

Altair shrugged. "I wanted to put Ravoux in an uncomfortable situation."

I sighed as I walked away.

"Did you actually want to go around with that guy?" Altair followed behind me.

"Does it matter? The date you and I *apparently* have has overwritten any potential plans."

The familiar conflicted, contemplative expression arrested Altair's face, but he said nothing as he continued to follow behind me.

"A rather interesting, indirect manner of asking someone out, Altair."

I raised my eyes to meet his gaze, expecting to encounter his smirk. Instead, I met his intense, penetrating stare, as if he never looked away from me for a moment. My heart fluttered, causing a skipped beat.

I averted my gaze.

To conceal my flushed cheeks, I glanced downward. The ambience enveloped me in a mix of anticipation and Altair's faint scent of pine.

Determined to escape the stifling silence, I asked, "I'm guessing you have a particular plan or idea?"

As if my question didn't register in his mind, he asked, "Have you thought about it?"

He didn't need to mention our partnership with The Lovers for me to understand his question.

"I have." To distract myself from everything that happened that night, I avoided remembering the sensations—being encased in his arms, the possessive way he held me, his intoxicating lips.

Altair nodded, as if predicting my answer. His disheartened eyes revealed what he thought I would say.

I continued, "I've been thinking. It's not a bad idea for people to have major speculations about you and me right before winter break."

"Why?"

I shrugged. "We might gain the support of our generation. Think about it. If we both show affection for one another but pretend to hide it, people will sympathize when it's time to bring our union up to our families."

Altair looked at me with a puzzled expression, but the hint of hope in his eyes revealed he understood my answer.

"What are you saying?"

"I'm accepting the union. It could symbolize a new beginning for both of us and those we lead. It'll help if we have classmates support our union instead of our opposition."

I shrugged, "And technically, we've already started some commotions. You and I seem to be around each other more often than not."

Altair appeared taken aback. He seemed to process my words. "Wait. Lyra, are you sure?"

"I am."

Altair remained speechless—like a broken clock that needed fixing to tick again.

I continued talking, pretending to be nonchalant about my decision, "So, I think... after our classes, we should walk to one of the most isolated tables at Spades Café."

"It's one of the least busy cafes, though."

"Exactly. It's secluded enough to make it seem like we don't want to be seen, but it has enough eyes to cause rumors. For lunch, let's stick to being with our friend groups—It'll give the expression we're trying to keep our... relationship... a secret."

"Agreed, but in-between classes, let's walk near each other and disappear together."

My heart leaped into my throat. "Where would we go?"

With the knowing look Altair directed at me, I knew he wanted us to disappear into his dorm room.

"Do you know how crazy Crescencia would go if I were seen going into your dorm room every day? We can't even say we're working on a project anymore."

Not to mention Xander.

I shook my head and continued, "That corner behind the library—in the festival grounds that's quite secluded."

It was my little sanctuary at school when I waited for Altair's return after his two-week absence.

"And Altair, we'll head to class separately. Again, we're portraying two lovers who're clumsily hiding their secret."

"You seem to have thought it through," he said.

"I did. I even contemplated the negatives of it."

"What would those be...?"

"My parents. With word spreading, we'll face vehement opposition."

"*Our* parents," he corrected. "It's a union that could cause a war. I will not lie to you, Lyra. My family might seek to eliminate you when they find out we're together."

"Haven't they been seeking that already?"

Shame flickered through Altair's expression for a second before he composed himself.

"I'm sure your father will actively seek the same thing."

I pursed my lips. "My father is more civil than that."

"*Your* father? Civil?"

"Yes. Why the tone?"

Altair shook his head. "If anything, that guy will personally try to sever my head."

"Hey," I returned his tone. "We're different from your family and *you*."

He clenched his jaw. A disheartening look flashed through his eyes again, making me feel guilty, but I needed to create a boundary in the relationship. His presence already affected my heart.

I continued, "Remember, if we're to get allies, we have to *fool* everybody into thinking we're in love."

I meant for my words to hit him like venom-filled spit out of a snake's teeth. I wanted to imply I knew better. Like him, a man incapable of love, I felt no such emotion for him, either. We shared attraction, and if anything existed beyond that in his world, it only reached lust and infatuation. I could not put myself at risk for so little in return, as it would only lead me to heartache and failure.

Altair frowned in response. Slight dejection crossed his face, but my guilt vanished with his next words.

"You're terrible at pretense, little Lyra. You wear your authentic expressions on your face."

I averted my gaze and attempted to conceal my blushing face. His captivating hand, adorned with an elegant obsidian ring, interrupted my motion and filled my line of vision.

Altair lifted my chin.

The rosy hue grew more dominant across my cheeks, betraying my excitement. He didn't have his usual mischievous smirk. Instead, he gave me a serious expression that observed me deeply, making me positively nervous.

Altair's hand shifted from my chin towards one of my blushed cheeks. I turned away from his grasp, but he caught my face with his free hand, trapping it between his hands.

I wrapped his hands around mine and softly pushed them away.

Letting out a deep sigh, I tried to mask my genuine emotions with an unaffected demeanor. "You must've missed me immensely if you can't keep your gaze or your hands off me."

"Who misses who?" He paused. "You're the one who wrote a letter to me during my absence."

Altair looked away, contemplating something—possibly fighting an internal struggle.

He had warned me that a guy like him wasn't capable of loving anyone, but when he acted like that, he wavered my firm resolve and feelings for him.

Page of Wands

Spades Café saw more customers the week after we began frequenting it, and just as we planned, rumors spread.

"Looks like we need to find a new café spot," Altair spoke loud enough for those nearby to hear, yet low enough to seem like he wanted to keep it private.

I smiled. "There's nothing wrong with the crowd, Altair. We're *friends*."

Of course, the unexpected friendship label between the Princess of Deltrea and the Prince of Follyn caused quite the commotion.

I cast my eyes down and smiled sheepishly. Our performance aimed to impress the audience, yet I couldn't help but feel genuinely shy.

Giggles, gasps, and whispers about Altair and me carried over from the nearest table, so we eyed each other in amused victory.

Our smiles held mischief as we indulged in our drinks and sweets as usual. We didn't have to say much to each other. We learned to communicate through our eyes and expressions alone. I found it comical—especially when we got constant glances from whispering groups of students.

I observed him prepare a ridiculously sweet coffee as I sipped on my chamomile tea. Altair usually ordered dark chocolate cake, but today, he ordered a chocolate cake with chocolate frosting, chocolate cookie garnish, and chocolate chips as sprinkles.

"You eat things ridiculously sweet... for the cruel Prince of Follyn," I muttered.

Altair clenched his jaw but moved closer to ensure his next words were only for me to hear.

"You have quite the venomous tongue, little Lyra, but if you must know, sugar is as addicting as blood, and the cravings and withdrawal symptoms are just as intense."

"Is that so?" I raised an eyebrow.

Altair laughed heartily. I witnessed this beautiful, bright sight more often than not at this point—I once thought him incapable of laughter.

I glanced around the café and noticed other customers sharing my awe; they quieted down in astonishment and curiosity.

"No," he finally said between laughs. "Sweets are simply a personal addiction, but there is an adorable purity in your gullible reaction."

I rolled my eyes.

Altair resigned back into his chair, putting enough distance for him to raise his tone and feed the eavesdroppers and the gossipers. "I don't mean it in a bad way, Lyra. You really are a beautiful breath of fresh air."

Some of the fellow students around us forgot to retain their gasps.

I did my best to not glare at Altair. Not only did he perform impressively and make me blush like a fool, but Altair viewing me as gullible took a shot at my pride. The cunning devil got back at me for the sugar comment I made, so he struck at me while fulfilling our purpose of the dates.

*****

The following day, Spades Café reached capacity. Despite the wait-line outside the location, the usual corner table Altair and I often sat at remained unoccupied.

Fellow students eyed Altair and me as we made our way to the back of the line.

"Should we go somewhere else?" he asked, loud enough for some of our audience to hear.

I nodded.

When Altair and I walked far enough from any spectators, he spoke in a low voice beside me, "No matter where we go, we might be followed at this point."

"What if we alternate cafés every day?"

Altair thought about it for a moment. Then, he nodded. "Let's head to Hearts Café today."

I blushed. "Altair, everything they serve at Hearts is for-"

"Couples. We've distracted enough people and got them to head to Spades. Hearts shouldn't be crowded, but there should be just enough spectators to cause more of a commotion."

"Shouldn't we pretend to avoid Hearts like the plague? Remember, we're being clumsy about hiding our... relationship."

"What if we do both?"

I eyed him dubiously.

He continued, "Think about all the rumors that have spread. We've had an abundance of positive reactions."

I nodded. "Right, much more than I thought we'd have."

"We must feed that, Lyra. We can go to Hearts today, and once our trip to Hearts spreads, we avoid it. People are watchful. They'll notice us avoiding it. Those who spread the excitement will feel guilty that we have to hide. They'll root for us."

It was a simple plan, one that required a lot of patience and nurturing. It could definitely benefit us. We might even gain sympathy for hiding our secret.

Everything fell into place exactly as I wanted. Nevertheless, I had the innocent role to play first. I needed to pretend that guilt was beginning to eat away at me. "I don't know, Altair. Playing with the emotions of our schoolmates, I-"

"If you're agreeing to The Lovers, there's no other way. Unless..."

"Unless?"

Altair shook his head, but I knew what he was going to say. With The Lovers, we were looking at a faux relationship or a real one, but a romantic relationship regardless.

"Okay," I sighed. "I'll follow your lead. Take me to Hearts."

*****

Syrena and Alphonse spent more time together. At first, they observed Altair and me, but my brother didn't pry, and I'm assuming, through his suggestion, Syrena didn't either.

Once the rumors about Altair and me peaked, my brother, Syrena, and Robin could no longer ignore them.

Robin distanced himself. He avoided eye and verbal contact with me, and he no longer joined Alphonse, Syrena, and me at our regular lunch table in Crescencia Dining Hall.

One afternoon, Syrena suggested we take our food to a private space for us to talk. Alphonse raised his eyebrows at me, hinting at the approaching trouble. With a sigh, I collected my things and followed the two of them to a study room.

"So," Syrena began, "A Celestia and an Antares, huh?"

I glanced at my brother, but he looked down.

I sighed. "Exaggerated rumors spread like wildfire."

"Lyra, we're your best friends. Is he asking you to keep whatever you have with him a secret?"

I shook my head. "We *both* agreed to it."

Syrena gasped, and my brother looked at me with fearful surprise. While he acknowledged the rumors' potential truth, I knew he wished for my denial.

"Lyra, what in the world are you thinking?" Alphonse asked.

"You're seeing each other, aren't you?" Syrena asked.

I paced around the room. "I don't know. Something just happened, and we found out we liked to be in each other's company. One thing led to another, and-"

"What do you mean, one thing led to another? How long has this been going on?" Syrena looked astonished.

"Since the night of The Fall Festival, right?" My brother said.

I nodded.

"You're in a relationship with Antares?" My brother's tone reminded me of my father's when he interrogated me and wanted no-nonsense. It made me nervous.

"Well, not exactly. We're *friends*, I think."

"Friends?" Syrena asked.

"It sounds like you don't even know what you all are, Lyra."

"That's why I didn't say anything. I'm sorry."

Alphonse shrugged and crossed his arms in response.

"But," Syrena started. "You like him, right?"

Blushing, my heart leaped at the sudden question that caught me off guard—especially amidst all this make-believe.

I took a breath and slid my thumbs in my hair, running them down until I tucked my hair behind my ears. "I might, yes."

Syrena and Alphonse looked at each other.

"His family is cruel, Lyra, and he's being trained to be just the same." Syrena's tone sounded apologetic.

I shook my head. "He's different from the person everyone believes him to be. He's more complicated than that."

"You have an idea what he's capable of, yet you're entertaining the idea of forming something with this guy?" Disappointment weighed heavily in my brother's voice.

"I know better than anyone *what* he's capable of, but even like that, I think Altair and I owe it to ourselves to try something out. Unless I'm a total fool, and he's obviously toying with me."

Syrena shook her head. "No, I've known for a long time now that he's shown interest in you. I think we've all seen it—even Ian and Roselia."

"You're right, but what if his interest only stems from the fact that she's the Deltrean princess?"

Syrena shrugged. "We can't know for sure, but there is something genuine in the soft way he looks at you. His eyes always seem to look for you—I think I've told you this before."

I nodded. She did, on the day Alphonse first arrived at the academy.

"You know," Syrena eyed my brother and me, "Robin also has an idea as to what's going on between you and Altair."

"I figured," I responded.

"You know he has feelings for you, right? I'm sure he's made it obvious."

I nodded. "Well, I wasn't exactly sure, but I made speculations."

"Look, it's not my place to tell you what to do, but you should talk to him. Tell him what you just told us—for his sake."

Alphonse nodded in agreement. "He's told us he wasn't going to give up on you, Lyra. We're all friends—best friends, so this is something he needs to hear from you."

"Altair and I are just... *fond* of one another."

Syrena shook her head. "I think you mean *attracted*, but I don't know about you two being together. Apart from the obvious—your historical backgrounds and your families—you still fight a lot."

"There is *something* between us, and also, if we don't do this, if we don't end this division between our kingdoms once and for all, who will?"

A mysterious cloud of gray hovered between Altair and me. Sometimes, we got along. Recently, we kissed. More often than not, I looked for him, and I think he reciprocated my actions. We often wrote to each other, so despite being physically apart, we still communicated and maintained a sense of togetherness. We enjoyed each other's company despite how often we argued.

"You are both forming a relationship based on infatuation," Syrena said.

Did infatuation and attraction accurately describe our situation? Did the audience pick up on the unspoken chemistry between Altair and me? The presence of deep-rooted negativity made me question if my feelings could ever grow beyond whatever *this* was.

"Lyra," Syrena voiced her doubts. "You're always so kind, but I question whether Altair shares your genuine intentions for unity."

Knight of Pentacles

I noticed Robin and Alphonse writing notes to each other in one of my classes.

As soon as class ended, I called out to my brother.

Robin walked away with a few words of departure, but he only referred to my brother, not me. I watched his back as he walked away.

"He doesn't even acknowledge my presence anymore," the hurt came out in my voice.

My brother sighed, "Robin's hurt, too. It's difficult to see the girl you like with someone else—especially with—" My brother's eyes motioned to the exit of the classroom. Altair waited for me outside the classroom doors, even when we attended separate classes.

My brother lowered his voice, "I mean, even I think it sucks to see you with Antares."

I mouthed, "Shhh!" at him, but my brother shrugged with a frown. "I don't care. Let him hear."

My doofus brother held the folded paper he and Robin wrote to each other in—he probably planned to shred it to pieces.

As he reached for his backpack, I yanked the paper from his hands. He tried to yank it back at first, but when I ran with it, he didn't chase me. He stood rooted to the ground, giving me a monotonous, annoyed expression.

"Lyra, are you serious?"

"I have to know his thoughts, Alph!"

He shook his head in response. "If you hold any respect for your friendship with him, you'll do the right thing."

My brother walked out and past Altair.

"Is something the matter?" Altair asked as I walked out.

I shook my head. "Nothing to concern yourself with."

"Altair!" Roselia called after him.

He sighed and looked at me as if he sought approval. I raised an eyebrow and gave him a skeptical look.

"Go, but don't be long." I crossed my arms. "I'll wait here."

Altair walked over to Roselia while I opened the note between Robin and my brother.

I hate it. I hate seeing them together.

My brother's handwriting filled the next line, indicating that Robin started the note.

I'm sorry. I know, though. I don't like seeing it either, but what can we do?

I know they only sit together in one class, but in the others, they constantly exchange looks and notes. In the classes we don't share, he's outside waiting for her within seconds. We can't even talk to each other. I can't help but feel she left us for him, even after our group of friends protected her from Altair when she first arrived.

Don't think of it that way. I know Lyra, and she cherishes the friendships she has here. I think she's trying to go above protection and separation. Her heart is noble enough to try mending things with the Follyneans.

She's probably being fooled, and she made it easy for him.

I see why you'd think that. I don't trust Antares, either, and unfortunately, it may be as you say—that Lyra's values made it easy for him, but it's her noble heart I support, you know? I think it's needed in Deltrea.

On the contrary, Alphonse, I think it makes her weak, and if it leads to chaos for Deltrea and a win for Follyn, I wouldn't blame Deltrea's downfall on anyone but her.

My mouth gaped open.

So, that's how Robin perceived me.

I understood his feelings for me, but he lit a flame when he questioned my leadership and Deltrea's strength, attributing it to my actions. If he spewed these negative thoughts about me to others, my friends must have thought the same as him.

A pair of eyes watched my reaction to the paper in front of me, interrupting my thoughts.

I looked up to meet Robin's horrified stare.

He must have come back to the classroom after realizing his carelessness in forgetting the note. He likely hoped that the paper in my hands wasn't the one he shared with Alphonse.

Determined to confirm his fear, I crumbled up the paper, walked up to him, and threw it to his face.

"Here's your garbage," I said.

I turned on my heel and paced away from him, but his panicked footsteps followed me. "Lyra! Wait!"

Robin grabbed my wrist and pulled me towards him. "Lyra! Please hear me out!"

I pulled my arm away from his tight grasp. "Let go!"

Robin's eyes shifted to a glare as he made eye contact with someone behind me. His grip on me tightened.

"Lyra," Altair's voice called out from behind me.

I turned to face him—he glared at Robin under furrowed brows.

"Lyra!" Again, Robin pulled on my wrist to get me to face him. "If you leave now, I swear I will jump off a cliff."

I gasped. "Robin! Stop it!" I shook my head.

Memories of the knight in my past life flooded in. He had sacrificed himself for me once already.

"*Nothing* is worth your life, not even me," I whispered to him.

Altair positioned himself in front of me, pushing Robin away.

"Get your hands off her," he threatened.

Even though I faced Altair's back, I realized he did something that caused Robin's glare to turn into an expression of terror. A faint blue glow was reflected in Robin's eyes, causing him to loosen his grip on my wrist.

Throughout my entire life, I had never witnessed Altair's pupils transforming into slits, but that day, I discovered he possessed an ability he always avoided revealing.

Altair's defensive stance hinted at his preparedness for an attack.

"Altair!" I lightly held on to his upper arm.

The glow reflected in Robin's eyes disappeared.

Altair turned to face me; his normal sapphire eyes revealed nothing. I feigned ignorance and hoped my curious peering didn't show that I noticed.

I kept hold of his arm and motioned for him to walk with me. When I put distance between the two of them, I looked back at Robin. He remained rooted to his spot, and a sad and fearful expression shadowed his face as Altair and I walked away together. Something about it reminded me of Robin, the Follynean knight—the past version of him who stayed behind to confront Altair while I ran away.

In this life, our friendship held a significant place in my heart. Like the fleeting alliances we shared in our past lives, our connection found its way back to us. The melancholy gaze that arrested his face served as a brutal reminder of the blessing that rekindled this bond. We needed to reconcile and untangle our misunderstandings to mend our fractured friendship.

"I'll be right back," I mouthed at Robin.

Altair walked forward with a glare plastered across his face, but it softened into a gaze when he met my eyes.

"What's wrong?" He said to me as he threw victory glances at Robin—who still stood there, waiting for me.

I stopped our walk and spoke in a low tone, "Er, we're going to skip the café today, Altair."

Altair's expression shifted to something of genuine surprise. Then, he gave a frustrated sigh.

"He told me he was going to jump off a cliff!" I whispered to Altair with concern.

"Tell him to do it," Altair snickered.

"Altair!" I shook my head at the cruel prince's appearance.

He stared at me for a moment, and I returned his eye contact with an offensive look in my eyes.

He shook his head. "I don't want you with him." His eyes focused on my reddened wrist.

"He's one of my best friends. I have to talk to him."

Altair shook his head again. "I don't want him touching you."

"I'll tell him he can't touch me."

"Who's to say he'll listen?" he shook his head again. "You're not going with him."

"You don't get to dictate my actions, Altair."

He remained quiet for a moment, and a conflicted expression settled on his face.

"You're right, I'm not." He gestured at my wrist. "But-"

"Don't pretend to care, either," I interrupted.

"I *do*, though."

My heart leaped into my throat.

"Can you trust me enough to believe I know what I'm doing?"

"It's him I don't trust."

"Isn't it enough to trust *me*?"

Altair sighed in resignation and nodded. "Then, I'll wait for you."

"I don't know how long our conversation is going to take, Altair."

"I'll wait in my dorm room. If you don't come tonight..." He paused. "We'll meet after our break."

"Okay." I gave a nod, and he reluctantly parted from me.

*****

Robin and I walked through one of the university's empty hallways. School had finished for the semester, and everyone either went home or stayed around the college town to celebrate and enjoy a last day with friends.

"I'm sorry I grabbed your arm like that," Robin broke our silence. "You must be very mad at me."

I acknowledged with a nod. "I am upset. Instead of communicating with me, you, whom I consider one of my best friends, went to spew all these negatives about me behind my back."

"I know. You didn't deserve that. What I did was wrong. It was a betrayal, and I apologize with everything I am."

"How many others have you expressed these thoughts to? Syrena?"

Robin shook his head. "Just Alphonse."

"Do you really feel that way about me, Robin? Do you really believe I'll bring Deltrea to ruin?" I meant for my tone to sound accusatory, but it came out dejected.

He shook his head. "No. Of course not, Lyra! But I believe Antares is lying to you. I believe he wants to ruin you, and you're letting it happen!"

I shook my head.

Even though it caused him pain, he needed to get accustomed to the idea of a union between Altair and me. Somehow, I wanted to be honest with him about The Lovers, but I couldn't share such delicate information explicitly.

Therefore, I settled for a similarity. "Altair has feelings for me."

Surprise flashed through Robin's expression. "He's lying to you. That guy cannot love anybody."

"I see it in his eyes, Robin, and I think everyone sees it, too."

"Yes, but it's lust! He has a hidden agenda, and the lust he holds for you is a bonus to his plans."

"You don't know that. He's different from the idea we all had of him."

"Well, how do *you* feel about him, Lyra? Do you realize how much you're defending your supposed enemy?"

"I-" I couldn't say it. I couldn't utter the next words. Speaking them solidified their meaning.

"Please, Lyra. I need to hear it," my friend pleaded. "What do you really feel for him?"

"Why does it matter, Robin?" I averted my gaze.

"Because, Lyra, I'm in love with you," he said, his tone expressing pain.

I kept my eyes cast down. I couldn't look at him.

He continued, "I want to be with you."

Struggling to hold back tears, I pressed my lips together. His words weighed on my heart and clouded my thoughts. The thought of inflicting heartache upon my friend burdened my soul, but I owed honesty to our friendship. With a deep breath, I willed myself to speak the truth I held back.

"I have feelings for Altair," I confessed.

My words hung in the ambience.

The room grew quieter.

Anxiety filled the space in that moment of vulnerability, and the world paused, waiting for my admission to be heard.

"In fact," I continued, my voice wavering, "I might have fallen in love with him."

Robin gave a slight nod. He struggled to keep himself together. He tried to be strong, but I saw his Adam's apple in motion. With a gulp, he did his best to keep tears from coming out of his eyes. His effort to maintain composure became evident in every strained breath he took.

"That's big. That's very big. It's a relationship which could cause chaos," he said, pausing. "For your happiness, I really hope he's sincere about you, Lyra."

"I still love you, Robin. You're one of my best friends," I whispered.

He didn't respond.

I agreed to hear him out because I wanted that communication with him. Our friendship needed mending from the misunderstandings and anger. Initially, I looked for an ally, but he and Syrena grew to be more than that. I loved them enough to work on the friendship we built, and I wanted to continue building it.

"I'll give you space. I'll go." For the time being, this was all I could offer.

Just as I started turning away, he said, "You're going to meet up with him right now?"

I held his gaze, but I offered no response.

Robin nodded, understanding my silence as an affirmation to his question.

"Goodbye, my friend." Again, I turned to leave, but Robin caught my wrist. This time, he held it gently and ushered me to face him.

When I complied, he planted a swift kiss on my lips.

"I love you, too," he said, and a single tear came out of his eye.

*****

I made my way to Altair right as the sun set. My conversation with Robin didn't carry as long as I thought it would.

As I arrived at the dormitories, I wondered if I should tell him about the kiss from Robin. Maybe he wouldn't care, but I also considered the possibility that his pride could take a hit, and he might react impulsively. Then, another thought crossed my mind—the unlikely possibility that he felt possessive of me. The desire to test that slim likelihood intrigued me, considering such possessiveness might hold meaning.

Shaking my head, I fought against the forbidden subconscious thoughts that surfaced in my mind, and I knocked in rhythmic annoyance on Altair's door.

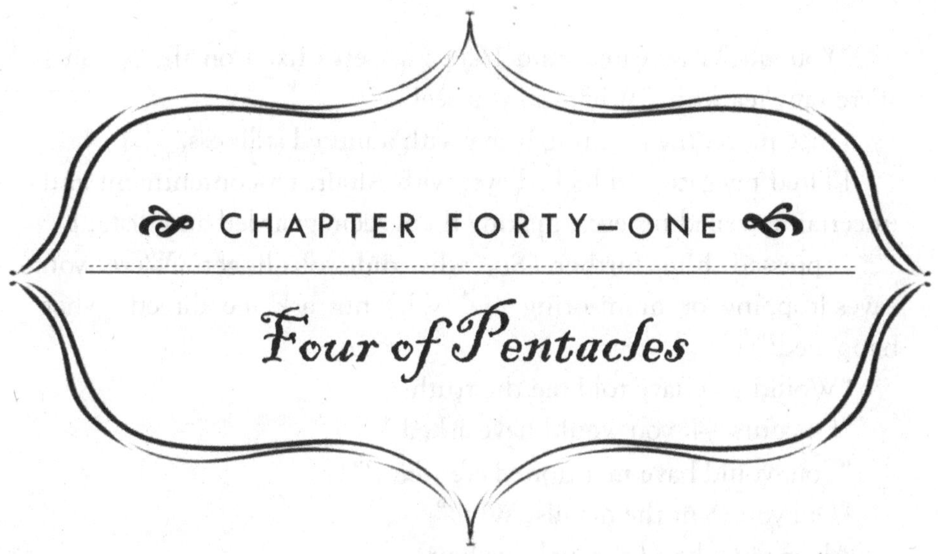

CHAPTER FORTY-ONE

Four of Pentacles

Altair seemed troubled. True to form, he remained silent, but his lack of eye contact alarmed me. His distant and evasive demeanor led me to suspect he might have gotten mad because I spent time with Robin.

When I saw a familiar crumpled paper on his coffee table, I realized Altair must have picked up the note I threw at Robin and read its contents.

"You just had to feed your curiosity, huh?"

Altair scowled. "It was on the ground."

"Is that why you're not yourself tonight?"

Altair's eyebrow furrowed, but he turned away to pour us tea before I got anymore glimpses of his face.

He sat beside me on his sofa, his gaze fixated on the tea he brought me.

"Altair, talk to me." I placed my hand on his, but his clenched jaw didn't relax.

I awaited his explanation, but the room's silence only deepened my worry.

Finally, he spoke, "I saw."

Altair didn't go into specifics, but it seemed like he alluded to Robin's kiss.

I sensed my heart dropping.

"You *saw*," I repeated, and I kept my eyes fixed on the spoon I stirred my tea with. "What did you see?"

Once more, the air hung heavy with a muted stillness.

I lifted my gaze and locked eyes with Altair. Discontentment and uncertainty veiled his eyes, making them seem guarded and distant.

I pressed him further. "So, why did you linger? Were you eavesdropping or monitoring me? Why not ask me directly what happened?"

"Would you have told me the truth?"

"Of course—if you would have asked."

"You would have mentioned *everything*?"

"Did you want the details? Why?"

Altair ran a hand through his hair.

"Why is it important I tell you *everything*, Altair?"

"Do you really need to ask?"

"I do. Yes."

"I thought you agreed to The Lovers," he declared, making my heart race. The frustration in Altair's tone only made me more hopeful that he felt a genuine spark of fondness towards me.

"The agreement to a card is different, and you know it."

"It entails the same thing, Lyra. Lovers. A relationship. Clearly, that means nothing to you."

Analyzing his tone and words, my chest fluttered with excitement. I took a deep breath to calm myself, reminding myself to be realistic, but I still wanted to probe his jealous emotions further.

"If you would have listened to my conversation with Robin, you would have understood that-"

"I listened. I heard everything I needed to hear."

"If that were the case, I don't think you'd be so angry."

"I'm not," Altair looked away as he said it.

"Okay. So then, it turns out you're jealous." It wasn't a question.

Altair vehemently shook his head and denied my guess. "No, I'm not jealous."

Despite his denial, I swore his expression conveyed jealousy. The ambiguity in his look hinted at a lack of comprehension of his own emotions.

"Which is it, then?"

"I don't know. Disappointment, I guess. I don't know." Altair shook his head again.

"Why disappointment?"

"I don't know." Altair hung his head. His elbows rested above his knees, and his closed hands acted as supports for his chin.

"I don't know," he repeated, but this time, his voice sounded hushed—as though he spoke the words to himself.

I let out a heavy sigh. "Alright. Tell me, what were you up to? You knew where I was and what I was doing. So why did you stay to listen to our conversation?"

The bittersweet frustration and the hopeful uncertainty in the ambience mingled with the satisfying scent of floral tea.

"I *didn't* wait around."

I fixed my gaze on him, studying his every move, but his lips stayed sealed. Tension thickened the air. An anxious silence gripped the room, and I yearned for him to shatter it, to explain. If my intuition proved correct, Altair's jealousy drove his silence and sparked this confrontation. His feelings would confirm the importance of our interactions and acknowledge the significance of *our* kiss.

He sighed. "I left after our last interaction. I came to my dorm and then..."

He paused.

As I observed him, I noticed a restless expression on his face and an unfamiliar touch of nerves.

"I made a discovery," Altair continued, his voice filled with urgency. "It was so important that I couldn't wait. I had to run back to get you."

"So, the seriousness of whatever seemed important faded away as soon as you encountered Robin and me?"

Altair shook his head and ran his hand over his hair.

"Then, what is it, Altair?"

I gasped when I noticed a deep scratch peeking out from under his button-up shirt. The uniform cardigan hid it from sight earlier.

I closed the distance between us and ran my fingers down to the scratch. Altair flinched.

"And this?" I asked.

Without realizing my unconscious motions, my hands settled on each side of his face. "This is recent! Is this why you ran back to me? Altair, talk to me. What happened?"

"Does it really matter?" He grabbed my hands and removed them from his face.

"It does to me."

"Why?"

Time froze as the room fell into a silent beat.

"Take off your shirt," I commanded.

Altair scoffed and turned away from me, his face flushed. He shook his head.

"If you don't take it off, I will take it off for you, and I might hurt you." I reached for the buttons, but before I touched him, Altair peeled his shirt off by yanking it off through his neck.

A bloody bandage covered the left side of his chest, but it fell short of the long gash that stretched from his chest up to his neck, where it peeked out.

I put my hands over my mouth. "Altair! What are you doing? We need to get you to the infirmary!"

"It's fine," he responded.

I turned towards the exit. "I'm getting a nurse over here."

"Hey, hey!" Altair caught me by the arm and got me to face him. "Lyra, for once, listen to me. It's fine. I have it under control."

"What, by drinking blood?" I snapped.

Altair shrugged. "It's in my nature... I'll have it taken care of soon."

"You haven't had it under control so far," I muttered. "If you will not let the nurses help you, then you have no choice but to let *me* help clean it for the time-being. Lay on your bed."

Altair contemplated his next words, but he said nothing as he complied with my demands.

"I always carry a little box with the most basic first-aid supplies in my backpack. Lucky for you, I have the hobby of studying herbs."

Altair remained silent, but he kept his distant, disheartened gaze on me.

I sensed his disdain from my kiss with Robin, so I tactfully diverted the conversation by shifting my attention to his injury.

I opened my little box of supplies as I scooted closer to Altair.

"Come," I reached towards his bare chest.

Altair slightly raised his eyebrows and pressed his lips into a thin line. He eyed me with skepticism.

"What? It's okay. I used to clean and close people's wounds all the time."

"For Von Almont?"

"Yes."

Again, Altair clenched his jaw.

I looked down at my materials and let out a little smile, unable to help myself at his reaction.

"Xander has... taught me much of what I know. He's helped me grow. Without him, I wouldn't be here right now. To be honest, I would have met a premature death if it weren't for him. He's kind and harsh when he needs to be, but he means well. Healing him is the very least I could do. He is my teacher and my friend. He is... the older brother I never had."

I offered a teasing smile. "Must I express my true feelings for someone else to put your mind at ease? Alphonse Forté, perhaps?"

Altair shook his head with no sign of conflict or distaste in his eyes when my brother's name came up. I couldn't decipher the meaning behind his confident and dismissive expression, but it left me unsettled.

"You're the oldest?" he asked.

I nodded. I am older by mere minutes.

Then, I remembered Altair wasn't supposed to know about Alphonse, so I improvised.

"I mean, of course. Oldest and only," I shrugged.

Altair remained silent. His eyes reflected deep thought as he gazed at me.

The oddness of his question triggered a cascade of over-thoughts in my mind, and I hoped he asked it in correlation to my comment about Xander, but my intuition set off alarm bells.

I brought our attention back to his wound. "This is going to sting. A lot."

Again, he gave no response and stared in silence as I cleaned his wound and wrapped a new bandage around it.

As I nearly finished, I met his eyes, but they brought me a sense of shame and guilt.

"You know, there's no need to look at me like that... I'm almost done fixing you," I said.

"You kissed Robin." His jaw clenched.

It shouldn't have come as a surprise to me that Altair didn't want to let go of the initial subject.

He continued, "I thought you believed a kiss was sacred."

If his words of jealousy reflected his true feelings, our relationship had undeniably changed. At the very least, a part of him felt possessive over me, which suggested something other than hate.

This realization brought a glimmer of hope. Perhaps, despite everything, there was a chance for us to transform this possessiveness into something more meaningful. Our connection had shifted, and I couldn't ignore the possibility that his feelings might be more complex and genuine than I had initially thought.

"I did not kiss Robin. He *stole* a kiss from me," I sighed. "A kiss *is* sacred. It's not something I'd willingly share with-" I looked at Altair—who held on to my every word. "Just anyone," I concluded.

"Then, what am I to you, Lyra?"

What could I say? I had already agreed to share The Lovers with him, a sacred and intimate agreement, so anything outside of the truth sounded like an excuse.

After all, Altair wasn't just anyone. He took my first life away, and now, he constantly occupied my mind. His kiss intensified his invasive thoughts against my soul.

Because of our sweet moments, I easily and unwisely fell for our own con. I reached a point where I deceived myself, desperately pretending I hadn't foolishly fallen in love with him.

I avoided eye contact and fiddled with my supplies. It was time for us to grow, but I wasn't sure we were ready for something that could break my heart if it failed. So, I kept the true extent of my feelings to myself.

"You are... Altair Antares, my childhood bully, the person who murdered my spirit countless times. You're my enemy, you're my opposition by default, and... you're my partner. You're the one I accepted to share The Lovers with, and I think you're my best friend."

My safest option was a friendship. This way, I protected what we had and gave us the space to develop naturally.

Anything beyond friendship risked deeper emotional hurt and heartbreak, and the thought of that weakness and distraction terrified me. I didn't want to face that fear in my life.

Altair faced me with that familiar, conflicted expression. Below his furrowed brows, his sapphire eyes searched mine for answers, reflecting an inner turmoil as he struggled to find the right words.

Finally, after a long moment of hesitation, he spoke, "More than *that*. I am your lover."

Altair reached into his pants pocket and pulled out The Lovers.

The card's eye was opened.

"How?" I heard the suspicion and surprise in my voice.

"Hell, if I know."

"No! Be honest with me! How-"

"I am. *This* is what I wanted to show you," he emphatically pointed The Lovers towards me.

I shook my head, "No. No, something is not making any sense."

"Lyra, look at me. I swear to you. I do not know how it happened." Altair grabbed my face in his hands, and the glowing string connecting my chest to Altair's shone significantly brighter than the first time.

I stared at it in astonishment, and after a moment, Altair, equally dumbfounded, let his hands fall from my face, causing the luminous bond to vanish once more.

"Did you hide a ritualistic circle in here the day we kissed? Or..."

Altair shook his head. "You can't hide a circle."

He was right. All circles gave off a blinding glow when the card successfully synchronized with its new master.

"So, then... how?"

"I don't know. I came back. I packed up, and as I waited for you, I unconsciously took it out to admire it and noticed its eye."

"Is it for you and me, though?"

Altair reached for my hand. When our fingertips touched, the incandescent link appeared.

We glanced at the string connecting our hearts.

"Do you want me to leave the card out in the open while you and I touch other people?"

I shook my head at Altair's suggestion; I knew better. The card only reacted openly to its masters, establishing permanence, regardless of my preference. The Lovers had reacted to us and awakened, but I couldn't understand how. Considering Altair's struggle to activate it in our past lives, I believed he spoke the truth.

"Why did you think to show me? Didn't you consider I might suspect you of deceit?"

Altair nodded. "Yes, but I was going to fulfill my part and tell you. Whatever you did with the knowledge, I would respect."

I sighed as I took a moment to observe the card.

"It seems it's been awakened, but it hasn't chosen a vessel." I held up my bracelet charm, which held Benjamin.

Alphonse contained Judgement in his kalimba. Just the same, I assumed Altair maintained his ability in his obsidian ring, but this card only observed us with its watchful eye.

These things are unpredictable sometimes. At least, we reserved the card for ourselves. These cards have a peculiar rule: once their eye opens, their loyalty remains unchanged until it seals again, which only happens with their master's death.

"I believe the rings needed for the ritual will serve as vessels," Altair said. "The Lovers hasn't given us its power, but it must have sensed a strong connection between us. Our bond must have been powerful enough to awaken and recognize us as its masters."

"Right. We gain its power after..."

"A lot of trials."

Altair's theory was scary but plausible, and as it sank in, I blushed. Denying what even a card confirmed would make us fools.

Lately, Altair found any excuse to touch me, focusing on my face or hands, and I always gave in. I wanted it. There was a connection there, a terrifying and addictive attraction. I didn't know how to handle it or hide my reddened face.

Altair's hand softly traced the nape of my neck, sending shivers down my spine as I melted into the moment. His other hand skillfully wove through my hair, gently twirling the ends with a tender grace.

I touched the glowing string protruding from his chest, but my fingers passed right through it. Instead, I brushed against his bare chest, my hand moving to stroke the sides of his fresh bandage.

After a few moments lost in the rosy trance, Altair's firm grip on my wrist abruptly halted my caresses. When I looked up to meet his eyes, I realized he inched much closer to me than I thought.

Altair's gaze fell towards my lips.

I turned away to break the moment, but Altair slowly leaned forward and kissed my cheek.

A small sigh escaped my lips at Altair's closeness, and he rewarded me with a trail of kisses on my face.

Despite my attempts to maintain composure, my emotions surged, drowning out any sense of logic. I couldn't push him away—I knew it would make him stop, but I didn't want that. Instead, I clung to his hair and mimicked his actions, planting a path of kisses along his face.

My lips moved towards his neck. He hesitated, then moved his head to the side, leaving his neck open for me. I indulged, planting a gentle kiss.

Altair gripped my chin and connected my lips with his. We moved in sync. His tongue entered my mouth and danced with mine. I returned the playful gesture in the same desperate rhythm of the flutters in my belly. His hand gripped the small of my back, pulling me closer. I arched my body towards him to devour his lips. Altair's other hand brushed my cheek gently before tangling itself in my hair.

I used one of my hands to grasp onto one of his shoulders, while my other hand clung to his hair.

I became captivated in the moment.

Altair moved away from my lips and started kissing my neck.

"Lyra," he whispered.

I couldn't help but gasp. Instead of pushing him away, I embraced his toned arms with all my desire and tightened my grip. Altair responded by wrapping his arms around me in a possessive hold.

"Altair," I whispered. "We need to stop. Your wound-"

I grunted when a sharp pain in my neck interrupted me. Altair sunk his teeth into my skin, but the pain vanished as quickly as it came, and an intense pleasure replaced it, leaving me flushed and craving more.

A soft moan escaped my lips. Upon doing so, Altair and I held each other even tighter, and my pleasure intensified. My hands instinctively traced the lines of his body, and with each touch, my craving for him grew stronger.

Altair gave a low groan, and I wrapped my legs around him.

I pulled on his silky hair, desperate for his mouth to abandon my neck and return to my lips, but he remained locked onto my neck, refusing to release his hold.

Despite understanding the dangers of Altair's relentless thirst, I found myself in blissful captivity of an intoxicating sensation which left me devoid of strength and resistance. My arms grew feeble, succumbing to the overpowering allure.

I surrendered and went completely limp until everything faded to black.

CHAPTER FORTY-THREE

Four of Wands

I opened my heavy eyelids to Altair's ceiling. The dimly lit room carried a faint aroma of lavender. Weariness settled over me, weighing down my limbs and clouding my thoughts. As I lay there, memories of Altair's bite on my neck flooded back.

"How are you feeling?"

Altair's mesmerizing voice left me breathless. I faced him and noticed he sat beside me on his bed. Without hesitation, I sat up straight.

Conflicting emotions consumed me as I met his eyes. I frowned, but the intensity of my glare wavered under the lingering sensation within me. Rhythmic buzzing reverberated in my chest, while a delicate flutter danced in my abdomen, a reminder of the pleasure from his bite.

I placed my hand on my neck and felt the evidence of his bite mark.

"I didn't mean-" He paused.

"See, I-" He paused again.

"The more I desire-" He paused once more. Altair struggled to find the right words to explain his actions.

Seeing my lack of response, he scratched his head and sighed.

"Let me see your wound," I said, keeping my glare on him.

"What?"

"Let me see your wound," I repeated, speaking faster this time.

"You heal after consuming blood, *so show me your wound.*" I wanted to emphasize my impatience in my repetitions.

Altair unbuttoned his shirt.

I tore away the bandages and discovered flawless, unmarked skin.

He healed completely.

I eyed him with my death glare.

"I'm sorry," Altair said, but his apology did little to calm my conflicted, upset, pleasure-filled, and excited emotions.

He kissed me. He bit me. He made me excruciatingly desire him— all of this after he eliminated me and took everything from me in my past life.

With a surge of conflicted frustration, I reached behind me and snatched the plush pillow, its soft fabric comforting against my fingertips. In one swift motion, I hurled it towards his face, the whooshing sound filling the air. I barely gave the pillow a chance to land on the bed before grabbing it again.

He flinched; his face contorted with remorse. "Right. I deserve-"

I interrupted his words by striking his face with the pillow again. This time, I refused to release my grip, pummeling him with hit after hit. The muffled thuds resonated with each strike.

My anger awakened The Magician. My eyes glowed as I readied myself to hit him with my ability.

"Whoa!" Altair scooted away.

Before he got off the bed, dizziness overwhelmed me.

Altair caught me as I fell forward and landed on top of him.

"Lyra, you need to relax."

"Get. Off. Me." I tried to push him away, but I couldn't keep myself up.

"You're the one on *me.*"

I groaned and attempted to push myself up, but my body gave out once again, and I fell back into Altair's arms.

He embraced me.

Confusion clouded my mind. Whether because of my dizziness or my enjoyment of the sensation, I refrained from making any further attempts to distance myself from him.

"I'm sorry," he whispered. "I know it was wrong."

"Is that why you kissed me? You wanted my blood?" I strained to get my words out.

"Absolutely not." He sounded offended. His voice carried undeniable sincerity, and his eyes held a captivating intensity that made me believe in his honesty, but my ego and my pride refused to accept his words at face value, prompting me to challenge him with doubtful questions.

"You wanted to heal?"

"No, Lyra. It's just... my nature."

"Your eyes didn't look red."

Altair sighed. "I couldn't help myself."

"Why?"

A long silence filled the room.

"I have a dulled sense of smell. It's flawed. I think it's because of my human side, but when we met again in Aquaenterra, your scent hit me like lightning. I knew I had stumbled upon Lyra Celestia. Your scent reminded me of when I was a child, longing to be near it, to indulge in it."

I frowned, and upon noticing my expression, Altair asked, "What is it?"

"I'm trying to figure out if that's a bad thing."

"Think of your most favorite scent in the world and why it attracts you. You are that for me."

The heat rose to my face.

"I'm coming to understand that an overwhelming attraction often accompanies an irrepressible thirst, especially when I must heal."

I remained silent, not uttering a single sound. Altair's words stirred sweet turmoil within me. I wondered if his attraction matched mine, but many unknowns remained, filling my mind with questions. As the conversation progressed, a growing fear ate at me—not because of who he was, but because of his vulnerability and sincerity, and the way he talked about attraction as if it were normal.

The old Lyra wanted to stop listening, but the new me refused to run. I wished to confront the emotions and conflicts that arose from our circumstances. As I waited for him to continue, our eyes remained locked. The weight of the silence thickened as I anticipated his next words.

"I let myself go thirsty days before All Hallows' Eve. The thirstier I became, the more intense my scent grew. By then, I had already tasted you. Lyra, I won't lie; it took immense self-control to keep myself from taking another bite that night."

"Can you smell... everybody's unique scent?"

"Yes, but certain ones are more alluring than others."

"Why did you neglect your own thirst?"

"I needed to differentiate specific scents."

I must've paled. The overthinking leviathan clouded my mind again. Could blood smell similar between siblings? Is this the reason he no longer seemed jealous of my brother? Did our scents show our blood relation?

"Did you accomplish what you intended to? Your mission was risky."

Altair shrugged. "I know how to be careful. I know exactly how long it takes before my eyes fade to their thirsty color."

He evaded my initial question.

"Altair, what did you discover that night?" I hoped for a reaction that revealed a mistake or information to confirm my suspicions or ease my mind.

Altair shook his head. "There was a different, overpowering scent in the ambience which skewed my sense of smell."

Of course! Alcohol must have influenced the situation. However, I couldn't shake the feeling that he had succeeded that night.

"I catch fragments of your scent in other people or in places you've been. It's hard to describe, but your scent always stands out. My sense of smell doesn't pick up aromas like a normal vampire. Many scents just blend, but yours dominates. I can always distinguish it. As a kid,

I hated my strong attraction to it. You weren't supposed to smell sweet to me, but you did. You had the most attractive scent I ever discovered. I wanted to be around you despite my family's wishes, and it made me angry. It confused me and left me unsure of how to handle the conflicting feelings. Even now, I still don't know what to do with it."

"As a child, how did you restrain yourself?"

"My thirst mingled with curiosity and genuine hatred. Pride consumed me, and my family's and my father's approval defined my life. Focusing on anything but you proved difficult, but the stakes loomed larger, and I clung to them."

"What about now? Are those things still important to you, Altair?"

"Yes, a child's curiosity is not as overpowering as an adult's attraction. The latter dominates. It invades. I became familiar with the emotion the moment I saw you in Aquaenterra. Then, with every eye contact and interaction in Crescencia, my attraction grew stronger. I held back and kept my secret until I tasted you. That's when my thirst for you intensified. As my attraction to you grows, you invade my thoughts more. I curse or rejoice because of you, driven by a thirst that mirrors my desires."

Altair caressed my face, his fingers guiding my chin upwards. I didn't tear my eyes away from his mesmerizing sapphire irises as I surrendered to his touch.

"Is it just with me?" I whispered.

Altair nodded. "Various scents attract vampires, but I learned that when they're captivated by a certain person, everything about that person—their scent, their blood—becomes more fulfilling. Flavorful. Addicting."

He continued, "I told you on the night we first kissed—you've become my weakness."

Altair's words resonated in the air, echoing the exact emotions I felt for him. The reminder of his confession and the lingering sensation of his bite left my blood pooling in my cheeks.

Again, we've caught ourselves in a dangerous conversation, I thought.

Instead of diverting from the conversation, I foolishly asked, "Why?"

"I think you know the answer to that, Lyra."

I shook my head. Perhaps I knew it, but I didn't want to search my subconscious for it. I didn't want to confirm *it* on my own.

"There's a reason The Lovers chose us, Lyra, and I doubt it's because of hatred. For me, that emotion faded long ago. And, you? Do you still hold on to it?"

I shook my head. "Altair, it's best if we stop discussing this."

"Why?"

"Because..." Facing my genuine love for you threatened my second downfall, bringing overwhelming fear and anxiety. Strong animosity towards you made it easier for me to stay focused and determined to carry out my plans. "Because... this is uncharted territory for us. For our families."

"You fear the unknown?"

"Doesn't everybody?"

"Not when it comes to you and me." His hand traveled from my chin to caress my lips.

"When I penetrate someone's skin with my bite, their emotions somewhat merge with mine. But when the reciprocation of affection exists, the synchronization of emotions consumes us both in a torrent of shared feelings. So, what you felt with my bite, I felt it, too," Altair murmured.

"I still feel it." He leaned in towards my face.

"Altair," his name escaped my lips in a soft, whispered breath. "That's all-the-more reason we can't cross this line."

"Lyra," he whispered, his voice filled with longing, "I'm about to drown you in kisses, but if you have even the slightest doubt, please walk away."

"Then, I should go."

"You should," he replied, but neither of us made a single motion.

Instead, I closed my eyes. Just like earlier, I felt our noses touch. Altair lingered in his position, waiting for me to decline his kiss, but

I had no self-control left to reject him. Perhaps he tried to find his resolve, too.

Altair pressed his lips to mine.

The kiss started slow and gentle, but it soon turned into an impatient longing. His hand caressed my cheek before sliding to the back of my head, where he tangled his fingers in my hair as our tongues intertwined.

As we briefly parted, my gaze traveled from his moist lips to his intoxicated, narrowed, glazed eyes. The intensity of his sapphire gaze mesmerized me, compelling me to press my lips against his once again. My hands slipped inside the bottom of his shirt, caressing his bare skin with my fingers.

He never separated his lips from mine as he settled himself on top of me on the bed. His hand mimicked my movements. When his hands found the bottom of my dress, he lifted it without pulling his fingers away from my bare thighs.

Desperate to remove Altair's clothing, I yearned to feel the warmth of his skin against mine with nothing between us. In response, Altair momentarily broke our kiss and stripped his shirt. I glimpsed his beautiful, chiseled torso before he linked his lips with mine again. My hands traveled across his chest, caressing the area where his injury should have been.

"Lyra," Altair breathed, but I didn't let him part from me. I persistently pressed my lips against his.

"My love," he whispered again, his voice tender. "Do you really want this with me?"

"Yes," I breathed, looking into his drunken gaze. He didn't realize how sweet he sounded when he called me "my love."

I wanted him so much.

The moment his lips and hands touched me, a delightful sigh escaped my throat. I savored the gentle caress of his hands as they traveled up my bare waist, finally resting at the lower curve of my breasts. Gripping his hand beneath my dress, I guided it to my breast—a silent invitation.

I relished the sensation of his hands caressing my breasts as I dug my nails into his bare back. I couldn't resist the urge to undress and entangle my body with his. I desired more of him—his essence, his warmth, his touch, his scent, and his taste.

The blissful feeling overwhelmed me with profound emotions, carving my heart deeper than when he bit into me.

Knock, knock, knock.

Altair and I looked at each other wide-eyed.

"Altair? You in there?" Ian's voice called out.

"Is Lyra with you?" Syrena was with him.

In an instant, Altair and I separated.

"I hear movement in there," Syrena said to Ian.

"Altair gave me a spare key."

"Wait, what if they're-"

"Er, yeah, I heard you! One sec!" Altair yelled out. It was the first time I had ever witnessed him so visibly shaken, so utterly surprised.

During Ian and Syrena's little outside conversation, Altair put his shirt back on and wrapped a scarf around my neck as I straightened myself out.

We greeted Syrena and Ian at the door.

"You interrupted our nap," Altair said.

I nodded.

Sensing a weird atmosphere, Ian and Syrena remained silent as they eyed us with suspicion.

A puzzled Ian broke the silence. "Why are you all out of breath?"

Syrena turned her smirking face away from us as she elbowed Ian.

"Oh." Realization hit him. "You were having sex."

"No!" Altair and I responded simultaneously.

"Your all's lips look all red and swollen, too, tho-"

Syrena interrupted Ian. "Guys, don't worry about it. Robin said you might be here, so I'll tell Alphonse and Roselia to wait. Sorry for interrupting!"

"We need to head back to Follyn, though, Altair," Ian said.

"They get it, Ian. Let's give them some privacy." Syrena rolled her eyes and dragged him away.

She spun back and added, "Also, Altair, your shirt is inside-out."

"No, Syrena. I'll go with you. Hold on!" I yelled behind me as I went back into Altair's dorm to gather my things.

"Enjoy yourselves! Bye, guys!" Their footsteps retreated.

Before I stepped out of his dorm, Altair caught my arm.

I needed to leave. If I stayed with him any longer, his begging eyes would hypnotize me, and I would walk right back into his arms. He didn't realize how much he had messed up my plans. He didn't know how deeply he had damaged my heart.

"Er," he began, "if you look from a certain angle, it's noticeable."

With my free hand, I instinctively covered the bite mark.

"I'll take care of it," I reassured him.

He nodded.

"Also…" Altair reached into a little drawer beside his bed, and he took out a little box. "I wanted to give you this."

I opened the pretty velvet black box with curiosity. An involuntary smile cracked through my lips. Follyn sold metal and crystal pinecones as little necklace pendants and bracelet charms. Each crystal color held a different meaning.

A turquoise pinecone indicated friendship. A clear charm wished the receiver good health. A purple pinecone symbolized success and new beginnings. A royal blue one communicated an apology. A brown pinecone stated thanks. A pink one expressed admiration, and a maroon charm declared love and passion.

The flutters in my core intensified when I laid eyes on my new maroon charm. I raised an eyebrow and gave Altair a teasing smirk. "Altair, do you realize what you're telling me with this?"

For the first time, a harsh blush took over Altair's cheeks, but he stayed silent.

I continued, "For the second time in post-Vegalia history, a Princess of Deltrea receives a gift from a Prince of Follyn. It's a powerful and beautiful gesture."

I removed my bracelet to insert my new charm. As I clasped it back on, I kept my face down to hide my blush before Altair noticed. A distinct aura of happiness surrounded us as we looked at my bracelet absentmindedly.

"Why did you hold on to the blue one for all these years? I thought you hated me."

"Did you just notice it?" I asked.

Altair shook his head. "I've wondered about it for a while now."

"It symbolized a human part of you that grasped uninfluenced emotions. Your sincerity accompanied it, so it meant a lot to me." I shifted my gaze from the charm to Altair. "But now, it's become something profound. You've become ingrained in my heart."

I tiptoed and planted a kiss on Altair's lips. "Thank you. I love it and I will cherish it always."

"You have a way of captivating me endlessly," Altair said, holding me in a final embrace.

"As do you."

"I'll write."

"I can't get anything from Follyn." My words carried disappointment.

"I'll find a way."

Before Xander and Alphonse came to claim me, I reluctantly parted from Altair's arms and left his dorm.

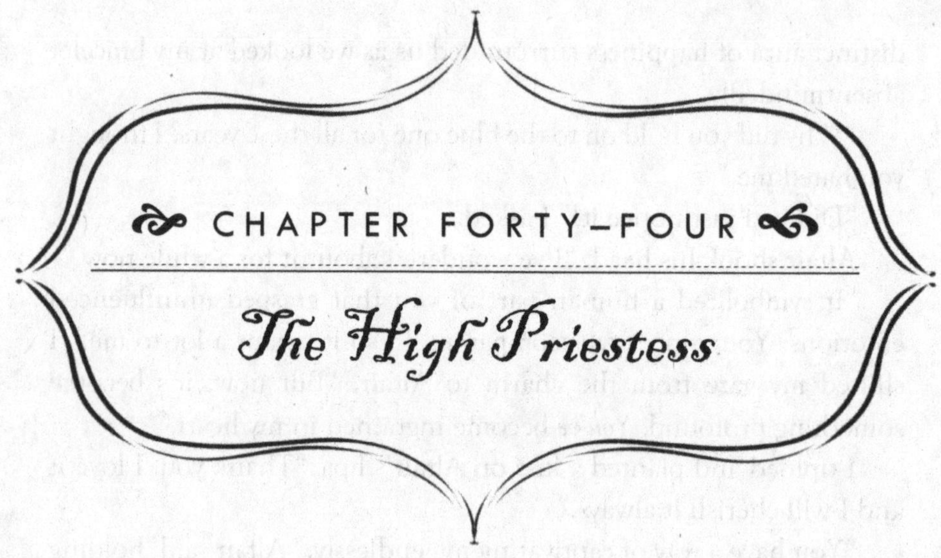

After a nightly walk around Deltrea Palace on the first weekend of Winter Break, I returned to my room to find my mother already inside. My journal—the one I exchanged daily with Altair—lay in front of her, and she was reading it with a fearful expression.

My heart sank at the realization.

"Why are you going through my things?" I yanked the notebook away from my mother. She clutched her chest.

My mother faced me with horrific disappointment. I looked around my ransacked room.

Despite my feelings of shame and betrayal, I calmed my tone for the sake of her heart. "Mother, what is this?"

Instead of answering, she said, "What does this mean, Lyra?"

"It's exactly what you think it means," I whispered, regretting my words.

My mother's eyes glowed; her pupils became slits. She looked at me with sadness, regret, and disappointment, and I knew what she intended to do.

Her card, The High Priestess, probed the victim's mind, causing excruciating pain and revealing every hidden thought. The moment her slit pupils locked eyes with someone, her power took effect. Therefore, in the millisecond I saw my mother's eyes glow, I shut mine.

With closed eyes, I attempted to flee my room, only to be caught and knocked down by my mother.

"What in the world are you thinking, Lyra?"

"What's going on here?" My father's voice filled me with dread as my mother and I screamed through our scuffle.

"Luciel! Help me hold her still! Alphonse, help me open her eyes!"

I struggled against the tight grip, which held me in its merciless clutches. My body squirmed. Each kick was a desperate plea for liberation, a wild attempt to escape the suffocating grasp of my captor. My screams echoed through the room, a piercing cry for help that fell on deaf ears.

"Have you gone mad, Cylane? She's our daughter!"

"HELP ME!" she yelled.

"You're being irrational!"

"Your daughter *is* romantically involved with Altair Antares!"

My brother gasped.

My mother continued, "I've had dreams, Luciel. Nightmares that warn me of tragedies to come. I've seen that boy—grown and motivated by a dark ambition that dooms us all."

My father gripped my arms. "This is a misunderstanding, right, Lyra?"

"It is, Father!"

"Look at this!" A thud echoed on the floor. I assumed my mother tossed my notebook towards my father, intending for him to examine the evidence. "I fear he will initiate his malicious endeavors by capturing our daughter's heart."

Though my eyes remained shut, I sensed my father's penetrating stare on me. How could I explain?

Because of the contents of my notebook, my parents would hide me from the world again. My plans would crumble, and unfortunately for all of us, I fell for the man I intended to deceive and ruin. This situation already complicated my family and original goals, and my plans to ally with Altair and infiltrate his territory would become impossible if I didn't act drastically. I needed to end this centuries-long feud with Follyn, and considering the circumstances, if I didn't act now, I risked facing a devastated Deltrea and a dead family much earlier than in my past timeline.

"Luciel, I have this strong feeling of unease. The dreams are vivid, as if they've happened! I've seen the devastation of our people. I've seen the fall of Deltrea, and, with the exception of Lyra, I've seen all of us dead."

My mother's heartbroken embrace tightened around me.

"Mother, it's not what you think," I said.

Finally, my father spoke softly, ignoring me. "Why didn't Xander say anything?"

"He did. Through him, I realized she and that boy may have been in a secret relationship, but we never imagined *this*!"

"Why didn't either of you tell me *anything*?"

"Because you're impulsive, Luciel." My mother sobbed.

"If what you're saying is true, then impulsivity was needed, Cylane!"

Again, he spoke, but this time, he directed his words at Alphonse, "Why didn't you say anything?"

"Don't blame him! He knew nothing!" I interrupted, but their silence showed they didn't want to listen to a word from me. My voice only reminded them of the disappointment and betrayal I caused.

I gasped when my father's grip on me tightened. "Do what you need to do, Cylane."

Again, I wriggled and protested in vain, but my mother forced my eyes open.

When I made eye contact with her, it felt as if hundreds of sharp needles traveled through my eyes into my brain. The enchanted needles probed every tiny nerve, digging out memories that flashed through my mind with excruciating agony.

I struggled to hear my own screams as I relived the painful events of my past life. The needles pierced my heart, searching for the conflicting emotions tied to Altair's image and memories.

"Cylane, that's enough!" My father's pleading voice echoed in my ears, blending with the murky boundaries between memories of the past and my current consciousness.

My mother witnessed every one of my thoughts unfold before her eyes—my goals, my desires, and every thread of emotions and thoughts that led to them.

I relived my lifetimes, and the pain from The High Priestess never subsided.

Knock knock knock!

Loud, frantic knocking echoed in the distance. The sound hid far in my memory or tucked away in my current subconscious. I couldn't tell.

"Cylane! You're hurting yourself!"

Mother? I thought. *My father sounds concerned. Is my mother okay?*

Suddenly, the excruciating pain stopped—only to be replaced with an agonizing ache all over my chest and my head. It hurt to close my eyes. It hurt to open them. The agony of breathing paralyzed me. I lacked the energy to rise from the ground. My body lay limp. Liquid oozed from my eyes at an alarming rate, but I lacked the energy to check if it was tears or blood.

It must've been blood, I thought. *All of those needles.*

"Cylane!" I saw my father hold my mother up. She sat down, haggard and ill. Her hands wiped her bloody nose, and crimson liquid dripped from her eyes.

"Mother, you need to lie down," Alphonse said.

"It's graver than I thought..." my mother's voice echoed away.

In those few seconds, my consciousness flickered in and out like a candle flame in a draft. I opened and closed my eyes, struggling to stay awake. It felt as if I was trapped in a time loop, caught between reality and darkness. I could catch fragments of my family's conversation, but then everything would go silent. This cycle of clarity and obscurity repeated itself throughout their conversation.

"We've lived before..." My mother's voice started, but before I heard more, my consciousness faded to black.

The next moment I opened my eyes, my mother stood against the bed frame. My father supported her fragile figure, and she continued speaking. "Lyra witnessed all our deaths, but after she got The World, she could..." Once again, everything vanished into darkness for a moment.

"...she tell us anything?" With my brother's voice in the background, my consciousness slipped away again.

As reality flickered back into view, I listened to the echoes of my mother's explanations. "...afraid of us getting captured and spilling the information... father's impulsivity... us away from harm's..."

"Is Antares a threat?" My father's voice echoed in the darkness.

My mother responded, "He's a... the scent of Lyra's blood... she suspects there's a chance he might know about Alphonse through the blood... considering how The Lovers accepted their union... don't think it's hatred on his part..."

A gnawing anxiety grew at the mention of The Lovers. How could I convince them that sharing The Lovers with Altair was the best thing we could do?

"She united with Antares through the power of The Lovers!?" My father's words interrupted my weak stream of thoughts.

"Can she get out of it?" my brother asked.

My mother's voice echoed through the ambience once again. "No, it's an enchanted card that's already awakened on their accounts. They're bonded together whether people..." Her words faded away into distance along with my consciousness.

The experience reminded me of being trapped in sleep paralysis. During moments of awakening, I caught glimpses of the room before unwillingly drifting back to sleep. I wanted to move, to help myself, but I remained helpless in a state of agonizing paralysis.

When their voices ventured into my awareness once more, I heard my father's next question. "How does she feel about Altair Antares?"

Knock! Knock! Knock!

The frantic knocking on my bedroom door held my consciousness in reality, and I listened to our lady-in-waiting's unusually agitated voice. "Your Majesties! Altair Antares is here! He is insistent..."

Impossible, I thought.

As I blacked out, I fought to keep my eyes open. I witnessed my father rushing out of the room. Summoning her final reserves of strength, my mother rose from the bed and trailed behind him.

Their actions made me realize I may have heard correctly.

As soon as they exited my bedroom door, I pressed my hands onto the soft carpet and, with trembling arms, I lifted my upper body.

An alarmed expression possessed my brother's face. "Lyra!"

"H-Help. Me-e," I responded, but my brother's expression stayed in place.

"I think you need to stay here," he said.

With the last bit of my energy, I summoned The Magician. I controlled Benjamin to kick open my balcony doors. I pushed my brother away and used the wind to assist me in gliding me over to the palace foyer.

As I suspected, Altair stood inside my palace, right by the entrance doors.

CHAPTER FORTY-FIVE

Queen of Cups

Altair took a determined, valiant stance in the foyer. He wore a long black coat over a loose-fitted black shirt neatly tucked into black slacks. Long black velvet boots fitted neatly over the pants. Altair also wore black gloves—I figured his obsidian rings lay underneath the gloves—I never saw his hands without them.

Anxiety and panic crept up my back. Altair displayed immense bravery or utter foolishness. Perhaps he held on to too much confidence. He underestimated my family and me, but I knew my parents' capabilities—not to mention my father's.

Xander's appearance below the stairs added another layer of concern. He looked different. As usual, he wore a disguise that concealed his true features. He looked more like a butler. A silver wig, and the silicone and makeup on his face made him look a lot older, and his eye color took on the incandescent hue from the eye drops I used back in Aquaenterra. He glared at Altair, standing on standby, waiting for a signal from my father.

Altair brazenly trespassed on our grounds. My mother's eyes fixated on him, reliving the horrifying moments when Altair mercilessly slaughtered our family. The weight of this knowledge opened a fresh wound in the hearts of everyone involved. My parents wanted to paint the foyer crimson—in his blood.

My mother looked exhausted and unstable, but she stood right beside my father—upright and steady at the top of the staircase leading to the foyer.

She held a look of suspicion and hostility as she looked down at Altair, but her eyes stayed normal. I doubted she could summon The High Priestess. Attempting it would cause her to collapse, exposing her weakened state. Worse, if she pushed herself further, it posed a risk to her health.

Despite the tense ambience, Altair's hardened expression didn't waver. He stood by our front doors with a glare that matched my father's. He came on a mission, and he looked to complete it without fail.

Using the wind, I glided towards Altair and positioned myself a few feet in front of him.

"Lyra!" My father yelled as he moved toward me.

His eyes glowed, and his pupils became slits. He readied himself to attack.

"Father, stop." My voice came out as a whisper.

Suddenly, I found myself devoid of strength. The winds failed to support me, and my knees buckled. My body collapsed to the floor, and the world turned black once again.

Except, I never hit the ground. Through heavy blinks, I saw Altair's face above me. He held me. He kept me from falling, and although my family was ready to attack, he took his eyes off them to catch me.

Liquid came out of my mouth and my nose. My overexertion while using The Magician drained me to the point of bleeding, leaving me physically and mentally exhausted.

Something familiar loitered in Altair's expression, though. It resembled the way he looked at me after he pierced my heart with his sword in our past lives. Horror hid behind his eyes, along with a hint of wrath and an overwhelming conflict. Then, his eyes took a burgundy tint to them.

I panicked.

At that moment, if Altair looked towards my father, my father wouldn't hesitate to slice Altair's head, and if, for any reason, he missed his mark, Xander would complete the task.

"Get your hands off my daughter!" The wrath and hatred in my father's voice made me fear for Altair's life.

When Altair made a slight motion—the slightest indication that he planned to face my father with his burgundy-colored eyes—I lifted my hands and caught his face to look only at me.

I leaned in close and whispered, "Leave."

"I'm not leaving you. I heard your screams."

My father's footsteps paced toward us.

"Father, I got it!" Alphonse's significant identity revelation interrupted my father's movements towards Altair and me. My mother covered her mouth in stricken astonishment. Altair suspected Alphonse's bloodline, but my brother just confirmed it.

Altair's face remained stoic, betraying no surprise when he heard my brother's voice. He didn't turn to see where it came from; he didn't have to. I had believed Altair only suspected Alphonse's identity, but he knew. Certainty arrested his eyes. Surely, our blood must have carried a similar scent.

Altair's gaze remained fixed on me

"Antares," my brother spoke. "I'll take over from here."

My brother's call made Altair look up.

"No!" I cried out.

"If you genuinely have any regard for my daughter, you should recognize the grave danger you expose her to, especially in your current state." My mother referred to Altair's burgundy irises.

I faced my family. Alphonse's eyes held a hint of fear and caution when he noticed Altair's eyes. My brother's arms remained stretched out to receive me, but I sensed Altair's hesitation as he held me. My brother meant well, but I knew that the moment he seized me, Xander would emerge from hiding, and go for the kill or capture.

Altair couldn't let me go. He risked facing a massive disadvantage without me in his arms. I was determined to stick with Altair and lead him away to ensure his safety. Otherwise, a war threatened to erupt, or Altair faced death. As a more favorable alternative, I'd end up hidden away.

Sweat formed on my brow. My mind raced through all the meticulous plans I crafted, searching for any loopholes or weaknesses that might hinder my success. Doubt crept in, whispering unsettling thoughts that threatened to undermine my confidence. The sudden opportunity to infiltrate Follyn caught me off guard, leaving me feeling unprepared. Anticipating that moment consumed my thoughts since I woke in my new life, yet now that it fell upon me, my body trembled with apprehension.

Timing mattered, and I wished I could've had more time to perfect my strategy, but I refused to let the chance slip away. Follyn contained a labyrinth of secrets. Layers of intrigue and treachery guarded Regnum Noctis. Infiltrating Regnum Noctis' walls meant gaining access to invaluable information that could turn the tides of power. Not for hostility, but for a new beginning for both of us—a better beginning. If Alphonse took me from Altair's arms, every force would work to separate me from Altair and Follyn's reach.

The World granted me a second chance. Now that I *knew* Altair, I envisioned a life where no leader, kingdom, or family faced extinction. Yet, danger loomed in our current reality, especially for Altair. If my father harmed him, he would spark a war, and I couldn't bear the thought. Together, Altair and I could reshape our world and forge a path of unity.

We proved the possibility existed.

He gave me hope.

I no longer harbored hatred for Altair.

The Lovers served as the symbolic representation of the inner transformation between us. I gathered my courage and took a leap of faith, driven by my love for the enigmatic Altair Antares.

It was time to leave my family.

"Take me away." I whispered my command with all the pain in my heart. I directed the low phrase towards Altair, and my voice echoed in his vampiric ears.

Altair returned his gaze to me, and a red glow took over his shifting, narrowing pupils.

Our foyer fell into a pitch-black darkness.

All light went out—as if the suffocating darkness of Altair's ability devoured it. The only glows around us were the hostile glowing eyes of my parents and the crimson tint of Altair's vampire eyes.

He looked like a veritable devil in his lair.

Just as quickly as he transformed Deltrean Palace into a black void, the breeze and cold air enveloped us. Altair ran outside with me in a princess-carry.

I didn't dare make a sound, and even if I wanted to, I couldn't attack. I lay limp in the arms of my enemy, overwhelmed by excruciating weakness. Altair moved swiftly, but the rapid clicking of my father's ability echoed close behind us.

Click. Click. Click. Click. Click.

My father's Wheel of Fortune spun relentlessly, and he attacked, blinded by Altair's darkness.

To Altair's confusion, I lifted myself, positioning the upper-half of my body over his shoulder to watch his back.

Temperance's chains clashed deafeningly, shattering the silence and revealing Xander's reckless assault in the darkness. I gasped as a chain traveled straight towards us.

"Left," I said, my voice low and hoarse. Altair understood me.

"I knew that man wasn't just a butler." Altair gritted his teeth. His family recognized Xander's loyalty to us, but because Xander often disguised himself, they probably never witnessed his true appearance.

Altair's increased speed did little to keep Xander and my father at bay. As they trailed behind us, their persistent attacks almost stopped our escape.

Drowsiness overcame me. My consciousness wavered, but when I stayed awake, I remained alert, keeping a watchful eye behind us while Altair carried me.

Despite the lack of visibility, the unsettling sound of crumbling dirt and anguished cries filled the air. The earth trembled with life around us as the dead emerged from their resting places. The air vibrated with an overwhelming presence, as if a legion of powerful forces claimed our vicinity. My blood ran cold as the pained groans of a multitude of creatures, sounding undead, echoed in the surrounding darkness. They shuffled closer to Altair and me, but I couldn't see them.

The cacophony they created served as a welcome diversion in the pitch-blackness, providing us with the cover we needed while my family persisted in chasing us.

Temperance's rattles grew fainter, and my tense body eased as Altair held me close.

We moved away, and I closed my eyes to recharge.

A new sound crept into my ears just before I faded away. The creepy familiarity snapped me back to the moment with alertness.

Once again, I faced Judgement. Now, my brother moved across the board.

The overpowering sounds of a high-pitched metallic humming dominated the chaotic ambience. It came in pauses and the same frequency. My brother seemed to tune something. Despite its softness, the sound reverberated in our ears and penetrated our cores, rendering us momentarily paralyzed by its overwhelming vibrations.

The first time the immobilization happened, the surrounding darkness wavered, and Altair and I came to an abrupt stop. As I clung to him in a state of paralysis, I felt his every movement and listened to his pained grunts as he fought against our shared immobility. His grip on me grew tighter.

As the confusion subsided, another wave of the same hum washed over us, immersing us in an unyielding darkness that seemed to sway and fluctuate. Altair pushed me further over his shoulder, his grunts of pain echoing through the air as he covered his ears.

In my state of confusion, I let out a laugh through my pain. The cruel twist of fate allowed me to witness Altair in agony because of Judgement, the very weapon once used by his most trusted ally against *me*.

Suddenly, a small woman jumped out of the ground where we stood and placed her long, red, black-finger nailed hands over my ears.

As the darkness wavered again, I saw the hole where she jumped out from. I shrieked at her appearance—eyes gleaming a golden hue with black slits for pupils, much like card users, but her irises lacked any glow. Her long, pointy tongue slithered from her grinning mouth, and pure evil glinted in her eyes.

As Altair sprinted, I noticed her hooves instead of feet. Since she stood short, her hooves floated above the ground, yet she remained tethered to Altair and me, gripping my ears tightly and sealing them from the sounds of Judgement.

"Altair!" I cried as I looked into the creature's evil eyes.

Again, the sounds of a tuning Judgement carried through our bodies—this time, taking my voice along with it. Altair grunted in pain as his body slowed and the darkness wavered again.

This time, melodies from a distinctive instrument modified the sounds of the ambience. The echoing strums of my brother's ukelele filled the air.

I always enjoyed listening to him play. His lively performances at home lifted our worries and stresses, and that familiar feeling took over my mind that night. The music held me in its thrall, halting my thoughts and resolving my conflicts. I lingered, mesmerized, trying to pinpoint the source of the captivating sound. The desire to watch the music man perform his art consumed my thoughts. Enchanted by the beautiful sound waves, I couldn't think of anything else. The world around me faded into the background, and I found myself spellbound by the master music man. I wondered why a swarm of people didn't surround us, eagerly enjoying the symphony he produced with just a few chords, but I didn't dwell on the thought because I spotted him.

Despite the considerable distance that separated us, my brother's figure rushed towards me. I struggled to maintain my balance as a wave of dizziness washed over me.

Somehow, I was on my feet.

My legs wobbled, threatening to give way beneath me. As I fought to stay upright, I caught sight of Alphonse clutching his ukulele, a look of concern etched across his face. The air carried an underlying urgency, and it brought a sense of dread that latched on to my shoulders, but my muddled head didn't understand why. Despite my unsteady state, my brother's exceptional performance remained freshly ingrained in my brain, and I couldn't think of anything more. Summoning every ounce of strength within me, I straightened myself, offering my triumphant brother a beaming smile.

"Lyra!"

I grasped the desperate echoes of a familiar voice calling out for me, but I couldn't remember who it belonged to.

I couldn't think. Judgment held me in a trance, my mind clouded and immobilized by its overwhelming power.

As I tried to shake my head, a familiar groan echoed around me.

"Altair," I whispered.

That's right. Altair and I escaped, didn't we? The coolness of his arms no longer enveloped me. I glanced beside me, hoping to find solace, but black emptiness took over my sight. Altair's absence left a void, a silence that echoed in my heart.

I couldn't understand how I heard his voice calling my name, though.

More groans tainted the surrounding silence until the melodies of my brother's ukulele drowned them out. While I wanted to enjoy his performance, my legs collapsed and I fell on the ground, facing away from my brother. My state of weakened paralysis allowed me to focus on the diminishing darkness and a familiar figure laying on the ground beside me.

The music subsided again.

Battling drowsiness and struggling with my blurry sight, I discerned Altair's form sprawled on the ground. His grunts of agony echoed through the air, his anguished expression twisting his face.

Then, my mother came into view, and I realized she caught him.

Despite being far away, she caught Altair's gaze and delved into his memories.

"No," I coughed out. This posed a great danger to my mother. If she didn't stop, this memory search could exhaust her and cause fatal consequences.

"Mother!" I heard the echoes of my brother's voice, laced with dread.

Darkness engulfed the atmosphere once more, but this time, I remained aware of my surroundings. This gloom resembled the familiar, dreading, draining void created by Altair, but as it dissipated, it seemed to take Altair with it because I no longer saw him.

When I looked towards my mother, a chill ran through my veins. A familiar figure dressed in black stood before her, and one of his black-gloved hands clutched his scythe. His black scarf danced in the wind, mirroring the trailing edges of his cloak, giving an eerie resemblance to a dark specter. He peered down at my mother, his face hidden beneath a distinctive raven mask.

In the desperate moment, I let out a breath as The Walking Plague's scythe pressed against my mother's neck, its sharp edge against her skin.

My desperate pleas for her went unanswered.

Her body gave out.

She did her best to hold back pained screams, and as bloodied tears came out of her eyes, she took a final look in my direction.

For the last time that night, my world vanished into an abyss of darkness.

*****

I woke up to an unfamiliar ceiling. Memories from the night of my escape engulfed me, causing a flood of heart wrenching emotions.

I got up and found myself in a living area with a lit fireplace. Altair sat in front of it.

I rushed over to him.

"What happened?" I grabbed Altair by the collar.

Altair's eyes held a sympathetic expression as he silently observed me—a silence that conveyed a lot of meaning and confirmed my worst fears. His gaze held guilt, sadness, and a mix of confusion and conflict. Even if Altair knew what to say, he couldn't vocalize his thoughts, and I didn't blame him. His severely bloodshot eyes meant my mother caught him with her endless probing needles.

Tears streamed down my face.

My mother.

My sweet, beloved mother, who did nothing but love me and worry about me. She never employed her ability unless she firmly believed it could be the difference between life and death. I experienced her unwavering support until the conclusion of my previous life, which led me to believe this time would be no different. Instead of an ending, I yearned for her presence by my side as we embarked on a tranquil era.

Lacking the energy to stand, I crouched on the floor, sobbing out all the pain I felt. One hand continued to grip Altair's shirt.

I steadied myself by planting my other palm to the ground.

Altair tried to lift me, but I pushed him away and remained in the same crouched stance. I didn't want to face him. I didn't want him to see my eyes, which reflected my sadness, loneliness, and weakness. The image of my pained face remained my secret to keep. I hid it. I dealt with it. In contrast, I allowed him to hear the sounds of my pain and sadness, only because I lacked the strength to control my emotions at that moment.

I sobbed and sobbed.

I knew what Altair's silence meant.

My mother was dead.

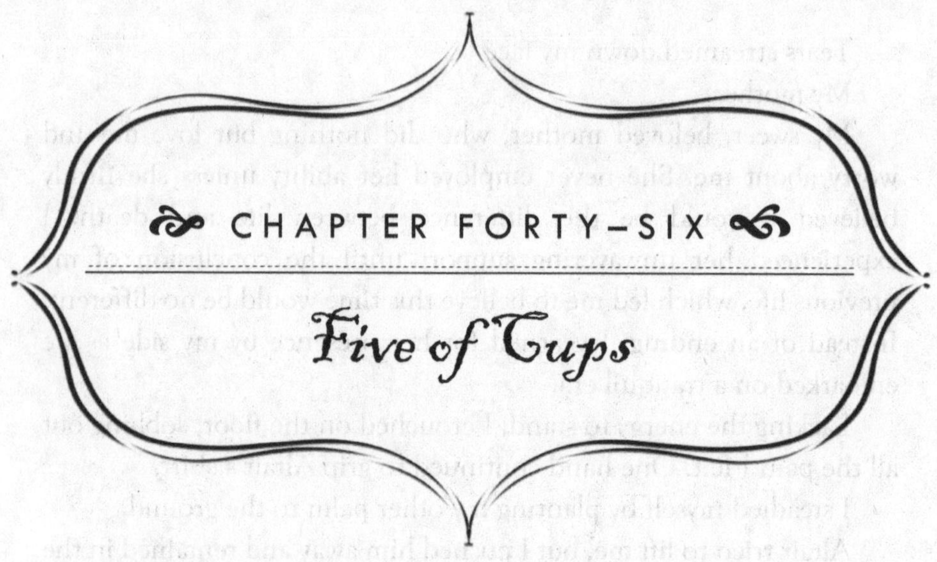

Altair and I stayed in a cabin near Follyn's outskirts. The land belonged to Aquaenterra, but Altair didn't want us to enter Follyn until I regained my strength.

We waited for word from his sisters. He advised them about bringing me into Follyn. More importantly, he constantly asked me to confirm my readiness to depart alongside him. I already crossed the point of no return—especially under the current circumstances. I couldn't let my father hide me, and I couldn't run. Living in Follyn would stall a war. It gave me the potential to show the world that Altair and I made a radical move. People would take our side.

I saw no option but to push forward.

"We'll be facing the same battles when you take me to Follyn," I whispered.

Altair paused, collecting his thoughts in silence. Then, he shook his head. "My mother might cause us trouble, but she yields to my decisions. My older sister, Solaris, she's different. She's always been different. She's never held unreasonable hatred. That's why my father refuses to let her be the next in line for the throne."

When I stayed quiet, he continued. "We'll have an ally."

"What about your other sister?"

"She-" Altair paused. "She could be overwhelming, at first. But she listens to me. If I tell her to behave, she will."

"What about your father?"

Altair's lips sealed shut, and a heavy silence settled over us.

*****

We barely spoke that week. I supposed he tried to give me space, maybe out of guilt.

I was left in a haze, unsure of what or how to feel.

When Altair's sister sent a carriage and coachman for us, he asked me again.

"You sure about coming with me to Follyn?"

No. I wasn't. Uncertainty clouded my mind, but I had no other choice. If things didn't work out peacefully between Altair and me, I still needed information from the inside. The Lovers gave me an edge, tying my destiny to Altair. I only needed enough time to gather details for Deltrea's success—the Antares family's weaknesses, strengths, the cards they possessed, and those they lacked. If Altair told the truth about his sister not hating without reason, my *innocence* might create a beneficial rift within their household.

I sighed. "We're aiming to unite, right? Not going now will worsen the conflict. If I join you, our nations have a fighting chance for a better future."

Although part of me wanted things to go that way, one of his own killed my mother, serving as a brutal reminder of my past.

This time, obvious doubt arrested Altair's expression. The fear of his skepticism ate away at my confidence.

*****

Much like Deltrea, Follynean knights heavily guarded the Follyn borders.

Their piercing gazes bore into me, a blend of curiosity and disdain on their faces. Regardless of their sentiments towards me, they had no alternative but to admit me into Follyn without opposition, given the commands of their crown prince.

We rode along a dirt path through a section of Follyn Forest. From the carriage window, darkness dominated my view.

Occasionally, I glimpsed the outlines of massive pine trees illuminated by our carriage lanterns.

The night was bitter.

"What's on your mind?" Altair's words interrupted my stream of consciousness.

His eyes betrayed his troubled thoughts, showing his concern. Maybe he knew I felt lonely. Perhaps he could sense the sadness I felt at leaving my home, the longing for my mother's voice, and the fear of the unknown turmoil waiting for me in Follyn. My mind drifted to *my ally*, my brother, Alphonse, and my heart sank into depths of dominating gloom as I imagined his heartbreak.

I shook my head and quickly suppressed any thoughts of my family, focusing on emptiness instead.

Speaking my true thoughts aloud would break me down in tears, a sight I refused to let anyone see—especially Altair, so I didn't say a word.

Instead, I reflected on my current actions. I made the choice to stop running—despite my fear—all for the sake of the possibility of a better future, but fear stood in my way. It produced a nerve-wracking and anxiety-inducing feeling in my body, but if I didn't take the initiative, who would?

My father acted too impulsively. My brother's determination never surpassed mine—it once did, in our past life, when I sought peace in abandonment and dodged my leadership duties. However, witnessing a future of significant loss forged in me an unimaginable determination to succeed.

I knew better. Therefore, it could only be *me*.

After a long silence, I responded to Altair, "The trees. They leave quite the impression even though the dark night makes them hard to see."

Altair studied me, but I didn't turn to face him. I kept my eyes on the carriage window.

I continued, "Even with moonlight, this place is pitch black."

"Are you afraid?" he asked.

I turned to face him. "Should I be?"

Altair kept his gaze on me, but he remained silent. Although I couldn't quite identify the emotions in his eyes, I perceived a hint of remorse.

I shrugged. "I wouldn't say... afraid."

To be honest, I was terrified, but my sadness—masked my fear.

"Lonely, perhaps," my soft voice carried through the melancholy ambience. "Here, I have no one."

I locked eyes with Altair, but he bowed his head and focused on the floor. He seemed hesitant to meet my gaze. He made no effort to convince me he could be a supportive companion, leaving me feeling more alone than I had initially thought.

When I needed him most, he started avoiding me, reflecting on our positions in this real-life chess game. We held leadership positions on opposing teams, each move deepening the divide between us. At least, I infiltrated Follyn.

Once again, an uncomfortable silence fell upon the carriage that led us to a kingdom of darkness. In those disheartening confines, I turned the question around on him.

"Are *you* afraid, Altair?"

He brought his head back up and locked his eyes with mine. "A little."

I furrowed my brow in a puzzled expression. "Why?"

At Altair's silence, I probed further. "We're in your territory. What are you worried about?"

"You."

"I can take care of myself even in a sea of hatred."

The carriage came to a sudden, violent halt. The forceful impact made me topple forward from my seat and propelled me towards Altair.

Despite the distance between us, despite the circumstances, despite the fact one of his own took away one of my most precious people, Altair gripped me in a tight embrace, shielding me from the surrounding chaos.

"Are you okay?" Concern laced his tone as he wrapped his arms tighter around me.

I pulled myself free from his grasp.

He scanned my body, perhaps checking if I was hurt. Then, he composed himself and got on his feet.

"Stay here," he commanded as he made his way out of the carriage.

"Like hell," I muttered as I followed him out.

"Prince Altair!" the coachman called out.

My eyes widened when familiar restraints ensnared the coachman, the two horses pulling the carriage, and the six guards riding behind us.

I became apprehensive. Xander had crossed the border. Even worse, he restrained nine living beings at once. He risked rapid energy depletion, and it wouldn't be favorable for his body to end up weak and limp in Follyn territory. Altair would kill him!

I loathed the idea of fighting against Xander, but I couldn't risk being taken back to Deltrea. If I returned to Deltrea, I might never make it back to Follyn, and Altair wouldn't remain passive.

One horse broke free from the restraints, but I realized these chains intended to confine me.

Using the leaves of the surrounding trees, I constructed a razor-sharp barrier to enclose Altair and myself. His slit pupils revealed his readiness to strike, but I blocked him from doing so when I created the barrier.

"Lyra!" Altair fumed.

The restraints tried to break through my barrier, but the thickness of my razor barricade made it difficult. With a firm grip on Altair's hand, we dashed towards the horse Xander had freed from Temperance's restraints.

As we ran forward, the shield remained with us, creating a protective barrier around the horse and ourselves.

I commanded Benjamin to absorb some of the fire from the carriage lanterns.

As my hand extended towards the horse's reins, Altair's words echoed in the air, "I'm not getting on."

"Then, you're staying. Guide the way, Benjamin!" I hopped on the horse and rode away, staying within my protective barrier.

Altair faced a diminishing shield as I moved further away from him. I expected him to come after me. I needed to lure him elsewhere, away from potential harm. I couldn't bear the thought of either of them getting hurt or, worse, losing their lives.

My heart raced as I contemplated the dangerous situation unfolding before me. The weight of responsibility pressed heavily on my shoulders, as the thought of witnessing a confrontation between him and Xander filled me with dread. My hands trembled slightly, betraying the anxiety that consumed me. The thought of the consequences of their confrontation loomed over me, casting a dark shadow on my thoughts.

Xander's restraints pursued me, as if he rode a horse nearby in the dark forest. I countered his restraints with the thick barrier of razor-sharp leaves that swirled around me.

I took a backward glance.

The darkness thickened, more oppressive than ever. Within the inky blackness, three enormous eyes snapped open, dominating the scene. From my distance, they seemed as vast as the towering pine trees surrounding us. I felt as though I floated in an endless black void, engulfed by three celestial bodies masquerading as eyes. Their erratic scanning of the area offered no solace.

One eye darted left, another right, and the third locked onto me with chilling intensity. The gaze of the eye fixed on me, along with the one to my right, burned with a sinister red glow. Those eyes weren't just watching—the red glow held a steady focus on their targets. The right eye locked on Xander, while the other focused on me. In front of these eyes, Altair mounted a black horse. A blue glow surrounded his reptilian-like slit pupils.

Altair's ability manipulated the uncanny eyes that followed us—I was certain of it. As he moved forward, the eyes moved with him. Strange creatures surrounded Altair and his horse, floating around him, forming a barrier and preventing Xander's restraints from affecting Altair.

These creatures, about a dozen in number, resembled the dancer Alphonse, Xander, and I encountered the night we acquired Judgement. These abnormal beings varied in size and emitted a suffocating, terrorizing energy that seeped into the marrow of our bones, causing dread, severe anxiety, and every variation of fear. The air around them rippled with malevolence, arresting the sinking feeling of fighting for survival against the unknown, as if the darkness itself watched in enjoyment.

Most of them glowed blood-red, their skin glistening as if dipped in blood. Some displayed long, tangled hair, while others revealed nearly bald scalps, with only a few thin, wiry strands sprouting. All displayed wide, bloody grins and hooves for feet, like grotesque parodies of horses. Half of the dozen crawled beside Altair on all fours, jerking with disturbing movements. The other half floated around him, glowing like malevolent balls of fire in the sky, their feet absent. Within those fiery spheres, masses of darkness writhed and pulsed, surpassing the forest's already oppressive darkness, like a black emptiness that devoured all light. The consuming darkness clung to Altair and the three ominous forest eyes.

A deeper sense of terror traveled with Altair. He brought heavy air, which carried the stench of decay and sulfur, and the chilling whispers of the demons filled the eerie silence. Altair's every movement exuded power, his presence commanded respect, and his eyes demonstrated authority. Shadows danced around him, seemingly at the mercy of their formidable captain. In his element, Altair lead in confidence and he harmonized with these demons.

My heart pounded. The horrifying scene behind me made my blood run cold. More than anything, I feared for Xander's life.

I needed to get us away from him.

I diverted from the path by taking a sharp left and heading straight into the darkness of the tall pines, hoping to lure Xander away and into a mess of trees.

"Lyra!" Xander's voice carried a mix of desperation, frustration, and disappointment.

I'm sorry, Xander.

Eight of Cups

Someone rode towards us.

She came upon us fast. I didn't stop, and neither did she. Despite evading each other, we made eye contact. Her eyes glowed green, with slit pupils—a card possessor.

"I'll take it from here, brother!" Her voice emitted a twisted excitement that made me shutter.

I stopped riding, only to turn around with a threatening death glare toward the woman who now threatened Xander's existence.

"Don't interfere, Lyra!" Altair charged towards me, and his creepy creatures followed. As if also following Altair's orders, my horse surprised me by galloping back towards Altair, thwarting my desire to intervene and fight the woman.

I gripped the reins, desperately trying to halt the horse, but it refused to obey. Its eyes glowed an eerie red. Beside me, Altair galloped fiercely. His pupils remained slits, and his army of devils swarmed around us.

"You possessed the horse!?" I exclaimed, but Altair did not respond.

Aided by his ability to see in the darkness, the pitch-black path posed no challenge for Altair as he rode through with ease.

"Stop! Altair!" I persisted, but my pleas fell on deaf ears. Altair rode on, and the possessed horse I rode followed him with loyalty.

"If anything happens to Xander, I *will* go back!" I exclaimed.

This caught Altair's attention. His slit-pupils faced me with anger. I flinched at his reaction, but I didn't avert my eyes.

I tried again. "Stop!"

"We'll talk when we arrive at Regnum Noctis!"

"I will jump off the horse!"

A frightening smirk cracked through Altair's face. A different intensity arrested his eyes, and he didn't have to look at me for dread to spread through my core.

The haunting image of Altair taking my brother's life played in my mind. Blood stained the ground. The sound of his final breath echoed, and the metallic smell of death filled the air. The memory of Altair aiding his sister in Xander's execution lingered in my consciousness. My senses remained haunted by the eerie glow of the moon, the image of his lifeless body, the echo of the crowd's reactions, and the scent of fear mingling with the crisp autumn air. The recollection of Altair plunging his sword into my chest pierced through me. The searing pain shot through my body, and the bitter taste of blood filled my mouth—vivid reminders of Altair's merciless cruelty.

When I moved my gaze from his twisted smirk, I saw one of the enormous red eyes on the left—the side away from Altair—targeting me. The creatures surrounded us to protect us, their twisted grins and blood-red eyes with slit pupils fixated on me. These creatures ran on all fours, and the idea of them catching me terrified me.

They weren't going to let me jump off to save anyone tonight.

I glanced behind me to face a second enormous eye in the darkness. The crimson pupil towered over me, targeting me. Its size consumed me.

All around me, I was watched.

Altair's smirk oozed confidence. The frightening sights of the unknown forest reminded me that all odds were against me, and unlike Altair, I couldn't see in the dark. Despite my fear and lack of superiority in numbers, I decided to fight against Altair's clutches and confront the woman chasing Xander. Despite the setback to my ambitions, I needed to get Xander home to save his life. I refused to lose anyone else.

Harnessing the winds, I conjured a gust so fierce that it swept me away. I rode a tornado, dangerously deterring anyone or anything nearby. The task proved difficult because I struggled to steady my legs and maintain balance.

Amid shaky confines, I allowed the wind to carry me higher and higher until the trees fell below me. Altair's loyal beings flew after me.

I summoned Benjamin, who levitated beside me, ready for battle. While I kept the tornado steady, I commanded Benjamin to absorb the balls of flame surrounding the shadow-figures. As he absorbed them, the figures shrieked and darted around me in frantic panic, as if the flames held their lifeline.

I dodged their frantic movements and realized they dropped brooms when Benjamin absorbed their flames.

"Are they like... witches?" I muttered to myself.

Using the winds of the tornado, I grabbed hold of one broom and steadied myself with it.

Figures, I thought. Hey, the broom helped. Riding the winds became easier.

"Lyra!" For the second time, I heard my name called in a desperate and frustrated tone, but this time, Altair's voice pierced the air.

I looked down but couldn't see him. Instead, I saw the enormous eyes targeting me. Just as I thought, they equaled the trees in magnitude. As I climbed higher than the trees, they followed suit. Altair wasn't going to let me off his sights.

As I ventured to the top of the forest, I used the fire Benjamin absorbed to light my way. Controlling the elements with my mind and hands, while also commanding Benjamin to use more of my ability, drained my stamina. Time was limited.

Guided by a faint light, I spotted slight movement in the forest. Using the winds, I hastened over to it.

I made out Xander's silhouette, and I manipulated the winds to bring him to me with rapid force, trapping him in my tornado. I lifted him higher and higher until he floated beside me.

Blood oozed from his eyes and nose. He teetered on the verge of fainting.

"Balance on the end of the broom, Xander."

Despite his disgust, he obeyed my instructions.

"Hold on to me," I commanded.

"The eyes-"

"I know."

Altair's massive eyes bore into me, yet his creatures halted their assault.

Out of the darkness, three shadow-figures materialized, clutching brooms and blazing orbs. Flames erupted from a circular lantern, casting a ghastly light on their forms. Ironic, considering these beings were darker than the pitch-black night.

Altair's decision to halt hostilities possibly signified his willingness to find middle ground. However, Xander risked being harmed if I didn't return to Follyn Forest after getting him to safety. Altair was quite impatient, so I knew I needed to act fast.

Xander's words interrupted my thoughts. "Come home."

Using my last ounce of strength, I directed the winds to transport us to one of the borders of Aquaenterra and Follyn. Once we passed the border, I dove and gently let Xander down.

His weakened state prevented him from calling out to me, but the remorse in his eyes made it clear he felt he had lost me.

"See you later," I mouthed to him.

I confronted the massive eyes that watched me and retreated into Follyn Forest with them.

I gasped at the sound of an organ, but when I opened my eyes, the sound dissipated. I sat up upon seeing an unfamiliar ceiling.

A little white marble coffee table stood at the front of the massive bed where I lay. In front of it, a black love seat faced me. An unknown woman sat on a chaise lounge to the right of the love seat. Dark brown hair, slightly lighter than Altair's, pinned in a semi-messy bun, crowned her head. Her warm-honey-toned skin and thickset, stocky frame gave her an intimidating presence. A pauldron and a long black side cape adorned her left shoulder. Two silver metallic belts crisscrossed her red corset, and another metallic belt wrapped around her tight black pants. Metal accents gleamed on the heels and toes of her black boots. A massive black sword rested against the window beside her.

She looked like she could crush me.

She sat on the chaise right beside an open window, but her face remained buried in the book she held in her hands. From the corner of her eye, she must've seen me get up, but she didn't look up from her book.

I stared at her for a few long moments before I cleared my throat.

She put her finger up and kept her eyes on the book. "Almost done."

I remained quiet, but nervous. The last thing I remembered was...

"Xander?!" I spoke aloud.

At my words, the woman removed a hairpin from her messy bun and placed it inside the book before closing it shut with a loud *thud*.

Finally, I locked with dark brown eyes and a friendly smile.

"I'm sorry. I couldn't put it down. The chapter ended brilliantly!"

I assumed she saw fear in my eyes. Before I responded, she spoke again. "As for Von Almont, he's fine. Altair told our sister Luna not to pursue him. He should still be in Aquaenterra. I'm sure he's received help by now."

Confidence and kindness shone in her eyes, but her words revealed her identity as a Follyn royal. This only meant one thing—it must be Solaris.

When I held my silence, she got up from the chaise.

"I'm Solaris Antares, Altair's oldest sister." She closed some of the distance between us to shake my hand.

A Follyn royal initiating a handshake with a Deltrea royal defied all precedents. Surely, she knew my identity. Stuck in my little conundrum, I stretched out my hand and shook hers.

"Lyra Celestia," I said.

She didn't flinch at the sound of my name, and her smile didn't waver.

"Altair told me you'd probably look like a scared rabbit," she shook her head. "My silly little brother doesn't understand the purity and beauty of innocence. Don't let him destroy that part of you. He's quite broken, but considering you and he defied societal norms and expectations, he isn't beyond saving. I used to find his beliefs, ideals, and loyalty to our parents annoying, but now I admire him for letting it all go for the Princess of Deltrea."

Her words made me flinch.

"Please don't take it as an insult. I should've made brave choices, too, but I guess life's all about learning and growth, right?"

I nodded.

She continued, "I see why, though. You are very beautiful."

While Solaris' words somewhat alleviated the tension, the distant sound of an organ broke the tranquility and put me on high alert. My heart raced upon recognizing its familiar melody.

"The organ," I said aloud, keeping my eyes on Solaris.

"We have one in our ballroom."

"I'm assuming they allow guests in there?"

Solaris shook her head.

"Then, who is playing the organ?" If it was Corvus Noir, I wanted to lay my hands on the grotesque visage of my mother's murderer.

Solaris remained silent for a moment before turning towards the window. "Sort of... a family friend, I suppose."

She couldn't quite hold eye contact as she said this.

"Where is Altair?" I asked.

"With my father," said Solaris. "They're in the presidential suite."

"Where are we?"

"We're in a room opposite the presidential suite. Don't worry, no one will bother us here. When Follyn's royals are in this hall, it becomes strictly prohibited for anyone to enter. My parents usually reserve the presidential suite, and when they're not here, we take it over. Unfortunately, the old man is pretty upset at Altair's disobedience, so he's in there using it." Solaris rolled her eyes.

"So, this is basically an abandoned hallway?" I asked.

"It's a private hallway," Solaris corrected. "They will probably stay in there for quite some time. He's trying to convince our father to spare your life, you know."

I glared at her. "You all don't scare me."

"I'm not your enemy, Lyra. I stay away from my father's business."

The organ continued playing.

I loathed the eerie melody. It was the same one Corvus Noir played right before Altair pressed his sword through my chest. There was no mistake about it. Once again, I listened to the forsaken melodies of that murderer.

The fury inside me grew. Sitting there and listening to him play his victory theme drove me mad.

I quickly got myself up from the bed.

As soon as I stood, dizziness and light-headedness kicked in. Despite my weakening knees, I pushed myself to stay upright and walk towards the door.

A big, firm hand grabbed my wrist. "Whoa. Where are you going?" Solaris asked.

My pride urged me to defy and frustrate her, but her kindness made me hesitant to sever ties with a possible acquaintance. I also believed she wouldn't simply let me leave. Her presence had purpose. Altair had probably tasked her with monitoring me.

I kept my guard up, but I figured I needed to test the waters and see how far we could go in terms of communication.

"I'd like to go watch the organ player."

She shook her head. "Everyone is forbidden from entering the ballroom and the basement. The ballroom is open to the public only when there's an event."

"Why is the organ player in there? Also, I'm not exactly the public, Solaris."

"You're right, but we don't go in there when we hear the organ playing. It's a family friend, and he likes his privacy. Considering how loyal he is to us, we permit it."

My current emotions both puzzled and upset me. "None of you know what he looks like without the mask?"

Solaris understood my implications. She knew I wouldn't be easily fooled, so she didn't confirm or deny anything further. Instead, she gave a remorseful shrug. "It's orders."

"It's Corvus Noir, isn't it?" I asked.

Solaris sighed. "I won't lie to you, Lyra, it is. But for everyone's safety, I hope you can refrain from approaching him. The situation is tense as it is."

"Why is Corvus Noir here?"

"He's always around."

Frustration mounted, and my jaw clenched tightly. With a determined stride, I made my way towards the door.

"Where are you going?"

"I'm going to face him."

Again, Solaris grabbed my arm. "I wouldn't do that if I were you, Lyra."

"Let me go," I warned.

"Respecting his privacy helps us maintain his loyalty. Losing Noir's loyalty could cause my father to act irrationally against you and yours. He values Noir's help, and Noir isn't too happy about your presence here, either. Altair is trying to set things right, and I support that, but your impulses shouldn't guide you."

I eyed her with suspicion. "Blind hatred breeds evil deeds."

"Indeed," Solaris released my arm. "I won't stop you, Lyra, but please, take my words into consideration."

I scoffed, "Won't Altair be furious that you let me go?"

"Perhaps, but Altair isn't my master, and he's not your master, either."

I nodded and headed towards the door.

"Lyra," she called out just before I turned the knob. "One last word of caution: It's late into the night, so be mindful of the hushed silence that envelops the sleeping guests. Be especially cautious, as many Follynean attendees harbor deep anger towards Altair for bringing you here, and, as you wisely noted, blind hatred can drive individuals to commit unspeakable acts."

Word always spread too fast in the corridors of Regnum Noctis.

I opened the door and left the room.

I faced a dimly lit hallway. The walls, crafted from black marble, boasted intricate patterns of white and beige streaks. A unique black-and-white checkered pattern covered the floor, with tiles arranged in a diamond shape instead of squares. A long black carpet adorned the hallway, showcasing elegant white floral patterns. Intricate white shapes wove within the black outlines of the carpet.

The hallway's outline showcased horned creatures and gargoyles leading to the stairs.

I walked through the sets of stairs and endless hallways, my thoughts and emotions running through my head. The organ in the distance continued playing, but I turned on my heel because I acknowledged Solaris' correctness. Despite the overwhelming surge of negative emotions, a voice of reason made me listen. Seeking Corvus Noir unsettled me, as it could unleash chaos upon this place, and the present moment did not suit such disruption. The land I found myself in belonged to the Follyneans, and their numbers far surpassed mine.

I returned to my room. Solaris was gone.

I closed my eyes to sleep, but my thoughts haunted me once more. Hearing that bastard play the same melody he played when Altair Antares took my life in my past life didn't help.

I struggled to sleep while the melody persisted.

Would this be my last night? I wondered. *Would Altair strike again as Death played his melody?*

The music ceased.

I opened my eyes and exhaled, but my breath brought no relief.

I lifted myself, feeling the soft mattress beneath me as I sat upright in bed. In my previous life, Altair Antares had found me when the organ stopped. Tonight, the room was devoid of immediate threats, yet an abundance of threats surrounded me outside of it.

I pondered whether his talk with his father had gone well.

Amidst the silence, I sat motionless, deep in my reverie, as the minutes slipped by.

When I sank back into the softness of the bed, I positioned myself to face the door, its wooden frame casting faint shadows in the dimly lit room. As I nestled under the weight of my blankets, I pulled them up towards my face. My eyes peeked out from behind them, surveying the room beyond the safety of my covers. Despite my efforts to calm down, relaxation eluded me.

The absence of noise was deafening.

As more time passed, I grew more restless, unable to shake off my persistent vigilance. Despite my initial reluctance, I sat up once more with the weight of restless frustration.

I rose from bed, shed my nightie, dressed, and left the room.

As I glanced into the silent corridor of the lavish hotel, a sense of dread washed over my frustration. Aside from Solaris, who may have retreated into one of the next rooms, I was all alone up there with the most dominant, evil forces of Follyn.

In front of me, a single double-door stood in the middle of the opposite hallway.

Silence surrounded the area.

I pressed my ear against the door but heard nothing.

Should I sneak in? I thought, but it would be prudent to plan my approach before confronting Dante, the King of Follyn.

Instead, I crossed my arms and paced outside the door until I heard a pained, horrified grunt from inside.

My intuition set off alarms.

Altair, I thought. *Was his father capable of hurting him?*

I reached for the knob.

To my surprise, I found the door unlocked, so I entered the large room without making a sound.

A lounging area with a lit fireplace stood to my right. The calming crackling of the fire contradicted the eerie aura of the ambience. To my left, I saw a large dining table.

I stepped further into the room.

A hallway stretched out in front of the dining table. Sound emerged from the doorless room at the end of the hallway. Altair and another person came into view through the open frame, but I froze when Altair's piercing gaze met mine as he glanced up from what I presumed to be his father's lifeless body. His crimson eyes glowed, and his ability highlighted the reddish color around his slit pupils. They glimmered in the night's darkness.

My mind tried to make sense of my visual: Altair drank the corpse's blood dry, and his eyes highlighted the predatory features of his kind. They glowed with his deadly ability and reveled in the lifelessness. In the timeless silence, our eyes locked into a wordless exchange that stretched into eternity. I didn't dare remove my eyes from him.

"Altair?" My voice carried the weight of his name as I whispered it.

No words came out of his mouth.

"Is that your father?" The tone of my shaken voice carried a sense of reluctance and caution.

After an endless wait, he responded with a subtle nod.

"Did you...?" I licked my lips. "Did you do this to your father?"

Once again, Altair's response echoed with silence as he nodded.

Anxiety arose from the depths of his unspoken words. Did those evil forces from his ability possess him? The man before me embodied the devil from my past life. He personified the true Prince of Follyn that everybody described.

"Why?" My voice escaped my lips in a soft whisper.

What in the world would possess you to assassinate your own father? I thought.

Altair remained silent, becoming one with the dense ambience that surrounded him. He removed his piercing glare from my eyes to look down at his finished work with a cold, detached expression. He stretched a hand towards the table beside the crimson-colored sofa, and he picked up a white handkerchief and wiped his face clean of blood. After cleaning himself, he grabbed the same piece of cloth and wiped the hilt of the bloodied dagger resting on the sofa next to his father, but he left the blood on the blade. He tossed it back down next to his father—abandoning the murder weapon at the scene of the crime.

That's when it clicked.

"You're going to blame Deltrea." It wasn't a question.

Altair smirked. "You thought I'd let Von Almont get away with his scene?"

"So, you murdered your own father?"

My words touched a nerve.

Altair charged towards me.

"Don't come near me!"

He stopped in his tracks. Then, he spoke with harsh disdain in his tone. "You saved Von Almont, Lyra! And you shouldn't have! He deserves to rot with the corpses of the underworld!"

My eyes glowed. In the quick moment that I summoned Benjamin and motioned him towards the fireplace far behind me, Altair lunged at me with fierce adrenaline.

With my back turned to him, I ran to escape from his presence.

I faced the fireplace and outstretched an arm towards it, attempting to capture the flames in my palms, utilizing every bit of my limited strength. Before my hands got ahold of any fire, and before Benjamin turned towards me with a mouthful of flames, Altair wrapped his arms around my stomach from behind. With remarkable ease and swiftness, he lifted me off the ground, maneuvered me away from the fireplace, and opened the door facing the dining table.

"You really believe you can challenge me with no stamina?"

"Let me go!" I wriggled to escape his grasp, but the effort proved futile.

"You thought I'd remain oblivious to your intentions?"

"What are you talking about?" My voice cut through the air, sharp and harsh, ready to fight for my life.

Altair planted me back on the ground. Then, he grabbed my wrist and turned me to face him. "You took my victory away from me."

Dread and apprehension permeated my body, but I kept my eyes locked on his slit, crimson irises, hoping he didn't refer to our past.

No, it was impossible.

He couldn't remember it because *I* awakened The World.

Altair's words pierced through my fearful thoughts. "This time, I will take back the victory you stole with The World, and my triumph will echo through every corner of the kingdoms."

END OF PART I

❧ ACKNOWLEDGEMENTS ❧

During my time as a teacher, I had the honor of witnessing students grow a motivation to build themselves for a bright future, as if a spark had ignited in their hearts.

Sometimes that spark was ignited by a teacher, sometimes through friendship, sometimes through romance, and sometimes by a need to prove a point to themselves and their doubters. Therefore, I wanted to include the light-heartedness of friendships, the heartbreak of betrayal, the difficulty of death, the guidance of teachers and parents, the bond of siblings, the growth of romance, and the life-changing attitudes and decisions made by characters who strive to achieve something important, beginning with facing their fears.

Working in a Title I school, I witnessed the daily hardships my students faced. Fiction provided them with an escape—a transport to a fantasy world far removed from their realities. Despite their struggles, not only did they connect to themes and lessons in fiction, but they enjoyed the stories.

My students particularly loved stories with horror elements. Despite their shyness and aversion to writing, they were enthusiastic about writing journals about horror experiences. They enjoyed the thrill and eagerly shared their supernatural stories in class. Even those who disliked reading engaged most with darker and gothic stories. Among our favorites were Poe's "Masque of the Red Death," "The Pit and the Pendulum," "The Tell-Tale Heart;" Shirley Jackson's "The Lottery;" Shakespeare's *Macbeth* and *Romeo and Juliet*; Kurt Vonnegut's "Harrison Bergeron;" and Bram Stoker's *Dracula*.

I wanted to allude to some of the ideas, authors, stories, and concepts we explored in class. I aimed to capture the essence of the works of fiction that my students and I enjoyed.

That being said, a thank you to my students for all the moments and for all they taught me. My children, it was an honor to be your teacher.

I'd also like to thank a few people who have been instrumental in this journey:

To my readers, thank you so much for picking up my book! It has been my lifelong dream to become an author, and you've made that dream a reality. I truly hope you've enjoyed the story so far! With all my heart, I thank you for your support and for taking a chance on *The Witch's Arcana*.

To the love of my life, Rudy. Thank you for always being my main pillar of support and for being my partner in everything I do. Thank you for being my first reader.

To my parents, Laura and Alfonso. Thank you for all the sacrifices you've made to make sure my siblings and I were always taken care of, even through the toughest times. Mom, thank you for the bedtime stories, for reading to me as a child, and for teaching me to create fun stories from nothing. Thank you both for being wonderful parents and giving me the best siblings in the world.

To my little sister, Sabrina. Thank you for being my second reader and for encouraging me to move forward, even when I felt like putting this project aside for weeks at a time. Without your motivational words, this project might still be a work-in-progress.

To my brothers, Alfonso and Adrian. Some of my bursts of creativity came from the things we did together in our childhood. I am blessed and wouldn't have wanted life to go any other way.

Everything I do is for you six. Thank you for believing in me. You all give my life *that* meaning.

To my cousins: Andrea, Brandon, David, Elizabeth, Alexander, Catherine, Edward, Fancy Nancy, Jerry, and Ruby for always being very supportive and for their unique goofiness. Life is a different adventure when we're all together. Andrea, thank you for teaching me to write all the odd ideas in my twelve-year-old mind. I cringe when I look at my teenage writings, but that's where it all started. Alexander, I strived to be as creative and intelligent as you. You were an older brother, my mentor, and my biggest inspiration growing up. I remember being about ten years old, watching in astonishment as you read a Harry Potter book in a single day. After that, I challenged myself with the same goal. Binge-reading became a habit I still carry. The same goes for the piano; you taught me my first song, the Harry Potter theme. When I told you about my writing hobby and the works I needed to complete, you were very excited. You even said you wanted to be one of my first readers for this project. I wish I would have gotten the chance to share this with you. Rest in peace, my dear cousin.

To my cousin, Edith, for taking my pictures with so much enthusiasm, excitement, and vision. Her daughter, Daiana, for drawing the first fan-art.

To my uncle, Andres, for the business advice. Thank you, Pops!

To my in-laws for welcoming me into their family and for their love and support.

To Joshua, Jesus, and Adrian for being my brothers without the blood relation and believing in my work.

To Brianna and Rachel for being my beta testers.

To Dinorah and Devenny, thank you for the feedback, support, and encouragement on this journey. Dino, for giving it to me straight. Dev, for inspiring me to take a path of reflection and growth, and for helping me see the worth and the voice of one's spirit and creativity.

To my fellow coworkers at Toyota of Laredo for cheering me on and encouraging me to complete this project. You lovelies know who you are.

To Laurie, for being *that* teacher.

To my ELA teachers and professors, for instilling in me a passion for English literature.

Finally, I'd like to thank my favorite artists, Twenty One Pilots, for creating music that makes the fight easier and inspires creativity, especially on tough days. Listening to "Jumpsuit" every morning during my first semester of teaching helped calm my nerves. When I felt it was time to leave teaching, I played "Choker" on repeat, and "Next Semester" came out a few months after I left, so it hit me hard, too. Then, "Oldies Station" came in clutch as I worked on this project. Thank you for making us feel heard and seen. Thank you for inspiring my husband, my sister, my brother-in-law, and me to keep pushing through. Houston, TX. 09/04/2024.

S. L. VELA graduated from Texas A&M International University with a Bachelor of Arts in English. She lives in Texas with her husband and their lionhead rabbit, Benjamin. This is her first novel.